A
MOST ENGLISH
PRINCESS

Dear Mary —
I hope you will enjoy this
story — she was a

A MOST ENGLISH PRINCESS

A Novel of Queen Victoria's Daughter

woman both lucky and
quite unlucky but

CLARE McHUGH

valiant throughout!

C. McHugh

12/20

WILLIAM MORROW
An Imprint of HarperCollinsPublishers

P.S.™ is a trademark of HarperCollins Publishers.

FIRST EDITION

Designed by Diahann Sturge

Title page and part opener art © Yakov Oskanov / Shutterstock, Inc.

Library of Congress Cataloging-in-Publication Data has been applied for.

ISBN 978-0-06-299760-9

20 21 22 23 24 LSC 10 9 8 7 6 5 4 3 2 1

for
JEMMA ROSE LASSWELL
brilliant daughter

May your life, which has begun beautifully, expand still further to the good of others and the contentment of your own mind! True inward happiness is to be sought only in the internal consciousness of effort systematically directed to good and useful ends.

—Prince Albert to his daughter Victoria, the Princess Royal, on the occasion of her twenty-first birthday, November 21, 1861

The unification of Germany by the now defunct and almost forgotten Kingdom of Prussia was at once inevitable and absurd, artificial and harmful.

—German historian Golo Mann, 1971

Cast of Characters

In England: The Royal Family

Mama, Queen Victoria, born 1819

Papa, Prince Albert, the Prince Consort, formerly
Prince of Saxe-Coburg and Gotha, born 1819

Grandmamma, the Duchess of Kent, Mama's mother, Papa's
aunt, earlier Princess of Saxe-Coburg-Saalfeld, born 1786

Vicky, Victoria, the Princess Royal, born 1840

Bertie, Albert Edward, the Prince of Wales,
born 1841, later King Edward VII

Princess Alice, born 1843, later the Grand Duchess of Hesse

Affie, Prince Alfred, born 1844

Lenchen, Princess Helena, born 1846

Princess Louise, born 1848

Prince Arthur, born 1850

Prince Leopold, born 1853

Princess Beatrice, born 1857

In England: The Royal Household

Laddle, Sarah, the Lady Lyttelton, governess to the royal children, born 1787

Baron Christian Friedrich Stockmar, adviser to Prince Albert, born 1787

Tilla, Sarah Anne Hildyard, governess to the princesses Victoria and Alice, born circa 1829

Henry Ponsonby, equerry to Prince Albert, later private secretary to Queen Victoria, born 1825

Mary Bulteel, lady-in-waiting to Queen Victoria, later married to Henry Ponsonby, born 1832

Fritz, Frederick Ponsonby, second son of Henry and Mary Ponsonby, equerry to Queen Victoria and later private secretary to King Edward VII, born 1867

In Prussia: The Royal Family

King Friedrich Wilhelm IV, born 1795

Queen Elisabeth, King Friedrich Wilhelm IV's wife, earlier Princess of Bavaria, born 1801

Prince Wilhelm, brother of King Friedrich Wilhelm IV, later the Prince Regent, later King Wilhelm I, later Kaiser Wilhelm I, born 1797

Princess Augusta, wife of Prince Wilhelm, earlier Princess of Saxe-Weimar, later Queen Augusta, later Kaiserin Augusta, born 1811

Fritz, Prince Friedrich, son of Prince Wilhelm
and Princess Augusta, later Crown Prince of
Prussia, later Kaiser Friedrich III, born 1831

Princess Louise, daughter of Prince Wilhelm and Princess
Augusta, later Grand Duchess of Baden, born 1838

Prince Karl, younger brother of King
Friedrich Wilhelm IV, born 1801

Grand Duchess Alexandrine of Mecklenburg-Schwerin,
younger sister of the king of Prussia, born 1803

Prince Albrecht, younger brother of King
Friedrich Wilhelm IV, born 1809

Fritz Karl, Prince Friedrich Karl, son of Prince Karl, born 1828

Anna, Princess Maria Anna, daughter of Prince Karl,
later the Landgravine of Hesse, born 1836

Marianne, Princess Maria Anna of Anhalt-
Dessau, wife of Fritz Karl, born 1837

Crown Princess Olga of Württemberg, earlier Grand Duchess
of Russia, niece of King Friedrich Wilhelm IV, born 1822

The Children of the Crown Prince and Princess of Prussia
Willy, William, Prince Friedrich Wilhelm,
born 1859, later Kaiser Wilhelm II

Charlotte, Princess Charlotte, born 1860

Henry, Prince Heinrich, born 1862

Siggy, Prince Sigismund, born 1864

Moretta, Princess Victoria, born 1866

Waldie, Prince Waldemar, born 1868

Sophie, Princess Sophia, born 1870

Mossy, Princess Margaret, born 1872

In Prussia: The Royal Household

General Helmuth von Moltke, aide-de-camp to Prince Friedrich, later chief of the army staff, later Prussian field marshal, born 1800

The young baron, Baron Ernest Alfred Stockmar, son of Baron Christian Stockmar, private secretary to Princess Victoria, born 1823

Dr. Wegner, court physician, born circa 1815

Wally, Walburga Hohenthal, later Lady Paget, lady-in-waiting to Princess Victoria, born 1839

Marie, Countess Marie zu Lynar, lady-in-waiting to Princess Victoria, born 1840

Also Appearing

Lord John Russell, the prime minister, born 1792

Napoléon III, emperor of the French, earlier president of France, born 1808

Empress Eugénie, wife of Napoléon, born 1826

Herr Otto von Bismarck-Schönhausen, later Count von Bismarck, later Prince von Bismarck, minister-president of Prussia, chancellor of the German Empire, born 1815

Ernest, Duke of Saxe-Coburg and Gotha, older brother of Prince Albert, born 1818

Sir James Clark, court physician, born 1788

Adie, Adelheid, Duchess of Augustenburg, earlier
Princess of Hohenlohe-Langenburg, niece of Queen
Victoria, cousin of Princess Victoria, born 1835

Fritz, the Duke of Augustenburg, husband of Adie,
claimant to the throne of Schleswig-Holstein, born 1829

Alix, Princess Alexandra of Denmark, later Princess
of Wales, later queen consort, born 1844

Mr. Robert Morier, British diplomat, born 1826

Mr. Augustus Loftus, later Lord Loftus, British
ambassador to Prussia, born 1817

Dr. Georg Hinzpeter, tutor to the children of the
Crown Prince and Crown Princess, born 1827

Poultney Bigelow, an American author
and journalist, born 1855

Prologue

Kronberg im Taunus, February 1901

$\mathcal{F}$ritz Ponsonby shifts uncomfortably in the corner of the carriage, trying to find an easeful place to rest his head, and pulls his overcoat tighter. Even with the luxuries provided the royal party—a large private yacht for the channel crossing and plush sleeping compartments on the train to Frankfurt—the trip overnight from London has been taxing, and he feels queasy and his temples throb. Private secretary to the new king, he'll have a full day's work to do when they arrive. Beside him, softly snoring, is Francis Laking, a Harley Street physician, whom the king enlisted for this visit to his ailing sister, the dowager empress of Germany. The morning sun shines brightly but the air is very cold. He listens to the jingle of harnesses and the clopping of horses' hooves as they pull five carriages up the hill. Finally, his eyes close.

A sharp turn to the left, and Ponsonby is jostled awake. Laking, too. The carriage judders to a stop at a high iron gate and soldiers approach on both sides, peering in the windows. After the vehicle lurches forward again, Ponsonby can see helmeted men marching four abreast in a courtyard on the left. Ahead, under an ornate stone entrance portico, he spies a cluster of officers. As the first carriage—the king's—trundles up to the door, the whole file halts. Ponsonby cranes his neck and watches two footmen dart forward to help out the honored guest. A small band somewhere out of sight strikes up a hearty, unrecognizable oompah-pah tune.

"No 'God Save the King'?" asks Laking.

"Not Wilhelm's style," Ponsonby answers. "Only he is lord and master in Germany."

A stocky figure Ponsonby recognizes instantly as the German kaiser steps forward to embrace his uncle. In brown tweeds and soft homburg hat, the English king looks strangely incongruous, mousy, a mere civilian surrounded by military brass.

"We have come to an armed camp," the doctor observes.

"Apparently so," Ponsonby replies.

THE KING PLANS to stay at Schloss Friedrichshof, his sister's castle near the village of Kronberg, for only six days. He won't absent himself from England any longer, during these, the first weeks of his reign, when so many in London watch to see how he will be different from his mother, Queen Victoria, who occupied the throne for sixty-three years.

Ponsonby can't suppress a smile as he's escorted across the baronial, wood-beamed entrance hall and up a set of wide red carpeted stairs. What a contrast this royal residence is with the king's own home in Norfolk—poky, stuffy Sandringham, reminiscent of an undistinguished Scottish golf hotel. From the outside the *Schloss* looks like an amalgam of an Italian Renaissance palazzo and a medieval castle, with a Gothic roof and tower, and Tudor-style timber framing on the side wings. But inside it's modern country house deluxe: light oak paneling; vaulted ceilings painted cream; well-proportioned, airy rooms furnished handsomely with elegant Biedermeier pieces and velvet-upholstered chairs. Entering his third-floor room, he notices the white-tiled bathroom off to the left, and ahead a broad, curtained bed that he longs to crawl into; beside that a plush roll-arm sofa, two tall windows overlooking the Taunus mountains, and a desk set in front of a large stone fireplace. Someone, thoughtfully, has lit a fire.

His valet, Barlow, is hanging three suits and his dinner jacket in the wardrobe on the far side of the bed. Ponsonby sits down in the desk chair and sighs. No possibility of a nap. He feels oppressed already by the voluminous paperwork that will arrive daily from London, need careful reading, and require answers dispatched back to the capital, and to British legations abroad. He inquired about bringing along an equerry, or at least a shorthand clerk, but the king refused—pronouncing, "Fritz, this is a purely personal visit." The new sovereign hasn't yet grasped that he is never off duty and traveling with a small staff is no longer practical.

Still, Ponsonby didn't insist, so now he's stuck.

ONCE DR. LAKING examines the dowager empress, he confirms that her cancer has advanced beyond cure, to the bones. He has turned his efforts to easing her constant, agonizing pain, since the German doctors seem to have little relief to offer. Because she is too weak to leave her suite, the king spends an hour there with her each morning, and another in the afternoon. Ponsonby pictures the diminutive empress instructing and advising, even shaking an admonitory finger at her brother from time to time, while he smokes and listens with an affectionate smile.

On the afternoon of the third day, Ponsonby is deciphering a telegram from Whitehall at his desk when a footman knocks and enters to say the empress wishes to speak with him. Getting up to follow the man, his stomach twists anxiously—not the worries of a nervous courtier but the dread of a fond acquaintance, for the empress is his godmother, and he's known her most of his life. Mortal illness will have changed her, and indeed, ushered into a sunny, apricot-colored lounge a few minutes later, he encounters a shrunken figure, clad in a simple gray smock, a black crocheted shawl over her shoulders, sitting supported by cushions on a chintz sofa, head bobbing slightly. Her face is yellow and swollen, her eyes closed, and her mouth fixed in an ugly grimace.

"*Warten Sie mal*," says a nurse, standing next to the sofa. "She's just had an injection. It requires some short time to take effect."

Ponsonby's throat tightens and his nose starts to run. Twenty years previously on a spring afternoon the empress, then a mere crown princess, came on a visit to his mother's workroom in the Norman Tower at Windsor and he saw her for the first time. He recalls her light rose scent, the red woolen dress and dainty hat she wore, her kindness to him, an ungainly and self-conscious youth. Ever after—they've met on two dozen or so occasions—he felt that somehow she'd taken his measure and concluded he was capable, worthy of notice. Terrible to see her skeletal, barely upright, and confined to the faintly sour fug of this sickroom.

She opens her eyes and looks up. "Fritz, dear," the empress whispers, "forgive me. I have been slow to properly welcome you to Friedrichshof." She closes her eyes again.

"Your home is beautiful," Ponsonby says.

"Please sit," she says, reaching a trembling, wasted arm over the cushion tower to indicate a place on the right. "I will speak to my godson now, *Fräulein*, thank you," she says to the nurse.

He's settled beside her, and the empress lays a hand on his forearm. Her sweet smile evokes her former self.

"I watched my father build two splendid houses. I was so fortunate to have the chance to build one of my own," she said.

"You were more inspired by Balmoral here, I would say, than Osborne."

"Yes, although nowhere is lovelier than Osborne."

"You were not tempted to build at the German seaside?"

"With Bad Homburg so close, I could count on a stream of English guests, my brother most constant." She smiles again. The famous casino at the Rhineland spa town of Bad Homburg—five miles distant—was frequented for years by the erstwhile Prince of Wales.

"It's a great pleasure for all of us to be here," Ponsonby says.

"My brother and I have had excellent talks. But I don't quite take in that he is king now."

"His Royal Highness is himself still adjusting, I believe."

"And not to be with my mother at the end. I cannot tell you how I suffered when the news came." She shakes her head.

"I imagine, Your Royal Highness."

"I try to believe that the queen and I were together so much and so often that it doesn't matter that I was absent in the last days."

"Yes."

"My son boasts he cradled his dying grandmother." The empress's tone is ironical.

"He maneuvered himself into position by the bed and sat propping her up with his right arm, my mother recounts."

"Determined to be foremost even at that bedside!" she exclaims.

Picturing the kaiser pushing in at a most inappropriate moment, they both laugh.

Maybe their merriment alarmed the nurse, for now she's back. "You mustn't stay long. She's easily tired," she tells Ponsonby sternly.

But the empress raises her hand slowly. "No, no. I need a few more minutes."

The nurse scowls and departs. The empress closes her eyes and sits silent for a while. Gathering strength perhaps. When she opens them again she says, almost casually, "I need you to do something for me, Fritz dear. I need you to take charge of my letters and take them back to England."

"Letters?"

"Letters I received, and those I sent to my father and my mother, during the years I've lived here. When I was last in England I retrieved from Windsor the ones I wrote. I thought to use them for a book. No time now."

Ponsonby looks away. Too distressing to acknowledge that.

She pats his arm. "Dear Fritz. Listen now. Tonight, late, I will have them brought to your room."

He nods.

"No one must know that they will be taken away. When I am dead my son will send men to search my papers, taking what he wants burned. Remember, after my husband . . ."

He nods again, recalling that dreadful episode at the Neues Palais, nearly thirteen years ago now.

"Keep them, and in future, well, I hardly know. May I give them to your care?"

"A pleasure, ma'am, I'm happy to do so." He hears his voice quavering.

She responds with another light pat. "And if I don't see you again, you will greet your mother," she says.

"Yes."

"And do not despair."

"No."

"The Catholics call that the unpardonable sin. As your god-mother, I can instruct in such matters." She smiles. It's remarkable: she looks so dreadful and then her smile is from the soul, still aglow.

He's on the edge of a sob but fights it back. He must answer her dignity with his own. "Yes, Your Royal Highness."

"Goodbye, Fritz, God bless you."

He rises to his feet and bows before leaving.

IT SHOULDN'T COME as a surprise, Ponsonby supposes, back at his desk, that the antipathy long extant between mother and son endures, even now that she's on death's doorstep. The two look at the world completely differently. Such a tragedy, all liberal Europe agrees, that the empress's late husband, Kaiser Friedrich, enjoyed only the shortest of reigns. And since that noble man was replaced by his son, the continent's most powerful nation has a volatile, attention-seeking man-boy at the helm, constantly flexing his muscles. Far from floating above politics, he shame-lessly supports right-wing parties. Bismarck, whose wars forged the German Empire, afterward used his diplomatic wiles to keep the peace. No German minister today has his finesse, and all must contend with their erratic, irascible kaiser.

Outside his window, Ponsonby hears the rhythmic, leathery stomping sound of soldiers marching in parade, as they do here at all hours. The troops are not the local garrison, he understands, but members of the kaiser's personal guard dispatched from Berlin now that the empress's illness has entered its terminal stage. A half-dozen plain-clothed men called "pursers" have been installed inside the castle, in an office off the main hall, and they seem to do nothing all day but prowl the passageways and spy on the comings and goings of the empress's guests. Ponsonby encounters them from time to time, traveling in pairs. The men smile, but malevolent purpose stews below their courtesy. It will be a delicate thing, removing the empress's letters from the castle undetected.

DINNER IS SERVED as usual at eight, the king at the head of the table with Princess Sophie and Princess Moretta, two of the empress's daughters, on either side of him. They dote on "dear Uncle Bertie," laughing at his remarks, vying to refill his whiskey glass. The kaiser sits at the foot, holding forth on a new naval ship design. He has brought along scrap paper and between courses sketches out the vessels' features for his dinner companions—General von Kessel and Rear Admiral von Müller—who appear to hang on every word, every drawing. Ponsonby understands that, in private, the German military leaders mock their blustering, intemperate kaiser, but tonight these men make a very convincing show of fealty.

After dinner, when the rest of the party heads to the library to smoke and play cards, Ponsonby returns upstairs. He attempts to focus on the documents and telegrams piled on his desk, but he's distracted, watching the clock. Time crawls. The clock strikes midnight and then one. Maybe he misunderstood the empress.

A quiet knock. "*Herein,*" he says.

Four men come into the room, each pair carrying between them a large box, the size of a trunk but flatter and wider. The boxes are covered with black oilcloth and bound with heavy beige cord, obviously new. Affixed to the side of each box is a blank white label. The men are stablemen, dressed in open shirts, wool

trousers, and tall boots. They lay the boxes down at the far end
of the room and leave without a word to him. It's like a strange,
mute play of two minutes' duration.

When the empress spoke of letters, Ponsonby imagined a half-
dozen bulky packets that could be concealed in his personal luggage. These boxes will have to be explained.

Ponsonby finally rises from the chair and writes on the label of
one "Books with care." On the other "China with care." Then he
adds his address: Cell Farm, Old Windsor, England.

THE NEXT MORNING, when Ponsonby emerges from the bathroom,
still drying his face with a towel, his valet is standing staring at
the boxes. "What are these, sir?" Barlow asks.

He gives his cheeks a final rub, tosses the towel on a side
chair, and says offhandedly: "Ah, Barlow, these are some things
I bought as we passed through Bad Homburg. When we are departing put them in the back passage with the dispatch boxes and
my portmanteaux."

"Certainly," he says, uncertainly.

A quarter of an hour later, Mr. Fehr knocks on his door. Fehr is
the king's courier, in charge of moving everything and everyone
attached to the sovereign efficiently from one place to another.
Barlow has obviously wasted no time passing on his concerns.

"I must say I am surprised, sir, that, as very clear instructions
were given to all the servants that items that came into the castle
had to be reviewed by me or by the chief purser, we now appear
to have two boxes of goods that no one has previously inspected.
How exactly did this happen?" Fehr asks.

Scanning his mind for a response, Ponsonby alights on indignation. "Isn't it enough, Fehr, that every time I return to England
I am grilled by Custom House officers who want a list of every
single thing of value I have acquired abroad? And then they dispute the value I put on each? Now I am obligated to justify my
purchases to you, standing in my bedroom? Is that what you are
asking me to do? The whole song and dance right here?"

Fehr looks shocked. The king's upstanding private secretary, whose father was the queen's upstanding private secretary for thirty years before him, is attempting a bit of petty smuggling? It takes a minute but then Fehr adjusts. "Oh, yes, of course, sir, I understand, sir. We will just keep it between us, sir, and don't concern yourself with the Custom House men this time. I will handle them," he says.

"Much obliged, Fehr," says Ponsonby, walking him to the door, where they shake hands. As he watches Fehr retreat down the hallway, he wonders what the man imagines the boxes contain.

Rattled, he lays his forearms down on the desk to rest his head for ten minutes before returning to work.

ON THE MORNING, two days later, when the king is departing for London, the kaiser sees them off. He presides at the foot of the stairs talking loudly about the relative merits of the German railroads versus the English ones, and his own prowess as a railway engineer and, for that matter, as a sailor and a horseman. The king is still upstairs saying a final goodbye to his sister, and Ponsonby listens and nods. Out of the corner of his eye, he monitors suitcases, dispatch boxes, baskets, and trunks passing through from the back landing, across the entrance hall, and out the front door, where three wagons wait to be filled. At last, the two boxes containing the letters go by, looking conspicuously different from everything else. Ponsonby sees servants place them, one on top of the other, on the back of the last wagon. The grooms throw canvas covers over the first two wagons, and tie these down, but the third wagon, closest to the door, remains uncovered. Surely someone will notice the anomalous boxes and insist on investigating? He spots Fehr out there, chatting with the grooms, at one point casually leaning his elbow on the top box.

The kaiser drones on, oblivious to the loaded wagons other than to welcome evidence that the English visitors are leaving. He can't imagine that Ponsonby, essentially a servant, would dare intrigue against him here, in Germany, where all quiver at his command. As for the empress, he long ago sidelined her, and now she is dying. The kaiser's not thought his mother might call upon the loyalty and discretion of a friend to remove from beneath his nose letters he'd like to destroy forever.

Ponsonby is swaying slightly, straining to betray nothing as the anxious moment stretches on and on. Then, without warning, a pair of grooms throw a cover on the last wagon, and it rolls away. Exhilaration and relief course through him. Together they—he and she—have thumbed their noses at the odious kaiser. In future those who seek to pass judgment on his godmother will have to contend with her own testimony.

The first carriage, ready for passengers, rolls in under the portico. Fehr bustles through the door and whisks by Ponsonby with a brief nod, heading for the back hall. There's a heavy step on the stairs, and Ponsonby looks up to see the king descending, his nieces following behind, white handkerchiefs pressed to their weeping eyes. The king's face is grim and set. He gives his nephew a quick, wordless embrace. Then he takes Ponsonby by the elbow and says, "Come, ride with me. I want to speak of other things now." And they are off.

LATE THE NEXT afternoon Ponsonby arrives at Windsor railway station with all his luggage, having been helped onto the local train at Paddington by a skeptical Barlow and a friendly porter. He had wired ahead to his wife and asked her to send the local drayman to the station with his wagon. At Cell Farm his wife looks on as he and the driver, between them, ferry the boxes up the stairs and into the attic, and stack them under the eaves.

The boxes remain there, unremembered and unremarked upon, for twenty-seven years.

PART I

Daughter

1

The Isle of Wight, June 1847

*V*icky stood in the dining room of Osborne House, legs wide apart, balled fists on her hips, striking what Mama called her "little madame attitude." She scowled up at a large painting on the wall. Some months ago Papa had declared it time a portrait be made of them all, and she recalled the artist, Herr Winterhalter, coming to Windsor to do sketches of everyone in the family. But she'd never imagined the finished picture would look anything like this.

Herr Winterhalter had placed Bertie right in the center next to Mama—who had her arm around his shoulders—while Vicky was pushed far down into the bottom corner, watching over Lenchen in her cradle. It was as if Bertie were eldest and best, which was certainly not true.

Vicky was the oldest in the family, and the cleverest, everyone knew. Mama and Papa often wished aloud that Bertie would be more like Vicky. In the mornings, when she and Bertie went to visit Mama and Papa in their tall bed hung with emerald-green curtains, and Papa read poetry aloud to them or talked about the Greeks and the Romans, Bertie would fiddle with the wooden soldier he carried in his pocket and sometimes pluck at the knots of the silk bedcover. Mama snapped: "Bertie, don't fidget while Papa is speaking. Look at your sister, she is not fidgeting."

At such moments Vicky would beam at Papa and he would beam right back. He didn't have to worry about *her* not listening. What a good and pretty girl she was, Papa often said. And while Mama never praised as much, she liked to summon Vicky to sing for her ladies, or recite, or speak in French. Her accent was much admired, also the way she could express herself so clearly in English and in German.

Of course, Bertie spoke German, too—they all did. Papa had come from Germany to marry Mama. She called him "angel" and because of him, Mama said, she had forgotten all about her sad childhood, when, without brothers or sisters, she'd lived with only Grandmamma and her governess for company in Kensington Palace. Her own father had died and Grandmamma had been very anxious to keep Mama, who was heir to the throne, far away from "bad influences."

"Why were you heir?" Vicky had asked her once.

"Because my uncle King William had no children," Mama said.

"How did Grandmamma keep the bad influences out? Did she lock the door?"

Mama laughed. "This is too complicated for a child to understand, Puss. Grandmamma tried, I will say that."

Now Mama was queen, and Papa helped her. Perhaps because she'd had no papa, Mama could be very irritable. And she didn't seem to care for little children, though she had so many. After Vicky, who was six, came Bertie, five, and Alice, four. Then Affie, really Alfred, who was two, and a new baby, Lenchen, whose proper name was Helena. Because she was eldest, Vicky was the Princess Royal, so much better than being plain Princess Alice like her little sister. But Bertie was a boy, the oldest boy, and that appeared to be best of all. Mama called him "the nation's child" and Papa talked about his "special destiny."

How very aggravating—vexing and not right. As Vicky stared at Herr Winterhalter's picture she began to wonder how things could be arranged differently. Papa always said royal persons must be dutiful and committed to the welfare of the nation. Mightn't it be her duty to explain to him the better way? No use talking about this with Mama. She never had patience for long, serious discussions, as Papa did.

Vicky cast her eyes around the room, thinking. Like the picture, most everything in it was new. The long mahogany dining table gleamed, highly polished, with eight matching chairs lining either side, like soldiers at attention awaiting people to come in to eat and converse. A thick flowered carpet had been laid down underfoot. The walls were painted a rich blue, the color of the Most Noble Order of the Garter, the senior knighthood of England. Papa had designed this house on the Isle of Wight for them because he didn't like how at Windsor there were no proper walled gardens for children to play in, and ministers and tradesmen paraded in and out all day long—which was so very disruptive. He pronounced: "We are a growing family and we need a home that is comfortable, peaceful, and most of all private." But Papa had made sure Osborne House was properly regal and fittingly decorated. One of his very favorite pieces, a Roman bust of a lady, had been placed in a white alcove on the dining room's far wall, directly opposite a large window. Vicky admired how graceful and confident the lady looked, wearing a diadem, presiding over the whole high, elegant space.

Now she walked over to the window and peered out at the terrace and the lawn that rolled down to the sea. The sun shone and she could catch tantalizing glimpses of sparkling water between the far trees. She could ask Papa to take her to the beach. That was a good idea. To talk and to look for shells. Vicky had started a collection, and Papa's eyes were sharp—he always spotted good ones. She hurried off to find him.

A SHORT TIME later they set off hand in hand. "Only a few ladies before Mama have been queen," Vicky began as they walked down the gravel path.

"*Ja*, if you mean queens in their own right and not married to kings," Papa replied.

"Why?"

"Because a king's sons have precedence over a king's daughters in the succession; you know this. Remember Henry the Eighth and how he searched and searched for a wife who would bear him a son?"

"But in the end Elizabeth was queen. And she was very able and commanding."

"After her younger brother, Edward, died, and her elder sister too, she ascended, *ja*."

"Papa, I am the elder sister of Bertie," she said, glancing up to check he was listening to this important point.

"That's true."

"And as it was good that Elizabeth was queen, don't you think it would be good for me to be?"

"To be queen of England?"

"Yes, after Mama."

"So you wish to kill off not only poor Bertie, but Affie as well?" her father asked lightly.

"I do not wish them to die," she explained. "I think the rule should be the eldest is always heir. That's fairest."

"Oh, Puss." She saw him smiling now. He shouldn't.

"This works especially well for our family," she told him. "Because I am clever and Bertie, well, he's rather silly."

Papa laughed now.

"Bertie doesn't care about what you and I care about, Papa," Vicky went on, not liking the laugh. "Books and poetry and behaving properly." In truth she frequently wished not to behave properly, but appearing less naughty than Bertie had many advantages.

"Ah, this matters not," her father said.

"Why not? Bertie won't mind. He thinks I will be queen someday and he'll be like you and help. He often says this!"

"He's a little boy still."

"That's why now is a good time to change things. You could tell the prime minister. He always listens to you."

Papa laughed again and squeezed her hand. "Don't worry," he said. "You'll have your own important job to do. Mama and I discuss it sometimes—the best future for the queen of England's eldest daughter."

"So you don't want me as Mama's heir? You prefer it be Bertie?" She dropped his hand and stopped walking to stare directly up at him.

He stopped too, and looked down at her, serious now.

"Ah, *liebe* Vicky, your question is not reasonable. God made you and your brother as you are. One a girl and the other a boy. It is our duty—mine and Mama's—to educate you and bring you up honorably and arrange for a purposeful life equal to the high station to which you have been born."

"So you don't choose me?"

"You can't be chosen."

"Can't?"

"Males will always come first in the succession," he said.

Her brows squeezed together and her arms and hands tightened. She was so much better than Bertie. Papa knew that, and yet he didn't care? He was happy she'd be pushed aside? Something deep inside her chest seemed to rip and she began to cry. Papa crouched down and she felt him catch her raised wrists before she could beat her fists against him.

"Vicky, no, no, *mein Kind*. You mustn't cry."

"It's so unfair."

"Your life will be beautiful."

She just wept.

"I promise, your position will be worthy of not only who you are but how you are," said Papa, trying to embrace her, but she wriggled away from him.

"Your excellent mind and your determination—these cannot be wasted," he said next.

She cried more.

"The world is very big, and I will find the right place for you. Please, Vicky, won't you stop crying?"

Through tears she saw him, at her eye level, gazing over sympathetically, and she did love him although what he said was very wrong.

"I suppose I might," she said finally, the ripped feeling beginning to fade.

He held out his white cotton handkerchief, and she took it. After a minute he asked: "Aren't we going to look for shells, after all?"

"No, I want to go and sit on the oak bench."

Dozens of trees had been cut down during the building of the house, and Papa had had one made into a long bench, with a high back, for the beach.

Sitting down side by side, they looked out at the sea—today a wavy carpet of blue and green patches with occasional flecks of white where the wind stirred it up.

"What do you think will happen, Papa?"

"To you?" he asked. His voice was gentle.

"Yes, me."

"Perhaps you will marry a king who lives in a different country, where they need you. Only God can guide us."

Vicky considered this. If she were queen she'd sit on a throne like the enormous one in Buckingham Palace where Mama sat sometimes. But who would be beside her? Would he look like Papa? She hoped he wouldn't look like those naughty uncles of Mama's, the old kings of England. They'd had fat red faces and wore stiff white wigs. She wouldn't want to marry anyone like that.

She leaned against Papa, resting her cheek on the scratchy wool of his jacket sleeve. After a minute he put his arm around her, pulling her closer. The afternoon was breezy, and puffy cloud castles glided by above. In her mind's eye all the days of her future stretched out ahead so far she couldn't see the end, but she felt herself embarked, being carried slowly forward on the stream of time, buoyant and alive.

2

Windsor and the Isle of Wight, 1848

*P*apa required everything to be correct; he often used that word. And Mama preferred things nice and quiet and she hated to be fussed. But Laddle was different. She'd sit by the window doing her cross-stitch and let Vicky and Bertie overturn the toy chest on the nursery floor. She'd watch as they set up opposing armies of wooden soldiers and laugh when they mowed them down with sweeping arms. Laddle, whom everyone else called Lady Lyttelton, lived with them in the nursery, taught them to read and write, and told them stories from the Bible. Her thick hair was brown and wavy, arranged splendidly on the back of her head. Her smile was serene, but her eyes saw everything. One rainy afternoon, Bertie and Vicky dropped the cows and sheep and horses from the toy farm out the window to see which animal fell quickest. "Now Flora has to go and bring back all of those toys, children, and get wet along the way. It hardly seems fair, does it?" she asked.

"What else is Flora doing?" Vicky answered back.

Laddle tut-tutted and said: "I expect better from you, Princessy." Which made Vicky stomp away until it was time for tea. But mostly she and Laddle were friends. At the end of the

day they said prayers together and discussed God's command-
ments. Laddle was very "high," Vicky had heard, although what
that exactly meant she wasn't sure. Something about the sort of
religion Laddle preferred. Her teacher liked to say that in life
nothing was more important than being kind. And Vicky always
thought, yes, but how very nice and important it was to be the
Princess Royal.

On a side table in his study at Windsor, Papa kept open a large
atlas with smooth, heavy pages that Vicky liked to stroke, and
carefully turn over, one after another. Because it was such a fancy
book, it had a lovely clean, woody smell. The large map of Europe stretched over two adjacent leaves, and sometimes Papa
asked them to find Britain, and Vicky and Bertie could point to
it, high in the left corner, the island nation colored a pretty shade
of pink. Papa would put his finger on a teeny-tiny green place
lower down, near the binding, and say: "That's *meine Heimat,
Kinder.* That's Coburg."

"But where is Germany?" Vicky asked one day. "Isn't Coburg
in Germany?"

Papa shook his head. "That's the problem, Puss. Germany isn't
one nation. In almost forty different lands people speak German.
All these," he said, and he traced a big circle on the open pages.

"Germany should be united like Britain, or like France," he
continued, pointing to the yellow country right across the narrow
band of water from Britain. "The French are the neighbors of the
Germans but France has been one nation for a long time and has
become very strong. Earlier in this century France invaded Germany and managed to get all the way over here, to Russia." Papa
pointed to a large gray country on the right.

"Then what happened?" Bertie asked.

"The Russians fought and pushed them out. Then the Prussians joined in. Prussians are Germans who have sizable territory along the Rhine, but mostly here in the east." He pointed
to a potato-shaped country colored bright blue. "The Prussians

eventually allied with the British and at the battle of Waterloo the French were defeated."

"Are the French still our enemies?" asked Bertie.

"No, we are friends now," Papa said. "And that's a good thing."

"Are we friends with all Germans?" asked Vicky.

"Some are easier to get on with than others," said Papa, smiling.

"Do you wish you lived back in Coburg?" asked Bertie.

"*Ach,* I miss it sometimes, very much."

"But your duty is here, Papa, in England, with Mama and with us," said Vicky sternly.

"That's true," Papa said. "Still, I can never forget the dear home place."

PAPA HAD ONE particular friend, Baron Stockmar, who was German too, and also from Coburg. But he was queer looking, much shorter than Papa, with a wrinkled face and spindly bowlegs. One day when he came to Windsor he and Papa went into the library, and hours passed.

Vicky got impatient. "We will invade, Bertie," she said.

"Won't Papa be angry?" asked Bertie.

"He's talked long enough with the baron," she said. "It's our turn now."

They ran along the passageway and burst in through the library door. The men went right on conversing. She shouted: "Here we are. Don't you want to sing with us?"

They paid no attention. She nudged Bertie toward the pianoforte.

"Go and play," said Vicky.

Bertie ran over and began banging on the keys.

Then Papa stood up. "This is not a moment to play music," he said, and he walked over to the piano, closing the lid after pushing Bertie's little hands away.

"Let's show the baron what you've learned since last time he was here," Papa said. Vicky loved this. The baron would ask questions and Vicky and Bertie would answer. Mostly it was she who answered. Bertie didn't know many Bible verses, and she had more history, too—she could say all the English kings and queens.

She ran to the sofa to perch between the baron and Papa, sitting up straight and ready. But this time the baron asked something odd: "Who is the most admirable being in the world?"

Vicky immediately said, "My papa," and cuddled closer to him.

Bertie, who had squeezed in between Vicky and the baron, looked troubled. Finally, he said, "Mrs. Bumps."

Papa laughed a big, ringing laugh.

"Who is this Mrs. Bumps?" asked the baron.

"She's not a person," scoffed Vicky.

"She's a dog, a golden retriever who belongs to Colonel Seymour, one of the equerries," said Papa, still grinning.

"Why did you choose her, Prince?" the baron asked.

"She is friendly and has a beautiful coat. Seymour gave her a collar that has a little picture of Mama attached to it. That makes her noble," he replied solemnly.

"Not a good answer at all," said Vicky. "We need other, different questions. Surely you can do better, Baron."

"You are very commanding, little princess," said the baron, smiling.

"I am not little princess. I am the Princess Royal," said Vicky.

There was a knock on the door and a footman entered. "The carriage is at the door, Highness."

"*Kinder,* we will have time later for other questions," said Papa. "I'm going out with the baron. You return to the nursery." Putting a hand on each of their backs, he propelled them gently forward.

Bertie ran ahead, and as Vicky trailed behind she overheard the baron say: "The heir, he has a fine disposition, Prince. That is something."

BACK AT OSBORNE for the summer, Papa declared they were old enough to learn to swim, and he had a bathing area marked out with ropes on their beach. She learned quickly, but Bertie and

Alice clutched at Papa for days. Finally, they could swim too, and clamored to go often. Even Mama liked to bathe, and Papa had had a special bathing machine constructed for her. She climbed up stairs into a little wooden hut to change clothes, then the hut rolled down the sloping rails of the bathing pier so she could step out the other side and slide right into the sea.

Bathing cheered Mama up. She had had another baby, called Louise, and she complained she was still very unwell. Papa urged her to rest and enjoy the sunshine and do her painting *en plein air*. Mama loved painting and had had a small easel made for Vicky exactly like her big one. The art master, Monsieur Corbould, came occasionally from the Royal Academy in London to give them lessons. So strange to see Mama following closely what he said, trying earnestly to improve. Mama listened to Papa of course, but really only to him and Monsieur Corbould.

Papa and Mama never wasted time inside when the weather was fine. But on wet days Vicky would find them working at their side-by-side desks in the upstairs study. Large despatch boxes from London sat open on the floor next to Papa's desk, and he'd take papers out to read, and then he'd pass them to Mama to sign. She would be writing a letter, to her half sister Feodora in Germany, or to Grandmamma, the Duchess of Kent, back at Windsor. She'd put the letter aside when Papa told her to sign a paper, writing "VR" in large initials and rolling over them with the rocking blotter. On some papers Papa would write, in pencil, comments he thought Mama should add. Mama would carefully copy over Papa's words with a pen in her own handwriting. After the ink had dried, Mama would erase any trace of Papa's pencil. "You are so very clever, my darling, thank you," she'd say, or just lean over to kiss his cheek.

One morning Lord Russell, the prime minister, arrived at Osborne with some other ministers. They milled about in the front hall, while Vicky and Bertie sat unseen behind the half-open door to the billiards room.

"Russell, after such a long journey it would be courteous if

Their Royal Highnesses received us immediately," said a tall, thin man, still wearing his top hat.

"Patience, Graham. The queen is likely retrieving her husband from the grounds. He's forever busy with one project or another," the prime minister replied.

"Why not simply converse with her?"

"No point. Haven't you heard me say it a hundred times? She has the title, he does the work."

All the men chuckled.

Vicky didn't like that, the sound of their laughing about the queen.

"She works, too, doesn't she?" Vicky asked Papa later, recounting the exchange.

"Indeed she does, and she has much good sense," he said.

"But sometimes Mama says she wouldn't know what to do if you were not here."

"Mama didn't have the education I did, Vicky, so it is important that I advise her. What is more, I am a man, and I watch out that those other men, the ministers, they do not try to be a little *pfiffig*—tricky—with her."

"She is queen! She orders them what to do!"

"It's not so simple. Sometimes they are sneaky. They propose plans that are not wise. Or pretend that they can do what they want without consulting her."

"They would dare?" She put her hands on her hips and looked up, indignant.

"As queen she rules together with the prime minister, the Parliament, and the ministers. It's a delicate dance, and when everyone dances the correct steps, then things are smooth. But I look carefully at what they do and keep them from treading on Mama's toes or taking the wrong steps."

"You have to guard her against naughty ministers?"

"Protect and defend her. Also uphold standards. The sovereign cannot expect to long enjoy his, or her, elevated position without doing that."

"I would do that if I were queen."

"Perhaps it will fall to you, as it has to me, Vicky, to share in the work."

"And keep things correct?"

"To use your life and your position for the general good," he said, smiling his lovely, kind smile.

ON A HOT day in June Papa announced a special guest was arriving. His name was Prince Wilhelm of Prussia and Papa said the children should call him Uncle Prussia, because he was royal as they were, and a distant cousin. Vicky imagined a jolly, affable man in a suit of bright blue, like the color of Prussia in Papa's map book. Instead Uncle Prussia turned out to be bulky and stern, with large bushy gray side whiskers, wearing a gray army uniform.

Papa urged her to talk to the prince and make him feel welcome. So she told him about her pony Trixie, her lessons with Laddle, and how Papa had taken them to the farm next door to Osborne House to see the sheep being washed before shearing.

"Those sheep hated their baths and they squealed, and tried to get away," she told Uncle Prussia, paddling her arms to show how the animals scrambled. "One escaped and went running down the lane, and only after the farmer's boy ran after and jumped on top of its wet back could he drag it back."

Bertie and Alice remembered that naughty sheep, and they laughed and laughed. But Prince Wilhelm appeared perplexed by everything she said.

When Papa came to the nursery to say good night she told him the prince must be hard of hearing or didn't understand her German.

"No, Puss, I believe you surprise him," her father said. "He's not sure what to make of such a lively, confident girl as you are."

"He doesn't like girls like me?"

"He definitely should. But, *liebe* Vicky, you are *einmalig*—like no one else."

"Is that good?"

"Very, very good."

UNCLE PRUSSIA WAS restless indoors and preferred to be out riding and hunting, always wearing his same gray uniform. He insisted on taking the largest horse from the Osborne stable. Papa and the grooms organized a special Prussian-style shoot for him: lots of deer from all over the island were herded together in a pen, and then when Uncle Prussia was ready, the grooms drove the deer toward him and he shot them. He killed a tremendous number.

Bertie had gone with Papa to watch, and he came back to the nursery very sad. "Those deer didn't have a chance," he said.

In the evenings Papa talked to Prince Wilhelm for hours about Germany. "It's all very interesting," Papa told them one morning after Uncle Prussia had gone out. "We discuss the united nation that must come into being. Prussia should take the lead."

"Angel, do you think he is actually listening to what you have to say?" Mama asked.

"Of course he is listening. What could be more important to him than the attainment of liberty and prosperity for all Germans?" Her father looked miffed.

"I only notice that Wilhelm is a very traditional man, and given that he was essentially chased out of Berlin, these modern notions of yours may not be in keeping with his own," Mama said.

"Nonsense," said Papa.

Vicky couldn't imagine the formidable prince's being chased out of anywhere. "What happened to Uncle Prussia?" she asked.

"He was the senior general on the spot when, three months ago, uprisings broke out in Berlin, Prussia's capital," Papa said.

Mama shivered. "We're so fortunate to have had no such uprisings here."

"Indeed, *Weibchen,* and that's because your government is basically sound, and includes the people's representatives," Papa said. "The same cannot be said of Prussia. Yet."

"I still don't understand why Uncle Prussia left," Vicky said.

"He ordered his troops to fire on the rioters and three hundred were killed. Afterward, his brother, the king, forced him to leave the country for his own safety. The revolutionaries wanted him executed."

What a nasty, frightening word—execute. "They wished to chop off his head?" she asked anxiously.

"Or some such," said her father, flicking his hand, surprisingly unconcerned.

"So he can never go home? He'll stay with us forever?" she asked, not pleased.

"The Prussians have to sort themselves out."

"Doesn't he have his own family?"

"He does, but they stayed behind in Prussia," said Papa.

"We dined twice with his wife when she visited London a few years ago," said Mama. "She's called Princess Augusta and she's from Weimar."

"Weimar is where the writer Goethe was born, Vicky," said Papa. "Some of the most famous poets, musicians, and artists in the whole world are German. Yet when it comes to governance we Germans have not been fortunate. We must pray things improve."

THE PRINCE DID depart Osborne some weeks later. Papa said he'd gone to London, to live at the Prussian legation, where he could follow events in Berlin more closely.

And later Papa told them Prince Wilhelm had returned home. He shook his head. "For a brief moment it looked like things were really progressing in Prussia. Now they are going backward."

"Don't fret, angel," Mama said. "The old ways can't last forever. Don't you always say that?"

"Yes, but it's no good if the new ways are just the old ways dressed up differently," her father said.

Vicky imagined Uncle Prussia traveling back to Prussia on a boat. He'd taken off his uniform and was walking the deck, swinging a cane, wearing a smart tailcoat and striped trousers, the clothes Lord Russell and the other ministers wore. But his face was stern as ever.

AT CHRISTMAS VICKY found on the present table at Windsor a large wooden crate that Mama said had come from Berlin.

Inside were three dozen Prussian toy soldiers, beautifully crafted in lead, meant for Bertie. Vicky received dollhouse-sized replicas of fruit and vegetable stalls. She admired the careful painting on the tiny round tomatoes, oranges, and pears. Mama read from the accompanying letter: "Tell the Princess Royal we have such shops in Berlin. And we hope the Prince of Wales will enjoy playing with our soldiers. We send you and Albert and all your beautiful children fond wishes, and many thanks for your hospitality. We hope to meet again one day soon. *Frohe Weihnachten*, Wilhelm and Augusta."

3

London, Spring 1851

*N*ow that Bertie had turned nine, Papa declared he was too old to be supervised by Laddle in the nursery and needed a proper tutor to educate him for his future. A washed-out, pained-looking man who had formerly taught at Eton College, called Mr. Birch, was employed to instruct her brother, but Bertie didn't like his lessons and being forced to sit and study for hours at a time. Sometimes he'd get so fed up he'd knock over the pile of books in front of him, crawl under the table, and refuse to come out. Papa would fume and Mr. Birch would look even more pinched and disconsolate.

Baron Stockmar had said that because Vicky was very able, her education could not be ignored, and Alice showed promise too, so he hired a young woman, a Miss Hildyard, a parson's daughter from Norfolk, to teach them both. After Alice mangled the name at first meeting, their new teacher was forevermore called Tillayard, or just Tilla.

Vicky thought Tilla resembled a clever, ardent bird. She had keen, small brown eyes and wore her shiny crow-black hair smooth over her ears and fastened up in a simple bun. Tilla worshipped Shakespeare, knew every chapter of English history, and could recite reams of verse. Also, she was passionate about politics, the rights of man, and all the rapid progress that, she told them, was the hallmark of the age.

"Imagine, girls, how for centuries people believed that tomorrow would be just like today and yesterday," she said. "But industrial inventions and scientific discoveries are advancing the way everyone lives. Who knows how far civilization will progress in your lifetimes?"

Papa, too, believed in the promise of the future, and he was planning a great exhibition to put on display everything that Britain—and the world—had to offer that was new. There would be huge machinery—steam-powered lifts, mechanical printing presses, and giant railroad locomotives—along with cunning inventions like a folding piano, a carriage drawn by kites, and various velocipedes that men could pedal, sitting atop two wheels or three.

To house these marvels a new building was being erected in Hyde Park. When Papa first took them to see, there was nothing there but a huge, ugly skeleton of thin iron poles, stretching much longer than the front of Buckingham Palace and reaching high over the grass, bushes, even two tall elms. The next time they went workmen were placing wide panes of glass between the iron poles. And finally, they visited one cool April evening, when the structure was complete and lit up on the inside. The newspapermen called it "the Crystal Palace" and Vicky understood why: it glowed with white-yellow luminosity in the darkening park, a strange, magical fairy form like nothing she'd ever seen before.

With the official opening of the exhibition fast approaching, Papa invited Prince Wilhelm back to England.

"I want him to see what's possible in a strong, modern nation, where men are unfettered to pursue progress," he announced at supper one Sunday. "If Germany were united, it could step up beside Britain and lead Europe."

"Angel, why not invite Princess Augusta as well?" Mama said. "And the son, said to be a handsome lad?"

Papa smiled. "He's a Prussian, thus he's a soldier, like his father, his grandfather, his great-grandfather before him . . ."

"Still, I think we should see him," Mama said, smiling back.

"*Kinder*, would you like to meet some young Germans?"

"Yes, I would," said Vicky.

"Tell them to bring more excellent toy soldiers," said Bertie.

It was soon fixed. Prince Wilhelm and Princess Augusta would come accompanied by their two children: the older was the boy, aged nineteen, Friedrich Wilhelm, called Fritz, and the younger a girl named Louise, aged twelve.

"You will be responsible for showing them around, Vicky," Papa said.

ON THE MORNING of the day the Prussians were to arrive, Vicky was up early, sitting on the edge of her bed, impatient for Flora to come and take the knotted rags out of her hair. She had asked for ringlets for the occasion, and although the knobby ties all over her skull had made it hard to fall asleep, the discomfort was worth it. The moment Flora was done, Vicky hurried over to the glass to stare at herself: her springy brown curls and big blue eyes looking back at her pleased her, and once she got out of her nightgown and into her new white muslin dress, she knew she'd look very nice and Papa and many others would admire her.

Flora had laid out a pink sash to wear, but Alice and Lenchen had the same, and Vicky didn't want to match. When Flora turned her back, Vicky fished a teal blue sash out of the wardrobe, tied it as best she could, and then left the nursery, heading for the Queen's Gallery, intending to watch out the window for Papa. He had gone to the London Bridge railway station to pick up their guests.

Passing along the corridor, she heard Mama's anxious voice floating out of her suite.

"Why does this flounce on the right droop?"

"Let me pin it up," said Mrs. Moon, the head seamstress.

"And the neckline definitely sits too low," Mama said.

Vicky heard the seamstress reply: "We can pull that higher from the back."

Vicky crossed the open doorway, and Mama called out: "Puss, I want to see you!"

She slid reluctantly into the room.

"Your sash is loose. Come here, turn round," said her mother.

Mama pulled and tugged, then she snapped: "Someone help me with this."

Mrs. Moon needed only a moment to tie a tight bow at the back of the dress.

Mama sighed. "Pretty, but just emphasizes how there's no waist there at all. She's the shape of a suet dumpling."

"Ah, ma'am, she's a young girl still," Mrs. Moon said.

"True," Mama replied, gazing dolefully at Vicky.

Vicky felt suddenly cast down, as if Mama had taken a pin and popped the balloon of her excitement for the day. Her mother often complained aloud about her own appearance—longing to be taller, fairer, and more slender. And while she'd smile when guests declared that Vicky was Her Majesty in miniature, in private their resemblance worried Mama, and she'd fret over her daughter's looks as well. Papa disapproved of all such talk.

"Obsession with appearance is the preoccupation of a shallow mind," he'd scold.

"How like a man to think so," Mama would retort.

Now a lady's maid brought in Mama's jewelry case, and her mother started fussing about which necklace to wear. Vicky took the chance to slip away. As she walked down the hallway, she smoothed down the front of her skirt and wagged her head from side to side to feel the lovely bouncy ringlets. Her new pointy-toed white shoes tapped sharply on the varnished wood floor. Mama hadn't been nice to say that she looked like a dumpling, not nice at all, but she mustn't think about that now. She had her job to do. Papa had said: "I rely on you to be a gracious and charming hostess, Vicky."

WHEN A HALF hour later she and Bertie were escorted by a footman into the Chinese Drawing Room, where the Prussian royals, now arrived, stood with Mama and Papa, her first thought was how tall they all appeared. Uncle Prussia she recognized immediately, his stern face framed on both sides by thick gray whiskers, and next to him stood a young man, surely Fritz. Father and son had the same big nose and square jaw, but Fritz sported neither whiskers nor mustache and had instead lots of wavy golden hair and a fine, smooth complexion. His expression and the way he tilted his blond head seemed somehow bashful. But when she smiled at him, he grinned and stepped forward, reaching for her hand and raising it to his lips to kiss.

Vicky felt gratified to be so greeted, and then Papa ruined it by laughing.

"Perhaps, as we are family, we can dispense with such formality."

"The prince is only my distant cousin, Papa," Vicky told him sternly.

"That's true," her father replied with a smile.

"I am very happy to meet you, Princess," said Fritz in slow, heavily accented English.

"Can we not speak German?" said Vicky quickly, in that language. *Können wir nicht Deutsch sprechen?*

"In England, we will speak English," declared the woman, surely Princess Augusta, who stood on Uncle Prussia's other side, wearing a dark purple dress trimmed with black feathers. She had a long, solemn face; a small, pursed mouth; and hooded eyes, close together. She was looking Vicky up and down, assessing.

"How very short you are for ten," the princess said.

Vicky felt again, as before with Mama, a sharp, deflating prick, followed by a flush of shame and a wave of sulkiness. She couldn't make herself any taller, could she? But she mustn't be distracted. She curtsied and said: "I am very pleased to meet you, Aunt

Prussia. Welcome to England. Please present me to your daughter." Out of the corner of her eye she sensed Papa beaming.

Princess Louise hovered close to her mother's right arm. Wan, and wearing an unfortunate beige dress, she was quite a bit taller than Vicky but appeared ill at ease. Thin, lanky, mouse-brown hair was pulled off her face and fastened, half up and half down, at the back of her head.

"Yes, this is Louise," said her mother brusquely as the girl bobbed at Vicky. "You two girls will be friends I hope."

"I have so looked forward to your visit," Vicky said. "First, you must meet my brother. Bertie, come here."

She beckoned to Bertie, who, having bowed to Uncle and Aunt Prussia, had drifted off to the side. Now he stepped over.

"Let's tell Louise about our preparations," Vicky said.

"Preparations?" said Bertie cluelessly.

"Last evening we set things up in the nursery, don't you remember? We got out the big dollhouse and the brick castle and the miniature shops from Berlin and arranged everything as a town."

"Yes, that's right," Bertie said to Louise. "We hoped it might look like a Prussian town. I ringed it with my Prussian soldiers. That's the best part."

Louise didn't respond. Was she offended?

"Maybe you think yourself too old for such things? I know you are twelve," said Vicky hurriedly.

"I like dollhouses. Soldiers, not," she said in a whispery voice.

"We have several other dollhouses, too, and of course many dolls," Vicky said.

Louise made no reply.

"And if we get tired of dolls we can paint. I love to paint. Do you?" Vicky said.

Again, Louise said nothing.

Fritz came around from the other side of his parents to stand behind his sister. "It is kind that Vicky and Bertie think about you, *nicht wahr*, Loulee?" he said in an encouraging voice.

Mute Louise nodded.

"And the other children are upstairs waiting," said Vicky, still anxious to get this girl to relax. "You know we have two little sisters? Really, it's three if you count the baby, our Louise, and a little brother, Affie."

"And tell her about the mare, Vicky," prompted Bertie.

"Yes, the mare. Your father rode so much at Osborne, we imagined you must fancy it as well and Papa had the grooms bring one of the nicest horses from Windsor for you. She's called Elsie."

"We can ride in the park," said Bertie.

The princess gave a small smile. "I do like to ride."

"*Das ist sehr schön,*" said Fritz, putting his hands on Louise's shoulders and smiling at Bertie and Vicky. "We can enjoy riding and many things together, here in London."

BUT TRULY, LOUISE was exasperating. Vicky felt sure she wouldn't be this timid visiting a foreign country. They took the princess up to the nursery to meet the little children and see the Prussian town they'd set out, and the other toys and books. At first it was fine and Louise got down on her knees to help Vicky rearrange some furniture in the dollhouse. Yet when Bertie and Affie began to quarrel over a wooden bayonet, and ended up tussling on the floor, Louise, wincing and dismayed, asked to be taken back down directly.

It was a relief to find Fritz good-natured at supper, served informally in Mama's yellow sitting room. Vicky sat next to him and they chatted together in German despite his mother's edict. He loved dogs as she did, but greyhounds were his favorite, not spaniels, which she preferred. He told her about his beloved horse, called Firefly, which he rode on maneuvers and in dressage competitions. He liked to read, but books about history and military strategy, not novels or plays or poetry.

"Perhaps next year when I study at Bonn I will have time for such things," he said.

"How sad you have to wait so long. My papa says that poetry is food for the soul and everyone must indulge regularly."

Fritz smiled. "Your father, he was also a student once at Bonn, *nicht wahr?*"

"Yes, before he came to England to marry Mama. He has a special green-shaded lamp on his desk from Bonn."

"Now he has become an Englishman and is no longer a German."

"I wouldn't say that," Vicky interjected. She'd been told how, when Papa first arrived, many of Mama's family and her ministers had been very suspicious of him. Now everyone respected him. An excellent statesman and counselor, he was called, a man of action who had single-handedly mounted the exhibition when no one believed it could be done.

She glanced down the table to see Papa at the head, conversing intently with Princess Augusta. "Papa is still a proud German," she told Fritz. "He's constantly speaking of what must happen in Germany. I know he's happy that your parents have come so he can discuss those things with them, and also so you all can see the exhibition. It's completely marvelous."

"Your father described it a bit on the ride from the station."

"I've been twice already. I've made a list of what to take you to see and in which order."

"You will be an excellent guide, no question," Fritz said, grinning in his friendly way.

She smiled back. He had such lovely wavy hair—bright blond, like Alice's favorite doll, Ada. Vicky felt like reaching up and touching it. Ada's hair was stiff and bristly; Fritz's was likely softer. She wondered if Louise felt angry that her older brother had gotten the hair that was so much better for a girl, when she was stuck with such thin, colorless locks. Vicky leaned forward to see around Fritz to where Louise was sitting on his other side. She had stopped eating and, clearly tired after their long day of travel, was resting her head against Fritz's shoulder. No, it didn't seem like the Prussian princess resented her brother—Louise appeared in fact to quite adore him.

ON THE NEXT morning, she and Bertie stood just outside the courtyard door, near Mama, busy talking with her cousins the Duke of Cambridge and his plump sister Mary, who were joining them for the day. Grandmamma had arrived as well, and she admired Vicky's attire: a shell-pink silk dress with a wreath of rosebuds for her hair.

"You look very pretty, dear, and I always like to see you and your mother match."

"But Mama's gown is watered silk, with diamonds sewn on, and it's a darker shade of pink," Vicky said.

"Yes, quite the same," her grandmother insisted.

No use arguing with Grandmamma; she was so often muddled. But she cooed over Bertie in the kilt and Highland hat that Mama and Papa had bought for him in Scotland. Then she asked for the younger children.

"Mama and Papa decided they'd better stay home, because it will be hot and crowded at the exhibition."

"Crowded? Not on the first day," said Grandmamma.

Vicky exchanged an exasperated look with Bertie. The servants reported the city teemed with people from all over England who had come to see the show.

Now here was Papa stepping out the door with the Prussians. Prince Wilhelm and Fritz, tall and resplendent in white dress uniforms trimmed with gold, walked beside him. Following behind, Louise looked pretty in a lemon-yellow dress. Princess Augusta wore dark blue.

Vicky held the two exhibition catalogs that Papa had had bound in red satin especially for Uncle and Aunt Prussia. She stepped toward them and curtsied.

"These programs are for you," she said.

The prince and princess took them without smiling or expressing thanks. Quite ungracious, Vicky thought. When they began to open the programs, Papa said: "No, we must go now, come this way."

Their parents walking on toward the carriages, Fritz and Louise lingered.

Suddenly she was nervous. "I'm sorry we have only the two special catalogs. I'm sure Uncle and Aunt Prussia will share," she said.

"I have a different question," said Fritz, smiling. "Will we two ride there together with you two? We hope so!"

"Oh, no," exclaimed Vicky. "You are obliged to go in the carriage with your parents. Bertie and I are to ride with Papa and Mama in the first one."

"Too bad," said Fritz. "*Komm*, Loulee, we will see Vicky and Bertie there. For our personal tour." He winked at Vicky before shepherding his sister toward the line of open landaus, painted the sovereign's color, chocolate brown, and each driven by a pair of coachmen in the royal livery, scarlet and dark blue. She watched them walk away, Princess Louise slipping her hand into her brother's. It had never occurred to Vicky until just then that having an older brother might be a lovely thing.

FROM THE MOMENT the file of carriages turned out of the palace gates, huge crowds lining both sides of the road cheered and waved, making such a racket that Vicky could barely hear Mama and Papa speaking to each other on the seat opposite. Mama kept squeezing Papa's hand and beaming at him. He looked stunned. From time to time Vicky heard calls of "The Princess Royal!" and she made a point of leaning forward and waving vigorously in that direction. She wondered if there had ever before been this many people out in London. Maybe for Mama's coronation.

They pulled up outside the Crystal Palace, which towered above them, mammoth. Vicky watched the Prussians get out of their carriage, and gaze up, and crane their necks to take in all four floors of glass, crowned by the glorious arched roof.

As Prince Wilhelm led his family toward them, he was shaking his head.

"I thought you exaggerated, Albert," he said to Papa in German.

"But it's truly a remarkable structure. How long did it take to construct?"

"Only four months, once the design was set," Papa said. "A new factory in Staffordshire can manufacture glass in large single sheets with a mechanized pouring process. You will notice only a few panes are not the standard size. Those were custom cut."

The prince stood transfixed, looking up. Fritz, beside him, pointed at the roof.

"So the roof is like the walls, completely glass? The entire length of the building?" Fritz asked.

"*Ja*, and when we go inside, you will see, it's as bright as day," Papa replied.

As if on cue, the sun broke through the morning's low clouds, and they walked up to the entrance in the sunshine, policemen holding back the happy, noisy throng.

Inside, a quieter, more reverent assembly stood to greet them. An invitation to the opening ceremony had become the most sought-after commodity in London, Papa had said. Members of Parliament, bankers and businessmen, lords and ladies, all clamored to attend. As the royal party processed up the center aisle toward the stage, Vicky saw on either side of them gentlemen in tailcoats and tall hats, and women, too, in their finery, silk dresses with wide hoop skirts laden with ribbons and lace, most holding small parasols to shade themselves.

Bertie beside her, she followed Mama and Papa up the four red-carpeted stairs onto the stage, while a chorus in the distance sang an oratorio Papa had composed for the occasion. Papa pointed to seats for them on the right of the dais and escorted Mama to a huge Indian chair covered in rugs that sat under a blue and gold canopy. He then took his place, standing at her left, as the last notes of music faded away. A pause. A blare of trumpets. And the organ began "God Save the Queen."

The rest of their group had seats in the front row, facing the stage. Vicky felt her chest swell with pride and excitement. Everyone had come to witness this glorious achievement of her papa's, with her mama presiding and celebrating her nation—the best, most advanced in the world. No wonder the Prussians looked so awestruck.

The lord mayor of London walked up the stairs and proclaimed that this "Great Exhibition of the Works of Industry of All Nations" was not only a triumph for Britain but a beacon of hope, promising peace and cooperation for all of humankind. When it was Papa's turn to speak, the applause was thunderous. At one point he tried to share credit with Mr. Henry Cole, his colleague from the Royal Society, and he summoned that paunchy, gray-haired gentleman to the stage. But the audience had no time for Cole. Instead a man in the second row shouted out: "Three cheers for the prince," and led the crowd in "Hip-hip-hooray."

Next, foreign dignitaries lined up to be presented to the queen, including a Chinese man in a long yellow silk coat who prostrated himself at her feet and had to be lifted away by two guards. Later Vicky heard he hadn't been a dignitary at all, but was the captain of a junk moored in the Thames who had desired to meet the famous Victoria. But in the moment, she thought that maybe ambassadors from Eastern countries always expressed reverence this way.

Bertie swung his legs restlessly and whispered that he couldn't wait for this endless proceeding to be over, and Vicky was about to scold him when a gong sounded and Mama rose and declared the exhibition open. A tremendous rustling of skirts and pushing back of chairs could be heard as the crowd got up and headed toward the exhibits. The Cambridges and the Prussians mounted the stage.

"Excellent, excellent," said the Duke of Cambridge, thumping Papa on the back.

Cousin Mary kissed Mama's cheek. "Your husband is the man of the hour."

Mama flushed.

"And how warmly the people cheered you, Victoria, all the way from the palace," said Aunt Prussia.

"There must have been two hundred thousand people, maybe three hundred thousand, out today," Prince Wilhelm said to Papa. "You never see a crowd that size in Berlin."

Papa smiled. "The police tell me more than half a million. Perhaps as many as seven hundred thousand."

"And all so joyful and happy," said Augusta. "They love their queen."

Vicky felt it only right that Uncle and Aunt Prussia be impressed—she supposed they were not used to the same at home. She had recently asked Tilla what happened when Prince Wilhelm went back to Prussia: did he still have to worry about people trying to execute him?

"I don't think he worries about that anymore, Vicky," Tilla had explained. "The Junkers—the conservative Prussians—prevailed after the revolution. Very disappointing for many German liberals, including your father and Baron Stockmar, who had hoped Prince Wilhelm's brother the king would establish a true constitutional monarchy, like our British one. That hasn't happened. There's a new Prussian constitution, yes, but it doesn't empower parliament much."

"Don't those Junkers want Prussia to be better?"

"They obviously hold a different view of what would be better. To them the Hohenzollern dynasty was appointed by God to rule, and they believe nothing should challenge their divine authority."

Now, as Vicky watched Prince Wilhelm and his wife, both so haughty, she could see they considered themselves superior to most people. But divine? Meant by God to rule one day? That seemed too unreasonable even for them. Kings and queens in England had believed that once, she knew, but in the olden days. Not now.

Mama was nodding at something Princess Augusta was saying when suddenly she looked around, bewildered. "Where is the duchess?" Mama asked. "Vicky, have you seen Grandmamma?"

Vicky stepped to the left to get a clear view of the other dignitaries still crowded in front of the stage but saw no sign of her grandmother.

"She must have gone off somewhere," Vicky said.

A sharp intake of breath from Princess Augusta. "Goodness, has she been kidnapped? Held by radicals or criminals?"

Vicky, Bertie, and Mama all laughed.

"My mother can be a real goose, Augusta," Mama said. "But no harm will come to her in London. Bertie, go and find her."

Bertie sped away—pleased, Vicky was sure, to have a job that released him from all the boring talk. She edged around the Prussian parents and the Cambridges to where Fritz and Louise stood.

They too looked alarmed. "Your grandmother is lost?" asked Fritz.

"For the moment. I'm sure Bertie will locate her, and meanwhile I will take you to see the exhibits."

FROM THE START Fritz was gratifyingly attentive, but Louise didn't always listen as closely as she should have to Vicky's explanations.

"Why are we even looking at this?" she complained when they reached the cotton-cleaning machine.

Vicky felt annoyed, but Fritz joked: "It's painful, then, Loulee, is it? Inserting new knowledge into your brain?" he said. He lightly tapped his sister's head with his index finger.

Louise smiled at him and hung on his arm.

Just then Bertie caught up. He'd found Grandmamma chatting cheerfully with a policeman, who had had no idea who she was, and had taken her back to Mama.

"Let's visit the French exhibit," Vicky said. "Lots of china and tapestries; you will like it, Louise."

Louise did, and then Bertie suggested the clock and watch exhibit, which they all enjoyed, laughing at the alarm clock attached to a bed, which, at the stroke of six A.M., would lift up the mattress and dump the hapless sleeper on the floor. Fritz was intrigued by the small electric clocks for sale, and he resolved to come back later to buy one for his student room in Bonn. Bertie dragged them to see his favorite item in the whole show, a defensive umbrella with a hidden stiletto at its tip, which Fritz also found engrossing. Vicky got impatient when Bertie and Fritz next spent long minutes marveling over a sportsman's knife with eighty blades sent by the city of Sheffield. Finally, she was able to lead them to a very special place—a small upstairs gallery lined with stained glass, a contribution from Venetian glassblowers. The sun, shining through the panes, made beams of every color, and Louise giggled as she passed her hands through and saw the brilliant shades on her skin.

Two hours later, back at the stage where they were to meet Mama and Papa, Princess Augusta and Prince Wilhelm were already waiting. But the Prussian couple barely acknowledged them.

"Such a waste that you spent the whole time with Bernstorff. Others wanted to converse," Princess Augusta was telling her husband, her long face a study in disapproval.

"I had much to discuss with our ambassador," her husband replied without looking at her. He was surveying the hall impatiently.

"Albert was eager to introduce you to some of the parliamentarians attending today," Augusta continued.

"There will be enough time for that later," said Prince Wilhelm, still looking away.

"You shouldn't miss such opportunities to—" Augusta began.

"Be still now!" the prince snapped, glaring at his wife. "I have no need of your direction."

Vicky glanced up and saw Fritz, cheeks flushed, staring straight ahead, pretending, she guessed, that he couldn't hear his parents bickering. Louise looked down, absorbed, it appeared, in moving a pebble with the toe of her shoe. Vicky was relieved when, a minute later, Mama and Papa arrived and it was time to go.

As THE ROYAL party walked toward the door, loud applause rippled through the crowd. Numerous people offered flowers

to the queen, and because today she had only her family and a
few guards escorting her—no ladies—she passed the bouquets
back to Princess Mary of Cambridge and to Vicky, who before
long held a half dozen in her arms. Just at the door a man presented Mama with a handkerchief, but as soon as she touched
it, it turned into a posy of fabric flowers. Mama started with
surprise—and then she laughed.

"A special tribute very much in keeping with the day," declared
Papa. They all waited while he spoke with the inventor and
turned the device upside down to see the mechanism.

Fritz was beside Vicky, and he said quietly: "That gentleman
should not play tricks on the queen."

"Mama's so often getting tributes. Flowers, of course, and
people come to Windsor with their splendid hams and bolts of
new cotton cloth, all sorts of things," Vicky said.

"Gifts are appropriate, but making the royal person look undignified is never correct," said Fritz.

Vicky looked up at him. Rather an odd remark for a young
man to make. She noticed how uprightly Fritz carried himself,
spine very straight, shoulders back, chin up.

"I don't think we believe this in England," she said as they
walked on.

"Your mother and father must recognize the distinctions of
rank," he said.

"Papa says royal persons are distinct in that they have grave
responsibilities and must meet the highest standards of duty and
propriety," she said.

"Natürlich," replied Fritz

"Papa also says that simple, natural manners best suit everyone," she continued.

"Royal persons aren't like everyone else," Fritz said.

"I suppose not. Still, if you are royal and you aren't honorable,
then you're as low as any common cur. You've never read the
Tennyson?"

"No."

"Oh, I forgot, you don't read poetry. Alfred Tennyson is a wonderful English poet. Papa loves him, and Tilla, my teacher, does too. I learned his poem 'Lady Clara Vere de Vere' for Mama's birthday. In it a wicked noble lady flirts with a good country boy and drives him mad. Terrible! She is highborn but she does wrong."

She recited in English: "*'Tis only noble to be good. / Kind hearts are more than coronets / And simple faith than Norman blood.*"

"I don't understand," said Fritz.

"It's about what makes true nobility. Mama likes to quote this. You must read the whole poem when you get home."

"If you say so." She saw he was smiling now, although still walking in his soldierly way, chin up, head thrown back.

"You want to be good, don't you, Fritz? Everyone should want that."

"*Doch,* I try," he said with a small smile.

"And because we are highborn we are not hungry, nor living in a hovel. So we are especially obligated to be virtuous."

Now Fritz laughed.

"You don't agree?" she asked.

"I do. But you are so funny. Church is the usual place for such sentiments."

Vicky frowned. "You never talk about serious matters outside of church?"

"Sometimes. But not with sweet and earnest little girls," he said, laughing again. "You're like the young Jesus in the Temple, preaching to the elders."

"I'm not."

"It's charming. What will you instruct next?"

"Don't tease, and I don't like to be called little."

"What do you prefer? To be 'big Vicky'? 'Big-enough Vicky'?"

"Neither of those."

They had reached the carriages. She scowled up at him, her arms still full of flowers.

"Oh, now you are angry," he said. "Please, Vicky, I did not mean to offend you." He kept smiling merrily, and finally she couldn't help but soften her frown.

"There, good, I see you forgive me," he announced.

"I don't really," she replied.

He cocked his head. "A little bit, maybe. And you are correct, serious matters should be discussed. Even out of church."

"Only if the persons speaking of them are sincere," said Vicky, glowering again. He shouldn't mock her.

"In future I promise to be. I imagine you've thought over many consequential matters," he said, feigning sober concentration, while his eyes still glittered with fun.

She was about to remonstrate, but she heard Mama call out: "Come, Vicky."

In his careful, guttural English, Fritz said: "Thank you for the exhibition very well to me showing."

He clicked his heels and bowed. As she walked away she resolved to instruct him later on where the verbs in English sentences went.

THE PRUSSIANS STAYED in England for three weeks, and Mama and Papa laid on a busy program of outings, recreation, and state dinners. Vicky, Bertie, and Louise came along for visits to the National Portrait Gallery, the Palace of Westminster, Madame Tussauds, and back to the exhibition. But they were excluded from the dinners and trips to the opera or the theater. When Vicky saw Fritz heading out one evening, she told him it was very unfair.

"You don't miss much, some of the dinners are particularly dull," he told her.

"Still, I would like to go," she insisted.

"And tell the important men what's what?" he joked. It seemed he couldn't help teasing her, and Louise too. Sometimes, when they were out seeing the sights, Fritz would nudge his sister and say: "Smile, Loulee, it's a holiday!"

But most of the time Fritz was either riding with his father and equerries from the Prussian legation or sitting in Papa's study, discussing German history and politics. Papa had taken a great liking to him.

"The boy has promise!" Papa said to Mama late one afternoon. The Prussians had gone up to dress for dinner, but her parents lingered in the drawing room, the tea things still laid out on a low table. Vicky sat curled up in the window seat.

"Yes, he's a pleasant young man, but so unseasoned. His mother tells me this is his first trip abroad," Mama said, feeding a bit of spice cake to the spaniel Percy.

"Too busy with military training," said Papa. "But now he's headed to Bonn."

"Where he will prove a poor scholar, Augusta says."

Vicky piped up. "That's unkind. Fritz seems clever enough."

Papa smiled at her. "You like him then, Puss. He's got a good mind?"

"He took a great interest in everything at the exhibition. Louise only cared about the pretty things. And we discussed virtue. I told him to read Tennyson."

Mama and Papa laughed.

"You're improving him then?" Papa asked.

"Maybe a little," Vicky said.

"His mother is sure he needs it," said Mama.

"Perhaps it's the habit of mothers to dwell on the deficiencies of their sons," Papa said.

"Yes, I know something about that," said Mama, and they both laughed again.

FOR THE FINAL week of the visit they traveled to Osborne. Louise finally cheered up in the Swiss Cottage, a children's playhouse Papa had had built complete with working kitchen. She and Vicky baked a cake together. Bertie taught Louise to play skittles on the lawn, and they all caught butterflies.

Fritz took long walks on the beach with Papa, and sometimes Princess Augusta joined. "At least they're out of doors now. Much healthier than lurking in the study for hour after hour," Mama observed.

In the evenings, Vicky and Bertie and Louise ate supper with the adults in the dining room, under Herr Winterhalter's picture. The conversation often stretched for two hours or more. While the other children grew bored, slumping in their chairs, Vicky was generally interested. Princess Augusta and Papa appeared to agree on everything, while Uncle Prussia frequently shook his head over their "irredeemably liberal views."

One night, Augusta announced to her husband: "When you are king you need to commit to true parliamentary government. Prussia and Germany deserve it!"

"And what do you plan for me and for your son?" the prince lashed out, gesturing angrily at Fritz, who was flinching at his place across the table. "That we be powerless? Mere figureheads? Pathetic eunuchs?"

Papa turned to her and Bertie. "*Kinder, raus*—upstairs now," he said, and pointed at the door.

Louise was right behind them as they retreated from the room.

"What's a eunuch?" Bertie asked Vicky.

"I'm not sure. Maybe a choirboy?" She looked over at the Prussian princess—perhaps she could tell them. But Louise's face was closed up tight, and she said nothing as they climbed the stairs.

THE NEXT NIGHT Mama announced: "No politics at the table this evening, I decree."

Vicky thought Uncle and Aunt Prussia might sulk, but instead they tried to be jolly. Prince Wilhelm described how the wily German warrior Hermann trapped three Roman legions in the Teutoburg Forest in A.D. 9, and smashed them to pieces, forcing the Romans to withdraw forever from Magna Germania. Bertie was enthralled. Princess Augusta talked about her childhood at Weimar and the genius Goethe, who had been her grandfather's tutor and wrote love letters to her mother. Afterward they all trooped into the music room and Mama sat down at the piano, rustling through the sheets on the stand.

"Nothing here I like. Look in the chest and choose something, Puss."

Vicky pulled open the top, shallow drawer and found the score to one of her mother's favorites: Bach's "Jesu, Joy of Man's Desiring."

"Very good, very uplifting," said Mama. "And you can turn the pages."

Mama began, struggling at first, but then finding a smooth way through the beautiful lilting melody. Vicky stood next to her, swaying slightly in time. It was a warm evening and the windows had been propped open. Suddenly a huge gust of wind blew in and Vicky was too late to stop all the music from flying into the air and littering the room. Both Mama and Papa sprang up to retrieve dozens of pages off the floor. The Prussians looked on, horrified, Princess Augusta and Prince Wilhelm stiff in their chairs. Vicky whispered to Fritz, "Are they angry?"

"Why does no one call the servants?" he whispered back.

But Mama and Papa continued gathering up the sheets and she bent down to help. When they had all the music put back properly, Mama resumed playing, unperturbed.

AFTER THE VISIT ended, with fond goodbyes exchanged along with promises to write, Papa declared it all a great success. Vicky heard him say to Mama that the Prussian rigidity and preoccupation with protocol was "just a bit old-fashioned." Strange that her father, who always praised a modern outlook, didn't expect better of Uncle and Aunt Prussia. And she felt sorry for Fritz, and even for exasperating Louise, obliged to live with parents who were not so nice to them. She wondered if in Prussia all the adults were very stern and haughty like Prince Wilhelm and his wife.

A few months later, Vicky was surprised to be handed a letter on heavy cream paper, addressed to her in a large, foreign-looking hand.

"From Fritz," said Papa. "He wants you to know what he's reading."

It was a short letter, about poetry mostly, written in stiff, terse German. Later she asked Mama: "Must I write back? I'm not sure what to say."

"Not immediately perhaps, but eventually, it would be polite," she said. Then she added: "And you like Fritz, don't you?"

"Yes, although not how he teases sometimes."

Mama laughed. "Don't you know this yet? Young men tease the girls they like."

4

Paris, August 1855

*F*ar away in the Crimea, Britain fought a bloody war against tyrannical Russia. France, so often in the past England's enemy, was now an ally, and English and French soldiers battled side by side. To celebrate this newfound friendship, Emperor Napoléon III had come to London with his beautiful Spanish-born wife, Empress Eugénie. And, when they were leaving, they invited the queen and her family to make a reciprocal visit to Paris.

At first, Mama didn't want Vicky and Bertie to join. But Papa argued that because they were now fourteen and thirteen, it was time they saw somewhere beyond England. Also, the emperor expected them. An excitable little man, like a bantam rooster, and very exclamative, he had declared: "We are transforming Paris into the most magnificent city in Europe! In the world! Your children must see it! We will give a ball in your honor!"

While Mama frowned for much of the crossing to Boulogne, she looked delighted as they drove down the Rue de Rivoli in open landaus, en route to be formally received at the Hôtel de Ville. Despite a melting sun, large crowds had come out to cheer the British queen, her husband, her heir, and the Princess Royal.

Vicky's favorite place in Paris was the room assigned to her on the second floor of the Palace of St. Cloud. At home she shared with Alice, so it was thrilling to have a room of her own. And beside the bed, she discovered a wooden door that led out into a walled roof garden, lined with flowering bushes and delicate orange trees. At the far end of the garden there was, set in a narrow, arched opening, a small ironwork terrace from which one could look down upon all of wondrous cream-gray Paris below.

In a corner of the bedroom stood a life-size doll wearing a ball gown—white net over peach silk, trimmed with pale peach roses.

"This gown I designed for you, Vicky," the empress had said when she escorted them in.

"So lovely. I do hope it fits," said Vicky, quite dazzled by the sight. Examining it more closely, she could see how the doll's light brown hair had been styled the way she wore her own, parted in the middle, slightly bouffant at the sides, and drawn back from the face.

"*Mais oui*," said Eugénie. "The doll is your exact size. I asked my maid to obtain your measurements when we stayed in London. And then the dressmakers assembled the doll and used it to cut the dress."

Mama had looked on most disapprovingly but said nothing.

Later Mama had complained: "We brought along a perfectly fine dress for you."

"Mama, I could hardly wear that now that the empress has had one made for me specially."

"I suppose not, but this is just why I didn't want you and your brother to come to Paris. Much too much ostentation. Imagine all this fuss over a gown for a young girl!"

Papa smiled. "Still, a first ball, it's a special occasion."

Vicky felt a bit in awe of the lavish garment. A half-dozen tiers of white lace flounces encircled the skirt, each trimmed with the narrowest width of peach-colored velvet ribbon. Small posies of delicate fabric flowers were attached to the sleeves and to the bodice, and at the lowest point of the V-neck. The gown sat daringly low off both shoulders, leaving half her back bare. The empress had advised she wear no jewelry. "Your fresh beauty does not require it," she trilled in her melodious, sweetly accented English.

When Vicky descended the St. Cloud stairs on the night of the ball, the rest of the family awaited her. Bertie whistled. And even Mama was admiring. "I suppose that's really what the French are good at—clothes," she said as they walked toward the carriage.

They drove for a half an hour through the summer twilight to the Palace of Versailles. A small troop of Zouaves, dressed in comical red pantaloons and red stocking caps, met them and led the way by torchlight through several cavernous reception rooms and into La Galerie des Glaces. Vicky gasped—it was like entering a vast, jewel-encrusted treasure chest, with towering, arched glass doors open to the garden on one side, and immense mirrors reflecting them on the other. Hundreds of opulently dressed people packed the glittering, ornate space, which echoed with cacophonous chatter and smelled of face powder, gardenias, and sweat. Loud cymbals banged to announce their arrival, and there was a burst of exclamation followed by a whooshing of skirts as everyone turned around at once to stare.

The guests formed a spontaneous aisle, down which scurried Emperor Napoléon. "Your Majesty," he said, bowing to Mama. "You will, of course, grant me the first dance?"

And Vicky watched them go off, a matched pair of miniature monarchs, and the music began. A short time later, Vicky had her turn being partnered by the emperor. And then Papa. And then the British consul Lord Ainsworth. And then a Spanish prince whose name she never caught. Waltzing around the floor, she felt swept up onto an impossibly high plane of glamour. Was this true life? The dizzying, stirring, enchanted brightness must have been the summit of what anyone could experience. Regular existence was a dull substitute, to be endured until one was raised again into this dimension of pleasure and fascination, surrounded by other dancers, carried forward by the music, excitement making the very air vibrate. Catching sight of herself in the mirrored wall, she saw that, flushed and perspiring from exertion, several loose strands of hair dangling in her face, she looked pretty— amazingly, improbably, unquestionably pretty.

IN THE MIDDLE of the evening came a break in the dancing. Vicky and Bertie found two gilt chairs in a window bay and sat down to watch the huge assembly mingle and talk. A small string quartet played softly at the far end of the hall, and enormous chande- liers blazed above. Several of Eugénie's ladies came to cluck and coo over "*la petite princesse*" and marvel at her complexion—"*un bon teint anglais.*" Vicky, in turn, admired these ladies intensely, dressed as they were in pale pastel silks overlaid with Valenci- ennes lace, their sculptural white shoulders exposed, their full skirts smoothly swinging left and right like tolling bells. None was more beautiful than the empress herself, tall and willowy, mounds of curly dark hair piled artfully on the top of her head, a single ivory rose tucked behind her ear. Vicky attempted to fol- low that elegant head as it bobbed through the crowd.

Bertie said: "I think Papa wants you."

She looked to the right and saw her father beckoning with a wave, so she got up and walked toward him.

Papa, neat and compact in his black Hussars uniform, stood next to a very tall, pale gentleman, with a large balding head and a full brown mustache, who was wearing a rusty black dinner jacket, buttons straining a bit over his substantial midsection.

"Vicky, may I present Herr Otto von Bismarck-Schönhausen. Sir, my daughter, the Princess Royal."

Vicky, looking up, stretched out her right arm. Large, alert hazel eyes gazed down at her from under a jutting brow. She esti- mated this man's age to be forty. He bowed his head; grasped her hand with cool, dry fingers; and raised it to kiss.

"A delight, Your Highness," he said in English. His thin, high voice surprised her, coming from such a big body.

"Herr Bismarck is the Prussian ambassador to the German Confederation's assembly, as you will remember, Vicky," said Papa.

In fact, the name meant nothing to her, but, pretending to know, she said: "Yes, of course, you're at the Frankfurt Diet, where German leaders meet to plan a unified future."

Bismarck snorted. "Not so much planning. Much politicking, complaining, and making endless speeches."

"Surely that last suits you, sir?" asked her father. "Accounts of your talents as an orator have reached even London."

"I must fall back on something, Prince. I was not handed a royal position as you were," Bismarck said.

If Papa found that remark insulting, he didn't betray it, replying levelly: "A successful future for united Germany—negotiated at Frankfurt or elsewhere—requires more progressive leadership in Prussia."

"The successful future of Prussia is my sole concern," Bismarck declared. Turning his intent gaze back to Vicky, he asked: "Is it true, Princess, that you are acquainted with members of our royal house?"

"Prince Wilhelm and his family spent a holiday with us at the time of the London exhibition, four years ago, yes."

"Did you find Prince Friedrich handsome? He is much admired in Berlin," said Bismarck.

"I enjoyed the company of both the prince and his sister Princess Louise in England," she replied.

He laughed. "Very polite! But you ignore my question."

"Not entirely," she said. What did Papa think of this cheek? Glancing left, she saw her father had been pulled away by a man who was now whispering something furiously in his ear.

"You must be a cautious young woman, anxious to please," Bismarck replied.

"I may hope to please as a general rule," she said. "But I don't lie."

"Yet I am still not clear: did you find Prince Friedrich handsome or not?" he said, pressing her.

"As I recall, Prince Friedrich was well spoken and fine looking. A gentleman. A credit to his family and country," she said.

Bismarck smirked. "Your father told me you were a young woman of spirit. I'm disappointed this is all I will hear from you." He bowed. "Nonetheless, a pleasure—"

"Please tell me, Herr Bismarck," said Vicky, curious now about this odd, belligerent character. "Your English is quite good. Where did you learn it?"

"I attended university with a marvelous American man, John Motley, still my friend. He came to Hanover with barely a word of German. I liked him, and forced to speak only in English, I improved."

"Did you pick up American views?"

Bismarck smiled. "I cannot think of one American idea I endorse. Certainly not republicanism."

"What of equality of men? That's something Americans believe in."

"I believe a few great men are far worthier than the total mass of all others."

"However, the principle of equality before the law does not concern a man's intrinsic powers of mind and body," Vicky said.

Bismarck raised his heavy eyebrows. "That is correct, Princess."

"Do you not believe that every man should be subject to the same laws and be treated equally?"

"I do."

"So were you simply being outrageous, sir? While accusing me of excessive tact?" A deft thrust, she was sure.

Now he grinned. "Clever as you are, Princess, you should concede that coy mincing is never preferable to having strong convictions and putting them forward."

"I was not being coy earlier, rather discreet and polite."

"Should good manners disguise the feelings and opinions that people don't dare speak?"

This man was really too much. "In the guise of an innocent

inquiry you were attempting to draw me out on a subject I am not prepared to address."

"Not prepared, or not willing?"

"There, sir, you do it again, goading me." She regarded him sternly. "That is truly ill mannered."

Bismarck laughed. "I am caught out, I suppose." He gave a small bow. "Please understand, Princess, I am not a native speaker of English," he continued. "I do not understand all the, how do you call it—the subtleties."

"Perhaps you need then to come to England and further improve your English," she countered.

"I have. I have made two trips there. I admire your country. But the English don't admire Prussians as a rule, and this I resent."

"I don't believe you are correct, sir."

"No? Let's ask your father. Prince, I was just saying that there's a profound anti-Prussian bias in your wife's realm."

Papa had rejoined them. "The government is unhappy with Prussia for sitting on its hands in the war."

"I am speaking not of Westminster politicians, but of the common man. Most Englishmen never imagine that Prussians might be as clever, enterprising, and literate as they themselves are."

"Germans in general are admired," Papa replied. "But Prussia needs to modernize."

"Back to this! Prince, you have an arrogant preoccupation with our domestic affairs. Royal authority in Prussia survived the revolution. The country is strong and stable. And Prussians feel proud of their country—its cohesion, its discipline, its strength."

"Its army," said Papa.

"Can you imagine Britain without the magnificent Royal Navy? The army is our equivalent. You recognize that, Princess, don't you?" he asked, smiling at Vicky—not a kind smile, wolfish really, but somehow stimulating.

"Of course, although the Royal Navy supports a growing empire, while the Prussian army, what good is it doing?" she threw back.

"A preposterous question. It defends Prussia," said Bismarck. "And does so capably led by men like Prince Wilhelm and your dashing Prince Friedrich."

"He is not my—" she started to reply.

Papa cut in: "Sir, Germans do not want to be dominated by a militaristic Prussia."

"You see into the hearts of millions of men, Prince? You don't even live in Germany any longer!"

"I'm lucky to live in a nation with the most enlightened, most liberal parliamentary government in Europe. I dream of seeing the same in Germany."

"Fine sentiments, but they do not find favor in Berlin, where all important men desire to conserve the Prussian system. Think for a minute as I do, unsentimentally. Are you capable of that?"

Papa frowned.

Bismarck continued: "Prussia is the largest and strongest pure German state. It makes up much of north Germany. No German unity is possible without it. Let the small German states be absorbed into greater Prussia."

Papa shook his head. "The Austrians will never allow that, and it's not the fate that the world hopes for Germany."

"You remain a Coburger, Prince."

"If you mean a moderate, a liberal, a patriot of the greater German nation—"

"I mean a naïve idealist, co-opted by smug English Whigs, who doesn't realize that Prussia cannot, and will not, stay a small power forever," Bismarck said.

Papa drew back and gave the man a frosty stare. "I bid you good evening, sir," he said in a clipped voice.

Vicky was amazed: this man dared to taunt Papa? On whose authority? Maybe only his own. Bismarck turned to her, bowed, and said cheerfully: "I am enchanted, Princess. Your conversation brightened this entire evening."

Flattered but also flustered, Vicky struggled to remain cool as she replied, "Good evening, Herr Bismarck."

As if reading her mind, he laughed. "Ah, your father's daughter, first and foremost, is that it? I hope, and I suspect, we will meet again, Your Highness."

"Come, Vicky," Papa said. He took her arm and, turning away sharply, left the tall Junker laughing behind them.

Her father wordlessly deposited her with Bertie and went to find Mama.

VICKY'S HEAD WAS still swirling from the dancing, the conversing, the sheer spectacle, when several hours after midnight, the four of them clambered into the carriage to return to the palace at St. Cloud. Bertie dozed off immediately. Mama's cheeks were bright pink and her eyes glistened.

"I drank a tremendous amount of champagne, angel," she said. And then she chatted gaily, for ten minutes, neither seeking nor allowing any interruption. Didn't they agree the dancing was splendid? And the music divine? And the flowers, what beautiful flowers, especially the huge arrangements along the walls, roses and dahlias and gardenias arranged ingeniously together. The ballroom had gotten far too hot of course. But the fireworks! Such a glorious way to conclude the evening. Had they ever seen anything so extraordinary as the final, special display, the one in her honor, a fiery Windsor Castle in the air?

Abruptly, she closed her eyes and slept.

For a long moment neither Vicky nor Papa spoke. She sat with her back to the driver while her father, opposite, appeared deep in thought. He looked out the window, idly fiddling with the bottom button of his jacket.

"Papa?"

"*Ja?*"

"That man we met: Herr Bismarck. He was very strange."

"He's notorious," said Papa.

"And so rude to you."

Her father shook his head. "A mistake, perhaps, to debate with him. I had heard he was ill mannered and arrogant. Count

Walewski came up to warn me that he is quite mad. But I was curious."

"Why does he suspect he will meet me again?"

"Why not? The queen of England's eldest daughter, she will be traveling again in Europe."

"Is that what he meant? Really?"

Papa paused before saying, "No, perhaps not."

"And he kept asking me what I thought of Prince Friedrich—Fritz."

Papa gazed at her for a long moment, a fond look on his face.

"You understand, Vicky, there's always talk about who you might marry one day. Last month someone at the Royal Society congratulated me on your engagement to Prince Ernest of Hanover."

"Isn't he nine years old? And I've never even met him," she said, indignant.

"Ja, absurd. But we have all met Fritz and you know I think him a fine young man. And you? Are you kindly disposed?" he asked.

In truth, Fritz existed in her mind only in a hazy way: tall, soldierly, jokey, with difficult parents and an awkward younger sister. Their correspondence had petered out. Sometimes Grandmamma, who read all the German papers, insisted that Vicky look at an illustration of Fritz reviewing troops in Koblenz, or out with his fellows from a student riding club in Bonn. But in these pictures he'd always be wearing a hat or a helmet, so it was hard to see his face. Although he did seem to have grown mustaches.

"I am not sure," she said finally.

Papa smiled. "It's not necessary that you know, Puss. You are so young. It's best that first you be confirmed and then we can begin to think seriously about arranging your marriage."

"That's a long time from now," she said. She felt both relieved and a bit impatient. She wasn't a child. Hadn't she just attended a ball? Sparred with a notorious statesman?

"Eighteen months will pass quickly," Papa said.

They rode on in silence for a few moments. The warm, fragrant air lofted in through the open windows, and Vicky thought France smelled different than England, more flowery. Of course she would be married someday. And she wanted to be—to have an important position, and to have her own family. But how it would feel to be someone's wife, she couldn't imagine. And it made her a bit anxious to think that machinations might already be under way to determine her husband.

"Did you have me meet Herr Bismarck because maybe Fritz and I . . ." She trailed off, too shy to spell it out.

"Prussia is a nation on the rise, there's no doubt, and I wanted this prominent Prussian to know you. But such a bellicose character! Terribly extreme. Tomorrow, I must write to the baron to describe the encounter, and Lord Clarendon too."

At the mention of the foreign secretary, Vicky knew Papa was reverting to habitual fretting over German politics. And now they were driving through the gates of St. Cloud.

Papa shook Mama's shoulder. "Wake up, *Weibchen*, we have arrived."

Vicky glanced over at Bertie beside her. He'd opened his eyes and was gazing dreamily out the window. They sat waiting for Mama and Papa to climb down.

Their parents out of earshot, Bertie murmured, "Don't you think, Vicky, that Paris is the most marvelous place ever?"

"Yes, wonderful."

"I asked the empress if we could stay longer."

"You did what? Mama will never agree!" she softly shrieked at her brother.

"I said she and Papa don't have to stay, they could go back. Just you and I might remain."

"And? How did she answer?" What a thrill to linger at the French court, unsupervised, Mama's censorious face nowhere to be seen. She'd join the flock of ladies around Eugénie, chat in

French all day, acquire more stylish clothes, maybe even one of those small velvet hats they favored, worn tilted over one eye.

"I told her there are six other children, and no one would miss you and me, but the empress just laughed," her brother admitted. "She thinks our parents could not do without us, even for a single day."

"A shame," sighed Vicky.

"Yes," said Bertie. "It will be awfully dull at home."

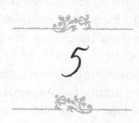

5

Balmoral, September 1855

*T*hey returned from France to Balmoral, the castle in the Highlands of Scotland that Papa had built for them.

In years past Vicky had enjoyed their Scottish holidays, but as Bertie had predicted, Balmoral now felt like the wet and dreary far end of the earth. So irritating to listen to Mama go on and on about how pleased she was to be done with the French trip and home with just the family. Each morning her mother put on a plain wool dress, covered that with a tartan shawl, and ventured out in the drizzle on pony treks with Papa, who stalked deer and directed the expansion of the parterre. All the rustic pursuits on offer seemed very tiresome to Vicky, and the six weeks of their stay stretched ahead interminably.

Tilla was away, and Papa hated to see Vicky at a loose end. "Time for a serious intellectual endeavor," he declared one sodden afternoon. "Why not write an essay summarizing the history of the constitution in Britain?" Vicky vowed to make a start but felt no true interest in the project. Instead she spent hours closeted in her bedroom rereading *La Danseuse*, her favorite romantic novel, set in Paris. Other times she just stared at the miniature portrait Empress Eugénie had given her as a parting gift. Would she ever have one-tenth the beauty? A modicum of the charm? It seemed like too much to hope for.

She thought sometimes, too, about strange Herr Bismarck. He'd been atrocious to Papa, definitely, but she felt a little glow when she recalled his describing her as enchanting.

On the Tuesday of the first week of September, Vicky went down late to breakfast. Morning meals were always laid out in the smaller of the two dining rooms, where the walls were covered in the green and blue Campbell military tartan and a huge stag head loomed over the table in a way that Vicky found discomforting.

Papa was reading a German newspaper, Bertie slathering butter on his toast, but Mama seemed agitated, nervously tucking stray strands of hair into her back roll. She gave Vicky a worried look as she took her place.

"I read, Vicky, that Fritz plans a trip to Ostend, in Belgium, for the bathing," said Papa, glancing out from behind his paper.

"Oh yes?" Vicky replied, eyes on an empty serving dish. "Are all the eggs eaten up?"

Now Papa put down his paper and both parents gazed at her in an odd, expectant way.

"In truth, Vicky, Fritz is coming here," Papa said.

"To Balmoral?"

"Yes."

"But he can't bathe here," observed Vicky uncomprehendingly.

"He wouldn't come to bathe!" said Mama. "Why do you think him so misinformed?"

Now Vicky stared at her father, the implications dawning. He gave a small nod, acknowledging them.

"I know," said Bertie, "Fritz is coming to see Vicky."

"In part," said Papa.

"And the rest of the family, too," said Mama. "And Scotland, and the Highlands. All of it." She waved her hand impatiently.

"He will be here on Friday," said Papa.

"In three days?" asked Vicky.

"I think he's eager to arrive," Papa said, smiling. "He will stay a fortnight."

Vicky, suddenly tongue-tied and blushing, hated how they were all peering at her, trying to read her reaction. She wished to ask why Fritz was coming now, but she couldn't wait to be out of this room.

"I want to take Fanny out for a ride," she said abruptly.

"But you've eaten nothing," said Mama.

"I'm not hungry."

"That's fine, Puss, off you go," said Papa.

SHE WENT DOWN the corridor, turned right into the vestibule, and went out the garden door in a daze. Hadn't Papa said in Paris he'd wait until after her confirmation to begin arranging her marriage? Had something changed? Had he resolved in the last weeks that Fritz was the best choice? Was this Papa and Mama's way of thrusting the Prussian prince upon her? She couldn't imagine they'd insist she marry a man she didn't care for. Mama in particular talked constantly about the blessings of a husband one adored. But they clearly favored the match, which meant they would prefer that she go along. And could she? Would she?

The day was cool and gray, with low clouds. Passing the large glasshouse, she wished fervently she could remember Fritz better. She couldn't marry any man, prince or not, unless she fell in love with him first. She was firm on this. But maybe she would fail to recognize love or be deceived somehow. She'd been reading how Thérèse, the main character in *La Danseuse*, adored handsome Pierre, but he turned out to be a criminal. Fritz couldn't be a criminal, he was highly appropriate for her, but, still, how would she know for certain to choose him?

So preoccupied was she with this thought that she was startled to find she'd arrived in front of the stables. Malcolm the grooms-man led out her favorite chestnut mare, Fanny, and as she waited for him to fetch a saddle she hugged the horse around the neck. "You're so lovely," she said aloud, stroking Fanny and running her fingers through the horse's mane. How beautiful animals were, but how vulnerable. She couldn't bear it if any harm befell Fanny. Would it feel the same to be in love with a man?

When she rode out of the yard, down to the bridle path along the river, she brooded further. If she didn't like Fritz, or if he didn't like her, he couldn't be just taken to the door and sent away—he'd be with them for two weeks. And how awkward that would be, the two of them forced to endure each other's company for days, just longing for the visit to be over. And then something else dawned on her. Princess Augusta so admired England and Papa and Mama—her parents sometimes talked about this— perhaps she had ordered Fritz to come now and propose to her. Which meant he might meet Vicky again, find her not at all desirable, and yet feel compelled to ask her to become his wife. She shook her head. In that case she would refuse him, definitely. She didn't want to be married to someone who wasn't passionately attached to her. And while she was no paragon like Empress Eugénie, she had good points. She numbered them in her mind as she rode on toward the village: large blue eyes; small, well-shaped nose and mouth; and pointed chin. She felt particularly proud of her chin since Mama's receded. And she had grown to be a full two inches taller than Mama—still short, but not startlingly so. And she recalled how Eugénie's ladies had oohed and aahed endlessly over her fair complexion.

She sighed. Skin didn't seem like something a man would care much about, she had to admit. The hard truth was that she was not slender, which she knew did matter, very much. Also, Mama claimed she waddled when she walked. It was inescapable. If Fritz intended only to marry a tall, willowy, graceful woman, then she wouldn't do. She pulled on the reins sharply to turn Fanny back toward home.

In public these days, when people scrutinized her, trying to see how closely this rare creature, a princess, resembled other mortals, she often worried she looked unworthy of her high station. Stepping out of the carriage when they arrived in Paris, she realized that Mama might be a great queen, but she was also a squat little person in a white, overlarge bonnet. And Vicky was hardly more chic. Only at the Versailles ball, wearing a gown of Eugénie's design, had she ever felt truly elegant. And yet, appearing in London or Windsor, she was often praised. Mama and Papa relied on her to help entertain guests, to stand next to them at receptions and teas. She liked to talk to statesmen and inventors and writers who came to the palace. Papa frequently commended her for putting people at ease, asking them about themselves, and conversing in a natural way. She remembered how, when she'd met the American ambassador James Buchanan in May, they'd discussed slavery. He'd favored compromise with the plantation owners of the American South—an odious idea, she knew, because she had read *Uncle Tom's Cabin* with Tilla. And while they'd disagreed, Mr. Buchanan had bowed to her as he left and said: "You possess an excellent head and a heart as big as a mountain, Princess. Both will serve you well."

Perhaps she wasn't a great beauty, but she did have the training and poise for a public position—which had to count for something. And if she said she didn't want to marry Fritz she wouldn't have to. Papa would understand, even though he had said in the carriage how Prussia was a country on the rise. Would it be nice to rise with Prussia? Vicky thought it might be. But to link her destiny with a nation's—without first falling in love with the nation's prince—would be a hollow, empty, unsatisfactory thing. That much she was quite sure of.

BERTIE WAS WAITING for her back in the stable yard, sitting on the top rail of the fence.

"I am happy to be meeting Fritz again. Aren't you?" he said, jumping down.

"I suppose," Vicky replied as she slid off Fanny.

"Do you think he's for you?" Bertie teased in a singsong voice. "For you, forever?"

"Stop it."

"You know what Grandmamma told me?" Bertie continued after Malcolm had taken the bridle from her and led Fanny away. "She says that Aunt Prussia got worried when she read about the ball at Versailles. The German papers wrote flattering things about you, and now she's nervous some other prince might snap you up before Fritz can get a look in."

Vicky gaped at him. "Really?" So, her suspicions were not groundless.

"That's what Grandmamma says," he replied with a broad smile.

"She says a lot of silly things."

"But it sounds right. Look at Mama and Papa all aflutter. Fritz must be coming with serious intent."

"Goodness."

Bertie laughed. "You've become a prize to be competed for, Puss. Let's hope Fritz doesn't mind how bossy you are."

"I'm not bossy."

Bertie laughed again. "Yes, you are. And husbands always like to boss their wives."

"How do you know?"

"It's just the way of things."

"As if you know anything about the way of things."

"On this point, dear sister, I'm confident I'm correct."

They walked back to the castle together, Bertie nattering on about what rides they might take with the prince, while Vicky pondered how strange it was, really, that something so monumental was about to begin. But thrilling, too, and she thought she could manage. She hoped she could.

BARON STOCKMAR HAD arrived from London, and he and Papa spent much of the next two days conversing together in the library. Mama fretted, constantly complaining aloud that Vicky's laugh was too piercing, her figure not impressive, her waddle worse than ever. Tilla had returned and Vicky and Alice had started regular lessons again, but her mother kept pulling Vicky away to have new dresses fitted, one navy with white braid trim, the other red and green plaid.

She didn't like the second at all. "Something about the shape is not flattering. I look like a small plaid ball on top of a larger plaid ball," she told Alice, modeling the dress for her sister in their bedroom. "And don't you think it clashes with the decor?"

Papa had designed tartan-patterned carpets that were installed on the stairs and along the passageways, and tartan wallpaper for many walls.

"I think it's a fine dress," said Alice.

"I dislike it intensely. But when I tell Mama, she won't listen," said Vicky.

"I can't understand what the fuss is about. Fritz might be nice, but it's not as if you are going to marry him any time soon. You are much too young to get married," said Alice.

"Some women get married when they are sixteen."

"You aren't even fifteen yet."

"I will be in two months."

"Ugh, you don't want to have babies, do you? Once you get married that happens immediately. Look at Lady Susan Lascelles, she was married last winter and I heard Mama say she's going to have a baby any day now."

Vicky hadn't considered that. It was true, she did not feel prepared to have a baby. And she wasn't even sure what went into it. A husband and wife shared a bed and after that the wife might have a baby. But what took place, exactly, in the bed?

"I'm not going to marry him right away," she said to Alice airily, trying to sound knowing. "But I do want to see what he's like. Papa already thinks so highly of him."

Alice glared. "You're not going to marry someone because of that, are you? Papa thinking highly? As if Fritz were the new chancellor of the Exchequer or something."

Why was her sister deliberately misunderstanding her? "No,

of course not, I'm only going to marry someone I fall in love with and really find wonderful," Vicky said.

Later she tried to think of men who were wonderful. Papa, of course, so noble and good. And her favorite of Papa's equerries, Henry Ponsonby, who always challenged her with riddles he saved up especially for her. The art master Monsieur Corbould had big, black, romantic eyes that she admired. Emperor Napoléon was charming, but so short and overzealous. Herr Bismarck had a certain charisma, but he was neither good-looking nor honorable, also hopelessly old. All of these men were old.

Fritz was nearly twenty-four, she knew, but that wasn't so old as to be out of the question. And clearly, he didn't think she was too young, or else he wouldn't bother coming, would he?

ON FRIDAY AFTERNOON Mama told Vicky and Bertie to wait upstairs while she and Papa greeted Fritz and his aide-de-camp General Helmuth von Moltke. And then they would be called for.

From out of the lounge windows she watched the two carriages of the Prussian party come up the drive and rattle under the carriage porch, but because of the angle, she couldn't see the occupants getting out. She sat down in a straight chair; Bertie lolled on the sofa opposite. Every muscle in her body felt taut, and she couldn't swallow properly—her throat had closed up. Gazing over at her brother, she envied him his unconcern. He was whistling and fiddling with a jackknife.

He noticed her looking at him. "Don't agonize, Vicky, he won't bite you."

"Of course not. I'm not worried about that," she answered waspishly.

"Don't worry at all. He's nice. I remember," said Bertie.

That was hardly the point. What if Fritz took one look at her and wished he'd never come? What if they had nothing, absolutely nothing, to say to each other? It could all be hideously embarrassing and awkward.

Just then a footman came to fetch them and they followed him out of the room. Vicky took a deep breath as she turned into the stairwell. No occasion in her whole life had felt so momentous.

Fritz stood in the front gallery with Mama and Papa on either side of him. When her mother caught sight of her descending the stairs, she trilled, in German, in an odd, nervous voice: "And here is Vicky."

Mama's tone—like a shopkeeper ashamed of the wares she'd put out for sale—instantly irritated Vicky, but as soon as she took in Fritz she forgot that. Tall, broad-shouldered, with a thick, tawny mustache, the Prussian prince looked so appealing. Yes, this was definitely the teasing youth who had come to the exhibition—square jawed, handsome, with glorious blond wavy hair—however, now Fritz was much more substantial, a grown man, and very dignified.

He smiled, somewhat shyly, and she felt, in a rush, protective of him. She had her whole family around her for this fraught encounter, and he was practically alone.

"Vicky," he said, reaching out his right hand and grasping her left.

"I am happy to see you again, Fritz."

"I, too, to see you. You are so changed."

He gazed down at her.

"No longer a child, of course," said Papa.

"Which is no surprise, as it was so many years ago when we last met," said Mama, her voice tremulous still.

"I didn't expect such a beauty." *So eine Schönheit.* Fritz continued to stare.

Some knot in Vicky's stomach that she hadn't even realized was there released, and she could feel her spirit blossoming open to him. And the blood rose in her cheeks.

"I thought I didn't remember you, Fritz, but now that I see you, of course I know you," she said. Did that even make sense?

He seemed to understand her, and nodded.

Bertie said: "I never forgot you at all, Fritz."

Everyone laughed. "Come, let's go into the drawing room," said Papa, herding them in that direction.

BEFORE THEY SAT down, Papa introduced her to General von Moltke, a man of about fifty, who clicked his heels and bowed over her hand to kiss it. The general struck her as a fatherly type, with wise eyes and effortless courtesy. He took a chair off to the side, while Fritz sat down on the sofa, sitting on the seat's edge, holding himself upright, chest out, shoulders and head back, chin slightly raised. Vicky chose a small armchair on his left, her parents on the sofa across. She still felt shaky, but she also sensed the prince's extreme nervousness and longed to put him at ease. They had done the hard part, the first minutes, when they were revealed to each other. Now if only they could relax a bit and become acquainted. Hard to do with Mama and Papa looking on.

"Your dear parents are well, I trust?" Mama began.

"Quite well, ma'am, and sorry not to visit along with me," Fritz replied.

"And your sister?" said Mama.

"Do you not know? Louise is engaged to Friedrich, Prince Regent of Baden. They will marry next spring."

Mama shrieked and flapped her hands. "Imagine that! I had heard about the possibility, but to have it confirmed, how wonderful," she exclaimed. "Vicky, isn't that wonderful?"

"Yes, I wish them joy," she said. Her mother should get ahold of herself too. Vicky turned to Fritz: "Is Louise seventeen now?"

"Almost. And finished with books, she says, forever and ever. Loulee never liked studies, as perhaps you recall," he said.

"I recall she enjoyed riding and baking."

"As it happens, still among her favorite pastimes," Fritz said. They locked eyes for a moment and exchanged smiles, acknowledging the peculiarities of Louise.

While her mother and father asked the prince other questions, catching up on the health of various German royal relations, Vicky studied him. Herr Bismarck had said he was much admired in Prussia, and no wonder; he looked the part of a prince—tall, golden, very manly. But he spoke softly, gestured restrainedly, and looked out at the world cautiously, from the back of his eyes. From time to time he glanced over at her, as if checking to see she was still there.

Bertie kept scuffling his feet on the carpet, and Vicky knew her brother had no patience for this conversation. At a momentary lull Bertie put in: "We have several hunters for you to choose from, Fritz."

"The deer stalking is excellent here," Papa said. "Vicky, why don't you and Bertie take Fritz out for a look around, and you can pass by the stables."

Mama nodded. "Yes, yes, go on," she said, making a shooing motion with her hands.

AS THEY WALKED along the gravel path that flanked the garden, Bertie launched into a detailed story about a recent hunt with Papa in Glen Harris.

"Do you hunt, Vicky?" Fritz asked, interrupting this account.

"I'll go along when Papa asks me to, but actually, I find hunting rather tiresome," she said.

"And she has no idea which deer are which, Fritz. She's hopeless," said Bertie.

"Red, roe, fallow, sika—all the same to me," she said.

Fritz laughed. "I, too, am not knowledgeable about deer. When I hunt it is usually for wild boar."

"Aren't boar blind, thus they can't see you coming?" Vicky asked.

Fritz laughed again. "You think perhaps they make easy marks?"

"Well, is it true?"

"Who knows what they really see, but they certainly sense you near them. And they can be dangerous when they charge. A friend of mine once walked between a sow and her litter and had to scramble up a tree to get away from the angry mother boar," he said, grinning at her. He already seemed more at ease, out of doors, away from Mama and Papa.

"I am only interested in the animals one keeps and cares for. Dogs, and especially horses," Vicky said. "You must meet Fanny."

At the stables Bertie went searching for the grooms while she took Fritz to the mare's stall. He stroked her chestnut flanks and admired her intelligent expression. Vicky spotted a patch of mud on Fanny's leg and reached up to the high shelf where the currycomb and brush sat.

"You groom your own horse?" asked Fritz as she stooped down to clean off the dirt.

"Not generally, but I've spent lots of time in the stables since we came to Scotland. Sometimes I prefer Fanny's company to my brothers' and sisters'. She's peaceful, they're noisy and obstreperous."

"I lived with horses when I was small," Fritz said. "I was nine when I started cavalry training. For the first months we slept right in the barns. So wonderful. We learned everything about how to take care of them."

"Didn't you tell me about your horse when you came to London? Was he called Firefly? I like that name." They were still speaking German, so she used the German word, *Leuchtkäfer*. She put the brush and comb back on the shelf and looked next for the hoof polish. It was easier to talk naturally to Fritz while occupied with something.

"*Ach,* noble Firefly. He was such a good beast. He died last year. I ride a few different horses now, none as good as him." Fritz now leaned against the stall wall.

"Too bad you haven't found a replacement," she said. No polish, but she did find a rag, so she bent back down to rub Fanny's front hooves.

"Maybe I never will. I had Firefly as a colt, and I grew up with him. I didn't have all those brothers and sisters as you do. He was my best companion."

"Did you ever wish you had more than just a single sister?" she asked.

"I never thought much about it," said Fritz. Glancing up, she saw him smiling sheepishly. "Perhaps that makes me an unimaginative fellow. I have a cousin the same age as me. He's called Fritz

Karl, and we often played together. Except when our fathers fell out, which happened quite often."

"I used to long for Mama and Papa to invite more children to come play with us," she said, straightening up and putting the rag back. "Sometimes they did, but mostly they expected us to amuse each other. We are now eight, you heard?"

"*Ja*, two new brothers, is that correct?"

"Arthur is five and Leopold two."

"I remember how proud your parents were of their large family," said Fritz. "Very affectionate—all of you."

"Mama and Papa both say they had lonely childhoods. Perhaps that's why they had so many children. To make up for that."

Fritz still leaned against the wall, and as she stroked Fanny between the ears, she could sense him gazing intently at her, as if trying to absorb every detail. Odd, but not unpleasant.

Bertie called out, summoning them to inspect the hunters. And soon after, Papa turned up at the stables to reclaim Fritz for tea in his study with the baron. Vicky watched the two men walking away, Fritz bending his head low to hear better what Papa, so much shorter, had to say. She felt a cautious kind of elation. Maybe, just maybe, Fritz was the one for her.

OVER DINNER VICKY described their Paris trip and Fritz voiced regrets at having traveled so little. He was a bit shocked she'd read *Immensee*, a German novel about a thwarted love affair. "Vicky has a good mind," said Papa. "I could trust her to see the deeper meanings." Both Mama and Papa had begun to relax— Mama in particular relieved, Vicky imagined, that Fritz didn't regard her daughter as a dwarfish troll. Papa told the story of his own awkward arrival in England to meet his future wife. "I hardly knew what to expect," he recounted. "She was already queen and I only the second son of an obscure German duke with not a *Pfennig* to my name. I walked up the castle steps at Windsor in a daze. But then I looked up and I beheld a vision. A beautiful, fragile girl with huge blue eyes and soft brown hair, she stood there quite defenseless, and I immediately wanted to love and protect her. I took the last steps at a run so I could seize her hand in mine."

Mama, smiling and blushing, added: "And from that never-to-be-forgotten day to this, we have never looked back, have we, my dearest angel? We have never had any second thoughts."

"Certainly, there have been difficulties," Papa said quickly, pretending to be stern, and everyone at the table laughed.

"It's true, my temper is not always the best," Mama said, "and, of course, dear Albert has had to endure the reversal of the right order of things, as I am queen regnant. But my dearest tolerates that, and so much more, while he steers the ship of state for me and for the nation."

Her parents beamed at each other across the table. Vicky was accustomed to Mama and Papa's gushing about how they met and fell in love, but maybe Fritz would find it indecorous. She reached out for her glass, at the same time stealing a glance at the prince sitting at her right. She noticed that, far from disapproving, he seemed charmed, smiling widely at his host and hostess.

PAPA MONOPOLIZED FRITZ most of the next day, discussing politics with him in his study, but eventually he was set free and came looking for Vicky.

"What would you like to do now?" she asked him. "And you mustn't say riding, as you can see it's pouring with rain."

"*Ja, ja*, not nice weather. Maybe chess?"

"Chess is in Papa's study. Didn't you just escape from there? Let's go find the ludo board."

"I don't know that game."

"I will teach you. It's easy. And I'm extremely good." She said this thoughtlessly, the way she would speak to Bertie, and immediately felt embarrassed.

But Fritz just smiled. "At least you warn me," he said.

It took three games until he won one, and then they moved on to draughts. Once she explained how to play, Fritz declared draughts resembled a German game called Dame. "And I am very good at that," he said.

He immediately beat her, twice. "Let's play again," he proposed, setting up the board for a third time.

"No, I think not."

"You don't like to lose?"

"I'm bored of games now and I see a glimpse of sun. I can show you the garden."

"I think you are not a good loser." He cocked his head, looking at her. For a moment she tried to think of some offhand response, but only the truth came to mind.

"Have you ever met anyone who doesn't prefer to win?" she asked him. "Too many timid girls say, oh, go ahead, I'm not good at this, I can't beat you. They are just pretending. They would like to win but don't have the courage to say it. They prefer to simper."

He laughed. "Hard to imagine a simpering Vicky."

THE NEXT DAY they went out riding with Bertie, and afterward Fritz asked to go up to the nursery to meet the little children. Lenchen, aged nine, and Louise, aged seven, started out very shy. They whispered answers to Fritz's questions about their favorite books and colors and things to eat. But they were pleased when he asked to be introduced to all the dolls by name. His attention never wavered even when Louise ran off to dig out some old ones that had been tossed into the bottom of a wardrobe. Then he gave little Arthur and Leopold rides on his back. They shrieked with delight and pounded on him, demanding more turns.

Fritz looked entirely comfortable on all fours on the nursery floor. Vicky was growing used to his size—he was not only taller than Papa but broader too—but he moved so easefully, like a large cat, with a lovely loping stride. Also, he was very strong. Affie came in when he heard the commotion, and at one point Fritz had the eleven-year-old Affie hanging off the back of his shoulders while holding both the little boys, one in each arm.

"Enough of this roughhousing, children," said Vicky. "Let's sing for Fritz."

She went over to the upright piano and started to play, singing: *"Oh dear, what can the matter be? Dear, dear, what can the matter be? Oh dear, what can the matter be? Johnny's so long at the fair."*

Of course, the Prussian prince didn't know the words to that song, or "My Bonnie Lies Over the Ocean," or "Sing a Song of Sixpence." But he grinned as Vicky's brothers and sisters all joined in and made quite a racket singing. Little Leopold jumped up and down to the music in the middle of the room, and glancing back, Vicky saw beyond him to the doorway, where two of the nursemaids were looking in wide-eyed, staring at this blond foreigner standing amid all the children, trying to follow along with English tunes.

THEY FELL INTO a routine. Fritz spent the mornings and the period right after luncheon speaking with Papa in the study or accompanying him on hunts or treks around the estate. But after that, Vicky's lessons also done, she and Fritz would have three hours together before supper. She often loitered outside the study door waiting for him. One afternoon, she asked Fritz if he didn't find all the political talk tedious. "Oh no, dear Vicky," he said. "Your father has so much knowledge and he is taking so much care to explain matters to me, I am very grateful." Still, she wished Papa would share his protégé with her more generously.

In Fritz's company, her dissatisfaction with Balmoral disappeared. She loved to walk together up to the Crathie bridge and back, Bertie and Affie racing ahead. Once, she nearly slipped traversing a muddy turn in the path, and he reached out to grab her hand and steady her. He didn't let go, so they walked along for a few minutes hand in hand, and her heart soared. It felt thrilling, so intimate, to have her small hand in his much larger, stronger one. But she worried they were not supposed to behave like this, as they were not engaged. And maybe she was clinging too hard and he would think her forward. So she dropped his hand, attempting to disguise the dropping by pointing at the Crathie church tower ahead. It dated back three centuries, she informed him.

They rode together often, and on rainy days took over a cozy corner in the lounge. Tilla and Alice chaperoned then, but would retreat to the adjoining music room, leaving the door ajar. Vicky kept thinking of books and poems she wanted to share, and plucked several volumes off the shelves every day. She'd read aloud to Fritz in English, he to her in German. But most often they just conversed. At the table with Mama and Papa, Fritz could be quite reticent even when General von Moltke prompted him to talk about his soldiering, his riding prizes, the loyalty he engendered among his men. But as the days passed Fritz opened up to her, telling her about friends he'd made in Bonn, some of his misadventures on maneuvers, his early memories.

One afternoon Fritz said: "Your father told me you and he met von Bismarck in Paris."

"Yes, he was extremely rude to Papa—in the end rather charming to me."

Fritz frowned. "He's a false character, not ever to be trusted. My mother hates him."

"Hates him? Why? Because he's not a liberal?"

Fritz sighed. "It's an ugly story." Vicky saw him hesitate, as if reluctant to pollute their pleasant intercourse with the account. But she looked over expectantly, and he began.

"You know about March of '48—the violence in Berlin?"

She nodded.

"Rioters surrounded our palace, shouting for my father's head, in revenge for the deaths of the men killed earlier. Father instructed me to take a scissors and clip off his whiskers so he wouldn't be recognized, and then he left via the cellars, through a hidden passage that leads to the embankment."

"And then he came to England."

"*Ja*, eventually we heard he was in England, but we received no letter for two weeks. The generals brought in more troops and the fighting continued. We were confined to the palace, me and Mama and Louise. We watched one battle from the window. Horrible, watching men get shot and bleed to death."

Fritz looked down at the floor and was silent for a long minute. Vicky's heart wrenched in pity, but she was not sure what to say. Before she uttered a word, he continued.

"On the fourth or fifth day, my uncle the king thought it best to go out and talk to the revolutionaries. To find a peaceful resolution. He wasn't opposed to all the things they demanded—some reforms appealed to him. But my other uncle, Karl, my father's younger brother, was enraged. He opposed the king giving in at all. Bismarck, his friend, convinced Uncle Karl that they should go together to see my mother. The two of them found their way through the streets disguised as workmen, wearing broad-brimmed hats decorated with the rebel cockade—black, red, and gold. Mama was astonished when they turned up. She's never liked Uncle Karl. He's a reactionary, with a terrible temper, and always intriguing. They had a proposition for her: the king had clearly gone mad, my father had been forced to flee, so the time was right to compel the king to abdicate in favor of me. I was six-teen years old. Uncle Karl told Mama he would act as regent for the next five years, and she needn't worry, he'd defend my throne for me capably. Apparently, they were very pleased with them-selves and with the whole scheme and were shocked when my mother refused. She even laughed at them. She should forget her allegiance to the king, ignore the rightful claims of her husband, and agree to the elevation of her son on their say-so? They must think her very stupid or very craven, she told them. But Bismarck didn't give up. Next, he tried to flatter her, to tell her that as she was so assured and intelligent, she should be regent, not Karl. Right in front of my uncle, he proposed this new plan. He had no doubt that he could convince her to commit treason, conspiring in the overthrow of the king."

"Goodness me." Vicky imagined Bismarck wheedling, cajoling, attempting to lure Fritz's mother into doing something she knew was wrong. Yes, Vicky thought, it wasn't beyond him.

"Mama insisted both men leave, and she immediately told the king and then later my father and everyone at court exactly what had happened. After order was restored, and the king and his ministers had regained control, she expected Bismarck would be jailed or banished or otherwise punished. But he suffered no consequences at all! He claimed that it had been my mother who'd proposed the king abdicate and my father renounce the throne. Uncle Karl said the same. Her account was dismissed as the lies of a hysterical woman. I reckon my father knows Mama is telling the truth, but he's let it all go. He just avoids Bismarck, even though my uncle the king continues to maintain that he's useful, as a most skillful defender of Prussian interests. And now Bismarck sits in Frankfurt, infuriating the Austrians with his taunts, his constant proclamations that Prussia must be first in Germany."

Vicky felt abashed that she'd let herself be flattered by Bismarck, even while he acted contemptuously toward Papa.

"Mama considers Bismarck far worse than the other Junkers he claims to speak for," Fritz continued, his voice rising. "She thinks the only cause he advances is greater power and influence for himself, and that he respects no principles and has no scruples."

"It's terrible the king and the others didn't believe her," said Vicky.

Fritz gave a sad shrug. "Not only is she a woman, she's known to favor reform."

"And dreadful that your father didn't defend her."

Fritz looked rueful. "Have you forgotten how they are together? Not like your mother and father."

"I do recall your parents sometimes quarreling," she said.

"I learned something recently from my aunt. Before he met my mother, my father fell in love with a beautiful Polish princess named Elise Radziwill, but his own father forbade their marriage, because Elise was not of the blood. And then she died."

"How sad!" Vicky exclaimed.

"*Ja*, I think Father chose Mama out of duty," Fritz said and Vicky felt a sudden flash of sympathy for snooty Aunt Prussia, married to a man who didn't really want her.

Fritz continued: "But we've never discussed this and Father's never mentioned Elise to me. We are not close."

He looked suddenly so cast down that Vicky searched her mind for something comforting to say.

"I think Papa considers you almost a son now," she said, forgetting for a moment what that implied. And when she realized, she blushed and wasn't sure where to look.

Fritz didn't tease, thankfully, just said: "I admire your father and the way he lives his life. I hope it's true that I have earned his affection."

THE VERY SAME evening, as she passed their private sitting room on the way down to supper, she overheard her parents discussing Fritz.

"No one has made enough fuss over that young man," Mama was saying. "He's less confident than he should be. I like his mother, always very complimentary to us, but who could forget what a cold fish she is."

"His parents haven't been so loving to him," said Papa, "but they're hardly loving to each other."

"Very unfortunate," said Mama.

"Still, Fritz is a gentleman, a soldier, a scholar—well, mostly a soldier—with no hint of dissipation." Papa abhorred bad behavior by men of rank.

"And I think Vicky is very taken with him," Mama said.

"*Ja*, do you see the coy way she dips her head and looks at him from under batting lashes?"

They both laughed.

"I hardly dare believe it, but I sense he admires her too, don't you?" Mama said.

"I do. Although he says nothing to me of his intentions. And I haven't insisted."

Vicky heard her mother sigh. "It's very nervous making. She's still so young, too young to properly know her mind. Maybe any question of an engagement should be left another year. He can return next autumn."

"Time to go down now," said Papa.

Her mother just went on musingly: "But if he leaves now with nothing said, he could choose someone else."

"That someone else—whoever she might be—will not be your daughter," said Papa. "Come, *Weibchen*, time to go down."

Vicky darted along the passageway and into the back gallery before they could emerge and catch her eavesdropping.

THAT NIGHT, TRYING to fall asleep in her bed next to Alice's, Vicky realized that if Fritz were to go away now without proposing, she would be crushed. Yet he might very well do that, she thought, rolling over restlessly, because of some misplaced notion that they hadn't been long acquainted and she wasn't old enough, as Mama said, "to properly know her mind." But how would being older change her feelings? She was sure now she wanted to be Fritz's wife. She loved him: his manliness, his golden good looks, the lovely, easeful way he moved. She felt a physical stab of something—a strange ache—when she watched him swing himself onto a horse or trot down the staircase in front of her, lightly carrying his tall frame on his long legs. And Fritz was like parched ground, ready to soak up affection. She could give him gallons of that, because talking to him, reading with him, listening to him, was the most absorbing, most gratifying, most pleasurable thing she could ever think to do. She took enormous pride in the fact that he, quite a shy person, confided so readily in her.

She knew, too, she would always be proud to have Fritz as her husband. In truth, she was still amazed that he found her beautiful, and she never grew tired of the way he gazed at her sometimes as if he wanted to drink in every detail. She wondered if, should they marry, people would see them as a mismatch, physically: he so handsome and arresting, she small and rather ordinary looking. But what other people thought shouldn't matter. The essential thing was that she loved Fritz, desired to be with him, and could help and support him, which he would need. If only he understood this and wouldn't let silly irrelevant things like her age distract and deter him.

THE NEXT MORNING, arriving downstairs, she spied Fritz conversing intently with Mama and Papa at the end of the hall outside the study. She approached, but Mama waved her off. In the dining room, sitting restlessly under the looming stag's head, Vicky waited for them to come in for breakfast, but they never did. When she trudged back upstairs for lessons, she was miffed to see the study door firmly closed against her. No doubt they were talking about her, and it was hateful to be kept out. What if Fritz was telling Mama and Papa that he admired her but considered her not right to be his wife? Would they just nod and accept that?

She could barely pay attention to Tilla, so preoccupied was she with the conversation going on downstairs. She practically bolted out of her chair when told it was time for luncheon, but on the stairs she instructed herself to stay serene and composed. It wouldn't do to seem overanxious. When she came into the dining room and saw Mama sitting in her place, wiping away a tear while simultaneously smiling, Vicky sighed with relief. Something good had been decided, clearly. Papa wore that stunned expression that overtook him at moments of strong emotion. And Fritz? He just looked very pleased with himself. She took her seat beside him, and he immediately reached over for her hand and squeezed it. Only on the path had he ever held her hand. If he wasn't rejecting her, then what was it?

Bertie and Alice appeared unaware of the palpable change in the air and dug into their meal. Vicky felt impatient with the conspiracy of silence among Papa and Mama and Fritz.

"Is there news from Berlin?" she asked, fishing.

"No news from Berlin," replied Fritz, grinning.

"One day I hope we have news of true reform in Berlin," began Papa ponderously.

"Vicky dear, do eat up," Mama cut in. "I hate to see food going to waste."

The adults turned the conversation to a most unromantic subject: the duchies of Schleswig and Holstein, German speaking but currently ruled by the Danes. General von Moltke, who had for a time served in the Danish military before entering the army of Prussia, debated with Papa and Fritz how this valuable territory might join the greater German nation. Usually Vicky enjoyed discussing politics, but today she had no interest. At least Mama kept beaming at her. How long until she would know exactly why?

Only at the end of the meal did Papa say, "Fritz and I have a hunting plan for the afternoon. But I think tomorrow we should go on a family expedition up Craig-na-Ban."

This hill, a few miles from the castle, offered a gently sloped trail to a high summit, where one could view the countryside in all directions.

Fritz turned to her, smiling. "It will be a lovely outing, don't you think?"

Vicky supposed she hadn't any choice but to nod, smile, and endure until tomorrow, but how aggravating to be treated like a child, and to be made to wait to be told something other people already knew.

VICKY AGAIN FOUND it hard to sleep. When the next day dawned clear and cold, with frost visible on the lawns and fir branches, she dressed carefully in a crimson riding habit, and a new shawl in her favorite clan MacDonald tartan over that. She wondered, leaving her bedroom, if she would return engaged.

Downstairs in the main hall they waited for the grooms to bring around the ponies. Mama laughed and smiled, her typical nervous manner evaporated on this bright morning. And a grinning Fritz once again reached for her hand, and squeezed it as they stood by the door. Affie, thrilled to be included on the outing, careened between and around everyone, chasing the two Labrador hunting dogs.

As soon as they set off in the sunshine, Fritz suggested they get out in front of the others. Kicking the ponies into a canter, they crossed the Dee bridge first and reached the upward rise far ahead.

"I think I love everything about Balmoral," Fritz said.

"Everything?"

"I love the mountains, I love the air, I love the people."

"But do you remember Osborne? I love that even more."

"I do remember Osborne, and the beautiful sea there. I hope to visit again."

They rode along in companionable silence for a few minutes.

Then Fritz began: "When I was at home, Vicky, after our trip to the exhibition, I laughed sometimes when I thought of you."

Vicky glanced over at him. He sat astride the pony in a relaxed, easeful way, the reins held negligently in one hand. He was looking out into the distance, smiling.

"You were so alive and so determined," he continued. "Confident of course, but also generous. It's not so often you meet a small girl like that. Then imagine how it felt to come here, as I did, nervously, a bit uncertain, more than a little resistant—since it was my mother's command that I must come and meet you again exactly now, no time to waste!"

He was gazing over at her now, smiling, and she flushed.

"And I arrive and I find that the same child who amused me has grown into a beautiful young woman. Who has captivated me."

She felt tears sting her eyes. It was too much, to hear him spell out his admiration. But she mustn't cry. She mustn't. She wanted to be poised.

"Let's get off the ponies," he said.

Vicky slid to the ground and looked behind her. The rest of the family trailed by a good half mile now, traversing the edge of the valley below.

Fritz searched for something in the grass. After a moment he bent down and picked something, a sprig of white heather.

"Your father tells me that this plant is good luck," he said.

"Yes, you carry it with you for success in the hunt," she said.

"Please take this. I wish to have the good luck to be together with you always. Will you come to Prussia with me, *Liebste*?"

"On a visit?"

"On a visit that will last a lifetime."

She heard his words, and she took the heather from his outstretched hand, but it took a moment before she felt a confused rush of warmth, a roar in her ears, a flood of sensation overtaking her. She struggled to steady herself and looked away before she found words to answer.

"Yes, I mean, I would like that. Of course." How ridiculous she sounded.

He smiled. "So your answer is yes? You will marry me?"

"Yes, yes, yes." And she nodded fervently.

He reached out and stroked her cheek. His fingers felt cold, but the gesture was gentle, almost reverent. She managed to look him full in the face and saw he had tears in his eyes.

"Yesterday I asked your parents if I might join your family and to my immense joy they agreed," he said. "However, they worry you're so young, you can't know your heart. I begged them for an opportunity to speak to you and finally they allowed it. May I?" he asked, and bent to kiss her without waiting for the answer.

His lips pressed against her mouth. Soft and warm and pleasurably insistent. How exhilarating to be a woman a man wished to touch. That it should be Fritz touching her, desiring her, was astonishing, revelatory. She began to tremble, even as she tried to kiss him back. She felt a peculiar surge of excitement rise and blood rush into hidden corners of herself.

When finally they broke apart, he said: "Your parents insist we wait until after your confirmation to announce the engagement."

Still shaking, Vicky said, "Which is more than a year from now."

"And they will not permit us to marry for another year after that."

"Goodness!"

"*Ja*, but I will visit. We will never be apart long."

Fritz placed his hands on her shoulders, and he gazed down at her, quite obviously exultant. Vicky felt excited as well—she had wished for exactly this—yet her arms quivered and her legs seemed inadequate to hold her up. A married lady? Such an adult thing to be, and she wondered for a moment how she'd cope. And living in Prussia, so far away? Of course, she'd not be getting married for some time, and Fritz would be her husband and she trusted Fritz. So many people would be pleased she had picked him. Had it been fated, for years, from the time of the exhibition? In any case there would be a huge fuss over the engagement. What would Tilla say? And Alice? She wanted to write immediately and tell Laddle.

They could hear the rest of the party approaching now. Fritz let go of her, but they stood close together, Vicky still clutching the sprig of heather. Papa was in front. When he saw their faces, he smiled a gentle smile. Vicky could hear Mama scolding Bertie for stealing Affie's cap, but then she too caught sight of them, and she stopped her pony. Vicky nodded slightly as the two exchanged a wordless, loaded look. Mama shook her head as if in disbelieving wonder at the beauty and the glory of it all.

PART II

Bride

6

Windsor and London, October 1855–November 1856

*P*apa was adamant—no one was to know she was now engaged. "We always said you had to be sixteen—and confirmed—to begin planning your marriage, and that's still the case."

"But it's all decided, Papa," said Vicky. "And you are so pleased."

"Yes, within the family it's decided, but not officially."

"I don't think it will stay a secret very long, angel," said Mama.

"There's no reason to inform anyone at the moment," he insisted.

The three of them were conferring in Papa's Windsor study, the whole family having returned to the castle from chilly Scotland the day before. On this morning, fog filled the Thames Valley and pressed up against the windows—the clock had just chimed eleven but it was impossible to see anything of the Great Park outside. Vicky tried to imagine what Fritz might be doing at this very moment, and where exactly. She began to envision wafting through the ghostly mist and landing, lightly, on two feet, directly in front of him. After he recovered from his astonishment, he'd bend down to kiss her . . .

Stern words yanked her from the daydream. "Are you listening,

Vicky? What's needed now is for you to be prepared for your future."

"Yes, Papa." She quickly nodded.

"Is everyone aware you expect this matter to remain private?" asked Mama.

"Of course," said her father, irritated. "Remind your mother that discretion is vital."

"I will, angel, although the duchess hardly sees anyone. Whereas those in Berlin . . ."

"Fritz and Augusta and Wilhelm will respect my wishes in this regard," said Papa.

"I wouldn't wonder if it's the talk of the court there already," said Mama, shaking her head. "And I fear poor Fritz feels hard done by."

As soon as Fritz had left Balmoral, he had written to Papa and Mama to express second thoughts. He couldn't bear a wait of more than two years. Mightn't he come back in the spring, present Vicky with a ring, and fix the wedding for next November, the month she'd turn sixteen?

Absolutely not, declared Papa. And Mama concurred. "He's fortunate we don't demand you're eighteen before you're a bride."

Now Papa said: "He may be downcast, but he won't break his word. And, Vicky, you are to speak to nobody about this outside the family."

FRITZ'S IMPATIENCE WAS thrilling—and Vicky wrote him long letters daily lamenting their separation. She described to Alice and Bertie how painful it was to live without him, and sometimes teared up. But when she was honest with herself, she didn't feel impatient for the wedding. It was exciting enough to be engaged, promised to a man as attractive as Fritz, with the prospect of a great position to occupy in future. The somewhat daunting prospect of actually being married she pushed out of her mind. She could come to grips with that in future, nearer the time.

And although her betrothal remained private, pleasing changes ensued. Now she frequently dined with her parents, rather than upstairs with the other children. Mama had become affectionate and confiding, telling Vicky the court gossip as if they were two friends and urging her to read Fritz's letters aloud so that they could dissect them together.

Papa stopped going out during the week in order to spend the two hours between seven and nine with Vicky, together studying government, law, political philosophy, and history. He requested she write a weekly essay analyzing current events in Europe, which she would then read aloud so he might critique her thinking and her prose.

"Vicky, you must understand your special mission," he often said. "The national union of the German peoples has been frustrated too long. Prussia is powerful enough to make it happen, but the crown must cede vital powers to the elected parliament to bind the common man to the government and counter radical thinking. If you and Fritz endorse and foster this evolution, it will come into being that much more quickly and to the benefit of all." How inspiring to hear Papa speak like this.

Mama had told Tilla about the secret engagement, and her teacher always requested to hear Papa's views recounted the next morning, which absorbed a good part of lessons. "All we learn is politics and government these days," Alice complained. "I want to study other things as well."

But her sister did not truly appreciate that Papa's training was vital, so she might exert the proper influence. Vicky imagined herself in future, sitting at the foot of a long table, Fritz at the head, with fascinating men and women gathered around conversing on the issues of the day. She and Fritz would invite the best minds in Berlin to their home, and then, when Fritz was king of Prussia, he'd have these people to advise him, along with herself. She would always be his closest counselor, his wisest friend, as well as his wife. She'd be widely admired for her perspicacity and modern outlook, and handsome Fritz would hover attentively at her side, anxious for her input, waiting on her words of guidance.

"That's Queen Victoria's daughter," people would murmur, "but so clever and farseeing like her father." She could picture it all.

AFTER NEW YEAR, news of the engagement leaked, much to Papa's indignation. Mama blamed his older brother, Duke Ernest of Saxe-Coburg, who had a wide circle of friends in Germany and a great fondness for gossip, and in whom Papa should never have confided. To Vicky it mattered only that the proposed match was very hostilely received. According to the *Times* Prussia was "a wretched German state" and the Hohenzollerns, Fritz's family, "a paltry dynasty." The editors of the *Morning Post* chastised the queen and her husband for "shipping off noble princess Victoria to live amidst the repressive Berlin camarilla" and predicted she would be forced to return home years hence "a sad and wretched exile." *Punch* even published a cartoon of a black Prussian eagle that had Fritz's mustached face, circling the crenellated tower of Windsor Castle, where Mama stood, wearing her crown. The caption read: "Shoo off the predator, Ma'am."

Berlin newspapers responded in kind: The British royal family was self-satisfied and arrogant. English people habitually sneered at Prussians. With his pick of admirable German princesses, Prince Friedrich had no reason to go abroad for a wife. The English marriage was a mistake.

Mama was distraught and Papa pained. He issued a statement to the newspapers: "No consideration would have induced the Queen or myself to imperil the happiness of our eldest daughter by a marriage in which she could not have scope to practice the constitutional principles in which she has been raised."

When she and Tilla attended a science lecture at the South Kensington Museum a few days later, Vicky worried the men and women in the audience were silently disparaging her marriage plans. She wished to clamber up on a chair and explain to the crowd that Fritz wasn't a predatory prince from a reactionary nation, but an upstanding young man who had learned at Papa's knee about the principles of liberal democracy. Also that the

Prussia of today wouldn't endure forever and that Fritz, with her help, would promote change. Papa liked to say that the dream of Prussian reform should be a dream people in England shared. If Prussia became a country more like Britain, and united all of Germany, then Germany would be a most useful ally for Britain. British people should understand this.

A WEEK LATER came another blow: asked by a German journalist what he thought of the match, Uncle Prussia declared Vicky would make Fritz a fine wife if she left the Englishwoman at home and became a Prussian.

Her irate parents summoned Lord Clarendon, the foreign secretary, to Windsor the very next day. And Papa refused to let Vicky join the meeting. Vicky sat shaking and infuriated at her desk in the schoolroom the whole of the morning, wishing she had the nerve to abandon her lessons, run back downstairs, and burst into the library where Mama and Papa were receiving the minister.

Tilla had them reading the second act of *Hamlet*, which didn't help Vicky keep her mind off matters. She always pictured the romantic Danish prince looking something like Fritz. And then their teacher announced they would go over some very tedious Latin conjugations, after eating the sandwiches that had been sent up from the kitchen.

They had just opened their Latin texts when a footman arrived to announce that her parents wanted to see Vicky in the library. It was a blustery January day, and as she descended the wide stone stairs she shivered, both nervous and cold. She found Mama and Papa sitting close to the fire, looking very somber.

Her father pointed at a straight-backed chair and she sat.

"Vicky, your mother believes we may have been too precipitous," he said.

"What do you mean?" said Vicky. "About Fritz? Why would you think that?" She stared, astonished, at her mother.

"Prince Wilhelm's words were offensive and unacceptable to me," said Mama.

"But that was Fritz's father talking, not Fritz!" Vicky retorted.

"Stay calm now," said Papa. "On Lord Clarendon's advice, Mama and I have written to Prince Wilhelm this morning demanding an explanation. I suspect his comment was impulsive, nothing more than his natural chauvinism trotted out for public consumption."

"Still, unless he understands how very lucky he is that you will be his son's wife, we cannot agree to go on with the engagement," Mama pronounced.

"Break it off? No, no, I won't do that. You can't force me," Vicky said. She heard a note of wild panic in her voice. The bottom had fallen out of her stomach.

Her mother put up her hand and looked at her sternly. "Puss, you know I like Fritz. For all that he could be more assertive, he's a fine young man who is passionately attached to you."

Mama paused, perhaps, Vicky thought, wondering anew why this might be so. But then her mother's expression softened.

"And there is nothing I want more for you in this world than a marriage as loving and fulfilling as mine has been." Her mother glanced at Papa before continuing. "But I fear now that Prussia will be too unwelcoming. Imagine Prince Wilhelm declaring you shouldn't be English! You will always be English, and the Princess Royal. I will not have my daughter living anywhere this is not recognized and celebrated. A match like this works only if both sides are delighted with it. We need to think again if Fritz is the right husband for you."

Vicky shook her head vehemently. How could this be happening? They'd been overjoyed when Fritz proposed. Now everything was to be smashed to bits over some careless words of silly Uncle Prussia?

She looked, beseechingly, at her father. "Papa, please don't allow this. I love Fritz, he's wonderful, and he loves me so much. He'd die if you told him there will be no marriage."

"He would be extremely disappointed, Puss, I am certain. But die, probably not. Let's wait and let Prince Wilhelm explain himself."

"We will accept nothing less than a full and contrite apology," said Mama. "You always assume Wilhelm more sagacious than he really is, Albert."

"And you always think the worst of him. Meanwhile, Vicky, you will stop writing to Fritz."

She shook her head again, but her father looked fixedly at her, so stern she felt she had no option but to acquiesce: "Yes, Papa."

"It will emerge, I expect, that Prince Wilhelm meant no harm," said Papa.

"What do you mean, no harm? By insulting us?" asked Mama.

"I doubt he sees it that way. He sought to reassure his country-men that Vicky will embrace her new homeland."

"And I will," said Vicky hotly.

"Your loyalty to Fritz is touching, Vicky," said Papa. "Still, Berlin is a labyrinth. I am doing my best to prepare you, but your mother is right. We need to be certain of full family support—"

"You shouldn't worry! Fritz will always be with me," she inter-rupted.

"Even so, navigating a foreign court in a foreign country will take tact and perseverance and a good deal of courage."

"You think I'm lacking? Is that what you think?" she asked. Again, that wild, panicky voice. She was gripping the sides of the chair seat so tightly her hands hurt.

"You are dauntless as a rule, Vicky," said Papa with a small smile.

Mama reached over and patted her arm. "Your father and I are only trying to protect you."

"This is not protecting me," she replied, testy.

"Let's wait and see," said Mama.

Both parents were looking at her kindly. Still she hated how smug and self-righteous they were, as if only they knew best.

"Can I go back upstairs now?" Maybe she sounded petulant and childish—but this was unendurable.

A WEEK PASSED. Fritz sent long letters from Silesia, where he'd gone on maneuvers. He clearly had no idea a storm had erupted.

Only in his last missive did he implore Vicky to answer: why had there been no letter from her for days?

Vicky stacked his five unanswered letters on her bureau and often sat on the edge of her bed staring at the mute pile. What if she were never allowed to write to Fritz again? What if the next letter he received from London was a formal note from Papa telling him their engagement was canceled? Would he think she never really loved him? Oh, she couldn't bear the thought. She wept in earnest and rocked back and forth.

On Wednesday afternoon, when Vicky went to Mama's sitting room, she found her mother surrounded by her ladies and very cheerful.

"Puss, you will dine down with us tonight," her mother said. Her eyes shone and she shook her shoulders slightly, the way she always did when excited.

"What has happened?" Vicky asked quickly.

"It's good news, but wait until we're at the table. Papa will explain all."

Her parents were already sitting at their regular places when Vicky reached the dining room. She saw immediately at the third place, perched on the plate, an oblong black leather case with a gold clasp.

After walking over she said: "Should I open this?"

"Of course," said Papa. "It's for you."

"But what about—" she began, anxious for the news.

"First, look at your gift," her father said. Still standing, Vicky picked up the case and clicked the clasp open—finding inside a long strand of pearls. She lifted up the necklace, letting it dangle from her fingers. The pearls, dozens and dozens of them, all matching in size, spilled down lustrously, pink-white orbs gleaming in the candlelight.

"Prince Wilhelm sent this necklace for you via messenger. He asked me to tell you how very pleased he is that you will be his daughter," said Papa. "He also sent a lengthy letter addressed to me and Mama." Her father paused.

"And?" asked Vicky.

"As I suspected, his concern is that you become a loyal Prussian—as Fritz's wife no other allegiance would be fitting. He wanted to state that to the public. But because of various sensitivities—"

He paused again, fiddling with the fork in front of him.

"Whose sensitivities?" she asked.

"Some Prussians are suspicious that a new strong English influence in the country will accompany your marriage. Wilhelm intended to address those fears. Now he concedes that perhaps his phrasing was not ideal. Your royal English lineage and English title are hardly a deficit in his eyes."

"I should think not," Mama said, pursing her mouth.

Papa continued: "It's one reason he believes his son has made an excellent choice. And he knows you to be an obedient young woman who will comport herself appropriately."

Vicky felt a surge of relief, like a warm wave, cross her chest. "So he satisfied you? Both of you?"

"*Jawohl*," said Papa, nodding.

"All's well that ends well, Puss," Mama said, beaming now. "Sit down. Standing there you look like Juliet waiting to see if she will be allowed her Romeo."

But something still bothered Vicky. "He expects me to be obedient?" she couldn't help blurting it out.

Her parents laughed.

"Prince Wilhelm is a military man," said Papa.

"And you're not marrying *him*," said Mama.

Vicky sat down and more carefully examined the necklace. She could hardly contain it in the palm of one hand, it was so lavish in length and the number of pearls—like something Mama would wear. How strange that she had become, too, a woman on whom tributes of expensive jewelry were bestowed.

"I imagine you desire to write immediately to Fritz?" Papa asked. "Shall we forgo study this evening so you can do that instead?"

"Yes, Papa," she said. With her parents' recommitting to her engagement, it didn't seem wise to dispute Uncle Prussia's notion of her further. But she didn't like it.

MAMA SAID THE necklace wasn't suitable for every day, and if she ever ventured into Vicky and Alice's room—which fortunately she rarely did—she would have been irate to see that instead of putting the pearls carefully away in their case, Vicky hung them off the corner of Fritz's framed portrait, one he'd recently sent her, of him looking spectacularly handsome in his Horse Guards uniform. And Vicky had laid the dry, crumpled sprig of white heather from the day of her engagement in front of the picture. This small shrine occupied the left-hand corner of her bureau now, beside the looking glass, the spot where she'd piled Fritz's letters when she'd been forbidden to reply to them. Sometimes she whispered to him; more often she just stared at his face.

Her heart would race and her stomach lurch when she imagined seeing him again in the flesh. She'd envision what he'd say to her and how he'd touch her and the glamourous, grown-up way they would converse and walk side by side. Right there, alone in her and Alice's bedroom, where no one could see, she'd dance and sway in place and spin around in excitement. She'd gaze at her flushed face in the glass, smooth her hair, and then start again. The pleasure of her imaginings was so keen that she didn't indulge all the time. She enjoyed them best when she could put aside any fears about the future and feel strong, enviable, and assured. Then dreaming about her and Fritz together would set her off, and she'd sail ecstatically, flitting, skimming, and diving through all the bliss and passion and euphoria he aroused in her, before she came back to earth sated and content until the time came for another flight.

HOW AWKWARD AND tense it turned out to be when Fritz actually did return to England—to Osborne in May. He was so very attentive—as she had thought she wanted—always sitting next to her on the sofa, grasping her elbow as they went down steps, lifting her onto her horse although she could get up perfectly well by herself. "He never lets you out of his sight," laughed Mary Bulteel. Mary was one of Mama's ladies, officially, but her mother had asked Mary to wait on Vicky these days, and they had become good friends.

"He's so puppy-doggish, those huge hands and feet and lavishing all that affection," her lady added. Mary, eight years older than Vicky, had dark hair, a beaky face, and slightly protruding eyes. Not pretty, but with a clever look and a cheerful disposition.

"We have been separated for months!" Vicky protested.

"I am not being critical, dear princess. It's remarkable. I expected a military man, very correct and Prussian."

"He is that too, but not so much around me."

"Clearly not."

She didn't admit to Mary, or to anyone else, that Fritz's avidity made her self-conscious, even alarmed her at times. His second day at Osborne, when Bertie had left them alone in the billiards room for a moment, Fritz had pulled her against him in a tight clinch and kissed her mouth hard, almost roughly, their teeth knocking. He let her go when the door opened again, and they both pretended nothing had happened, but she felt unnerved. As they left the room to go into luncheon he whispered: "I'm sorry, I couldn't stop myself."

Which was flattering. But he was galloping ahead of her with his ardor, and she worried how it would be: married and lying together every night. What would he demand? She tried to remind herself that Fritz would never want to upset her. After the billiards room incident, he did exert better self-control. He would stare intently into her face sometimes, and she realized that he longed to kiss her, but he never did again, except on the day he departed. He loved to hold one of her hands in both of his for many minutes at a time, examining first the palm, and then the back, heaping praise on the small size, white skin, sweet dimples, as he turned the hand over and over. His fingers were a little rough, but the lightly grazing sensation of his touch was tantalizing, especially when he gently stroked each of her fingers and then carefully, deliberately, interwove them with his own. He claimed her hands were the softest he'd ever felt. Once he pressed her palm against his cheek and said, "When I am back home I hope I can recall this touch perfectly."

Such a tender moment, and Vicky hoped her blushing nervousness hadn't spoiled it. She had thought to return the gesture, to put her other hand on top of his or reach out and stroke his cheek. But she hesitated, unsure. Would that be welcome? How difficult to manage the feelings of a grown man—she sensed a crouching animal inside him that she was not adept at handling. After he left she vowed to do better in future. She didn't want to be anxious or frightened of Fritz.

TO CELEBRATE HER sixteenth birthday on November 21, Mama and Papa had decided to hold a ball, and of course Fritz would attend. He arrived five days beforehand, pale and tired after a rough channel crossing, and Vicky felt a surge of sympathy for him as he walked into the Green Drawing Room at Windsor. They were so cozy and at ease on this cold, dark autumnal afternoon—Papa, Mama, Bertie, Alice, and she—gathered in the golden lamplight, enjoying the warmth of the fire. And in he came, a tall and rather stiff outsider, still nearly a stranger to them. With everyone present she found herself tongue-tied, although she longed to throw her arms around him and declare how thrilling it was, after six months apart, to once again stand together in the same room. She did manage to take his hand after he kissed her decorously, on the cheek. She held on to it as they walked into supper.

At the table Papa quizzed Fritz about matters back home. Had he met with liberal members of the Prussian diet? Was he keeping up with the debate on reforming the Prussian courts? "I am occupied with my army command," Fritz answered. "And as long as my uncle is alive not much can be accomplished."

"Nonsense," snapped Papa. "You are heir apparent after your

father and have a responsibility to be well informed, align yourself with men of ability, and seek constantly to encourage progress."

Fritz looked sheepish and had no answer. What a relief when Mama said reprovingly: "Now, angel, Fritz has come for the ball, and to spend time with Vicky, not to be lectured on his duties."

"*Na, gut,* and we will have plenty of opportunity to talk more in coming days." Papa nodded, but Vicky noticed the three vertical creases between her father's eyebrows, always in evidence when he worried.

THE DAY BEFORE the ball, they moved to Buckingham Palace and Mrs. Moon came that afternoon, for the final fitting of Vicky's white silk ball gown. At tea, Mama and Vicky debated for nearly a half an hour whether she should wear cornflowers or white roses in her hair, before finally agreeing cornflowers would best bring out the blue embroidery detailing on the dress. Mama fretted over how Vicky could fit in all her partners. She would have to accommodate her cousin the Duke of Cambridge, and also the bad-tempered Duke of Wellington, son of the Waterloo hero. And certainly the young Duke of Argyll, who was helping Papa found the new Imperial College in Knightsbridge. Vicky asked about William, Earl of Burlington. A young man of nineteen who was Bertie's best friend outside the family, the earl rode with them sometimes at Windsor. He'd often voiced his desire to dance once with Vicky before she disappeared forever into the wilds of Prussia. Should she not give him a polka?

Papa smiled forbearingly through all this chatter, but Fritz appeared cross and out of sorts. Vicky wondered what could be the matter.

Finally, she got up from the sofa and motioned to him. "Fritz, come and look out the window with me."

He obediently rose and joined her as she leaned on the deep sill.

"Are you ill?" she whispered to him.

"No," he whispered back.

"Then what is it?"

For a long moment he remained silent, then, in full voice, he said: "Do you really intend to dance with other men at this ball? Other men besides me and your father?"

She laughed. "Of course! It's a ball for me. It would be odd if I didn't dance with my guests."

Fritz's face hardened, his jaw tense and twitching, his eyes staring straight out the window, with no particular object.

A mistake, perhaps, to laugh, but how could he fail to understand?

"Perhaps it's different in Berlin," she explained. "Here in England young women, especially when they first appear in society, meet and dance with gentlemen who ask. The hardest part is to keep track of who is promised which dance. And in my case there are so many considerations of course because of Mama . . ."

She trailed off. She could tell he wasn't mollified.

"In Prussia once a woman is engaged, she does not dance with other men," Fritz said. "After the wedding she might, only if her husband approves."

Vicky was confused. Did he expect her to conform to Prussian custom here? And their engagement had still not been formally announced, nor the wedding date fixed. Papa wanted a dowry for her to pass through Parliament before settling on that.

"Fritz, I believe I must do it the English way, especially as the ball is for me. I thought to give you the first dance, and let's add the last, too. If that's acceptable to Mama. Come, we'll ask her," Vicky said, tugging on his hand, eager for her mother's help coping with disgruntled Fritz.

He just kept staring out the window. Finally, he said, "No, perhaps I will speak to your father later. That is better."

Dropping her hand, he stalked away. Papa looked up when he heard the door to the sitting room open and close.

"Fritz is going out?" he asked.

Vicky, disturbed and embarrassed, couldn't confess the truth, so she said: "He wants to answer some letters before supper."

FOR THE BALL Fritz wore the striking, bright red tunic and white trousers of his Horse Guards uniform, but also a tight, forced smile Vicky hated. While he danced the first dance with her, he answered her questions in the curtest way possible and ventured no remarks of his own. He'd disappeared by the time the last dance began, and when Papa saw her stranded, he left Mama on the side amid a bevy of guests and drew her onto the floor.

"Fritz told me he hasn't felt well since his arrival. He's likely gone upstairs to bed and didn't want to concern you," Papa said. It was clear that Fritz hadn't brought up the English dancing customs with him. "In any case, it's all been a great success. Torrington pronounced it a highlight of the winter season."

While Vicky supposed she should be pleased that Papa's friend, the society eminence Lord Torrington, approved of the ball, Fritz's mood had spoiled it for her. When, the next morning, Fritz didn't turn up for breakfast, she thought in a panic that perhaps he'd call off their engagement. At the same time, she knew he was being absurd. It was hardly disloyal, or unseemly, to dance with noblemen of her acquaintance at a ball in her honor. And what of herself? Was she not an independent being who could venture out into the world and come back to her love? Would he want to imprison her after they married? Keep her from natural relations with others? That would be dreadful. She wouldn't, couldn't, do that.

A steady rain was falling on this dark and gusty morning. Tilla excused her from lessons so she might start on the reams of thank-you notes she owed for gifts she'd been sent. Together with Mary, Vicky headed up to an infrequently used room on the third floor where there was a large table. Even in that high room, with a pair of four-paned windows looking out on the courtyard, the light was dim and Vicky requested candles. The footman returned promptly with two tall tapers, which he lit and placed on the end of the table where she and Mary sat across from each other.

Vicky wore a new dress of soft gray muslin with a lace collar. It had pretty, full sleeves and a flounce of lace that peeked out under both wide cuffs. How disappointing Fritz wasn't here to see her in it. Maybe he'd gone to the Prussian legation, or could he have left London? Hard to imagine he'd depart without telling Mama and Papa—so terribly rude. But this hostile Fritz was someone she hadn't previously met, and who knew what he was capable of? She felt anxious, and also impatient to be done with her writing task. Even with the lit tapers it was hard to see.

Standing up, she leaned over the table, reaching to pull back the woolen drape a few extra inches, to get more light. In the small draft stirred up by her abrupt, hasty pulling, one taper flared and the tip of the flame brushed the bottom of her right sleeve as she drew in her arm. In an instant, the whole sleeve was ablaze. Vicky stared into the garish brightness, paralyzed, until Mary screamed. Clumsily Vicky backed away from table and fell to the floor trying to smother her right arm, her flesh horribly smarting and shriveling. A loud scrape of chair legs, a scurry, and Mary stood above, holding the hearth rug.

"Roll left, Princess," Mary said urgently. Vicky managed it, and Mary swooped down and covered the burning sleeve with the rug, throwing herself on top, to extinguish the last of the flames.

After a pause, Mary toppled off of her, breathing heavily. They lay on the floor, and Vicky looked over her shoulder into her lady's white, terrified face.

"I'm all right, Mary," Vicky said, even though her upper arm was agony and she felt dazed from shock.

"Thank God you weren't alone. Thank God, thank God," said Mary, beginning to sob.

Now they heard a man's striding step in the passageway and Henry Ponsonby poked his head in the door.

"What's happening? I heard a scream—"

"Thank goodness, Henry, it's you," said Mary. "Go immediately and tell Miss Hildyard the princess is injured. And then find the queen and her ladies, explain the doctor must be called, for there's been an accident with a candle." Mary sat up as she said this.

Within three minutes Tilla was there, chest heaving—she'd run up the stairs. Alice followed, her eyes large and apprehensive. Tilla and Mary helped Vicky up and had her sit down on the wide leather settee. The sleeve of her dress was completely burned away. Vicky could see a large angry red stretch of seared skin all along the back of her arm. The smell of burnt cloth filled the air, and throbbing, blistering pain befuddled her.

"A shame about my nice new dress," said Vicky slowly. "I wonder if Mrs. Moon can make another."

The room filled up quickly. Mama, her hand at her mouth, flew in through the door, Henry Ponsonby and two ladies behind. Dr. Clark arrived with his assistant, and in the end Vicky counted three different footmen who came and went, fetching cool water, and then compresses, and then butter at the doctor's request. She watched, trembling a bit and nonplussed, as Dr. Clark scissored off the remnants of the sleeve, bathed and cooled her arm, applied butter and another salve from his bag, and wrapped a white bandage from the upper wrist to the right shoulder. He urged her to stretch out on the settee. A maid brought in a blanket.

"The princess must be left in peace," the doctor declared to the company, and looking down added, "Do you prefer to go to your room?"

She shook her head. She might faint on the way downstairs.

"Everyone please depart, excepting yourself, ma'am." He bowed to Mama.

Just then Fritz appeared in the doorway. For a long moment he simply stood there, staring at Vicky, aghast.

"*Hallo*," she called out. She almost laughed with relief to see he had clearly not caught a boat train for Folkestone. From the mixture of fear, dismay, and abashment on his face, she guessed he'd been sulking somewhere, heard the commotion, and come running.

She beamed at him, and he walked over to kneel beside the sofa while Mama herded everyone out of the room, leaving them alone for a minute, although Vicky could see her mother and Mary lingering just outside, speaking with Dr. Clark.

"Your dress caught fire?" Fritz said in a strangled, anxious voice.

"Yes, the sleeve, but Mary was with me and it was quite quickly put out. Dr. Clark says I've a bad burn on my arm, but it will heal. And with luck, not much scarring."

He nodded, ashen.

She continued to smile, to bolster and hearten him, and finally he gave a small smile back.

"Where have you been?" she asked quietly.

"I went to go riding."

"In the rain? Isn't it raining?"

"*Doch*, so instead I just sat in the stables for a while. A groom told me the doctor had been sent for. He didn't know why, or for whom, but when I came in again a maid said it was you, you had burned yourself. I was so full of dread at that moment. I ran up here convinced you were terribly hurt."

He picked up her left hand and kissed it.

Vicky felt emboldened after her escape. "Fritz, will you leave off now, with your bad temper?"

Fritz nodded, and then he shook his head, muddled and obviously upset with himself. "I shouldn't have— I don't know. What I want to say to you, *mein Schatz,* is that when I see your face, I feel I have come home."

She managed to hold his gaze, steady, listening.

"And so, because of that I am . . . I was not happy," he said. "I will be much happier when we are married and you belong to me, to no one else."

She was surprised to see a tear on his cheek, and she reached out to rub it away, gently, with her thumb. And then she traced the whole line of his cheekbone. First one side and then the other. Lovely man.

Mama bustled in and clapped her hands, taking charge. She reeled off her commands. Vicky must stay quiet and recover. Mary would find a book to read aloud to her while she rested here. They would cancel their evening plans for the theater, which was just as well since Papa had been occupied the entire day at the Imperial College and would be exhausted.

"Fritz, dear, you go to the nursery," Mama said. "Reassure them all that Vicky is fine."

"*Jawohl*," he said, getting to his feet, and then he asked Vicky: "You still feel a lot of pain?"

Her arm throbbed and ached, but she shook her head. "It's not so bad."

His eyes glowed down at her; he was smitten.

"Thank you, Fritz," said Mama. Vicky listened as her mother chivvied him out of the room, saying: "Having so many children is such a great strain, you know."

7

London, January 1858

*W*ith the wedding only a few weeks ahead, and her parting from the family imminent, Vicky endeavored to spend some time each afternoon with Beatrice, Mama's new baby, eight months old. Beatrice had a favorite yarn ball, which Vicky rolled across the nursery floor, clapping as the baby crawled furiously after it. Vicky taught her peek-a-boo and made her a first book, each page of heavy paper dedicated to a letter of the alphabet, illustrated with a small watercolor, and stitched together with thick red thread. Just sitting with Beatrice nestled heavy in her lap calmed Vicky. And she hoped she was imprinting herself on the tiny girl's memory. "I worry she will never think of me as a sister," she said to Alice. "I will be like some aunt or cousin to her always." Alice, already distraught over Vicky's leaving, burst into tears.

FOR A BRIEF moment, in October, it had appeared she and Fritz might not marry after all. The Prussian ambassador had told Lord Clarendon that the wedding could not take place as planned in London on January 25, because weddings of Hohenzollern heirs were always held in Berlin. Papa drafted a letter to Prince Wilhelm demanding an explanation for this latest, most insulting dictate but tore it up in a rage. Best for Mama, he said, to write to Clarendon refusing to even consider a change in venue and directing her foreign minister to so inform the Prussians. Mama read out the concluding paragraph of her letter to Vicky: "Whatever may be the usual practice of Prussian princes, it is not every day that one marries the eldest daughter of the queen of England. The question therefore must be considered settled and closed."

Vicky couldn't fathom why the Prussians were only now raising this objection, a full two years after her engagement. No one had bothered to ask Fritz his opinion. "It's likely that someone—the king, or maybe the queen or Uncle Karl—decided it looked bad, all of us traveling to England, and chose to make a fuss," he wrote.

But after Mama sent her letter and Clarendon conveyed the message, nothing was heard back on this subject, so planning for the wedding recommenced.

Then, in November, the king of Prussia, Fritz's uncle, suffered a serious stroke. He could no longer speak or walk properly, thus would not attend the ceremony. His wife, Queen Elisabeth, announced that because she didn't favor the English match she would also stay away. When Uncle Prussia wrote after Christmas to claim he was too busy doing his brother's job to leave Berlin, Papa sent a wire immediately to insist he be with them, and Fritz's father acquiesced, but the exchange distressed Papa terribly, and now he'd retreated to bed, fending off a cold he felt sure was coming on. Mama, at a peak of fretfulness, couldn't decide on a gown to wear for the wedding or which rooms the three dozen guests from Germany would sleep in.

As the days ticked down, Vicky found herself chanting in her head: "I love Fritz, I am marrying Fritz, the wedding will be splendid, all will be well." She couldn't crack, even a little. She had to find a dignified way through the whole charged occasion—jumping every hurdle and sailing through each public appearance. She owed this to her parents, to Fritz, to everyone. She was the Princess Royal.

And on the other side would be—what? The departure, which she more and more dreaded, but never mind. First, she had to navigate the wedding.

A LONG, SUNNY room near the kitchens at the back of the palace had been set aside for Mrs. Moon and her team of seamstresses. Vicky's trousseau included ten evening gowns, six ball dresses, three court dresses, a dozen day dresses, and several riding habits. The seamstresses sat at trestle tables stacked with lengths of velvet, silk, wool, cotton lawn, and the dull black crape intended for mourning. These women smiled shyly at Vicky when she came down for fittings, and she always thanked them for their careful work. Did they try, as she did, to imagine where she would be wearing all these lovely clothes? She'd seen a picture of the Berliner Schloss, the imposing baroque castle that was the home of the Hohenzollerns on the Spree Island in the middle of Berlin, but she had no sense of the inside. She'd studied illustrations of the royal residences in the Potsdam country district outside the city, many built by Friedrich the Great, and inspired by Versailles and other French palaces. Now in her mind all of Potsdam resembled an eighteenth-century fantasy village, populated with men in white powdered wigs like Fritz's distinguished great-great-granduncle. How rooms in Prussia would actually look and smell, she couldn't foresee, and how the food would taste and the way she would fill her days with Papa, Mama, Bertie, Alice, Tilla, and Mary far away, she had no idea. And it puzzled her that she didn't feel more alarmed by this. Perhaps because she couldn't quite believe she was going.

Ready or not, she'd be venturing forth into the unknown well equipped. Huge packing cases stood open beside the tables and were gradually filling up with shoes, stockings, shawls, bonnets, caps, mantillas, crinolines, and mackintoshes. Underwear had been ordered by the gross: twelve dozen shifts, twelve dozen pairs of drawers, twelve dozen nightgowns, plus eight dozen petticoats— as if there were no shops in Berlin, nor dressmakers at all.

Mrs. Moon labored over the wedding dress, doing much of the stitching herself. Mama had requested white antique moiré, a heavy watered silk, and on the skirt three deep flounces of Honiton lace worked with roses, shamrocks, and thistles, the emblems of England, Ireland, and Scotland. More lace on sleeves and bodice. The gown had a train three yards long, and the veil, trimmed with white satin, stretched nearly as far, to be held in place on the top of her head by a wreath of myrtle, the traditional German wedding flower. She'd also carry a bouquet of orange and myrtle blossoms, as Mama had done at her wedding eighteen years previously.

Mama desired Vicky's wedding to resemble hers and Papa's as much as possible, and the ceremony was to be held, as theirs had been, in the Chapel Royal, at St. James's Palace. Which was well omened, thought Vicky, since no married pair were as devoted. And she wondered, would she and Fritz in the future recount to their own children the story about how they met and courted? She expected they would. In her bewilderment about her new life in Prussia she always clung to that one most comforting thought—Fritz would be there with her.

SHE KNEW SHE should ask Mama what to expect when she and Fritz were finally sleeping in the same bed, on their honeymoon, which was to be at Windsor Castle. But she felt too bashful. And Mama herself dreaded discussing this, Vicky sensed. She couldn't upset her mother further in her current highly agitated state. And perhaps the matter should remain something private between her and Fritz, a secret discovery they made together? Mama had implied as much—that the bedroom was a couple's sacred sphere. Still, Vicky hated to be totally unprepared and run the risk of looking like a silly child in front of Fritz. She thought she might ask Tilla some questions, in the guise of scientific inquiry, of course, since her teacher had never been married. One afternoon during the first week of January, when lessons had finished and Alice had already left the schoolroom, Vicky lingered behind.

"We never studied much biology, Tilla," Vicky began.

"All that botany last summer when we were at Osborne," said Tilla, distracted, looking for something in the top drawer of her desk, rustling through papers.

"No, I mean human biology," Vicky said. She waited, uneasy. Tilla would probably guess now what she wanted to know.

"Oh, here it is," said Tilla, holding up a small gold key. "I have been looking for weeks for this key. It's to the glass bookcase in the passageway."

Vicky was tempted to drop the subject right then. But, having looked up, Tilla now registered what Vicky had said.

"Human biology? What do you mean, anatomy? Health?" she asked.

"Well, the health of babies and all that—"

"Babies?" Tilla appeared confused.

"Not caring for babies but . . ." Vicky flailed and found herself unable to look at Tilla. Instead her eyes began to roam around the room, seeking something else to talk about. A brownish-yellow water stain had appeared in a corner of the far wall; was Tilla aware of that? She had just opened her mouth to mention it when she heard a sharp intake of breath.

"Oh, yes, I've been meaning to show you something," her teacher said hurriedly. "To explain the marital relation. Let me see, where did I put it?"

Tilla opened a different drawer, on the right, and again riffled through papers. But the sound was more frantic this time, like a small animal burrowing in the dirt. Goodness, she should never have brought this up. Now Tilla was unnerved, and what on earth would she show her? Vicky just then recalled a dusty postcard, frayed at the corners, that Bertie had found once years ago on the floor of a train compartment and had shared with her when Mama and Papa weren't looking. It was a painting of a woman, her face turned up, laughing with her eyes nearly closed, while a gentleman standing behind her was sliding his hand down the front of her dress. Would it be something like that? Did her teacher believe she wanted to ogle such a picture?

"Here, here, I have it." Her teacher drew out a thin black book. She came around to the front of the desk and started flipping the pages quickly. Tilla's hands were trembling. Again, Vicky quite regretted she'd ever introduced the topic.

"You can show me later," said Vicky.

"No, no, I must show you now. You see, Princess, human male and female anatomies are different—"

Now Vicky could be dismissive. "Of course, as horses and dogs are," she said.

"And the male member, when aroused by, the, the presence of a female, becomes engorged with blood." Tilla had tilted the book so Vicky could look on and was pointing at a left-hand page, where Vicky saw a drawing, a diagram really, of a naked man. Goodness, the member looked large and droopy. Nothing like a boy baby's short little stalk. How awkward to have such a thing hanging between one's legs.

"And when erect it can be placed in the woman," said Tilla, speaking in a queer, rapid way, as she nervously tapped on the right-hand page, the drawing of female anatomy, which appeared stark without disguising hair. "Placed in her—" Tilla faltered.

"I know where," said Vicky sharply. And she supposed she did, although not exactly. And how long would the whole thing take? Must she do something particular while it was happening? Questions rushed into her head, but she couldn't bear to talk any further. Her cheeks had flushed and she felt idiotic. And she hated that she'd upset Tilla.

"It's fine, it will be fine, thank you," Vicky added.

Her teacher gave her an anxious, searching look and closed the book up abruptly. "It's all most natural, I understand," she said softly before walking back behind the desk.

Vicky wanted to assure her: we never need mention this again. But she left the room without another word, her teacher now sitting, disconcerted, in her chair. Surely Tilla couldn't be half as mortified as she herself was.

FRITZ'S MOTHER HAD proclaimed some months before that she'd enlisted a half-dozen "responsible matrons" to wait on Vicky after her arrival in Berlin. Papa had said no, noblewomen her own age must be chosen. Aunt Prussia had sent a list of names and Papa had invited the two youngest—Countess Walburga "Wally" Hohenthal, eighteen, and Countess Marie zu Lynar, seventeen—to Windsor for inspection. Auburn-haired Wally was tall and striking looking, the intelligent, orphaned daughter of a profligate general. She and Papa got into a long discussion about Roman architecture. Vicky felt faintly intimidated by her. Marie, a blonde, was quieter and less assertive but friendly and nearly as well-read as Wally. Papa declared the girls would be most suitable companions for Vicky and at the end of their three-day stay offered them posts. Mama laughed. "It will be the youngest court ever assembled in a European capital."

While Vicky was pleased that Papa had overruled Princess Augusta, and she supposed she'd enjoy getting to know Wally and Marie, she secretly longed for Mary to accompany her to Prussia. Mary—perpetually steady, cheerful, and practical—was never overwrought like Mama or Alice. She deferred to Vicky, of course, yet had a breezy, tactful way of making suggestions or giving advice. How reassuring it would be to have her in attendance in Berlin.

But her lady's widowed mother lived in the country and she had an older, unmarried sister who wasn't well. When not working Mary returned home to Hampshire to help care for her sister. It would be a terrible imposition to prevail upon her to come and live in Berlin, even for just a year or two. And then there was Mama, who would be very irritated to lose her. So Vicky had told herself she mustn't even raise the subject with Mary.

Then came a frigid morning ten days before the ceremony. The newspapers were full of speculation about the wedding. A few editors still grumbled that the young Princess Royal shouldn't be married off to the scion of a reactionary royal house, but most of the coverage was admiring, laudatory even. Mary had brought in the *Times* to show Vicky a large illustration of her and Fritz framed by a floral border shaped as a heart. "You're a romantic heroine now, the princess bride of everyone's imagining," she said with a light laugh.

Vicky examined the picture closely.

"You look lovely," Mary added kindly. "And isn't Prince Frederick's likeness splendid?"

Vicky nodded. Fritz at his noble, virile best. "Shall we get on with this task?" she heard her lady ask, but Vicky kept staring at the newspaper. More evidence the wedding was really, truly happening. They were standing in the ground-floor business room about to sort through some books Vicky intended to ship on ahead, and writing up an order list for more from the bookseller's, Mudie's. The servants were setting up extra tables and chairs in the State Dining Room just above for the first of three celebratory banquets, and the noise of dragging furniture grated on her nerves.

Vicky couldn't keep it in any longer. "Dearest Mary, you know you might come with me, with us, to Berlin," she said.

Mary appeared startled, but at least she didn't immediately exclaim "Oh, no!"

Heartened, Vicky continued: "You might enjoy it—to live abroad. It might only be a short while and think how interesting . . ." She trailed off, surprised that her voice trembled a bit.

Now Mary gave a rueful smile. "I worry I wouldn't fit in in Prussia."

"You? What about me?" blurted Vicky.

Mary didn't answer at first, instead stepping over to move one pile of books to the far side of the table. Then she turned and looked directly at Vicky. "I know how single-minded you can be, Princess. You'll do beautifully."

Something in Mary's face made Vicky think she felt sorry for her. She mustn't. "I intend to," Vicky said quickly. But then she added: "It's just that—of course a new court will be—well, I believe I could use your help, since from things the prince has said, I understand people in the Berlin court don't really get on."

"Princess, you know all about this. Think of all the quarreling here, over vital matters like costume," said Mary. And then they both laughed. Lady Churchill, Mama's lady of the bedchamber, had last week confronted some of the younger ladies, accusing them of disrespecting the queen by adopting the racy new continental style of wearing crinolines during the day, rather than layering petticoats under their skirts. Mama finally had to mandate that both looks were acceptable, in defiance of the now very put-out Lady Churchill.

"In Berlin, I think it's politics and various personal rivalries that cause trouble," Vicky said. "The prince has two uncles, Karl and Albrecht, who apparently don't speak to each for months at a time, and then suddenly burst out in loud argument over who is to go through a door first. Imagine!"

Mary shook her head. "A strange new world. But in your own home you will set the tone."

"When eventually we have a home," Vicky said. A palace in Berlin near the Berliner Schloss was being renovated for them but Fritz had reported many months of work remained, which would leave them where? With his parents?

She sighed. What was the scripture passage Papa liked to cite? "Sufficient unto the day is the evil thereof," which meant don't borrow trouble from the future. But it couldn't be denied, she would miss Mary terribly.

ON JANUARY 19 royal guests began arriving, the official events commenced, and from that day onward, Vicky had no more say in how her hours were spent, no more lessons with Tilla, no more play time with Beatrice nor chats with Mary. She marched through receptions, banquets, tea parties, drawing rooms, and public outings. She had to speak to everyone, and dozens and dozens of people passed before her eyes in a haze as she smiled and nodded and attempted to utter a few cogent words of greeting with Mama on one side, Grandmamma, often, on the other. Sometimes she felt she couldn't bear it another moment, but then she would sternly command herself to remain steady and attentive, as was her duty.

Papa's brother, Duke Ernest of Saxe-Coburg, was among the first to appear, accompanied by his beautiful wife, Alexandrine. Vicky had last seen her uncle three years previously, and now he marveled at her looks. "Your determined little face has grown quite lovely, my dear," said Uncle Ernest, chucking her under the chin before seizing her hands and stepping back to take a fuller look. "And an admirably curvaceous figure. The lucky Prussian must be eager to sample the delights on offer," he said with a raucous laugh. Vicky cringed. Wasn't that a very unsuitable remark? Her father's scowl confirmed it.

Since Queen Elisabeth had announced she would not attend, the Hohenzollern contingent had shrunk. But it was led, naturally, by Fritz's parents, whom she had last seen at the exhibition, nearly seven years previously. Prince Wilhelm, sixty-one, stooped a bit now, and Princess Augusta, forty-six, had small wrinkles fanning out from the corners of her tightly held mouth, and a wattle under her chin. Fritz's mother still carried herself imperiously, throwing her shoulders back and sailing into every room as if expecting all eyes to turn immediately to her. She barely addressed Vicky, although she bragged to everyone that the match had been her idea from the start. Fritz's father looked at her gravely from under bushy gray eyebrows, but Vicky could not relax with him. On his first evening in London he had remarked to her abruptly: "You will never have reason to doubt my son's devotion." She blushed and felt suddenly tongue-tied—a good thing Uncle Prussia didn't appear to expect an answer and immediately stumped off to speak with Papa.

So strange to see Louise again. Fritz had reported that his sister had grown more confident since her marriage, which was evident from the moment Louise first stepped into the Queen's Gallery on the arm of her husband, Friedrich, now Grand Duke of Baden—a stocky blond gentleman called, of course, Fritz. No longer an awkward, shy girl, the tall and vigorous Louise glided over to greet Vicky, eyes shining. She had a long face like her mother's, but none of the haughtiness, appearing instead forthright and kind. Her hair had darkened and thickened and it was arranged beautifully, rolled away from each temple. Something about the cast of Louise's well-spaced features reminded Vicky of Fritz—brother and sister didn't look much alike, but they shared an appealing sincerity entirely absent from their parents' faces.

After kissing Vicky on both cheeks, Louise confided in a low voice: "Fritz told me it wasn't politics or ambition that made him choose you. It was his heart. And I am so glad of this. He deserves all happiness."

Vicky squeezed her hand. "I hope we will see you often in Berlin," she told Louise. It was a shame that Fritz's sister and her husband spent most of their time in a palace in Karlsruhe, in the south of Germany.

Fritz's uncle Prince Karl, who had endeavored to push his oldest brother off the throne during the revolution, came as well. Karl looked perpetually scornful, his mouth curled into a pout, and Vicky overheard him complaining to Papa that London was so shabby and chaotic. His tall, dark wife, Princess Marie, was Princess Augusta's older sister, but they were not affectionate with each other, not like Vicky with Alice; one princess often contradicted or spoke over the other. Fritz's second uncle, Prince Albrecht, had not been invited, because just last summer he'd divorced his wife to wed the prettiest of her ladies. Fritz's father had a younger sister, Charlotte, married to Czar Nicholas of Russia. She too had not been asked, such was the lingering animosity between Russia and Britain. Prince Wilhelm's two other sisters stayed away out of solidarity with her.

Amid the crowds of English royals and other Germans— Mama's older half brother and half sister had come with their large families—the Hohenzollerns stood out for their height and their air of self-importance. Would she ever feel as if she were one of them? Hard to imagine.

VICKY GAVE A little shriek when, on the morning of the twenty-first, she suddenly spotted Laddle, surfacing amid the sea of faces, smiling fondly at her. Laddle's brown hair had turned quite gray now, and she lived in retirement with her daughter in Wiltshire, but she was still that steady personage Vicky remembered so well, square shouldered, with her mild but observant expression. Vicky was grateful when Mama agreed she might have a few minutes to spend alone with her. "Come and see the wedding presents, Laddle, there are a tremendous number," Vicky said, towing the dear lady by the hand.

As they walked down the gallery to the Chinese drawing room, Vicky rushed to describe how wonderful Fritz was, so loving and handsome, and of course he had formidable duties ahead of him, but she would be at his side to help. And Papa had worked tirelessly to prepare her for being a Prussian princess, one day queen.

"I pray that I am worthy to be his child, and Mama's," Vicky said.

"If you do your best, you will be more than worthy," Laddle answered.

"Prussia might be a bit regressive now, but it has huge possibilities. And the prince's mission and mine will be to foster reform." Maybe living in the depths of the country Laddle was out of touch with the question of the modern governance in Germany?

"Very admirable," Laddle said.

"I have two Prussian ladies to help me and I intend to get right to work. I aim to continue my studies, but I also hope to meet notable thinkers and politicians and artists in Berlin and entertain often when the prince and I have an establishment of our own. I desire to contribute to life in my new country immediately."

Her teacher laughed softly.

"You think this overly ambitious?" Vicky asked, indignant. "I speak excellent German, I have been trained for a public life, I have Papa's instruction."

"Princess, I never doubt your good intentions and strong will."

"Do you believe I'm not clever enough?" She surprised herself by confessing the fear aloud. Along with loneliness, she worried most about that.

The lady gave her a kind look. "It's not a question of clever-ness, or determination, my dear. Rather discernment and tact. And patience."

Vicky, still affronted, said: "I suppose you think like Papa that I can be too impulsive and too hasty. Is that it?"

For a long moment Laddle didn't reply. They continued to walk along, the clamor of the reception room slowly fading behind them.

"Princessy, no one is perfect," Laddle said finally. "Although I believe both your mother and father expect you to be. It's part of the enormous pride they take in you, their eldest, most cherished daughter."

"And I will make a success of things, Laddle. You shouldn't doubt it."

"Yes, but if you are convinced you know best, and believe you can constantly arrange matters to your liking while also enjoying the approval of others, you will inevitably be disappointed."

"No, of course, I wouldn't do that," Vicky said, not quite sure what Laddle meant.

"And while it's fine to be your father's ambassador, as a young woman in a foreign land, it will take time to gain influence and the trust of others."

Now Vicky understood: Laddle had forgotten she was no lon-ger a child! She laughed. "Don't pour cold water, Laddle! Yes, it will take time, but it will turn out well, you'll see. And Fritz is completely marvelous. Also, he needs me."

"I imagine," said Laddle. "And how are his parents?"

"You met them, didn't you, during the exhibition?"

"Briefly. Rather formal, I recall. Do they treat you affection-ately?"

"In truth we are not well acquainted. And they are formal. I must do more to win them over."

"Let them make the effort, too, my dear. You are, after all, giving up here"—Laddle pointed at the red-carpeted floor—"to go there."

How to explain Fritz's parents' peculiar Prussian pride to Laddle? It didn't seem possible, and in any case they had reached the drawing room. Her teacher was bound to be astonished by the gifts.

"You'll never believe all the jewels, Laddle," Vicky said. She took her first to see the diamond diadem sent by the king and queen of Prussia and then a beautiful necklace of diamonds and turquoise Uncle Leopold, the king of Belgium, had given her. There was a trio of three flower brooches from the emperor of Austria—the same setting worked in each of rubies, emeralds, and sapphires. And the king of Hanover had sent several heavy gold bracelets engraved with the seals of the houses of Hanover and Saxe-Coburg.

Laddle and she laughed over a pair of enormous crystal candelabra sent by Empress Eugénie and Emperor Napoléon. "I believe they stand nearly as tall as the emperor is himself," said Vicky.

After a quarter of an hour spent surveying the three laden tables, Laddle said: "I'm sure you're wanted now, Princess. Run on ahead, my dear, and God bless you."

Vicky hugged her and said: "I will see you later on, Laddle, and I will introduce you to the prince!"

FRITZ ARRIVED ON the twenty-third, two days after his parents. Vicky was standing in the yellow drawing room, surrounded by people, and suddenly he was there, at her elbow. A shock, really, to see him—this tall, impressive man about to become her husband—but a thrill too.

She broke away for a private word of welcome. Looking up, she noticed a strange expression on his face: tense and uncertain, sullen even. He said bitterly, "I see I am not needed here to get the merriment started."

For a moment she was so impatient with his reverting to his

previous jealous self that she almost stamped her foot. Then she imagined he felt as she did that the attention on them at the center of the wedding whirl was like physical pressure bearing down on their skulls, making any fears and irritations so much worse. Vicky took a deep breath and said: "Dear heart, only now am I truly happy, because now you are here." She squeezed his hand and gazed up at him with all the devotion she could muster.

His face relaxed, and he said in a rueful voice: "I've missed you."

"Think, we'll not be separated again," Vicky replied.

Fritz shook his head, as if not sure he believed it. They looked at each other for a long minute, absorbing. And then he grinned and bent down to kiss her swiftly on the lips.

At the lavish state ball that night, where, as Lord Clarendon said, there were "more princes than at the Congress of Vienna," she danced only with Fritz—except the final set, which Papa requested for himself, and for which his future son-in-law graciously relinquished her. She overheard Fritz telling Grandmamma: "I know how much she is giving up to be with me, and I promise to make her happy."

MAMA HAD FINALLY settled on a lilac silk gown with a short ermine train for the wedding, and on the morning of the ceremony she requested that Vicky join her in her suite so they could dress together. Vicky had no chance to feel nervous because Mama was herself very agitated, chiding anxiously that Vicky must take small, even steps in the chapel and not touch her hair unnecessarily or fiddle with her flowers. And no giggling. Mary and Lady Churchill came in to make a last check of their ensembles before they all went together to meet Papa and the eight bridesmaids in the throne room. Papa's chest was draped with chains of office and the cross of St. George affixed to a golden sash. His face looked tense, his brow clenched, but when she glided into his sight, his smile was doting. "You look lovely, *Liebchen,* a vision of purity and grace."

He directed them to the corner where Mr. Thomas Richard Williams, London's leading photographer, awaited. He bowed deeply at their approach. "A magnificent bride you are, Your Highness. Stand just here," he said, and arranged the three of them, Papa in the center, Vicky and Mama on either side of him, half-facing each other.

"Now, it's vital that you remain absolutely still for a half a minute while I expose the plate," Mr. Williams said. Vicky rested her folded white-gloved hands on the top tier of her dress and concentrated on breathing in and out of her nose, but she sensed Mama, across from her, trembling. She doubted the picture would turn out well.

Afterward Bertie and Affie came running up to them, both in Highland dress. Bertie looked particularly merry. "You won't believe the number of people outside," he announced. "At first light it was ten deep at the gates, but now you can see crowds halfway down the Mall."

As Vicky smiled at him, she thought how strange it was that from now on she'd live apart from Bertie. He was like the air she breathed, the water she swam in, her second self. She supposed Fritz would be that for her now. Still, he could never be as effortlessly familiar to her as her brother. She suddenly remembered Bertie, years ago, wading into a small stream at Osborne intent on building a dam. Pushing his floppy hair out of his eyes, calling back to her: "Take off your shoes, Puss, and your stockings too, don't just stand there."

No opportunity for musing further now. The room had filled with their guests—only Fritz and his parents were absent, having moved to the Prussian legation on Carlton House Terrace the night before. Soon it came time to go downstairs with her attendants, Mama and Papa ahead of her, accompanied by the boys and by Alice, Lenchen, and Louise, wearing matching pink satin dresses. In the courtyard eighteen carriages had lined up, ready to convey the large royal party. She and Mama had the last one.

Before climbing in, Vicky tipped her face up to the brilliant blue sky. Her wedding day was cold but so fine, she sensed the face of heaven beaming down approval.

It was only a mile's ride, yet far enough to share in the crowd's excitement at the spectacle. A troop of three hundred soldiers escorted them to St. James's, along with three dozen outriders. Drumrolls and trumpet blares sounded outside the chapel as Vicky stood waiting for a moment for Lord Palmerston to enter first with the sword of state, escorting Grandmamma, followed by Mama with all the children around her.

Papa offered his arm. Her bridesmaids lined up behind and picked up her long train. Out of the bright sunshine into the dark vestibule they went, and Vicky's eyes took a moment to adjust to the dim light, but then she saw the congregation rise. As the two of them started down the aisle, Papa's arm shaking under her hand, she spotted Fritz at the altar standing tall, wearing the dark blue tunic of the Prussian Guards, holding his gleaming silver helmet close to his side. A small flip of her heart, and then a surge of joy. She began walking forward eagerly, impatient with the slow pace the music demanded.

At the altar Fritz held out his hand and led her to kneel beside him. He placed his helmet down on the kneeler on his right. The Archbishop of Canterbury began. "We have come together in the present, the presence of the God—of God . . . ," he stuttered awkwardly.

"He's more nervous than we are," Fritz whispered. She smiled into his face and noticed that today he looked completely calm, all strain erased. She was to recall until her final hour how, as they spoke their vows, it was as though they were enclosed together in a bubble—immune to the tears and scowls and haughty looks of family around them and floating apart from the vast public enthrallment with their coupling. As they linked fates, joining their lives forever, Vicky was confident that Fritz felt exactly as she did—how right this was, not only for the world, but for the two of them, separate souls who had found safe haven in one another.

The chords of Mendelssohn's wedding march crashed into her ears as they led the procession out of the chapel, and Vicky was plunged once again into the hubbub of the occasion, being hugged and kissed by all the ladies, watching Fritz shake hands heartily with Papa, catching a glimpse of Prince Karl whispering something snide into Princess Marie's ear.

But at least for a moment she had experienced—memorably, piercingly—what it all signified.

8

Windsor, January 1858

$\mathscr{T}$hey returned to Buckingham Palace for a lavish wedding breakfast, numerous toasts, and finally the cutting of the six-foot-high wedding cake. Vicky spied Laddle in a corner of the Queen's Gallery after she and Fritz and their parents, having waved to the cheering crowds on the Mall, stepped back inside. She turned to Fritz to say he must meet her beloved first teacher, but someone called them away just then, and by the time she had her new husband's attention again, Laddle had disappeared.

At three that afternoon, when Vicky and Fritz climbed into an open carriage to drive away, Mama and Papa and Uncle and Aunt Prussia were the last to wish them well. Papa was silent. Mama looked nervous and gripped Vicky's hand. "It's a solemn day when a woman unites herself to a man," she told her. "God bless you, dearest, and God keep you. You have an excellent husband. Otherwise I couldn't bear it for you."

How like Mama to offer no reassurance when she could have used some, but Vicky willed herself to focus on the happy crowds that cheered them as they rode to the station. More people lined the rail route out of London, and Fritz and Vicky stood in the window of the slow-moving royal train, waving.

At Ealing junction her eye picked out of the throng an ordinary woman, quite young, wearing a worn gray cloak and a sagging bonnet, a little boy clinging to her skirts as the noisy train chugged past. What actually set her apart from that woman? She rode in a royal train and the other woman stood on an icy verge, and would soon head home to some small, shabby accommodation while Vicky spent the night in a castle. But were they not human both—dwelling in female forms, vulnerable to illness and disease, prey to countless other predations of fate? Today Vicky might have been the most fortunate young woman in the kingdom, but pain stalked everyone and nothing was certain.

The idea gripped her intensely before she scolded herself for morbid and silly thoughts, on this day of days.

AT WINDSOR STATION another open carriage waited for them. Schoolboys from Eton College had unhitched the four white ponies meant to drive it, and a half dozen had yoked themselves into place instead. These boys pulled them up the long hill to the castle, while scores of others ran alongside, cheering and yelling and throwing top hats in the air.

At the entrance, after they stepped down out of the carriage, Fritz grasped her around the waist and swiftly bore her aloft. He faced her to the right and then to the left, allowing all the boys to catch a last glimpse of his bride, their Princess Royal. Fritz's fingers dug into her flesh through her white velvet going-away dress and blue velvet cloak, and she was rather shocked. Looking into his face, after he placed her down, she saw how he was reveling in the whole rowdy, primitive scene—his cheeks red from the cold and his eyes gleaming with excitement. He might have been ten years older than most of these Eton boys, but he was exultant to share in their laddish high spirits.

Once inside the castle he said: "Let's race." And they ran up the two flights of stairs, Fritz first well ahead before deliberately slowing at the top to grab her hand. They stepped on the top landing together at the same moment and turned into the sitting room that Mama had set aside for them. They collapsed, panting, on the two sofas. Through an open door in the adjoining, redecorated room, Vicky could see the large bed with wooden headboard painted with the gold initials V and F intertwined. She felt suddenly trembly.

Servants brought in supper, and Fritz kept up a steady patter of jokes and comments. But now nervousness crept over Vicky and she had no appetite. How would she handle what came next? And what if Fritz was dissatisfied with her when he saw her without clothes? All her anxieties about her small, round figure came swarming into her mind and she sat frozen on the sofa, her mouth dry, her insides quavering. After two footmen cleared the plates away, she and Fritz were left completely alone. She could not look at him and she stared anxiously into the middle distance, twisting her new wedding ring around her finger. She heard him get up from the sofa opposite and sit down beside her. She forced herself to look up. He gazed down at her tenderly.

"You don't trust me?" he asked.

"I do."

"Then give me your hands." He held out his own, palms up.

When she put her hands on top of his, he squeezed them. "At this sacred moment, we will go slowly."

He led her by the hand into the bedroom and started to undo her hair. After a minute of his awkward fumbling, she had to help him dig out the smaller pins at the nape of her neck and uncoil the thick braid. When all her hair was loosened, falling to her waist, he buried his fingers in it, lifting it up and down to feel the weight. She managed to smile up at him and notice how his beard had grown in since last he'd shaved—it must have been early in the morning. She reached up and stroked his rough, bristly cheek.

"See," he said, "it's lovely to be alone together, *nicht wahr*?" Then he started unbuttoning the back of her dress, and she shivered a bit when he pulled it off her shoulders and down below her waist, along with her petticoats. After that he came around front and helped her step out of the billowing mass of fabric heaped on the floor.

She stood only in a chemise, with drawers underneath, and she let him lead her to sit on the edge of the bed. He bent down and removed her shoes and stockings for her, as if she were a child. Then he stood up straight, took a step back, and grinned. "You look so lovely like this, *Liebling*. I enjoy this sight more than you in your fancy wedding gown."

She was suddenly very nervous again, and began to shiver.

"No, no, you mustn't be frightened," he said quickly. "I think less light now as we get accustomed to each other."

After turning down the two gas lamps, he walked back toward the bed, sat down beside her, and hugged her against him, kissing the top of her head. Then he released her to pull off his boots and remove his jacket and shirt, throwing them onto the small horsehair chair next to the bed. She was surprised to see his chest was covered with dark golden hair. He stood up, wearing only his trousers.

"Here, *Liebe*," he said. He offered her his hand, so she could stand up too, and then he reached around and pulled back the bedclothes. "Let's lie down," he said, and he guided her so she lay in the middle of the bed.

He quickly unbuttoned his trousers and started to remove them, and she had to look away. She even closed her eyes. She sensed him stretching out beside her on the bed. She made herself turn and edge toward him although she was stiff with fear and self-consciousness. Finally, she opened her eyes, and he was lying on his side, smiling at her. His chest was like a wall of flesh, and she was too scared to examine him farther down. At least he did not seem disappointed—quite the opposite.

"Let me see how beautiful you are," he said, coaxing the chemise up over her head. "Ah," he said, "look at your lovely breasts, such a wonderful full shape, and so pink at the tips."

She wanted to cover her bust with her arm but instead allowed him to push her tenderly onto her back as he started caressing her and moving downward, kissing her body. So peculiar to see the top of his head with all its bright wavy hair, against the firm, white skin of her left breast.

Now he pulled himself up to kiss her deeply, his tongue, astonishingly, moving into her mouth, his hands cradling either side of her face. This wasn't so unpleasant, she thought to herself. But it was all going quite fast. She had no time to respond, nor any instinct for how she should act. She felt him pull down her drawers and tried to help him by kicking them away. It floated into her mind that he maybe had done this before, with someone else. She wondered, idly, who that woman might be, but she was strangely unperturbed. His eagerness for her, at this moment, was so clear.

"*Liebe*, I want to . . . ," he whispered, and somehow, awkwardly, he moved his left leg between hers, nudging them apart and pinning her body under his where he wanted it. Then he pushed into her, groaning softly. A lovely animal sound, she thought, and hardly minded the jab of pain. He propped himself up on his elbows, starting to move inside her, intent on his task, going steadily faster, his breath becoming sharper and shallower. He nuzzled her neck and then he groaned again, and she heard something like a sob catch at the back of his throat and he fell against her, shuddering for a moment, and then still.

For several minutes they remained like that. He on top, spent. She, eyes wide open, looking at the ceiling. So strange, but also, as Tilla had suggested, quite natural.

Then Vicky smiled to herself. She'd jumped over the last bridal hurdle and shown everyone how well she could do.

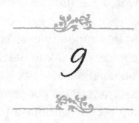

9

*V*icky insisted that she and Fritz go together to the Windsor station to meet Mama and Papa and the family when, two days later, everyone came to join the honeymoon couple for the weekend. Vicky wished her parents to see immediately that she was at ease with Fritz, now that they were truly man and wife. Mama's anxious face emerged from the railcar, but when Vicky waved cheerily, her mother was at once smiling, relieved. Back at the castle Fritz and she recounted how they'd ice-skated on the frozen lake, taken a sleigh ride along the banks of the Thames, and traipsed through the grounds of nearby Frogmore House in search of the snowy owl rumored to roost there. A glimpse of the bird in flight was said to be good luck, and Fritz thought he had spotted it, but Vicky said she couldn't be sure. "Whatever we saw, we are already living a very lucky life together," she heard Fritz tell Papa as the two men stood together in front of the fire in the Green Drawing Room.

Vicky noticed Papa smile then, but in general he seemed cast down. The next day, Friday, when Fritz went out with Bertie and Affie to skate in the afternoon, Papa requested Vicky come to his study to discuss a letter from Baron Stockmar.

The baron had skipped the wedding to go on ahead to Berlin and install his son as Vicky's private secretary. The young Baron Ernest von Stockmar would handle her correspondence, and the income granted her by Parliament, plus advise her on protocol. Fritz had at first rejected this appointment. As a Coburger, and the liberal Prince Albert's choice, Ernest von Stockmar would immediately be considered a political agent, Fritz said, raising the suspicions of the entire Berlin court. Papa countered that he would not allow Vicky to expatriate herself without a trusted man to advise her, and administer her dowry separate from any Hohenzollern monies. It had been a point of contention between the two men for several months the year previous, until at last Fritz had relented.

The elder Stockmar now reported that he had gone with his son to visit the Berliner Schloss, where Princess Augusta had determined it would be best for Fritz and Vicky to live until their new palace was ready.

"The apartments are apparently a bit musty," Papa said, standing by his desk, examining the letter in his hand. "Which is hardly surprising since the old king, Fritz's grandfather, was the last person to live there before he died twenty years ago. The king and queen apparently prefer Potsdam, and Wilhelm and Augusta have their own establishment farther along Unter den Linden. The *Schloss*'s receiving rooms are used for ceremonies, balls, receptions, and the like, and you and Fritz will be accommodated on the third floor."

"I'm sure Aunt Prussia wants us to be comfortable," Vicky said, vastly relieved that she would not be forced to share premises with Fritz's parents.

Her father glanced over at her, pained somehow. "*Hoffentlich,*" he said, and threw the letter down on his desk before walking, restless, over to the window, where he stood staring out.

"Vicky, I want to caution you about discretion," he said finally, still looking out. "Everyone in the court will be curious about you, especially at first. Speak candidly only to Fritz and his parents."

She felt her throat tighten. "Yes."

"But there's something else. Most concerning." He hesitated again, reluctant to go on.

When he turned his head, he looked directly into her eyes. "You are going to a place where you are very much needed as an example of moral living."

She nodded, uncertain what he meant.

"You know of Prince Albrecht's disgrace. But I hear other reports of shameful behavior among Fritz's family. Even Prince Wilhelm conducts himself in an indecent way, straying from his wife."

Vicky stared at Papa, startled, and in a strange way, embarrassed. She blushed. Now she appreciated, as she hadn't previously, how going to bed with a person could be quite thrilling, but she hadn't realized that an old gentleman like Uncle Prussia might do it. With other women. She'd spotted Fritz's father conversing gaily at the wedding breakfast with one of Princess Augusta's ladies—a Countess Louise Oriolla, who wore a bright orange gown, very daring. She'd never before witnessed Uncle Prussia in high spirits and asked Fritz: "Your father seems to like the countess very much. Are they cousins or just old acquaintances?"

"Neither," said Fritz tersely. "She's not a nice woman. I can't understand why my mother chose to bring her."

Now Papa sighed and walked back over to his desk and sat down. He picked up a pen and twiddled with it. "Above all, I expect you to use your time constructively," he said sternly. "Don't be idle and fritter away the days."

This conversation was becoming distressing, and she despaired at his tone.

"Papa, you're speaking like Berlin is impossible, and I will be indiscreet and compromised and waste my time, doing I don't know what, behaving badly and getting into difficulties. Why would you believe that?"

Tears flooded her eyes. Hadn't she managed the wedding so well? Made Fritz a very happy husband?

"No, Vicky," he said. "I know you are good and reasonable.

But it's much to cope with." He looked around and pulled over another chair for her next to his own. She sat down and blew her nose.

"I wouldn't allow you to go if I didn't think that Fritz would take care of you," Papa said finally.

Could she not also take care of herself? she thought irritably. But seeking to soothe her father, she answered: "Yes, and he will."

"Remember who you are and where you come from."

"Of course."

"I have thought about it so much, *liebe* Vicky. I am proud of what I have accomplished in England. But I desire progress in my own country. In Germany. And it will be of value to all Europe, should it happen . . ."

Vicky had heard him say some version of this so many times she simply nodded.

"And I can't do much myself, obviously, from London," he continued.

"Fritz and I can accomplish a great deal."

Ignoring that, he said: "The Prussians are a strange, belligerent lot. I sensed it more than ever at the wedding."

"But Fritz is wonderful, and together—"

"Fritz needs to stop playing at soldiers," Papa said sharply.

"I will encourage him. And he will remember everything you've taught."

"*Wir werden sehen.*" We will see.

He spoke so flatly, without conviction, that Vicky shook her head. She wanted to ask him why exactly he had lost confidence in Fritz and in her, too, but she couldn't bear to hear a list of her shortcomings.

Just then Mama came in, followed by Alice.

"Why are you two skulking in here?" Mama asked. "Have you forgotten we expect the Cambridges and the Sutherlands for tea? My mother has already arrived. This is no time to be closeting yourselves away."

Papa got up obediently and motioned for Vicky to follow. As

they walked out of the study, Vicky whispered to him: "Papa, you mustn't worry, I will manage."

ON THE MORNING of their departure for Prussia four days later, Vicky still lay in bed when Flora came in to gather the final bits and pieces to pack. It seemed a large stone had become lodged in her throat, and the task of speaking or getting up seemed too onerous. Fritz had dressed and gone downstairs long since.

If only she and Fritz could be instantly transported to Berlin, and there sit at desks side by side just like Mama and Papa's, ride out in the afternoons, enjoy quiet evenings of books and study together. Maybe then she wouldn't mind this cruel wrench from home so much. But instead they'd be traveling, and she'd be on display, for days and days. Lying there, she enumerated it: first the ride from Buckingham Palace to the London Bridge station, where they'd catch the train for Gravesend; next, boarding the royal yacht *Victoria and Albert* for the overnight crossing to Antwerp; and, after that, a week of public appearances across Belgium, Hanover, and Prussia.

A knock on the door, and Alice poked her head in.

"Darling, sweetest sister," Vicky called out.

Alice rushed to hug her and immediately began to sob. "I cannot bear it."

"Nor I," said Vicky as she sat up.

"I have something for you." Alice pulled from her pocket a little red leather diary. "Write down everything you do and when we're together again you'll tell me it all."

"Thank you," said Vicky, hugging Alice again. "Sit in here while I get dressed." She couldn't tarry any longer or encourage her sister in more tears. She had to get on.

She donned three wool petticoats to keep out the chill, and over that a navy-blue wool traveling dress. Dawes, her dresser, came in to put up her hair. Flora brought toast and tea. Alice had stopped crying, but when Mama walked in, sobbing, her sister was set off again.

"We must pull ourselves together," said Mama between sobs. "Your dear papa tells me that the servants are gathering in the Audience Room to see you off, and Papa and Fritz want to depart immediately afterward."

"Papa is resolved to come to Gravesend?"

"Yes, and Bertie and Affie, too."

Vicky glanced out the window. Snow had begun to fall. It was a long, cold way for her father and brothers, but at least she'd have their company a few hours more. With a final backward glance at the pretty blue bedroom—if only it could have been hers and Fritz's for a month or two more—she headed down the passageway holding Alice's hand, Mama behind, taking deep breaths to keep from crying.

Grandmamma stood in the Audience Room with all the little children around her, Mrs. Thurston holding Beatrice. Vicky reached out to take the baby for a final cuddle, but Beatrice, alarmed by the hubbub, clung to her nurse, screaming and kicking. Vicky bent down to hug her other brothers and sisters, each in turn.

And the servants! Heartbreaking to see them lined up so carefully, in five long rows, majordomos to kitchen maids, and everyone in between, regarding Vicky with such devotion. She tried to thank them properly, but she stuttered feebly. She noticed Henry Ponsonby standing to the side, and when she looked mournfully at him, he gave her the kindest smile, and a small nod as if to say: You will do splendidly. She wished to tell him she'd miss him, and his riddles, and his friendship, but it was too late. Fritz had come up beside her. "*Komm, mein Schatz*," he said as he took her elbow to steer her across the room and down the stairs, lined on each side with other members of the household. "Goodbye, goodbye," she managed to murmur.

Out in the courtyard where the carriages were waiting, it was so cold. Snow pelted down. Mama gave her a last kiss. Fritz wrapped a heavy shawl around her and carefully scooped her up and settled her into the carriage—an open landau, despite the weather. London would want to see her, Mama had decreed. Fritz came around on the other side and hoisted himself in. Papa and the boys clambered into the carriage behind. A band, standing at a short distance, struck up a march and they moved off. She couldn't bear to look back. Fritz laid his gloved hand over hers, clasped beneath the shawl.

Along the Mall and past Charing Cross, down Fleet Street and Cheapside and across London Bridge, people waved and cheered. Several large arches had been erected over the streets. On one was written, "Farewell, Fair Rose of England." Another said, "We give her to your care." Outside a public house on the Strand, workmen stood in the street clapping and stomping. One tall, redheaded lad ran alongside the carriage, pointed at Fritz, and yelled: "Be good to her, or we'll have her back." Fritz smiled tightly—she could tell he was displeased by the implication.

Vicky looked out at the dear gray streets, eyes dry, with an odd, hollowed-out ache in her stomach. Why, exactly, had she ever agreed to go? Who would she be when she was no longer here, in her native land? A Prussian princess, but not really. She'd never belong; she'd never be loved there the way she was here.

At Gravesend another band played at the side of the pier, and two hundred people waited to see them off. A bevy of young girls wearing white dresses and wreaths in their hair scattered flowers in front of Fritz and Vicky as they walked down to the boat. The yellow, pink, and purple blossoms landed on the slushy snow and were soon sodden and trampled upon. On the deck Fritz and she turned to face the crowd, and the lord mayor of London, come to do the farewell honors, shouted: "God save the prince and bride! God keep their lands allied!" Everyone roared approval.

Below, in the large queen's salon, Vicky, sure she was going to faint, sat down immediately without removing either bonnet or cloak. Papa and Fritz and the boys stood murmuring together for a few minutes while the servants carried in the bags they would need for the voyage. Vicky heard Papa say, "Time now," and her brothers, first Bertie and then Affie, came to kiss her. Bertie had recently become very spotty—now tears ran down his cheeks and he looked a dreadful sight. When her father looked sorrowfully down, Vicky rose to embrace him, and laying her face on his shirtfront, she began to cry, too.

"*Liebe* Vicky, I am surprised you suffer so. I thought you were excited to leave with Fritz. You told me not to worry," her father said.

"I could never really imagine how it would be, Papa, to go. Now it is much, much worse than I expected."

"We go along fine, *ja*? We plan and we are calm because we are prepared, but then the event is upon us and . . . we are overcome, *nicht wahr*?"

"Yes."

"I remember how it was, to leave home and all the feelings and experiences of one's youth. You leave behind that 'I' forever, Vicky, even as you make up another 'I' in your new home." He nodded slightly, as if to himself. "But the two are never completely separated. They cannot be. One 'I' is built on top of the other."

Papa, speaking in his most abstract way; she supposed he couldn't help it, but it made her weep harder.

"You are strong, Puss. You will be strong now," he said next.

Vicky tried to collect herself. She fished out a handkerchief tucked in her sleeve and wiped her eyes. "You will miss me, won't you, Papa?"

"So much. Now, take heart, the future beckons."

He leaned down to kiss her cheek. "*Auf Wiedersehen*," he said, and stepped out of the salon, closing the door behind him.

Vicky fell down onto the bed sobbing. As the yacht sailed down the river and out into the open sea, Fritz sat beside her, rubbing her back from time to time. She told him she couldn't bear to leave the salon and he agreed to go up and entertain their entourage over supper. After he left, she thought she must be sensible. She stood up and undressed without calling for her maid. She folded her clothes neatly and piled them on a chair. She wound up the tortoiseshell traveling clock that Grandmamma had given her and placed it on the bedside table alongside a small framed daguerreotype of Mama and Papa she had taken from Windsor.

Then she got into bed holding the red leather pocket diary that Alice had given her. She found the page for February 2 and wrote, "Today I left England forever." She put the pen and diary next to her parents' picture, turned down the lamp, and curled up tightly under the covers.

Many years later, Vicky found the diary in the back of a bureau drawer. Flicking through it, she saw and read that first entry. She flashed back to the stricken girl in the cabin on the royal yacht sailing into a new life. But now she drew a line through the word "forever" and wrote instead "for Prussia."

10

Berlin, February and March 1858

*V*icky entered Berlin for the first time riding in an antique state coach that Fritz called "the golden monkey cage" for the way it teetered and swayed, suspended between high waggling gilt wheels. As they passed through the Brandenburger Tor and down Unter den Linden, Fritz sat beside her naming the different divisions of cavalry, artillery, Horse Guards, and militia assembled to greet their future queen. Despite the frigid temperature, Vicky pushed open the window of the coach, the better to see and be seen.

Berlin had a raw, open-to-the-sky feeling about it, and their vehicle bumped violently over large, ill-fitting cobblestones. The buildings were mostly low and wide, made of sandy-colored or muddy-gray stone. Deep dirt gutters bordered the road, and large water pumps stood on the corners. Many of the side streets were unpaved—alleys of frozen, rutted mud today. But along this spacious boulevard the namesake lime trees, tall and bare branched, marched two abreast in elegant, motionless parade as they proceeded down the gentle slope toward the river Spree.

Ordinary citizens crowded between, behind, and on either side of the dense ranks of military men. Windows above were full of people and the Prussian flag—a black eagle on a white field with red and gold detailing—draped out over sills. Cheers and whistles reverberated in the air, and from time to time the coach came to a halt as Berliners surged around the police and into the road trying to catch a glimpse of the newlywed couple. The throngs on both sides, with high-raised arms and waving hats, looked to Vicky like tuffets of tall ruffling grass. Face after upturned face—ecstatic, delighted, rapt—passed beneath the coach's window.

While this was the rousing capstone of their journey, she had enjoyed the previous week more than she had expected. Uncle Leopold had hosted a splendid ball for her and Fritz in Brussels the night of their arrival in Belgium. And their progress across Europe had been convivial, with various local noblemen joining them on the train for short stretches—some distant cousins, others old German university friends of the Duke of Kent, Vicky's grandfather, or courtiers from the time of saintly Louise, queen of Prussia, Fritz's grandmother. Graf von Wrangel, the aged and very portly commander of the Prussian army, boarded the cars at Brunswick and gave a long recounting of Napoléon's defeat at Waterloo. He was still in attendance at Wittenberg, where the mayor presented them with a huge apple tart covered in meringue, a specialty of the town. Vicky placed it carefully on the seat opposite her, but later, when Wrangel stood to go, a sudden jolt of the train threw him on top of the tart, and she and Wally and Marie had to frantically wipe meringue off his backside before he was presentable again. At Magdeburg, where they all got down, guards strained to hold back effusive crowds as they entered the famous cathedral for a tour. At its conclusion they were advised to go out a side door, but there, momentarily unprotected, people rushed toward them and pressed in closely—some tearing lace off Vicky's skirt, to carry away as souvenirs. It happened so quickly she hadn't the chance to be frightened, and she told Fritz the lace could be easily mended. But her husband was incensed. General von Moltke had to take him aside and urge calm—just curiosity and national pride had fueled this frenzy of interest around the Princess Friedrich.

The atmosphere seemed equally fevered here in Berlin, but inside the coach, Wally and Marie sat opposite them, shivering. Like Vicky, both young women wore the low-cut ball gowns required of women for Prussian state occasions, and no wraps. Wally had folded her arms in front of her chest and clutched them to her. Marie had pushed herself back into a corner, looking for warmth, it seemed, from the thin walls of the vehicle.

Vicky said, in an attempt to be comforting: "We will arrive soon, I should think." Her teeth chattered.

Fritz nodded. "Soon."

Shuddering and knocked about, Vicky was, nonetheless, euphoric. In London, she had experienced plenty of joyful crowds, but here, honored as Fritz's wife, the promise of a new royal generation, she felt as if thousands of Prussians were lifting her high on a flood of well wishes, a crescendo of devotion. She swore to herself she would prove worthy of all this generous admiration.

And under the roars of welcome, Vicky sensed Berlin humming with energy and ambition—a city on the brink, as she herself was.

THEY HAD SPENT the night before at the Bellevue Palace on the western edge of the city. Fritz and she had sat up until midnight as he wrote out and went over a list of all his relatives to whom she'd be presented the next day—their names, their ages, and, in the case of the men, their military rank.

Fritz's uncle the king was too ill to receive her, but Vicky would finally meet Queen Elisabeth. "Once she knows you, she will love you, *Liebling*," said Fritz confidently. Vicky prayed that this proud, childless queen—born a princess of Bavaria but fiercely loyal to her husband and to Prussia—might at least come to accept her.

Of course, she would see Fritz's parents again, and his uncle and aunt Prince Karl and Princess Marie. Fritz warned that another aunt, Prince Wilhelm's sister the Grand Duchess Alexandrine of Mecklenburg-Schwerin, could be temperamental. And it was not clear if disgraced Prince Albrecht would be permitted to come to court—certainly his new wife would not appear. Fritz had over a dozen cousins on his father's side, and most lived in Berlin. He hoped Vicky would like his favorite, "dear Anna," who was Prince Karl's daughter and had been married recently to the Duke of Hesse-Kassel. Fritz's childhood companion had been Anna's older brother, Fritz Karl, now a general in the hussars. Another cousin, Crown Princess Olga of Württemberg, daughter of the czar of Russia, was known for her vocal anti-English views. "Like the queen, she will come around, *mein Schatz*. Watch and see," said Fritz.

Now Fritz pointed out the queen awaiting them at the top of the *Schloss*'s short staircase, flanked by his parents. Vicky, still elated from the cheers of the crowd, forgot to be nervous and stepped out of the carriage without waiting for Fritz's hand down. Lifting the hem of her heavy silver gown, she ran up the stairs. How splendid Prince Wilhelm looked in his white uniform with gold epaulets, the star of the Order of the Black Eagle, Prussia's highest rank of knights, pinned to his chest. She felt proud that he would be her father here in Prussia. She curtsied, rose slowly, and tilted her face, expecting his kiss, but Prince Wilhelm ignored her and instead called out to Fritz, coming up behind: "You're twenty minutes late, why?"

Startled and embarrassed, Vicky looked around in confusion, but Queen Elisabeth, a slender, intensely dignified-looking person, wearing a blue gown trimmed with white fur, came to her rescue. She exclaimed: "My dear, how pretty you look! And you have come so far in the cold. You must be frozen!"

Vicky smiled. *"Ich habe einem warmen Ort, mein Herz."* She laid her hand over her heart, her one warm spot, and curtsied again so low her knee brushed the ground. The queen extended her hand to help Vicky up and smiled, obviously very pleased. As they stepped back Wally whispered in Vicky's ear: *"Sehr gut gemacht."* If only Papa and Mama were here to see her managing so well.

After Fritz's mother kissed her perfunctorily, she instructed Vicky and her ladies to follow behind the rest of the party. They went into the high entrance hall of the *Schloss,* which smelled faintly of coal smoke, and then turned right to the Weisser Saal, a cavernous ballroom decorated in white and gold, elaborate baroque paintings filling tall panels on the walls, a dozen massive crystal chandeliers hanging from the ceiling. Vicky shivered. The air was only a little warmer inside than out, and across the room she could see the rest of Fritz's family sitting in chairs on a red velvet dais, all in a long row, none looking particularly amiable. Fritz detached himself from his parents and, offering her his arm, escorted her down the line. There were a few smiles, and some queries about the wedding and their trip from London, but for the most part the Prussian royals stared at her as if she were a strange creature in the zoo, come unfortunately to abide among them. Even the tall and striking Anna, who had an elegant oval face, slightly hooded green eyes, and lustrous brown hair, was barely courteous. Later Vicky was irked to spot her husband with Anna in a corner of the room laughing together over some private joke.

As the afternoon turned to evening and she engaged in one stilted, mildly antagonistic conversation after another, Vicky felt tempted to remind her new family that she had a German father and a half-German mother; and that her knowledge of German language, music, and history rivaled anyone's here; and, moreover, that her great-grandfather George the Third had sat atop a worldwide empire while the Hohenzollerns had struggled to hold on to Brandenburg-Prussia. But, straining to remain pleasant and even-tempered, she resisted saying any of this.

Of all those she met, the friendliest was Princess Marianne, Fritz Karl's young wife—a tall blonde, with round cheeks and a ready, dimpled smile. She and her husband hadn't come to the wedding because Marianne had recently given birth to her third child. "A beautiful baby girl, but as it's my third daughter, my husband is not pleased," the princess confessed to Vicky in a low voice.

"How lovely to already have a sizable family," Vicky replied. "I am the eldest of nine, you know."

"Everyone knows," says Marianne, laughing, "and people wonder if you will do the same as your mother."

"Time will tell!" said Vicky. "I hope to meet your daughters soon. I can explain I have four sisters, and I count myself very fortunate."

WHEN DINNER WAS over at nine, Fritz noticed Vicky's exhaustion and to her great relief whispered that she might go upstairs while he finished speaking with everyone. Wally and Marie had already explored the apartment that was to be hers and Fritz's, so they led her up the broad staircase to the third floor. Herr Weber, the lord steward of the household, called in German the *Hofmarschall*, came too, carrying a candelabra to light the way.

"This will be your room, Highness," Weber said as they entered a dark, damp-smelling chamber. Vicky couldn't discern much in the light of the candelabra, the only illumination, but there appeared to be a large bed, hung with dingy gray curtains and covered with a heavy blanket that resembled an old tapestry rug. Softer and cheerier bedclothes would be required immediately, she thought, before fully taking in the man's words.

"Isn't this the room for both of us—the prince as well?" she asked. In her parents' home, it was assumed that newlyweds shared a bedroom.

The *Hofmarschall* looked taken aback. Confused, Vicky turned to Wally, who said evenly, "Royal etiquette calls for separate bedrooms for married couples. In this enfilade the prince's bedroom is on the other side of the king's."

"The king sleeps here at the *Schloss*?" Vicky was further confused.

"The old king, Fritz's grandfather, died here, and the family likes to keep his room exactly as it was on his last day."

They filed into the neighboring room, even gloomier than the first, with a high, sooty ceiling, dark wood walls, a huge black oak bed, and tall-backed medieval-style carved wooden chairs, also black. Vicky almost laughed—this was all too dreary to be imagined. But she sensed no derisive response would be welcome—the *Hofmarschall* in particular was already leery of her. And good gracious, how cold it was up here. At least Weber acknowledged this, murmuring just then: "We must get the stoves started."

He hadn't thought of heat before now? Vicky felt aggravated but allowed him to carry on, leading the way out of the king's room into Fritz's room, a space decorated, maybe forty years previously, in a scheme of morose purple and dull gold. Beyond that was a sitting room, and after that a dank library, with several shelves filled with tall black and brown leather-bound books that looked to have never been opened.

"And where is the bathroom, and the water closet?" she asked.

Weber looked at her blankly. "There is neither, Princess. There is no need. The servants can bring you all the water you desire."

Vicky desired nothing more than a nice, hot bath, and she thought longingly of the large plumbed-in bathroom at Osborne, with its deep, mahogany-framed tub. But her two ladies, plus Weber and a gaggle of maids, were all peering at her, wary of her displeasure. Not the time to make a fuss, she thought, and retired without bathing.

Sometime after midnight she awoke in the musty bed with the gray curtains, and rolled over and reached out her arm in the dark. Such a relief to touch Fritz's warm flank and to hear his steady breathing. He hadn't left her alone for this first night in her strange new home, whatever etiquette dictated.

THE LACK OF modern facilities turned out to be the least of it. To the despair of her dresser, Dawes, the apartment had neither cupboards nor wardrobes. All of Vicky's beautiful dresses remained in their packing cases, from which they emerged crumpled and creased. As she was required to change into full evening dress on most nights, preparing became a tortuous procedure. Dawes had no place close by to iron clothes, and all water to wash and arrange her hair had to be carried up a vast distance from the other side of the *Schloss.*

With only a few candles and old lamps at hand, she strained to read and write after dark. To bathe she sat in two inches of tepid water in a tin tub—she never felt really clean. The stoves smoked, emitting scant warmth, and cold wind blew down the chimneys and into the rooms via the vast unused fireplaces.

She hated most how, to get from her room to the rest of the apartment, she had to cross the spooky, dusty death chamber. Unfortunately, the door separating her room and that one didn't close properly, so several times during the first week, while Vicky sat reading on her sofa, a draft blew open the door behind her, and she nearly jumped out of her skin.

Fritz finally inquired about having a bathroom and some cupboards built, but word came back from the queen that nothing could be touched in the Berliner Schloss. They'd be moving into the palace currently being renovated for them farther up Unter den Linden near the opera house by the end of the year, and that residence would have a bathroom and several water closets. So Fritz thought they should make do for the moment.

Vicky didn't like to complain to her parents, so far away and eager to hear that she was off to a brilliant start, but she did concede the *Schloss* was awfully cold and dark. Mama wrote back that hot rooms were dreadful, so Vicky should count herself lucky to be spared that torment. Papa urged her to get outdoors as much as possible and breathe in the invigorating, fresh air. Berlin was far chillier than England in February, and Vicky soon caught a cold with a hacking cough. Confined to bed for a week, she struggled to stay cheerful.

Hofmarschall Weber took offense at her simple requests—first to clean the stoves to give more heat, then to order new, larger lamps, and finally to fit the doors with better hinges and locks so they'd close quietly and firmly. He complained about her, and it was soon abroad in the court that *"die Engländerin,"* as she had been dubbed, found her spacious quarters most unsatisfactory. Gossips speculated she would soon return to London, and Wally and Marie were asked: Was it true? When exactly would Vicky depart? Her ladies laughed over this, and urged her to do the same, but Vicky found it distressing to be so maligned, with no way of defending herself.

Her best hours were spent alone with Fritz. They always breakfasted together, and on days when he didn't report to army headquarters he took Vicky for walks or rides through the Tiergarten, Berlin's large public park. Fritz said no other husband and wife in his family ever went out together—a princess might drive out with her lady-in-waiting and a prince with an aide-de-camp, and sometimes they might run into each other, but never intentionally. And royalty didn't frequent public places where there were lots of commoners.

Vicky always enjoyed being out in the city, encountering her new countrymen. Prussian faces tended to be square jawed, with high cheekbones and pale, waxy skin. There were fewer of the round, rosy, or freckled faces so typical in England. Some Prussians were blond like Fritz but plenty had light brown or red hair. When Berliners recognized Fritz and Vicky in the park, they stared—yet if Vicky smiled or waved or called out "*Guten Tag,*" people looked very pleased and greeted them cheerfully in return. One morning, she and Fritz were strolling along a stone path in the Tiergarten when a little girl of about eight rushed up beside her and wordlessly thrust into her hand a single white carnation, like something a gentleman might wear in his buttonhole. She turned to watch the girl run, long yellow plaits bouncing against her back, toward a man, her father surely, who stood some distance behind them on the same path. When Vicky waved, the man took off his hat and, with a wide sweep of his arm, bowed low.

Fritz laughed. "I doubt anyone else in the family would be so affectionately greeted, *mein Schatz.* You are already a great favorite."

Vicky was glad that ordinary Prussians liked her—if only more people at court did. Fritz's mother made no effort to get to know her, yet she demanded Vicky be in her train for all scheduled events during this, the busy winter season. Most evenings Prince Wilhelm and Princess Augusta hosted a formal dinner, starting at five P.M., followed by the theater, or a concert, or the opera. As dressing took at least an hour, Vicky would be forced to stop reading or painting at half past three, and she was never in bed before midnight. She laughed to think how Papa would cope. He hated late hours and always nodded off at nine thirty if he was still at the table or entertaining guests in the Windsor drawing room.

On Sunday the extended family went to church together, and then the day's large meal was served at two in the formal dining room of the Berliner Schloss and lasted most of the afternoon. Vicky kept hoping interesting people would be invited to dine— artists, musicians, and particularly politicians and journalists with whom she could discuss the current situation in Germany. Mama and Papa always welcomed such guests, but here the royal circle kept to itself.

Which was why it was particularly unfortunate that Fritz's relatives did not warm to her. Some were openly rude, particularly the Russian-born Crown Princess of Württemberg, who refused to address her and ostentatiously turned her back whenever Vicky walked into a room. "I believe she blames you for Britain's victory in the Crimean War," laughed Fritz after she complained to him. "Pay no attention."

But all the nasty looks and barbed comments—especially about her short stature, considered a kind of deformity—upset her. A week after she arrived the Grand Duchess Alexandrine of Mecklenburg-Schwerin, Fritz's aunt, approached with a question. "My ladies believe Queen Victoria told a falsehood about your age, and that you have not yet reached your sixteenth birthday," she said. "I assured them that the great lady would not lie. Who is correct?"

Vicky thought the duchess must be joking, but no, she gazed at Vicky, brows raised inquiringly, awaiting a reply.

"My birth in November 1840 was announced in all the London

newspapers and was the cause of great public celebration, my parents have told me," Vicky answered. "I am seventeen years and three months."

"Just as I supposed, your mother is not a fabricator!" said the duchess, looking pleased with herself.

"Of course not," said Vicky, astounded.

"You can hardly blame my poor ladies, though, you are so tiny and look, how shall I say, childlike? I suppose you won't be growing any taller at this point," said the duchess, "which is a pity."

And then Fritz's aunt raised both her hands and looked heavenward, as if to observe silently how mysterious were God's ways, and glided away, leaving Vicky fuming.

The young princes at court liked to tease her, pinching her from behind and, when she whirled around, pretending they had not. Prince Albrecht, Fritz's disgraced uncle, did appear, seeming in no way ashamed of himself, and he took special pleasure in interrogating Vicky about religion, because, he said, she was "reputedly so clever." She was never certain how to answer his queries. If she gave a precise reply—citing for instance which of Martin Luther's ninety-five theses rejected the use of indulgences to absolve sin—the prince laughed at her "scholarly pretensions." But if she answered offhandedly—opining that the Reformation was inconclusive on many matters of doctrine—he'd turn suddenly stern, asking if she took her faith so casually as to brush off the most important Protestant thinkers. She couldn't win.

Fritz Karl, often sarcastic to others, she noticed, was gracious to her. Still, Vicky hadn't felt at ease with Fritz's tall cousin ever since Fritz had told her how Fritz Karl, enraged after the birth of his third daughter, had boxed Marianne's ears. His wife still couldn't hear properly.

In frequent letters Mama warned Vicky against unwise, unguarded confidences and told her not to laugh in her unseemly, piercing way. Vicky was tempted to reply that as she had no friends, nor prospect of making any, there was little risk of sharing secrets, or, indeed, laughing. In the end she simply promised

Mama she was being careful. And Papa demanded that she take precedence, always, over Fritz's cousins since she was the Princess Royal of England. "You should be the third lady behind the queen and Princess Augusta at all times," he wrote. But Crown Princess Olga insisted that as the czar's daughter she should come before Vicky, and after lengthy debate with the young baron, Vicky and he decided to cede the point. "But let's not tell Papa," she told her adviser.

THE WEEKS OF winter passed very slowly, and well into March it was terribly cold. Vicky dreamed at night of Osborne, of following the winding, sun-dappled path to the sea, of walking through the bluebells in the woods behind the Swiss Cottage, of sitting with the family in the dining room under Herr Winterhalter's painting. She hadn't realized that homesickness would actually feel like being ill. Every morning she woke with a peculiar hollowed-out ache in her tummy, which came and went all day. Study was the only remedy. She devised a daily timetable and sent it to Papa for his approval. She resumed writing a weekly essay for him. And one evening Fritz brought home his old mathematics tutor from Bonn, Professor Anton Schellbach.

"The prince tells me you are an eager student," said the professor, bowing to her. On this rare night when they didn't have to go out, Vicky wore her favorite Scottish plaid dress and black velvet slippers, her hair loose and streaming down her back.

"I am indeed, Professor, and I have so much to learn about mathematics," she told him. "Perhaps we can meet regularly?"

Tuesday evenings were set aside for dear Professor S, as she called him, and she looked forward to seeing him all week long. She realized she was a little in love with him—even though he was old, perhaps fifty, and his droopy, hangdog face almost ugly. But she adored the deliberate way he spoke and was flattered that he, unlike the Prussian princes, clearly enjoyed her company. They discussed scientific and political progress, as well as tackling geometry. When he approved of something she said, he'd give a soft little nod and say, "*Welch raffinierte Gedanken.*" At her urging, Fritz introduced her to other teachers, including the classics scholar Christian Brandis, the archaeologist Ernst Curtius, and a philosopher, Karl Werder. "Prussia must be awakened to embrace its destiny and birth a new nation," Professor Werder said during one evening's discussion of the future of Germany. "With your marriage you will hasten that change." Nothing she had heard in Berlin had made her happier.

FRITZ'S PARENTS DISAPPROVED of how much time they spent with people of lower rank, but Vicky was confident Papa would applaud. Instead he wrote back: "Why doesn't Fritz have actual work to do? His father should scale back his military duties and have him sit on the Crown Council."

Vicky showed this letter to her husband. "My father doesn't want me involved in government," said Fritz. "I've asked before."

"Not want you? Why not?" she asked.

"I suppose he doesn't consider me very capable."

He looked so sad, and Vicky wasn't sure how to respond. She had come to see since her arrival that while Fritz was admired at court as an excellent soldier and amiable fellow—getting on with nearly everyone—he didn't have much influence, nor did he push himself forward. It didn't help that his parents rarely treated him affectionately, although he was always deferential and never embarrassed or contradicted them. So odd.

In his next letter Papa instructed her to speak to Fritz's parents about their son's future.

"Surely Wilhelm and Augusta don't want Fritz to arrive on the throne totally unprepared," her father wrote. "You must say something."

One night later that week Vicky found herself alone in a carriage with Princess Augusta en route to the opera and seized her chance.

"Aunt, Papa was just inquiring about Fritz's official duties. He thinks Fritz is ready for more."

"Does he indeed?"

"Yes, and he reminded me how when he arrived in England and longed to help Mama, he started with palace administration tasks and only then did he move on to other, more important things, like reading state papers. Fritz could take a similar path," Vicky said, pleased to have such a suitable plan to propose.

"Your father advised you to bring this up with me?" said Princess Augusta in a chilly tone of voice.

"Well, yes."

"And why is that?"

"Because you have the right opinions. I agree completely with what you said at dinner yesterday about the new restrictions on political speech being unacceptable." A little bit of flattery couldn't hurt, Vicky thought.

"And how is that relevant?" she asked, still cold.

"Because you and Fritz and I see so many things the same way. And as you are his mother you want the best for him."

Princess Augusta laughed, not gaily. "I'm not sure who is more naïve, you or your father."

Vicky, stung, quickly retorted: "Papa's suggestion is a good one!"

"Your father is an intelligent man who fails to understand how the court here works," she said.

"Why shouldn't Fritz do more?"

"I suppose that would suit you. You fancy then you too would have influence? Maybe more than I do?" Princess Augusta gave her a sharp look.

Her hostility shocked Vicky. "But Papa wants what's best for everyone. And for Prussia."

"I suggest your father stay out of what is not his concern."

They had arrived at the opera house and a coachman was opening the carriage door. Princess Augusta began to climb out and then turned to look back at Vicky.

"Don't interfere, it will only be damaging to Fritz in the end."

Her mother-in-law ignored her for the rest of the evening.

VICKY COULD HARDLY recount this exchange to Papa—he would be so insulted. Nor did she care to tell Fritz how she'd been rebuffed. And perhaps she had been naïve to ask Aunt Prussia for support rather than go straight to Fritz's father. She had come to see, now that she lived in Berlin, how besieged Princess Augusta's own position was. Fritz's mother led the court faction who agreed that Prussia must evolve, becoming less like Russia and more like Britain. But because she and her husband didn't get on, those who opposed her modern ideas felt free to openly deride her, with Fritz caught in the middle. While Fritz was known to lean to his mother's side in political arguments, and his marriage to Vicky had reinforced his liberal credentials, he spent his days working with his father and his cousin Fritz Karl in the army leadership. And he preferred to avoid conflicts whenever he could.

As for Fritz's father, he didn't concern himself much with questions of political reform. The army was always his first priority—he wanted Prussia to be strong. While Prince Wilhelm believed that Prussia was destined to lead Germany, he felt there was no hurry about it. What angered him was his anomalous position. Prince Wilhelm had all the responsibilities of kingship, without full authority, because his brother the king still clung to life and the queen watched beadily to ensure that no important decision was made without her husband's approval. As the king suffered from softening of the brain, the business of government often stalled. Fritz could be of great help to him, Vicky was sure, but how best to point this out?

At dinner that Sunday Vicky noticed Uncle Prussia had sat Wally next to him. Wally's late father had been his friend and army comrade, and everyone knew he favored her. Beautiful Wally—slender, tall, with creamy skin, lovely red-brown hair, and a vivacious, expressive face—excelled at the airy, slightly mocking conversational tone employed by so many at court. From across the room Vicky watched her lady tell the prince some long story, gesturing frequently with her fluttering white hands, while he chuckled and leaned back in his chair. Could Wally be his next conquest? No, Vicky thought, probably not. Wally had confessed that the earnings from her job were her only income. She needed to marry well, and as the prince's mistress she'd be out of bounds to other men. It was more likely that Wally was encouraging the prince's admiration without committing to him. Vicky sighed. She frequently felt unsophisticated and juvenile in Wally's company, although it was she who was the married woman. As she was so isolated, she had only a foggy sense of court gossip, but she worried that Wally's familiarity with Uncle Prussia reflected badly on her. Shouldn't her ladies be above reproach? Vicky sighed again. Her authority with her lady was undercut because she often depended on Wally for guidance—a state of affairs she could think of no good way to redress.

The next day she said to Wally: "You have such skill with Prince Wilhelm. I wish I could say the same."

"He's not difficult to get on with," Wally replied. "I think he relaxes more readily with people outside his family."

"He's very stern with Prince Friedrich. And not much better with me."

"Try to be less critical, Princess."

"What on earth do you mean?" she said, aiming to convey stern displeasure with her lady's familiarity.

"The prince, I believe, does not feel at ease with you because you don't think Prussia is as good as home, as you always call it."

"That's not true!" Vicky exclaimed.

"No? You constantly find fault."

"Only to point out how things could be improved. Such as, let me see . . . such as more pavements! We were nearly run down the other day by the Horse Guards. Don't you remember? We had to flatten ourselves against the barracks wall to let them pass."

Wally laughed. "When speaking with Prince Wilhelm, emphasize what you *like* about Berlin."

THE FAMILY ALWAYS milled around for a half hour before dinner on Sunday, and the next week, when Vicky spotted her father-in-law standing alone for a moment, she summoned up all her courage and approached him. So nerve-racking, even though she was doing what dearest Papa wanted.

"Are you aware, Uncle, that the Neues Museum here on Spree Island has recently received a splendid cache of Greek antiquities brought back from excavations on the Peloponnesus?" she began.

The prince looked down at her, immediately on guard.

"On Thursday Professor Curtius took me to see this array of sculpture and pottery," Vicky continued. "I am certain your schedule allows little time for museum visits, but you would gain much from seeing the pieces."

The prince grunted.

"And the professor plans to take a team from the University of Berlin to dig at Athens this summer. Have you heard? No person in all of Europe is better informed about ancient Greece than our Professor Curtius."

"Is that so?" said Uncle Prussia.

"Yes, in this field Prussians lead the—"

He suddenly interrupted. "Why is it your husband, my son, allows you to spend so much time with professors?"

"My outings with Professor Curtius are hardly improper!" she said with a titter. "Wally and Marie accompany me. And Baron Stockmar went along this time, too."

Prince Wilhelm glowered. As Fritz had predicted, his father disliked the young baron and resented having a Coburger in the Hohenzollern family circle.

"It's not impropriety I suspect," the prince said. "It's your zeal for more and more useless knowledge that I find ill becoming."

"The study of classical sculpture is not becoming? Would you prefer I remain ignorant of all these exciting discoveries? And stay out of the splendid Berlin museums?" She meant to sound bantering, the way Wally would. But her father-in-law's face darkened.

"A woman's duty is to dedicate herself to husband and home," he pronounced angrily.

Goodness. She hadn't even come to the point yet, and he was already irate.

"My husband, dear Fritz, must always be my priority. You are, of course, correct, Uncle," she said, tacking in a new direction. "And it's because of that I've been meaning to speak to you, to urge you to include him more in state matters. He is ready to attend the council, to read state papers, help you with administration. Papa says so."

Prince Wilhelm snorted. "Your father chooses you as a go-between? To send me messages about how to treat my family and run my government?"

"I'm not a messenger but Fritz's wife, and his most devoted advocate."

"It's not your place to opine on such matters."

"No? Shouldn't any woman, especially an educated one, strive to know what is going on? Take an interest? If I failed to do that, I'd probably bore Fritz. And what good would I be to the world?" She felt suddenly buoyed and less nervous. Debating like this, she enjoyed.

Prince Wilhelm raised his eyebrows and snorted again. "You may entertain yourself with such speeches, my dear, but they count for nothing with me."

"Nothing? You would prefer I never discuss anything of importance with you—you who are my father in Prussia?"

"I will always prefer that. Always."

She wondered suddenly if her father had ever pictured her being treated this way. No, he would never have imagined it, nor countenanced it, and that thought emboldened her. She forced herself to meet Uncle Prussia's eyes and said: "And you are not concerned, sir, that your dear son will arrive on the throne unprepared and unschooled?"

"It's ridiculous how you and Fritz still play at school," he snarled. "Let me tell you something you haven't learned: You are not your mother. This is not England. And you have no influence on the government here in Prussia. If you desire your marriage and your life to be a success, you will keep away from that which will never be any of your business."

He turned and strode off.

Vicky felt like she'd been smacked. The color rose in her cheeks and she could sense herself trembling, but she fought to be calm. His behavior toward her was neither just nor proper. She would not accept it as so. Yet, she must stay dignified; she could not betray her disquiet; she must remember who she was.

Fritz walked up to her.

"What were you discussing with my father?" he asked, wary. "He seems angry."

Vicky looked left and saw Prince Wilhelm berating one of the footmen. "He's tired of waiting so long for his dinner," she said.

She couldn't bear to reveal to her husband—or later, to Papa—how thoroughly and rancorously the prince had rejected her appeal. All through the meal, Fritz gave her concerned glances, sensing something wrong, but, surrounded by the family, he didn't inquire further. While the meal dragged on, Vicky pondered how she could possibly respond to the prince's rebuke. He saw her in such a different light than Papa did—as Fritz's wife and nothing more. How could she have a beneficial influence on her adopted country if he continued to dismiss her? It was such a conundrum. Dear Professor S had been teaching them about the ancient geometers, who tried to "square the circle." Here was her own intractable task.

When they got up from the table, Fritz bade his parents good night and Prince Wilhelm glared at them both. In the carriage, Fritz shook his head and sighed. "Father is so often in a bad temper these days."

11

Babelsberg, May 1858

*M*ama demanded letters at least three times a week, and she preferred Vicky to write daily. So many things her parents wouldn't understand and others that would only distress them— the quarrel between her and Prince Wilhelm foremost. But she did confess to her mother, as she felt she could to no one else, how passionately attached she had become to Fritz. In fact, it worried her. "I sometimes fear that there are some great trials or sorrows awaiting me, or I should not be allowed to enjoy happiness such as this," she wrote.

Mama hoped Vicky could now appreciate how wearisome it had been to share Papa with so many children—and how much she suffered when her first two years of married life had been blighted by pregnancies, expecting first Vicky and then Bertie. Mama prayed fervently Vicky would be spared such a trial for at least a year, especially since she was still only seventeen. Mama had been nearly twenty-one when she married.

Vicky loved little babies, and she hoped to have her own one day, but her intimacy with Fritz completely absorbed her for the moment.

THEY FINALLY LEFT the dreadful Berliner Schloss on the first of May and went to live at Schloss Babelsberg in Potsdam, a romantic, turreted castle set on the crest of a small wooded hill overlooking the river Havel. It was owned by her parents-in-law and crammed with the overlarge, heavy furniture that Princess Augusta favored, and the windows were overgrown with ivy and Virginia creeper, a Prussian style Vicky found gloomy. Still, at Babelsberg, she and Fritz had so much more time together, with the winter season over and a shorter trip for Fritz to make to headquarters. They were assigned separate bedrooms, but in practice Vicky spent the nights with Fritz in his cool, gray room on the north side of the house, making love for hours.

"So this is what a honeymoon feels like," Fritz joked one morning in bed. "Not squeezing the whole affair into two days, as English royal parents seem to think sufficient."

"Better late than never," Vicky said.

She'd watch Fritz rise out of bed each day to go to his dressing room, his muscular body so gorgeously proportioned, like the classical ideal, with broad shoulders and narrow, elegant hips. His catlike way of moving, lithe and agile, was particularly evident when he was naked. After he went to work, she'd sit at her desk and close her eyes to remember how he looked propped up on his two arms above her, and she'd smell the earthy odor of him still on her fingers. She worried that the servants noticed her watching the clock at night, wondering how early was too early to go upstairs. When they read together now, she always laid her head in his lap. And sometimes he'd put the book down as she stroked him through his trousers. All through the day she'd be yearning for him to once again be kissing her, laying his weight on top of her, his fingers grazing and arousing her. She still missed everything about England, except in England she hadn't had this.

Fritz laughed. "You're insatiable. But you never let me see you properly. I want you to rise up and parade yourself like Lady Godiva."

At first, she was too shy, but finally she agreed, late one evening.

Fritz turned up the lamps and propped himself up on three pillows for a clear view. And he gave a low whistle as she walked around to the front of the bed, first posing with her back to him, and then turning to face forward, gathering up her waist-long hair with one hand and lifting it up above her head.

"*Mein Schatz*, you are a beautiful eyeful," he said. "Get back here immediately."

AN UNFORTUNATE ACCIDENT on the narrow stairway ended the idyll. She was coming down while the lamplighter was going up, and when she moved quickly to make way for him, she missed the last step and landed her weight awkwardly on her right foot, and fell to the floor, spraining her ankle. When Fritz arrived home, he insisted on sending for Dr. Wegner, the court doctor. Vicky didn't trust this officious man. A confidant of Fritz's mother, he'd likely repeat to Princess Augusta everything he learned about them.

As he examined Vicky's ankle, he asked: "How did you fall?"

"I moved aside quickly to let a servant pass on the stairs and lost my balance."

"Strange. You weren't dizzy or distracted?"

"In truth, I was a bit dizzy. I was tired this afternoon and took a short nap. I had just gotten up to go out for a walk."

"Hmm." Dr. Wegner asked the maid to fetch a big basin of boiling water. He excused himself to retrieve some bandages and requested Fritz accompany him. Only Fritz returned.

"*Liebling*, Dr. Wegner wants to know when you last bled."

Fritz looked embarrassed, but he knew she'd prefer to discuss this with him rather than directly with the doctor.

"Not since we've come to Babelsberg, I think," Vicky said. "I've rather lost track. Maybe six weeks ago?"

They looked at each other for a moment in silence.

"All right, I will go and tell him," Fritz said.

Dr. Wegner came back after ten minutes with bandages. He

had Vicky soak her ankle in the hot water and then used the bandages to bind it up.

"Stay off your feet, Your Highness. I will return in a few days and examine your ankle. And we can discuss other matters."

Vicky lay on the sofa the next day, queerly light-headed, uninterested in painting or reading. She was embroidering a kneeler for the new English church in Berlin, but when Wally brought her sewing basket, crewelwork seemed like too much trouble. At supper she had no appetite and Fritz said: "I do not think you are perfectly well, *mein Schatz*," he said.

The next day passed much the same, and when he bent down to kiss her on the second evening she whispered, "Still no blood."

Dr. Wegner came on the third day and first conferred with Fritz. Then they came into her sitting room together and sat down in front of her.

"We must conclude, Princess, that you are expecting a child," the doctor said. "It is early, of course, and at the beginning pregnancies are delicate. You must rest and avoid strain so that the child can attach well in your womb."

"Suffering with a sprained ankle makes that easier," joked Fritz. He looked rather abashed.

Dr. Wegner unwrapped her bandages, inspected the ankle, and declared it better. "Tomorrow start walking on it briefly. First, fifteen minutes in the morning, maybe a half hour after luncheon."

The sun shone and Vicky longed to be back on her feet. But she complied with Dr. Wegner's instructions, as Fritz was so anxious she do so. She felt queasy and no food appealed. Fritz brought home the almond cake she loved from the bakery on Oberwallstrasse, and fresh grapes, and one day a tin of sardines. He waved the tin at her. "I understand expectant ladies desire all sorts of strange things to eat," he said.

"I have never liked sardines and I won't begin now," said Vicky.

"A shame," said her husband, who asked the kitchen maid to make toast and then proceeded to eat the whole can in front of Vicky, spreading the odorous fish on one slice after another.

"Eww. The smell is terrible," she said.

"But the taste is so delicious." Fritz grinned at her. It was he who was so delicious, thought Vicky with a pang. Dr. Wegner had also ordered abstinence.

Vicky didn't tell her parents about the baby. Mama would be furious, and Papa was agitated already, harrying Vicky for details of what exactly Prince Wilhelm planned to give Fritz to do. Vicky sent vague answers and he just wrote back more insistently. Had she and Fritz fallen out with his parents? Was Fritz resisting work? How were they getting along together?

And then Papa announced he would make a quick trip to Coburg. Could she meet him there in two weeks' time? He would show her his old home and they would talk. "These past months have marked your entrance from childhood into life," he wrote. "I need to see you and hear directly all your impressions."

Vicky, sitting at her desk, shrieked. Wally, across the room, reading a book, looked up, alarmed, as Vicky swiveled around in her chair. "Papa is coming!" she said, and waved the letter in the air.

Her lady smiled. But she could hardly know how much this meant. "You have to understand, Wally, Papa is my oracle," Vicky said. "He's the person on earth who knows me the best and understands better than anyone how I should live, work, be."

"He's a wise man, your father, and I remember his devotion to you, to all his family," said Wally. "But tell me, Princess, does your husband share this adulation?"

Vicky gave her lady a sharp look. "What do you mean? Of course he does. The prince has always idolized Papa."

THAT EVENING SHE dashed out of the drawing room when she heard Fritz come in.

"Dearest, you will never believe what has happened," she said as Fritz hugged her hello.

"Before you tell me, you must say how is your ankle. Should you be running about? You can't afford to fall again." He looked down with worried eyes.

"No, no, everything's fine. Come in and sit down and I can give you the wonderful news."

Fritz listened carefully: Papa's letter, his upcoming trip to Coburg, how thrilled she was to be seeing him again so soon.

"I can discuss with him all the problems here, now, in person," she said.

"Which problems?" asked Fritz.

"Well, such as how to go forward with obtaining more responsibility for you."

"I will discuss that with your father, but I can't go to Coburg now."

"Papa said he will most likely be coming back for a longer visit, with Mama, later in the summer, and then of course, he will come to Potsdam and you will see them both."

Fritz shook his head. "Is your ankle completely healed? And Dr. Wegner said that at the start of a pregnancy it is necessary to stay quiet. Perhaps not a good moment to travel."

"Coburg is not very far. And I can bring my ladies and Dawes. Goodness, maybe Dr. Wegner would like to come as well!" She beamed across at him, but he still seemed troubled, and he didn't say much as she chatted on about the trip over supper.

When they kissed good night Vicky said, "This is really so wonderful for me."

EARLY THE NEXT afternoon, she was at her desk working through some mathematics—dear Professor S was due later in the week—when a footman came in to announce that Dr. Wegner had arrived and asked to see her.

She stood to greet him but didn't offer him a chair.

"I hear, Princess, that you are considering a trip," he said, standing a few yards distant, next to the sofa.

"Yes, my father is coming from England to Coburg and has asked me to meet him there." Vicky felt very annoyed that Fritz had already told the doctor her plan, but at least she now could mollify him directly. "My ankle is so much better. You can see I stand without any pain. And even my appetite improves."

"Princess, I cannot recommend any travel at this time."

"Thank you for your advice. Since it is not a long way to Coburg I am confident I will be fine."

"No, you will stay home. That's best."

Vicky stared at him, incredulous. Did he believe she would miss out on seeing her father on his orders? That she should lie around in Babelsberg for weeks and weeks, and do nothing for the whole duration? Women in the fields hardly stopped working when they fell pregnant.

"Papa is expecting me and I will be going. I've quite decided. Thank you, doctor." She turned around sharply and sat back down at her desk, leaving him to see himself out.

FRITZ ARRIVED HOME that evening very low. As soon as he sat down across from her at the dining room table he said quietly, "You have a responsibility now, to me, and to the whole country, to take care of the baby who will be heir to the throne."

She felt sick. Even Fritz?

"I suppose," she said slowly, "that if you could be sure it was a girl, this baby, then you would be fine with me going?"

"I don't care if it is a boy or a girl. But it must be protected."

Fritz was suddenly formal, very Prussian.

"So you order me not to go to Coburg because you think that would not be protecting the baby?"

"*So ist es!* Dr. Wegner says it is not wise. Thus, you will not go."

It was all she could do not to throw her plate at Fritz. Instead, she hurled words.

"If I had understood that as soon as I was expecting a baby, my body would no longer belong to me but to the nation, I would not have allowed myself to become pregnant."

Fritz did not answer.

"I never envisioned I would be reduced to some kind of a mute vessel to create the next generation of Hohenzollerns."

Still no response.

"And I would never have come to this nasty, uncomfortable,

backward country to live with you if I had thought this would be your attitude."

Fritz had heard enough. He stood up.

"You are a child, and a very silly and selfish one," he said in a strange, cold voice quite unlike him. He strode out of the room, deliberately slamming the door behind him.

FRITZ DID NOT return that night or all the next day. Vicky woke up confident that she had been very ill used. And it was a relief to have told Fritz exactly what she thought. By midday she was less sure she'd acted honorably. That afternoon out walking by the river she wondered what she could say to Fritz next. To have voiced her dissatisfaction with Prussia was bad enough—although he knew she struggled with homesickness. Far worse was to say she regretted she'd married him. But how dare he side with the insufferable Dr. Wegner against her? And how nasty of him to echo his loathsome relations and call her a child. He'd been pleased enough to share his bed with said child.

She'd eaten supper and was already upstairs in her sitting room trying to concentrate on a new Trollope novel when she heard Fritz climbing the stairs. Still wearing his greatcoat and uniform, undone at the neck, he came in and sat down with a sigh in one of the massive brocade armchairs. He looked across at her grimly.

"Having listened to my parents argue all of my life, I had hoped to be spared such scenes once I was married," he said.

"I know."

"But you could not help yourself and you flung all those accusations at me."

"Because you are parroting Wegner. You are not listening to me."

"I am quite capable of having my own opinions, Vicky. I do not think it sensible to travel now."

"I can't bear not to see Papa."

"You should ask your father to come here."

"Then I would have to explain why."

"And so? You'll have to tell him soon enough."

"It will cause such a fuss. Mama will be in a complete fidget and Papa will be even more worried. I am not ready."

"I begin to wonder if you really care about the baby."

"Of course I do."

"And care for me."

"Fritz, I—"

"You speak all the time about Mama and Papa. Mama does this, Papa does that. You're anxious to know what Papa advises and always say we should write to Papa and see what he thinks. You wonder why people regard you as a child."

Vicky struggled not to cry. Fritz sat there, looking unkempt in a way he never looked, and she remembered his reverence for Papa at Balmoral, all the hours they spent together talking.

"How can you speak like that about them?" she asked. "You were just pretending to love them, all along?"

"No, I was not pretending. But I believed after our marriage it would be different."

"Why different? They are the same."

"I thought after I was your husband, you would turn to me, no longer to your father, always, for everything." His face looked bleak, and his words hung in the air.

For a long moment she felt stunned and then a bit ashamed and finally she had the urge to be placatory. She began to speak, slowly, in the softest, kindest way she could. Of course, Fritz was the person she relied on most—he was her protector and her dearest companion. While Papa would always be a precious and valued counselor, she happily surrendered her allegiance, in full, to Fritz.

At first he simply nodded, still glum. He stared into the distance for a minute or two. Then, when she was about to despair, he looked back at her, smiling slightly. "We cannot come apart now, can we? Now that we are starting a new family?" he asked.

"No, certainly not," she said and answered his smile with her own.

They agreed that Fritz would write to Mama and Papa, giving

them the news, as he was head of the household. Vicky giggled and told him he was in for it from Mama, and indeed her mother wrote back immediately bewailing the young bride's fate, and chastising Fritz for his selfishness and lack of understanding for all that Vicky would have to endure. Papa merely congratulated them both and agreed with Fritz that in the new circumstances he would amend his trip to spend two days with them at Babelsberg on the way home from Coburg.

Fritz rose at dawn on the day of Papa's arrival to fetch him from Grossbeeren station so he would be spared an hour's wait for the connection and Vicky could see him sooner. Once he arrived they took long walks together arm in arm along the Havel, and Vicky told him a somewhat modified account of everything that had happened since her move to Berlin. Papa listened carefully, and promised to contemplate best next steps and how Prince Wilhelm might be brought around. But her father declared that preparing for the birth was her most important job now, and Vicky agreed. He was delighted to see them in good health and in harmony with each other, and he pledged to bring Mama to Potsdam before the summer was over. She waved him goodbye with only a few tears.

12

Berlin, January 1859

*O*f all the indignities that giving birth no doubt entailed, Vicky dreaded most that she would be grunting, groaning, and pushing down conspicuously, while a large group of men looked on. Dr. Wegner, to start with, and Dr. Clark, too, Mama's doctor, whom she insisted on sending from London. Dr. Wegner requested that a Dr. Martin, recently appointed head of obstetrics at Berlin University, attend the birth. "Because this is the princess's first child and she is quite young," he explained. Fritz immediately agreed, and when Vicky protested that surely a third doctor wasn't necessary, he repeated Dr. Wegner's advice.

"You are young, *Liebling*, and doing this for the first time."

"I wish I could have only women around me."

"And me."

"And you, dear heart, with all your horse experience."

Fritz had witnessed the birth of many foals, and they joked: how different could it be, really, a baby?

But Fritz didn't disregard Vicky's squeamishness altogether. When Dr. Wegner brought Dr. Martin to meet them at their new home, the Königliches Palais, just before Christmas, the new doctor suggested he examine Vicky "to see how the baby is positioned."

Vicky flinched and squeezed Fritz's hand. She hated the whole idea of strange men touching her. She supposed it was inevitable during childbirth, but not beforehand. She'd never been examined below the waist by a doctor, and she was confident Fritz wouldn't allow his wife to be so indelicately probed. Indeed, he waved off the suggestion.

"No need for that now. Soon enough the baby will come," Fritz said.

The doctors both nodded and rose to go. Dr. Martin, a dark man with a jowly face and solid, fleshy hands, didn't leave before looking Vicky up and down.

Vicky felt compelled to speak: "My mother is smaller in stature than I, and she has had nine babies."

Dr. Martin gave a quick bow. "Of course, Princess. And the only measurement that can matter is the width of the mother's pelvis, which of course I cannot discern from here."

Vicky squeezed Fritz's hand again. How very disagreeable, having her private dimensions discussed. And Dr. Martin seemed uncouth.

At least Mrs. Innocent, Mama's midwife, who had come with Dr. Clark to Berlin, reassured her. "Nature takes its course and you ride along, with an occasional push, Your Highness."

Vicky prayed fervently this was true. She hadn't had an easy pregnancy. She had fallen again, late in the summer, when she caught her foot on a chair leg. She'd worried she'd hurt the baby until she felt it move for the first time two weeks later. But she was often tired, ill, and fretful. And she missed Mama. Her mother had always intended to come for this, her first confinement, but the timing made it impossible. The opening of Parliament took place in late January, when the baby was due. "Why in heaven's name did you choose a moment when we could not be with you?" Mama wrote.

But Fritz assured her he'd sustain her throughout.

"You will stay and keep people from walking in, when I haven't all my clothes on?" Vicky asked.

"Of course, *Liebling*. I will allow no immodesty," he said, smiling.

Wally and Marie were astonished—Prussian husbands did not attend births as a rule. "I could never keep him away," said Vicky. "He's so excited." And while her ladies assumed he longed for a son, Vicky could report honestly that Fritz did not care. But all along Vicky prayed secretly the baby was a boy. No better retort to her critics at court than the arrival of a healthy heir.

She experienced some intense cramping on both January 24 and 25, her first wedding anniversary, but each time the pain faded away. Mrs. Innocent told her that when cramps came with wetness down her legs she would know labor had properly begun. At eleven P.M. on January 26, she rose from her bed with severe pain and felt a warm gushing just as the midwife described. Fritz jumped up. "I must send now for Dr. Martin. He lives quite far out on Dorotheenstrasse."

Dr. Clark and Dr. Wegner were lodging in the palace along with Mrs. Innocent, so they were with Vicky within the hour. Dr. Wegner's assistant, Fräulein Stahl, soon arrived, and she had the maids cover the four-poster bed with heavy cotton covers and lay out flannel blankets to drape the new mother when the delivery was imminent. For the time being, Vicky walked around the suite with Fritz beside her, clutching at furniture when the pains came.

Mrs. Innocent kept saying: "Breathe deeply and steadily through the pain, Princess."

Quite soon she found that impossible. "I can't, I can't, it's so much. Like being ripped in two," she said.

By three A.M. Fritz had her lying down, and the agonizing waves kept coming and she'd scream.

"Please forgive me, darling, I can't control myself. I am failing," she told Fritz.

"Don't worry, *mein Schatz*, you will manage this. Try to breathe steadily."

But all she could do was scream and grab at the blankets—something, anything, to lessen her distress. It went on relentlessly, the ripping, wrenching sweeps of torment alternating with moments of relief when Fritz would lie next to her on the bed, she resting on her side and he behind, stroking her head and pushing her sweat-soaked hair off her brow.

Sometime in the night she heard Mrs. Innocent speaking to the doctors. "The princess is obviously experiencing great pain and yet the contractions aren't regular."

"This spasmodic action sometimes occurs, especially with a primigravida," said Dr. Clark.

"We must examine her now, to see where she is," Dr. Wegner said. "Prince, why don't you stretch her out and cover her."

Fritz pushed her over onto her back. "Here, *Liebe*, let's allow Dr. Wegner to look at you."

Another horrible, very sharp pain, and Vicky fought Fritz to roll over again on her side.

When that pain passed he shifted her gently onto her back with legs bent and knees spread apart under the blanket. It was left open at the bottom so Dr. Wegner could sit between her legs and examine her.

She felt a cold metal probe slide in and then heard his voice.

"*Ach*, the baby is not in the normal position. And the cervix has not dilated completely. Prince, we must call immediately for Dr. Martin."

"I wrote to him earlier," said Fritz. "I have no idea why he's not yet here."

Fritz and the doctors went off to confer in a corner of the room, and Mrs. Innocent appeared at Vicky's side.

"What is happening? Is something wrong with the baby?" Vicky asked her.

"Sometimes instead of being head down, babies are positioned so their bottoms or their legs will come out first."

"And this is how my baby is?"

"Yes, the doctor believes so."

"It's bad for baby?"

"More difficult to deliver, yes, but, Princess, leave that to the doctors. Focus now on breathing through the pain. Soon it will be time to push. You will need your strength."

Vicky began to cry. "But why? Why did this happen? Did I put baby in the wrong position? When I fell, maybe it got wedged in the wrong place?"

"Nonsense. Try to stay calm."

Another bad wave of pain. Vicky shrieked for Fritz. His face, furrowed with concern, hovered above her.

"Will baby die?"

"*Liebling*, please don't worry. I will carry you through."

Dr. Clark approached. "I believe that you will find this a help, Princess. Your mother used chloroform in her last two deliveries. Just breathe in." He put a damp handkerchief under her nose, and she inhaled. The smell was like sherry but sharper. After a few minutes, she started to float away into numbness.

She even slept for a while, but then there was a sharp contraction again and she screamed and thrashed on the bed. "I can't do this anymore. It's worse and worse," she told Mrs. Innocent.

She looked around for Fritz and saw him standing at the foot of the bed facing the door.

A strange dark man had come in, still wearing his overcoat and a gray bowler hat. Who was that? Maybe the undertaker? Come to measure her and baby for a coffin? Dr. Clark brought the wet handkerchief back under her nose. "Breathe in, Princess."

Fritz was talking, and the bowler-hat man took off his coat. Oh, Dr. Martin. Fräulein Stahl had brought a basin of water. He was washing his hands. Vicky closed her eyes.

She woke up again as Fritz moved her onto her back and down the bed. "Knees up, *Liebling*."

Now vile Dr. Martin was sitting on a stool between her legs and putting his fingers inside her. She would have hated this if she cared anymore, but she didn't. Baby was wrong, she was wrong, all she could hope was that the pain would stop.

"Frank breech. Right buttock presents," Dr. Martin said from far away.

"Tell me what this means," Fritz said.

Vicky tried to listen but her brain was hazy.

"As long as the delivery can be accomplished quickly, your wife will survive."

"And the baby?"

"A baby is always vulnerable in this position. May not be born alive."

"Think only of the mother. Do you hear me? My wife must live."

"Certainly, Prince. But it is my practice to try and save both mother and child."

"Remember what's at stake," Fritz snapped.

Odd to hear Fritz so overbearing. Not like him at all. *He must be very worried*, she thought idly, her consciousness dulled. She saw Dr. Martin talking and pointing at various people in the room as he pushed back his stool away from the bed, but then she slipped into a feverish dream. She was by the river at Babelsberg, water rushing past her, so much faster than it did in reality. If she waded in she'd be carried out to sea. Good, she'd like to float away. But then the scene shifted and she was in the ballroom at the Berliner Schloss and she had on only her long flannel nightgown and people stared. Dr. Martin was with her, wearing his bowler hat, holding her hand as if to guide her, but everyone at court was laughing and saying: *See that silly, stuck-up girl? She thought she could be a mother but all she did was kill her child.*

Mrs. Innocent shook her awake. "Doctor wants you to drink this medicine, it will help your womb expel the baby."

"I think baby is dead."

"Hush. Drink, now."

Vicky drank it down, a new pain rolled over her, and five minutes later she vomited.

The midwife and Fräulein Stahl wiped up the sick. Fritz came and sat next to her. He looked tearful.

"I am sorry, my dearest, I failed," she told him.

"No, no, Vicky, you have not."

The next pain was the worst yet. She arched her back and wailed. Dr. Martin directed Fritz to stand behind her and hold her head. "We don't want the princess hurting herself. Keep her fingers out of her mouth and her neck straight."

New cushions were brought to sit her up. Mrs. Innocent took one leg and Fräulein Stahl the other. Dr. Martin directed: "Now the princess needs another dose of secale cornutum. Dr. Wegner, please administer."

She reached for the cup of medicine the doctor offered. Her hand shook so much she could hardly keep the cup steady. Another huge contraction built within her and Vicky screamed, but she also felt something new, the urge to push.

"Bear down now, Princess, hard."

Fritz was stroking her head. "Good, that's good, Vicky *Liebling*."

The next pain and the next were so intense, she could not push. She could only writhe.

"She needs to be anesthetized fully so she will be still, if I am to turn the baby," said Dr. Martin.

Dr. Clark came up on her right, this time holding a glass bottle, open at the top. "Take full deep breaths in, Princess."

She inhaled. That sharp, sweet sherry smell again.

"Now again."

She inhaled once more. A giant pain tore through her. But then the numbing feeling—more enveloping now. Better, better. Fritz was shifting her onto her side and then, like a candle blown out, she lost consciousness.

SHE AWOKE SOMETIME later, so hot, and aching across her midsection, sticky blood between her legs. Fräulein Stahl, sitting next to the bed, saw her eyes open and called for Fritz.

She almost laughed at the sight of her husband—he looked like a wild man, hair standing up on end, mustache uncombed, and shirt splotched with blood.

"*Liebling*, the baby is alive, and it's a boy."

Vicky didn't fully comprehend.

"Then where is he?"

Fritz smiled. "Mrs. Innocent had some work to do, to get him to take his first breath. Slapping, hitting, turning upside down, but he finally cried, and then the doctors said he needed a warm bath. Fräulein Stahl has done that now, and they are wrapping him up."

"But you have seen him?"

"*Und ob!* A beautiful boy. Not big. But beautiful."

Five minutes later Mrs. Innocent passed Vicky a flannel sausage with a small face peeking out.

Vicky, strangely, felt little interest in the baby. That he'd come out of her, causing such agony, seemed unlikely and farcical. She held him for a minute, then thrust him back at the midwife. "I don't feel well," she told Dr. Wegner, who had followed Mrs. Innocent into the bedroom.

He nodded. "You have been through a very difficult ordeal, Princess. You must rest."

For the remaining part of that day, and the next, Vicky lay in bed, burning and feverish for hours, and shivering and shaking for hours more. She wondered if she, like Princess Charlotte, Mama's tragic cousin, would die following childbirth. It would be a shame, she thought in her delirium. She hadn't accomplished much in her life, privileged as it had been. She supposed she had brought pride and pleasure to her parents, and Fritz loved her. He'd be so sad to raise their son alone. She hoped not to abandon him, but all was beyond her: living, dying, shaking off her fever. Dr. Martin came to examine her, but she wouldn't allow it. She'd only accept Dr. Wegner. Fritz stayed behind to tell her that everyone agreed: Dr. Martin had saved the baby's life. Fritz's first note to him had been put in the post by accident, not delivered by hand, but when sent for again he'd come immediately and taken charge at the most perilous moment.

It didn't matter. Vicky hoped never to see that vulgar man again. She shuddered to think where his fingers had been. That he was the savior of her son only made her ashamed of her dislike and more eager to avoid him.

On the third day she felt a bit better and asked Mrs. Innocent to bring in the baby. He was heftier now, minuscule red cheeks round and filled out. A wet nurse named Frau Höffer had been feeding him, nearly every hour, the midwife reported. And as Vicky held the baby, he turned his little head toward her, tiny mouth open, obviously looking to suck. Vicky's breasts had become swollen and tender and now, the baby close, she felt a heavy rushing sensation in her chest. "That's the let-down," Mrs. Innocent said. "The milk for the baby is ready."

"Can I try to feed him?"

"Of course, Princess."

When Fritz came to check on her a half hour later, Vicky was sitting up in bed. First she'd nursed the baby from her left breast, and then she'd switched to the right. This she could do, and do well. The baby made sweet little satisfied snorts as he drank. "Mrs. Innocent says I have an excellent supply of milk," she told her beaming husband. "And baby latched on correctly from the start. What a clever boy."

LONGING TO BE alone and at peace with her newborn, Vicky had to cope with her infuriated mother-in-law. Princess Augusta came in person to tell her Prussian noblewomen never nursed, a revolting practice. That's what a wet nurse was for. Vicky tried to distract her, cooing over the baby and pointing out all his darling features, but the princess refused to be mollified, not even when Vicky told her that she and Fritz had decided to name the baby Friedrich Wilhelm Viktor Albert, after his father and his maternal grandparents.

"What else would he be called?" Princess Augusta retorted.

"In the family he will be known as William, or Willy. It wouldn't do to have another Fritz, would it?" Vicky asked, smiling, and hoping for an answering smile that never came.

Then Mama put in her two pennies' worth, just as disapproving.
"Such a repellent idea, darling child, you as a nurse. It has been the ruin of many a fine young lady," she wrote.

So Vicky mostly gave it up during the day and only nursed at night, when no one save Fritz could see. He understood how much it meant to her, and as she was still confined to bed, he brought Willy in at nine, at midnight, and again in the small hours. The three of them cuddled together while Vicky gave her son the breast.

"He prefers his mama to anyone else," she told Fritz. "I can tell."

SOON, ONLY THOSE stolen, private moments at night relieved Vicky's despair. Her torn-up nether parts didn't bother her much, as sore and uncomfortable as they were. Nor was she overcome with the tearfulness that her mother warned often arrived after a birth. This was much worse. There was something wrong with William's arm.

When swaddled he looked normal. But Mrs. Innocent gave Willy a daily bath and she noticed that the baby's left arm hung limp from its socket. She showed this to Fritz, who then asked Dr. Wegner to examine Willy closely, and he confirmed that the baby couldn't move the arm properly.

Fritz brought Dr. Wegner with him to break the news to Vicky. The physician explained that Willy's breech position at birth meant that Dr. Martin had been compelled to pull the arm down from above his head, and then use it to turn Willy's trunk so he could pry the baby from the womb. "But when I carefully investigate the collarbones, the shoulder joint, and the whole arm, Princess, no bone is out of place or broken, and all joints permit free movement in all the normal directions," the doctor said.

"So why does baby not have use of it?" she asked.

"I believe that during birth the pressure on the upper arm and the shoulder caused some local paralysis," he explained. "Indeed, there are slight traces of bruising on the skin in those areas."

Fritz looked steadily at Vicky as Dr. Wegner spoke.

She felt her throat constricting and a panicky fluttering in her stomach. She forced herself to say evenly: "What can be done to remedy this, doctor?"

"Time itself will heal the arm. But in the meantime, we will apply some cooling compresses to help the strained ligaments recover."

Fritz applauded Wegner's diagnosis and his treatment plan. And later, when they were alone, he urged Vicky not to worry.

"We have a beautiful baby boy we came close to losing. You need to have faith now that all will be well."

Vicky wished she could believe as Fritz believed, and share his conspicuous pride in his son, whom he called *"mein Junge."* Fritz marched around the palace with the baby in his arms, insisting everyone in the household, including the servants and visiting tradesmen in the kitchen, take a moment to admire the lovely boy. And he'd provide prompts: "You must notice his intelligent expression," he would say. Or "See how quickly he is growing."

And while a doting father, Fritz remained an adoring husband, who told Vicky she looked stronger and healthier every day. "I cannot wait until we can resume all of our favorite pastimes," he said to her with a wink. "And I'm going to find you a gentle new horse. You need to ease back into riding."

But Fritz's jokes, his solicitousness, and his pleasure in the baby just as he was could not relieve Vicky's persistent anxiety. She was sure William's arm had been wrenched irreparably during birth, and while Dr. Martin had done this, the real fault had been hers. Had she labored harder and stood up to the pain with more courage and nerve, she could have made the brutal extraction unnecessary. She had started to push but couldn't manage to continue. Willy had paid the price.

Sometimes she whispered to the baby, "I'm sorry." She begged Fritz to say nothing to anyone about it, and to instruct Mrs.

Innocent and Dr. Wegner to also stay quiet. And she couldn't bear to tell Mama and Papa. Maybe Dr. Wegner was right, maybe time would heal the injury, and she'd never have to mention it. But Vicky feared not. And she wondered to herself, in the quietest, darkest moments, could a one-armed man really be king of Prussia?

PART III

Wife

13

Berlin, March and April 1859

*D*uring Vicky's pregnancy, politics in Prussia had shifted. Back in November, when Queen Elisabeth had decided to take her frail, barely conscious husband to live in the milder climate of the Italian Tyrol, Prince Wilhelm had insisted he be made Prince Regent and formally assume all his brother's authority. He subsequently dismissed the archconservative minister-president Otto von Manteuffel and replaced him with Prince Charles Anton of Hohenzollern-Sigmaringen, a distant cousin, a Catholic, and a political moderate who had spent time in England.

Vicky rejoiced to see her father-in-law pushing Prussia in the direction Papa had so long advocated. And when some of the Manteuffel cabinet were also replaced, and his chief crony, the head of the Prussian police, was removed, she was even more pleased. Fritz downplayed the changes.

"Manteuffel was never a favorite of Father's. You heard the talk—he took bribes and ran various departments for personal profit," said Fritz.

"Still other ministers have been dismissed as well!"

"My father didn't bother discussing it with me," said Fritz, frowning. "But Moltke told me he's determined to have his own men, regardless of party, loyal to him, not the king. And he's made Albrecht von Roon minister of war. Trust me, there is no more ardent monarchist than Roon."

But Papa knew and admired Prince Charles Hohenzollern so shared in her excitement. He applauded *die Neue Ära*—the New Era—as the German papers called it, and intended, he told Vicky, to assist as much as he could. He began dedicating several hours each week to writing and sending long memoranda to Prince Wilhelm and Prince Hohenzollern on exactly how to govern Prussia.

At the beginning of March, at the first Sunday dinner with the family after her recovery, Fritz was away on maneuvers and she was seated with Fritz Karl and Marianne. Marianne had been so kind to Vicky before and after the baby's birth—calling regularly, knitting a beautiful blanket for Willy, giving her a salve for the stretched skin on her belly. Vicky felt happy to be dining with her and took the chance to celebrate all the news.

"Let's toast Prince Hohenzollern and his splendid administration," Vicky said.

"No tears for old Manteuffel, devoted servant of Prussia?" Fritz Karl smirked. Like so many Prussian princes he had no idea how to speak about anything serious with a woman.

"Certainly not," Vicky replied. "And good riddance to Herr Rolf Eckhard, as well."

"Remind me, who is he?" asked Marianne.

"The former chief of police," said Fritz Karl, sneering at his wife. "It's difficult to remain quite as badly informed as you are, Marianne."

"But you missed nothing not knowing him," said Vicky quickly. "He's vile."

"He was always bowing and scraping to me, which is what I like," said Fritz Karl.

"When I first arrived here, my letters from Mama, and mine to her, were often opened," Vicky said. "We've been using a courier in recent months to avoid the police spies. I hope we can stop that now."

Fritz Karl laughed. "Perhaps the postal workers opened your letters—eager to read about the doings of the great queen and her glamorous daughter."

"Surely those who work in the post office are too honorable to open the post," she said.

"The newspapermen perhaps bribe them?" suggested Fritz Karl.

"Or maybe the police sold the contents of the letters to journalists," countered Vicky. News of her pregnancy had appeared in the *Kreuzzeitung*, the most reactionary Junker newspaper, before anyone in Fritz's family had been told.

"Prussian police wouldn't do that," answered Fritz Karl.

It was silly to argue the point now that Eckhard had been removed; best be positive. "My father reports people in London come up to him to congratulate him—everyone's so delighted with the Prince Regent," she said.

"Of course, we are all agog about what people say in *London*," answered Fritz Karl, scoffing.

Vicky plowed on. "Men of talent, conservatives and liberals working together in coalition, it's exciting to see. *Prost*," she said, and raised her glass.

"What would you have them do first?" asked Fritz Karl after gulping down some wine. Now he sounded actually curious.

"Prince Hohenzollern must move to end the restricted franchise," she answered.

"And allow every nonentity on the street to vote?" said Fritz Karl. "You favor that?"

"Not every man, but many more. Everyone with a decent income or some small property," said Vicky. "As in England."

"I am amazed, my dear, that you know so much about this," Marianne said.

"Papa's training. I doubt anyone in Europe knows as much as he about constitutional practice," she said. "He is closely advising Prince Wilhelm now, which is so wonderful."

"I wish I understood it all better," said Marianne, sighing.

Fritz Karl rolled his eyes. "Bah—the English royals have been very weak, diluting their authority for centuries. It's hardly a model for us."

"The queen retains important moral and political influence, which is as it should be," Vicky replied.

"I admire you, Vicky. You speak of public affairs so confidently," said Marianne.

Vicky smiled at her—if only more people at court were as sweet as Marianne.

"In England they bring up princesses differently," said Fritz Karl. "You could never have managed, Marianne. You have no sense."

VICKY WAS SO put off by Fritz Karl's habitual contempt for his wife, she failed to realize that she'd said too much to him. He claimed to others at court she'd bragged about her father directing the Prince Regent and declared that "the New Era" would transform Prussia into a parliamentary democracy like Britain. Two days later, a long article condemning Vicky's pernicious opinions appeared in the *Kreuzzeitung*. Prince Karl and Prince Albrecht demanded Fritz publicly repudiate his wife's offensive views, and Fritz's father summoned Fritz to his office in the Wilhelmstrasse the next morning.

Vicky felt mortified to have brought trouble onto Fritz, but also infuriated to be so betrayed and attacked. Fritz was calm as he set off for the audience with his father. "I should have cautioned you to be more discreet, *Liebling*," he said. "My father's elevation, all his changes, it's stirred things up."

"What do you mean? Everyone should be overjoyed and nothing I said was—"

Fritz put up a hand to stop her explaining. "Let's see what my father orders."

When he returned in the late afternoon he asked Baron Stockmar to come and confer with them, and they gathered in the library of the Königliches Palais, in front of the large porcelain stove. It was still chilly in these first few days of spring. Vicky and the baron sat down on opposite ends of the green cut-velvet sofa, while Fritz chose a large leather chair near the warmth and crossed one long leg over the other. He sighed, and rubbed his temples before beginning.

"My father was calm. And he immediately declared it beneath my dignity to issue any kind of official disavowal of my wife's views," Fritz said.

"I should think so, given my views have been distorted," Vicky replied heatedly.

"However, as I expected, he instructed me to demand greater circumspection in future as these kinds of stories fuel suspicions and are damaging to the crown."

"I suppose we cannot be surprised that this would be his view," said the baron.

"I'm reprimanded for voicing *support* for his choices?" Vicky cut in.

Fritz nodded. "Father's clearly not comfortable being labeled a reformer. And he particularly dislikes any suggestion he's taking orders from Prince Albert."

"Although who could be a better guide? He's lucky to have Papa's help!" she retorted.

Now Fritz smiled, a bit sadly. "Promise me you will never utter those words anywhere else in Berlin, only here, in this room, to us," he said.

"I advise you hold yourself aloof from political discussions for the time being, Princess," said the baron.

It was infuriating. "What I said to Fritz Karl any sensible person would agree with! Or at least recognize it as a logical position to express—an end to corruption and an expansion of the franchise. I did not say Prussia would, or should, become a replica of Britain." She fervently wished she could remember her exact words but she was not in doubt of the gist. "I was extremely reasonable. Marianne thought it all very interesting."

Her husband shook his head. "Reasonable in England sounds radical in Prussia, especially at court."

"So my views are not welcome?"

"Not at the moment," Fritz said.

Vicky felt this verdict thud down on her chest. "It's the closed-mindedness I can't accept," she replied vehemently. "How much longer can the Prussian people's desire to participate in government be denied? Doing so will just incite violence and discontent. Maybe that's what Fritz Karl would prefer—riots, and hundreds of men killed in the streets, to repeat '48 all over again. And it's distressing in terms of the family. I always thought Fritz Karl was fond of you, and thus accepted me, your wife. Why would he behave this way?"

Fritz gave her a long, rueful look before answering, "You should understand something: plenty of people at court wish Fritz Karl were heir. He's reliably conservative, pro-Russian, not married to an Englishwoman—ideal."

"Thus, he feels free to malign us?" Vicky asked.

"I believe my cousin enjoys stirring the pot from time to time, for the attention, and to remind everyone of what they don't like about me," said Fritz. His mouth twisted in an odd way, as if he suddenly tasted something sour.

How despicable that her loyal, gallant husband had to put up with this kind of conniving—from members of his own family. "You have been very badly served by your cousin," Vicky said. "I hope you never speak to him again!"

"That's hardly realistic," said Fritz.

"That's what I would do," she exclaimed.

Fritz uncrossed his legs and rose. He said: "Baron, thank you for your counsel. I think I have told you everything relevant."

After Stockmar left the room, Fritz came and sat down next to her on the sofa. He picked up her right hand and started to study and caress it the way he used to do in their courtship days.

"It's a long story between me and Fritz Karl," he said after a minute. "I'm sure there are plenty of rivalries and jealousies in your mother's court, too."

"My parents never tolerate bad behavior, you know that." She felt a bit impatient—Fritz shouldn't just accept this as the status quo.

He looked up at her. "Perhaps you were not aware of every-thing that went on, being as you were, a child."

That word again. Was he implying she didn't know the essential nature of her own family home? Which was so much more ethical and upstanding than this treacherous court! She scowled and said:. "Even if that were true, I would still think it terrible, Fritz Karl's conniving and his disrespect. You need to tell him immediately that—"

Fritz cut her off. "The less said about this at the moment the better. It will blow over. You and I will go on as if nothing has happened."

"So you're happy for Fritz Karl to repeat lies about me and pay no price?"

Fritz's face tightened. "I need to work with Fritz Karl every day, and it's best to leave it. Now you know—"

"Yes, now I know that Fritz Karl is happy to stir up animosity against me, against us," she said bitterly, interrupting. "He's very nasty. How Marianne can bear to be married to him, I cannot think. And I hate that I will have to see him and pretend there's nothing wrong."

Fritz's expression softened. "*Leibling*, it takes time to navigate a new situation. You've only just arrived. You've recently been so ill."

"I've been here more than a year," she said bitterly.

"My father's elevation, all his changes—it's disruptive to the family," Fritz continued. "When everyone becomes accustomed to the regency, there will be less squabbling and less jockeying for advantage."

"And then I will be allowed to say what I like? Especially when I am right, as I was here?"

"I am not sure you and I will ever be able to say, completely, what we like, except to each other," said Fritz. He leaned over and kissed her gently, his mustache tickling her nose.

She smiled at him but added: "That makes me very unhappy."

"I will always want to know exactly what you think, *mein*

Schatz," he said. "And the time will come when I will rely on all of your finest advice."

SUCH A LOVELY gummy smile the baby had, everyone agreed, and Mrs. Hobbs, the English nursemaid Vicky had hired, told her William was an alert infant who had plenty of spirit. Mama heard of Fritz's "baby worship" and wrote instructing Vicky to discourage it. Vicky did nothing of the kind, still grateful that her husband saw nothing grievously amiss about their son. Meanwhile Dr. Wegner went on promising that with time—and careful handling—the arm would strengthen. Fräulein Stahl followed the doctor's directions assiduously, rinsing Willy's arm three times a day in cold brine, and afterward applying cool compresses, scented with peppermint leaf, to the shoulder and elbow joints. Forevermore, the smell of peppermint would transport Vicky back to the first months of Willy's life.

In the morning, when Mrs. Hobbs brought him into Vicky's sitting room in a basket, Willy would be chewing on the fingers of his right hand and snuffling and gurgling like any normal baby. Vicky would lay him on the sofa and watch him gaily wave his feet in the air. In that position everything looked as it should. But she never stopped obsessing over his arm. She remembered how Bertie and she used to run down the big hill at Osborne, arms outstretched like wings. Would Willy ever do that? And these days she found herself staring at other children as they clapped or banged on a toy with both hands. It was so miraculous, actually, having two arms and two legs fully functional—a wonder, but completely commonplace. Was only her son to be denied?

Starting when Willy was ten weeks old, Dr. Wegner bound the left arm in a half-bent position to his body for several hours a day. After three weeks, the doctor demonstrated how Willy's arm no longer dropped completely limp if raised and then released, and the baby could hold it rigid against his side. Dr. Wegner and Fritz regarded this as notable progress, but Vicky despaired because Willy still didn't lift the arm or bend it at the elbow on his own.

And as the weeks passed, his arm seemed to rotate and pull in, so that a peculiar, deep crease formed on his left side between the upper arm and the shoulder. When Mrs. Hobbs propped up Willy to sit, his head lolled, his right shoulder hunched forward, and he looked horribly lopsided. Vicky would snatch him up. She preferred to hold him in her arms rather than see him like that.

Mama and Papa longed to meet the baby, and she'd promised to bring him to England once he was three months old. But when Dr. Wegner advised against it, she was relieved. She couldn't keep William's impairment a secret forever, yet she quailed at the thought of presenting the baby, as he was now, to his grandparents. With luck, the arm would improve before they ever saw him.

Mama was extremely put out. She had expected Vicky and the baby for her fortieth birthday party at the end of May at Osborne. If Willy could not travel, then she demanded Vicky come alone. But Vicky required Prince Wilhelm's permission to leave Prussia, and she avoided asking him. It wasn't just the fuss over her indiscretion with Fritz Karl—although that was bad enough. Her shame and disquiet about the baby made her tremulous around her father-in-law. On the few occasions he had come to visit Willy, he'd said nothing critical, but Vicky imagined the proud old soldier couldn't be pleased that his grandson's arm was lame.

She had a further excuse not to bother Fritz's father—his attention was absorbed by a foreign crisis. Austria and France had begun wrangling over the crown lands of the Austrian Empire in Northern Italy. Fritz said the Austrians, Prussia's traditional allies, deserved Prussia's backing against France and the Italian nationalists, and he waited impatiently for his father's government to announce it. If war came, he would be ready. All his training had prepared him well, and the prospect of some actual fighting thrilled him. He'd already chosen which men and which horses to take on what promised to be a long campaign in Northern Italy.

The more Vicky listened to this, the more alarmed she became. What if Fritz left her and William and never came back? Imagine life as the widowed princess, *die Engländerin*, alone, with no throne to look forward to and a crippled son to care for. The Junkers would anoint Fritz Karl heir, and she and Willy would be dispatched to some broken-down palace in Potsdam, where she would live out her days friendless and despised.

THIS NIGHTMARISH POSSIBILITY was still preoccupying her when, one evening in the middle of April, at the annual royal diplomatic reception in the Weisser Saal, she spotted amid the crowd the tall figure of Otto von Bismarck.

Since her move to Berlin, Vicky had often heard the notorious Junker diplomat spoken of, praised for his adroit defense of Prussian interests and unstinting allegiance to the House of Hohenzollern. But many in the family, including Queen Elisabeth, deplored how he constantly insisted that Germany wasn't big enough for both Austria and Prussia. At the Frankfurt Diet Bismarck stirred up trouble with his high-handedness, his arrogant attacks on the Austrians for meddling in the affairs of the German Confederation, which, he said, should properly be Prussia's to direct. He wasn't authorized to say such things, and yet he persisted.

While Bismarck had been for many years a friend of the king's, he'd never bothered to ingratiate himself to Fritz's father. Still, Bismarck had apparently been surprised when, after he'd proposed himself as Manteuffel's natural replacement, the Prince Regent gave the minister-president job to Prince Hohenzollern. And then Bismarck, to his fury, was removed as Prussia's representative to Frankfurt and demoted to ambassador to Russia.

A few weeks previously at the opera, Vicky had heard Princess Augusta crowing: "It'll be a long, cold exile on the Neva for Herr Bismarck!" Fritz's mother was not a generous, forgiving type.

Now Vicky caught Bismarck's eye and smiled. He strolled over, an amused look on his face.

"Princess, this time I bow to you as your loyal subject," he said in English, and kissed her hand.

"You recall our meeting at Versailles then, sir?"

"Of course, Your Highness. How could I forget the precocious, spirited Princess Royal, her father's pride and joy? And imagine my delight when I heard I had been correct about your liking for Prince Friedrich, which at the time you tried, rather clumsily, to disguise."

She laughed and shook her head. "I was not disguising anything. I was just a girl."

"You are still a girl. And we needn't dispute something that's now been so satisfactorily resolved. I congratulate you on the birth of your son. All Prussia rejoices with you." He gave another bow, his elaborate politeness delivered with an ironical flourish.

"I understand you are moving to St. Petersburg," she said.

"Not my choice," he said tersely.

"Do you think well of the czar?"

"We have never met. But Russia is the natural ally of Prussia."

"I was told it was the Austrians with whom we enjoy an unbreakable bond of kinship," she said, teasing.

Bismarck scowled. "Too many in Berlin, including the Prince Regent, more's the pity, remain in thrall to this farcical Austrian allegiance."

"So, you won't welcome an Italian campaign?"

He snorted. With his flaring nostrils, tucked-in chin, and very large wide-set eyes, he resembled an edgy Thoroughbred, impatient to race.

"Quite the opposite," Bismarck said. "We should allow the Austrians to entangle themselves in war with France and then march south with our whole army, carrying our frontier posts in our knapsacks and setting them up again on the shores of Lake Constance."

She laughed again. "What a provocateur you are, Herr Bismarck." She knew she should be on guard against him, but she found his energetic declaiming of his brazen worldview stimulating. Conversation at court events was usually so tedious.

"I'm sincere. And some men here agree with me," he said, gesturing with his arm to the room at large.

"You can't count my husband among them," Vicky said.

Bismarck looked at her beadily. "Tell me: do you wish your husband to become a replica of your father?"

Vicky was taken aback; for a moment she wasn't sure how to answer. Then she said: "My father and my husband are great friends, that is well-known, and Prince Friedrich admires him tremendously."

Bismarck smirked. "Then your answer is yes?"

"What is your aim, sir? To try to discount my husband's views by implying they are English? Foisted upon him by me and my father?" she said.

"I am hardly alone in this suspicion."

"Which is absurd! Prince Friedrich's mother has been eager to see political advancement in Prussia for decades, since before she was married."

"I know something about the Princess Augusta's opinions," said Bismarck quite sourly.

"And the dream of a united Germany, committed to democracy and justice, is shared by all right-minded Germans," Vicky said. "It will be accomplished best by a Prussia the other states can look up to."

"You recite your early training like catechism, Princess, but you, like your father, have no understanding of what will actually be required to establish this mythic new nation you desire."

Vicky was warming to further debate when just then Fritz materialized at her side.

Bismarck bowed immediately. "*Guten Abend,* Your Highness," he said. Vicky watched how the man's features smoothed out as he stood erect again and looked at Fritz guardedly.

"Bismarck," Fritz replied, his tone cool. "I have come to collect the princess. The British ambassador has arrived, and she must be among the first to greet him." With that, he abruptly steered Vicky away by the elbow.

Vicky had no chance to say goodbye, and glancing back over her shoulder she saw Bismarck now appeared gloomy—his elemental vitality oddly damped down. More than three years were to pass before she would once more cast eyes on the man, and that particular dejected expression she was never to see on Bismarck's face again.

TENSE WEEKS OF wrangling followed, with Fritz and Fritz Karl eager to join the Austrian war effort immediately, and the Prince Regent and War Minister Roon reluctant to commit. Only when the small states of the German Confederation pleaded that resurgent France might next cross the Rhine and attack them did Fritz's father agree to mobilize the army of Prussia. Fritz received this news on the morning of the last day of April and rushed to his father's office. Later he sent a message asking Vicky to meet him that evening at the Berliner Schloss for a long-planned banquet honoring retiring army officers. At five, Vicky departed the palace with Marie for the familiar drive down Unter den Linden. The scent of the blossoming lime trees filled the warm air, and hours of daylight stretched ahead. Such portents of spring would typically have delighted Vicky, but instead she sat looking out of the carriage window stiff with dread.

The streets were crowded with soldiers. Some men wore white ceremonial tunics, but most were dressed in the drab, dark blue uniforms meant for battle. The flat caps of the Landwehr—the national militia—bobbed everywhere, hordes of them, and Vicky could also see plenty of the cavalrymen's spiked helmets and the infantry officers' tall fur hats, emblazoned with the death's-head symbol that she found distasteful. The militaristic spirit of Fritz's homeland was in full bloom, along with the limes.

Entering the large, echoing state banquet hall at the *Schloss,* Vicky discovered her husband surrounded by a scrum of officers, including Fritz Karl and General von Moltke. Fritz was talking animatedly, spreading his arms wide. The other men listened closely, even Fritz Karl, engrossed and deferential. Fritz looked as happy and excited as Vicky had ever seen him. Until this very minute she hadn't appreciated that he might love his work as much as he loved her. Perhaps more. The army had certainly been his first great passion.

General von Moltke broke free and approached her.

"Your Highness, *Guten Abend*," the general said with a bow.

Vicky smiled at him, relieved to see that he appeared untouched by war fever—still the paternal, sagacious, counselor she had first met at Balmoral. Fritz, she knew, confided in him more than in his own father. The Prince Regent had recently appointed Moltke army chief of staff. In the company of this old friend she could be candid.

"General, I must say, I am a bit overwhelmed," she admitted.

"All this excitement over the mobilization?" he asked.

"Yes, where will it all lead?"

"Your husband hopes it leads right to battlefields beyond the Rhine. Soon."

"That's what frightens me," she said with a shudder.

"We are some distance from that. Mobilization takes at least six weeks, maybe longer, because we haven't done this in more than ten years," he said, a brief smile crossing his face.

"My husband doesn't want to hear this, but I still hope war can be avoided."

"Perhaps it can be. The prince, I know, is eager for the chance to prove himself."

"That's all very well but so distressing for me! He said the other day how a soldier's life is the most becoming for a man. He seems unconcerned about what could happen to him."

"He is very brave," the general replied.

"He thinks nothing of his unhappy wife, whom he will leave all alone, here, in Berlin," she said. Tears filled her eyes—something about Moltke's kind, grave face made her feel undone.

The general called to Marie, who had been hovering discreetly a few yards behind. "Her Highness needs some water and a fresh handkerchief. Please find both for her."

He led Vicky to one of the wooden chairs set along the wall and sat down next to her.

"I understand your life in Berlin has proved quite demanding, Princess," the general said. "Perhaps more so than anyone antici- pated. But I watch you and the prince together and your marriage is, as your husband always says, a true love match. How few Ger- man princes and princesses can say that!"

"But now he is willing to abandon me," Vicky replied.

"Far from abandoning you, he is defending you. And your baby son. And all the people of Prussia. He sees this as his sa- cred duty."

"But, General, you remember in England, we always spoke about Prussia moving on. It isn't meant to be the German Sparta any longer, obsessed with making war against its neighbors, but the leader of a new Germany. And modernizing itself."

"*Vielleicht*—that may be so. But it will be a gradual evolution." Marie arrived with a glass of water and the handkerchief. Moltke took both and handed Vicky the handkerchief.

She wiped her eyes. "I am told this over and over again. How things take time. It's very tedious," Vicky said.

"You are a student of history, Princess. Can you name a nation that recast itself overnight? In England it took centuries and a bloody civil war to get to the current state."

"America?" she proposed.

"A special case, a new continent and an educated group of Englishmen with the distance, and the means, to go to war with the mother country and establish the government they designed. And look at them now—mired in tremendous difficulties over slavery." He passed her the water, which she sipped.

"Even the French are farther along than we are in Germany," Vicky countered.

"After a violent revolution, and, remember, when this Napoléon couldn't get himself reelected president, he promptly declared himself emperor. His current adventure in Italy is a distraction to get the French to overlook all they don't like about him."

"Perhaps."

"We must hope the Prince Regent can command Prussia and

the German Confederation in a short, victorious war against the French. Then he will be recognized as the leader of Germany."

"Do you think a short war is possible?" Vicky asked.

"*Ja*, especially if the Prince Regent has fine soldiers like his son—your husband—on the field."

Vicky sighed. Fritz was so often pushed aside and denigrated by his father. Now he had a vital role. Would she complain and wish it otherwise? Tinkly bells rang, announcing dinner.

"Let me escort you," the general said, taking the glass from her. As they walked toward the head table, she saw Fritz taking his place while still talking intently with an officer standing alongside.

She bade goodbye to Moltke and slipped into her chair on Fritz's other side. He turned. "*Mein Schatz*, we begin to make real progress."

"I saw you speaking with all those men."

"And there is more," he said, grinning.

"Yes?"

"My father called me into his private office this afternoon. He told me I am to attend council meetings from now on," he said, lowering his voice to a near whisper.

"Oh, Fritz, how wonderful."

"Because of the war of course, or the chance of war. He wants me in the room when military questions are discussed."

"You'll contribute so much," she said.

Fritz shook his head slightly. "He cautioned that I am not allowed to say anything. Just listen."

"Rather insulting!" Vicky wished for the millionth time that the Prince Regent had more confidence in his son. She sensed Fritz's essential gentleness disarmed his father. He didn't fully trust Fritz because he didn't fit the ideal of a Prussian warrior—being neither arrogant nor authoritarian.

"This is my father we're talking about. He never moves fast. And I am content to start like this."

Vicky resisted her instinct to protest further. "Then I am content, too," she said.

A footman stepped between them to pour wine into their glasses. When he moved away, Fritz leaned back to her, still smiling.

"Also, I mentioned to him that you hoped to make a quick trip to England."

"And?"

"He agreed. A good time for you to go, he said, as I will be so busy."

Vicky reached out for Fritz's hand under the table and squeezed it. "Mama will be so pleased, darling, but I will miss you and the baby."

"Don't worry about Willy. I will play with him plenty when I'm not working. My father said he hasn't seen enough of the beautiful boy. He's coming on Saturday afternoon specially to visit him."

Now the dinner was under way, and others expected their attention, so Vicky reluctantly broke off and turned to the elderly general on her right. After exchanging pleasantries on the sunny weather, she asked him about his Napoleonic Wars experiences.

Suddenly she felt light and buoyant. For the first time in weeks, maybe since before the baby was born, she relaxed.

The Prince Regent sat at the head of the long table, his white tunic draped in gold braid, across his chest a scarlet sash laden with medals. Between the second and third courses, she caught his eye, smiled, and then nodded—her way of thanking him, while saving them any awkward interaction. Her father-in-law's somber face softened a bit, and he nodded back at her.

She was quite sure that everything was neither forgiven nor forgotten. But tomorrow she could write to Mama and tell her she was coming home.

14

Windsor, Osborne, and Berlin, May–July 1859

*B*ack in England Mama and Papa kept exclaiming over her. She had grown beautiful, acquired so much poise, become overnight an adult. Mama admired her clothes. Papa asked for her views. They held dinner parties in her honor and insisted the prime minister and the foreign secretary come and listen to Vicky explain the current moment in Europe. She found it gratifying but also unsettling. Had she changed so much? She wrote to Fritz, "Mama has been treating me with a friendliness and warmth that I have hitherto not experienced."

Vicky missed Bertie, away in Rome with his tutor, and Mary, who had gone home on leave, but she had Alice, and to her sister, now aged sixteen, she wasn't someone different or important. When, on her first night home, Alice affectionately slipped her arm into Vicky's as they walked along the passageway, she realized, with a pang, that no lady in Berlin did that. Or might ever do it. She and Alice talked about books and the new plays. They sat together at the pianoforte and played pieces for four hands. While her little sisters and brothers clambered into Vicky's bed in the morning seeking cuddles and kisses, it was Alice who shared all her hours.

"I had imagined it would be a quiet visit," Vicky said to her sister one afternoon as they rode in a pony phaeton over to Frogmore to squeeze in tea with Grandmamma before the dinner that night for the chancellor of the Exchequer, Benjamin Disraeli.

"Never that, you're so in demand," said Alice, smiling. Her sister had grown taller in the fifteen months they'd been separated, but her blue eyes were as ever—round, beatific, and contemplative.

"It's not that I mind, really, but it's not what I expected," Vicky said.

"Mama and Papa have been very worried about you."

"Yes, worried I would behave badly and embarrass them. I heard this constantly in their letters."

"Mama did screech when she learned you sat on a sofa for William's christening. Maybe acceptable in Prussia, but never in England!"

"I couldn't have stood, had I wanted to. I was still very ill then," Vicky said.

"It's true then, having a baby is a misery?" asked her sister.

"Well, in my case. But I trust it will go better for you, and for me, next time."

Alice laughed lightly. "You know how Mama and Papa are, Vicky, always full of pronouncements. They fancy themselves a two-person council of propriety for the whole world. But most of the time when they talk about you, they fret. They worry your situation is not an easy one. I believe they feel guilty."

"Guilty? What for?"

"For letting you marry too young, and go to live so far away, you goose."

"But I am very happy with Fritz," she said, looking sharply at Alice. "You know that, don't you?"

Alice nodded. "I do. Still—"

"So many women are married to horrid men," she said, interrupting her sister. "I never really noticed this before, but now . . ." Vicky paused, thinking of Marianne. "Alice, you must be very careful about whom you choose!"

"Of course, and I will be, but Mama and Papa vow I will not marry until I am twenty-one. No need to think about it for the moment, they say."

Now it was Vicky's turn to laugh. "That's what they say. And I'm sure they mean it, but events could overtake them. Remember how Papa swore he wouldn't arrange my marriage until after I'd been confirmed?"

"And by that time you'd been engaged for months?"

"Over a year."

They both laughed.

"No one should worry about me," continued Vicky. "Because Fritz and I, we—we are so in love. In this way I am exactly like Mama. Both of us besotted with our husbands." She smiled to think of it.

"Yes, but are you happy in Berlin? You make it sound a very uncongenial place," said her sister.

Vicky sighed. "Wintertime is much the worse, shut up inside so much. And Aunt Prussia, she's very difficult and wants constant attending."

"Demanding every scrap of filial duty she feels entitled to?"

"Yes. And I feel little affection for her, although I try. Many at court assume because of her enlightened ideas we must be close. But in truth she prefers me never to speak."

"You'd think she would enjoy your companionship, with her own daughter living far away."

Vicky rolled her eyes. "Quite the opposite. She dictates but she never converses. And when I speak in company I feel her gaze upon me, resentful; she believes it unsuitable for me to venture my opinion. Only she should hold forth, and I'm the supporting prop, Mama and Papa's daughter, there to show everyone she enjoys a connection to the British crown. The other day she scolded me for discussing the foreign situation with the prince of Württemberg. But she does dote on William. I will grant that. Fritz laughs and says she's much fonder of the baby than she's ever been of him."

"How hurtful!"

"Fritz doesn't let it worry him. My darling concentrates on doing his duty by everyone and we have lovely times when we are alone." She blushed a bit—even with her sister she was too shy to spell it out.

"No other friends?"

"Not really, yet. I like Marianne, Fritz's cousin's wife. And some nice professors we've studied with."

Her sister's mouth turned down.

"You mustn't fret, Alice dear," Vicky added. "When I left England last year I was truly bereft. But Fritz has consoled me so lovingly and when I think of all that has happened to us since then, I give thanks to God that we have each other. Now here, parted from him, even though I'm home, it feels like being banished."

Alice reached over and squeezed her hand. "You will see him again soon. And meanwhile I am so, so happy to have you back."

AFTER A WEEK at Windsor, they traveled to Osborne for Mama's birthday. There, she finally spoke with her parents about William's arm.

"You understand that at the birth baby was positioned incorrectly—his feet were where his head needed to be?" she said.

Papa and Mama nodded.

"Dr. Martin had to swivel him around to extract him, and that's when his left arm was hurt."

"What was this Dr. Martin thinking, delivering baby in such a rough manner?" asked Mama.

"I believe he felt he had no choice, if the baby were to live," said Vicky.

"And what are the consequences?" asked Papa.

"At the moment Willy cannot move his left arm by himself, but it can be lifted and moved by others."

"Why have you kept this from us?!" asked her mother.

"Fritz and I thought it might quickly be better, Mama. And it still might. We didn't want to worry you."

"I am worried! And I am astonished you didn't insist on bringing baby with you. An English specialist must examine him immediately," she said.

"Dr. Wegner is managing, Mama."

"Who? The court doctor? That furtive-looking, thin man?"

"Yes, you met him in Potsdam last year."

"I told him he needs to come to England to be further trained!"

"Maybe so, but Dr. Wegner is a good man and a fine doctor. I've quite come around to him," she said, forcing herself to smile, to be reassuring. "And Willy is otherwise perfectly healthy and such a darling."

"Also handsome I hear!" her mother said.

"Yes, fat and bonny," Vicky said.

"Your own brothers are such a disappointment in that regard. Leopold is so particularly ugly I find. Nothing like you, angel." Mama gazed over at Papa fondly.

LATER, IN THE evening, alone with her father, Vicky was more candid. They sat on the south terrace, listening to the pleasant hiss and patter of the fountain.

"It worries me constantly, Papa."

"His arm doesn't appear normal?" her father asked.

"No, it's completely limp and the fingers curl inward, like a claw."

"But Wegner thinks this is temporary?"

"He sees small improvements. I would say minuscule. The arm is bathed and rubbed with spirits all the time, but little changes," she said.

"Bring in a specialist, as your mother suggests."

"But how can I? Wegner will be so offended."

"Don't assume that," Papa said, shaking his head. "He wants the best for baby, *nicht wahr*?"

"I think so, but you know how people are, Papa, at court, and especially in Berlin. They don't want to lose face."

"You can't sacrifice the baby's well-being out of an exaggerated regard for Wegner's dignity," her father said.

"If I consult someone else, am I not saying that I have no confidence in his treatments?"

"What does Fritz think?"

"He thinks Wegner is careful and conscientious but won't object if we ask another doctor's opinion," she said.

"Then you should."

"Of course, Fritz expects a German doctor. There's already nasty gossip in the court that I use an English nursemaid because I don't think Prussian ones good enough."

Papa sighed. "This animosity toward you is very distressing."

"If only you could witness it, Papa, it's so nasty. Especially Fritz's Russian relations—the pointed remarks made, the whispering in each other's ears, and the upturned eyes—as soon as I come into a room."

"I am very sorry to hear it," he said.

"And all the etiquette! I can hardly keep track. Just before I came away the king wrote to berate me for going out in the city in a landaulet. A proper carriage drawn by four horses must always be used in Berlin. And they must be black, four black horses!"

Now Papa laughed. "Ludicrous!"

"Yes, I can't take such things too seriously. But about Willy's arm, I agonize endlessly."

"Of course."

"And if I consult another doctor all Berlin will know there's something wrong with him and I will be loathed even more." She struggled not to cry.

Papa looked at her so sorrowfully she regretted her frankness.

"Perhaps I am overstating it," she added quickly. "I know doctors are discreet. It's just that everything there gets blown out of proportion, quite easily."

"It's vital to find the right doctor," her father said.

"The leading Berlin surgeon is a gentleman called Professor von Langenbeck. I met him once at the Science Academy. He's a very confident man, long-winded and somewhat pompous, but people say he is very skilled."

"The best surgeons are confident, even arrogant, I find," Papa said. "Perhaps you have to be, to be willing to cut people open."

"But will he be discreet?"

"Tell him immediately when he arrives that you expect this. A man of honor will respect a woman's—a mother's—wishes."

"So, I'm not wrong to pursue it?" she asked.

"Not at all. You should do what is best for the baby."

"Thank you, Papa. If only I had you beside me every day."

"You're coping well, Puss."

"I wouldn't say that."

"And could I really help you?" he asked. "I have scant influence in Berlin, I fear. The Prince Regent never responds to any of my memoranda."

"You will always be a help to me, Papa. What I can't stand now is the not knowing. I am haunted by the idea that poor baby's arm will remain crooked and paralyzed forever, and end up one half the length of the other. Willy might never be able to eat without someone cutting his food, nor ride. What about that? Can you imagine a Prussian prince who can't ride properly?"

"Willy is still quite small. I am sure there is much that can be done," he said.

"I hope so. But I don't *know* so."

Her father smiled. "Who can see the future? A curse, but maybe a blessing, too."

AFTER TALKING TO Papa, she found worries about Willy's arm didn't intrude constantly into her thoughts. And the weather turned very fine, so she and Alice, sometimes accompanied by Lenchen, walked for miles through the meadows or searched for shells on the beach. She took distinct pleasure in pointing out that her shell collection—stored in a desk in the pink bedroom that had been hers—still surpassed everyone else's.

And she spent hours with Mama looking at the pictures in the house. The Hohenzollerns had never collected art, so she had a renewed appreciation for all the wonderful paintings that hung on the walls in English royal residences.

For Mama's birthday she organized the children to recite and perform, as she had always done. Even baby Beatrice, two years old, stumbled through some lines of Wordsworth, praising the daffodil.

She woke up on her last day in England content. She loved Osborne more than ever, but it was so painful being separated from Fritz, and soon that pain would be over. She had missed the baby too, but mostly Fritz. When in Windsor she had visited the rooms where they spent their short honeymoon, and she laughed at the memory of herself as a nervous, bashful bride. She sat on the edge of the bed they'd shared and felt a wave of longing for him, his musky smell, his long muscular legs intertwined with hers, the strength of his arms as he pressed her against him. It was a good thing no one guessed what an insatiable woman she was, always hungry for her husband's intimate embrace.

VICKY WAS ANNOYED to find, back in Berlin, that Fritz spent all his time laboring over the mobilization and was rarely at home with her. The Austrians, who were losing the war in Italy, still haggled over alliance terms, not willing for Prussia to appear to be the senior partner. While infuriated by the pigheaded Austrians, Fritz didn't let this or anything else distract him from his task. All day long he met with men from the railways and the telegraph companies setting up the communication and supply lines to the west. In reflective moments, Vicky thought mournfully that Fritz's intense efforts were in support of a larger aim she wasn't sure she agreed with: killing more French soldiers in a shorter amount of time. Still, she supposed he was ensuring Prussian soldiers had the weapons, food, and medicines they needed to win. And although she remembered with a pang her old friends Emperor Napoléon and Empress Eugénie—only four years ago they had been together in Paris—this whole conflict was the fault of Eugénie's foolish husband. He should never have incited the Italians and made war against the Austrians. It was high time that Germans stuck together and fought back against the pernicious, predatory French.

She hoped people in England could see it similarly. "With God's help the engagement will be short and successful and Prussia will help the Austrians, while securing for itself the position of first among German nations," Vicky wrote to Papa. He didn't like the prospect of war either, but he joined in her prayers for its quick conclusion.

Even after Austria conceded that the Prince Regent would be senior commander, Fritz's father did not immediately declare war because he had only a quarter of the men he needed in place. The French and their Italian allies took advantage of this delay and engaged the Austrians near the town of Mantua on June 24. The Austrian emperor, Franz Joseph, led his troops personally, and he was beaten badly.

Fritz despaired. "We have allowed the enemy to get so far ahead of us."

"But when you are on the field, it won't matter," Vicky said.

"Hard to know," he said, looking gloomy.

Finally, a week later, a decision: Prussia would declare war against France on July 12. Fritz and his father planned a special dinner for army top commanders at the Königliches Palais on the eve of the announcement. "You don't mind holding it here?" Fritz asked. "Our dining room is so much nicer than that echoing barn of a hall at the *Schloss*."

"I don't mind at all," said Vicky. "I want to do something to help."

VICKY ACTED AS sole hostess since Fritz's mother had left Berlin, bitter and aggrieved. Princess Augusta thought her husband foolhardy to go to war against Europe's most powerful army, and she had told Fritz and Vicky the same. When they hadn't agreed with her, she had roundly abused them for their gullibility and departed to stay with Louise in Karlsruhe.

Fritz and Vicky decided that instead of the traditional long
table, their sixty guests would be accommodated more comfortably at eight round tables in front of a head table. The elegant
cream-colored room with fluted pilasters at each corner and four
high windows overlooking Unter den Linden needed little extra
light to keep it bright and festive on a long summer evening. Still,
she directed the servants to place, at either end of the head table,
the two large crystal candelabra that she and Fritz had received
as a wedding gift from Napoléon and Eugénie: an ironical gesture for her private amusement—though she planned to tell her
husband later, for a laugh.

Vicky didn't take a seat for the meal and instead circulated
among the tables, wishing each man a good supper and a successful campaign. So many praised Fritz and told her how proud
they were to fight alongside him. Vicky prayed fervently all these
handsome, brave men would return safely, and she found their
excitement and commitment contagious. Tears came to her eyes
when, just before the first course was served, a tall officer with a
fine tenor voice got up to sing the anthem of the Prussian army:

Üb'immer Treu und Redlichkeit bis an dein kühles Grab
Und weiche keinen Fingerbreit von Gottes Wegen ab

She suddenly felt so keenly the sterling virtues of Fritz's countrymen. The court was an ugly place, a distortion of the nation—
ordinary Prussians had no ridiculous pretensions; most aspired
to practice honesty and fidelity, as the words of the song said,
striving to be loyal to God's teaching, unto death. For a few long,
aching moments, she regretted she was not a man and could not
join these men and follow Fritz into battle.

At his seat of honor at the center of the head table, Prince
Wilhelm glowed with vigor and contentment. He rose to his feet
several times to propose toasts. Last, and most heartfelt, was
his tribute to Fritz. "My son has devoted himself to the preparations. A patriot and an excellent leader of men, he's a vital help

to me, his aging father. I know he will distinguish himself on the battlefield!" Every man in the room pounded fists on the table in minutes-long acclaim, and Fritz Karl stood to embrace Fritz—the two cousins, so often rivals, had become like brothers as they prepared to go off to war.

Two hours passed. The party grew raucous and noisy, the room filling with cigar and pipe smoke, and much wine and beer was consumed. Now the songs the men sang were drinking ditties that Vicky didn't recognize. Time to go to bed—no one would miss her. At the door, she nearly collided with a short, uniformed man in a pointed hat, a leather bag thrown across his chest. Clearly a messenger. She turned and watched as he cut quickly through the tables and handed an envelope to the Prince Regent. She saw her father-in-law open it and unfold the paper within. He gestured for quiet. Someone chimed on a glass, someone else shouted, "*Achtung!*" Prince Wilhelm stood up, swaying a bit, and all turned to him, expectant.

"I have just been informed," he said slowly in a low, deliberate voice, "that a peace treaty has been signed between the emperor of Austria and the emperor of France."

Total silence. Vicky's eyes darted to Fritz, and just as she'd feared, he appeared stricken. Fritz Karl, beside him, had covered his face with his hands.

THE WAR THAT didn't happen felt like a catastrophe. Melancholy weighed down Fritz, his father, and everyone at court in the weeks that followed. Late in the evenings Vicky would hear Fritz Karl in the drawing room downstairs, shouting about Austrian treachery—Franz Joseph had forged an early peace as revenge for Prussian insistence on leading the German troops. Fritz agreed, but he also despaired to Vicky over what had been the snail-like pace of mobilization. The vaunted Prussian military machine was, in truth, creaky and inefficient, and desperately needed modernizing. Fritz and his father began cataloging the improvements that could wait no longer.

Her husband also devoted hours to drilling the soldiers under his command, spending several nights a week at the barracks. Prince Wilhelm fell into a deep gloom, and everyone was afraid to speak to him. Fritz said his father felt angry and humiliated because in this, his first foray into foreign affairs as Prince Regent, he had antagonized Austria and done nothing to beat back renascent France.

Meanwhile, a Hanoverian nobleman, Rudolf von Bennigsen, established a new organization: the Nationalverein, a group of parliamentary deputies, professors, lawyers, and journalists. They announced their intention to ceaselessly lobby the Prussian government until the Prince Regent and Prince Charles Hohenzollern agreed to establish, in the territory of so-called Kleindeutschland— the German states without Austria—the United Kingdom of Germany, a constitutional monarchy with the Prussian king as king of Germany, the way King Victor Emmanuel of Sardinia was poised to become king of Italy.

Papa, writing furious letters to Vicky, wondered why Prince Wilhelm didn't just embrace the group's agenda and get on with it.

For the first time Vicky sensed her father lived too far away to see the situation clearly. While she was so vastly relieved that the war hadn't come, that Fritz had never left her, that he'd never been in danger, she hated that her frustrated husband, hopes dashed, had become very depressed. His face always looked heavy and joyless. Only playing with Willy cheered him a bit. He said to her one evening, seemingly out of the blue: "What if that was it? Maybe I missed my only chance to become the man I so much want to be."

"I don't understand, darling," Vicky said. "You have a long life ahead. There will be other chances. And you are needed for so many better—"

"It's true, you don't understand," he said, cutting her off. He was suddenly furious and got up and stalked out of the room. She was astonished. Why was he so offended? He wasn't born to be a soldier, or even a general like Moltke, but a king. Did it matter so much that he'd not gone to war now? Hadn't Papa always said he should stop caring exclusively about Prussia's army and concentrate on political reforms?

She went upstairs to their bedroom to get ready for bed. More than an hour passed as she waited for him to join her, anxiety growing. Perhaps she had misspoken. Better to have just listened and acknowledged his feelings without commenting. He was sorely disappointed. She knew that. If only he would come and she could soothe him.

She fell asleep and woke in the morning to find his side of the bed still made up, undisturbed. She walked down the short hallway to his dressing room, where he sometimes spent the night when she was unwell. And, yes, the bed there had been slept in, but he was nowhere in sight. She felt a stab of dismay. She longed to speak to him, if not to apologize exactly, at least to acknowledge she hadn't fully appreciated his state of mind.

Downstairs a footman told her the prince had finished breakfast and left the palace already. She sat down at her desk and tried to think if she should send him a message. To say what exactly? Just then a second footman came in with a note addressed to her in Fritz's hand. She opened it with shaking fingers.

"Dearest, forgive my foul temper. I will see you this evening and I will be restored," he had written.

That evening he kissed her and then recounted his day as if nothing had happened between them. She decided not to press the question. In the weeks that followed she listened carefully as he talked about the plans he was writing for the newly organized army and his descriptions of the frequent Crown Council meetings, at which the ministers argued over how to cope with the Austrians, the French, the disgruntled German nationalists. She began to understand why the Prince Regent wasn't leaping into nation-building as Papa hoped. She came to see that above all else Fritz's father desired never again to be caught unable to move his forces into place swiftly. He needed to feel competent in his *Kommandogewalt*, power of command, which, under the Prus-

sian constitution, was the monarch's alone, and included everything about how the army functioned. He was supreme warlord
of Prussia, as one day Fritz would be. And the two of them took
this duty more seriously than any other. Maybe in future, when,
years hence, they were king and queen, Vicky would be able to
nudge Fritz in a different direction. But that was not today. At
this moment, military reform was all Fritz and his father thought
about, all they cared about.

ON THE TWENTY-SEVENTH of July Vicky received Professor Langenbeck at the Königliches Palais. The doctor assured her of complete discretion, but otherwise his visit proved disappointing.

Willy, six months old now, was brought into the drawing room
by Mrs. Hobbs. Langenbeck requested that towels be spread out
on the side table and he spent a half hour examining the baby.
Cheerful Willy gurgled in a very winning way. Vicky watched
the doctor move the baby's arm in all directions, and look at the
other arm too, before flipping the baby over on his stomach and
spending much time massaging and pressing his finger into the
flesh between Willy's neck and the top of his shoulder.

"Your Highness, the prince is a robust little fellow, alert and
responsive," Langenbeck said finally.

"Yes, yes," said Vicky.

"The arm is a good deal better than Dr. Wegner led me to believe, and it is not so much smaller than the other. And the shoulder is not dislocated, nor are any bones broken," the doctor said.

"Still, he does not move it naturally."

"It moves a bit from the shoulder, but not the elbow."

She had heard all this before. "What do you believe the cause
to be?"

"I don't disagree with Dr. Wegner. There must have been bruising of the softer structures at the time of birth."

"Can these structures be restored?"

"More time and treatment will be needed."

Langenbeck made two suggestions. The first one, bizarre, was the so-called *animalische Bad*—animal bath. Twice a week, Fräulein Stahl was to put Willy's arm into a freshly slaughtered hare, so the warmth and vigor of the animal could be transferred to the arm. She laughed when she told Fritz about this, but her husband liked the idea. Vicky thought it horrid, and sure to be of no use, but Fritz was so keen, she couldn't refuse to try it.

Langenbeck also told them to bind Willy's good, right arm to his body for several hours a day, to force baby to use his left one instead. "As he begins to walk this will be particularly helpful, Your Highness, because the little chap will improve his balance and strengthen the left side and arm as much as his right."

The surgeon left with a courteous bow and many compliments to Vicky and Mrs. Hobbs on Willy's otherwise good health.

"He said nothing much at all," she wrote to Papa that evening. "He said he hoped it would come right soon and we should try binding the arm, but this sort of thing does not satisfy me. I want to know exactly what he thinks. What caused the injury? Why does it not improve? What will baby have to cope with in future? He said nothing of any of this."

She finished the letter, sealed it, and sat back in her chair. She was in such a strange, baffling position. She had joined a family, and a court, where she could not be candid and her opinions were not welcome. Yet, few people would be honest with her. Berlin's leading doctor wanted to reassure her, not inform her. Infuriating. She'd come to Prussia to put her life to good use, and even in this personal realm, she was thwarted. What way forward? She didn't know. So much for her purported cleverness. She sighed and turned out the desk lamp.

15

Coburg, September 1860

*A*lthough the dates did not align precisely, Vicky always chose
to believe that her second baby was conceived at Windsor. Fritz
had agreed to take a respite from work and accompany her to
Bertie's eighteenth-birthday celebration, and stepping onto English
soil on her husband's arm, her spirits soared. On the train up to
London, sitting at a little table across from Fritz, she watched the
benevolent green landscape rush by, savoring the sound of cheery
English voices and the taste of hot, strong English tea. She even
approved of the misty, mild November weather—back in Prussia
winter chill had set in already. At her old home, surrounded by
loving faces, she felt in such harmony with existence that every
gesture was natural and sure, every conversation sparkling, and her
intimacy with Fritz once again immersive. No wonder a new life
started to grow inside her.

The months of pregnancy followed on smoothly. She felt less
sick this time, and for the last stretch, she lived in Potsdam, where
they now had a summer residence of their own, the Neues Palais.
Frederick the Great's last architectural endeavor, this was a vast,
200-room structure crowned by an enormous green-copper
dome, with stucco walls painted to look like brick. But Vicky loved

the sunny residential apartments at the south end of the palace, and vowed to make them even more comfortable in years to come. Fritz requested Dr. Martin attend again, and the physician insisted on several internal examinations, to which Vicky submitted this time, and without complaint. From the start she was sure all would be well, and the labor, easy and relatively speedy, confirmed her intuition. Fritz rubbed her feet during the worst pains. Charlotte arrived at the end of a warm July evening and, presented to Vicky, looked every inch the perfect baby princess.

All very pleasing. Only a small circle of family and friends knew about Willy's arm, but any comment or question regarding it—however kindly meant—felt to Vicky like a reproach. Her beautiful girl garnered only praise.

Mama and Papa, impatient to meet both grandchildren, proposed a visit to Potsdam. But Fritz told her to put them off—the mood in Berlin and within his family had turned sour. Early in the summer the Prussian parliament had rejected the budget, which included increased funding for army reform, enraging the Prince Regent, who refused to countenance any modification to his plan. But Fritz's mother advised her husband he would do grave harm to the country if he defied his deputies' wishes, and the liberal papers preached the same. Should Prince Albert arrive and join the scolding chorus, Fritz worried his father would lash out, perhaps causing a permanent rift between Vicky's father and his own. Better Papa not come at all.

Vicky was struggling to think of an excuse to give her parents when a piece of sad family news solved her problem. Duchess Marie, Papa's stepmother and the wife of his late father, Ernest, Duke of Saxe-Coburg, died of an infection. The funeral service would be held in Coburg on September 20, so they agreed to meet there.

WHAT WOULD MAMA and Papa, with nine children of their own, think of her William? He understood everything said to him in German or in English, but at twenty months old, he did not use words, and he was often cross, agitated, and restless. He had learned to walk, but he moved unsteadily and often tumbled over. The good, right arm was bound to his body half the day—and that aggravated his poor balance and caused frequent tantrums. Despite the binding and regular *animalische Bäder,* his left arm still hung—stubbornly—limp and useless.

Vicky had fed baby Charlotte herself for a few days before passing her to a wet nurse. No point rowing with her mother and mother-in-law, and she had worried that Willy, already violently jealous, would scream to see the baby constantly at her mother's breast. Fritz loved *"die Kleinste,"* as he called Charlotte, but he didn't see her much. And he remained disheartened that the good feeling between him and his father, so remarkable last year, had disappeared.

Many in parliament distrusted Prince Wilhelm now as well, and they didn't want him succeeding the dying king, preferring to skip right to Fritz, who, they imagined, would compromise with the people's representatives and be less fixated on spending huge amounts on the army. When a bold group of deputies sought out Fritz at his barracks and told him of their desire to set aside the Prince Regent when the throne became vacant, he went directly to his father to report the plot. Rather than commend Fritz for his loyalty, Prince Wilhelm had called him a Judas and had barely spoken to him since.

Vicky suspected—and tried to convince Fritz—that his father didn't really believe his son would betray him. Rather, he hated that he was losing control in Prussia before he even ruled in his own right. While in public Fritz supported his father's military reforms—which he'd helped to write—in private, he was worried that the deadlock with parliament made Prussia look backward and autocratic, little better than the czar's Russia. Most of all, he wished he and his father were on better terms.

WHEN VICKY MET her parents off the train at Coburg, she noticed immediately that Papa was not well—his face was pale and drawn, and he bent over in an odd way as he walked along the platform. She waited to be alone with her mother in the upstairs sitting room at Schloss Ehrenburg, Duke Ernest's home, to inquire about him.

"He had an attack of stomach cramps, with a fever and chills, last week," Mama said, shaking her head, more irritated than dismayed.

"Why didn't you write to tell me?"

"He didn't want you to be concerned, as he would be seeing you so soon."

"He looks dreadful. Doesn't it worry you?"

"Yes, of course, but he so often moans and fusses. I never know when it's serious." Mama frowned. "And he exhausts himself with work. That's the real problem."

Standing there—pink-cheeked, bright-eyed—her mother looked the very picture of health. Vicky couldn't remember a time when she'd ever been ailing. Only when having a baby. Her mother's robust constitution must have been one reason she got impatient with Papa, who was so susceptible to illness, especially when under strain. Vicky hoped that here in his old home her father would soon improve.

PAPA DID LOOK somewhat better later that afternoon, when, after a nap, he joined them in the drawing room. Once they were all assembled—her parents, Uncle Ernest and Aunt Alexandrina, Fritz and herself—Vicky had Mrs. Hobbs bring Willy in to meet everyone. Dressed in a cunning little sailor's outfit that Mama had sent for him, he looked so angelic that Vicky had to smother a laugh. He was hardly the boy she knew. Mama and Papa marveled at his smooth white skin, his pleasing plumpness, his very fair curly hair and blue eyes. They took turns holding him and soon the whole company debated: whom did Willy most resemble? Mama couldn't decide between Fritz, Affie, and Papa himself. When Fritz suggested a likeness to his sister, Louise, Mama scoffed. Papa said the baby was so handsome he was surely meant for great things.

Mama agreed. "Perhaps he will be called William the Wise when he becomes king!"

Holding the baby, Papa examined his left arm, lifting it up a few times. But he made no comment. After Mama settled Willy on her lap, she turned to Vicky and said: "His left arm appears quite the same as the other. As he gets older, it will get stronger. Don't let it preoccupy you."

Willy sat patiently on his grandmother's knee for ten minutes, but then he reached out his right arm to his favorite person, his father, and squawked. Fritz walked across the room to pick him up. As Fritz swung him high into the air, Willy giggled delightedly. Then Fritz started to march in place and sing an army tune: *"Da war ein Soldat treu und wahr . . ."* Willy sang along as best he could and moved in time in Fritz's arms. Adorable.

Vicky gave Willy a hug and many kisses before he was taken off to have his supper. She felt very proud.

A TRAIN OF twenty-five had come with Mama and Papa to Coburg, so many dear, familiar faces among them. She caught sight of tall Henry Ponsonby at the station but had only time to wave. A few minutes later, following Mama and Papa toward the carriages, she encountered Mary. "Let's walk together in the garden this evening before dinner, dear Mary," Vicky said, squeezing the lady's hand. "It's been too long since we've really spoken."

She was astonished to come downstairs at six and find that Mary waited there with Henry beside her. Something about their glad expressions gave Vicky an inkling of their news.

"We're taking the opportunity to tell you in person," said Mary as soon as they were outside.

"The queen and Prince Albert do not yet know," continued Henry.

"But we plan to marry at Christmastime," finished Mary.

"How wonderful!" exclaimed Vicky. Mary must have been nearly twenty-eight now. Old not to be married.

"We give credit to you," said Henry, beaming with his character-istic good humor. "When you were gone from England we both missed you, and often spoke of you."

"I must frequently remind Henry of your dictate: a walk, to be a proper walk, must be of half an hour's duration. He's very feeble and sometimes attempts to retreat inside after a mere ten minutes, especially when it begins to rain." Mary looked up at her fiancé, pretending to be stern.

"And Mary will say she's read a book when actually she's only finished the first half and scanned the last chapters. A deception she told me you never practice, Princess," Henry said in a mock-earnest tone of his own.

Vicky laughed, delighted to think these lovely friends hadn't forgotten her.

Later that evening, catching Mary alone, Vicky said again how pleased she was to hear of their engagement.

"I fear your mother will be extremely vexed," Mary said. "She is quite used to me by this time and Henry would like to leave the court, at least temporarily, to join the foreign department and live abroad."

"She will miss you keenly, Mary, I have no doubt, but you have given her many years of devoted service. Now is your chance for happiness. You must take it."

"Thank you, Princess. I think we will be happy together. We laugh at all the same things."

"An admirable foundation for any marriage—and very English."

THE DUCHESS'S FUNERAL took place the next day—the weather appropriately wet and dreary. Their third day in Coburg dawned sunny and autumnally cool. At breakfast Papa looked very pale and his teacup trembled as he lifted it to his mouth, but he an-nounced they would visit the Rosenau, the hunting lodge several miles outside of Coburg where Papa and his brother had spent so much time growing up. "I have been impatient for you to see this, Vicky, the paradise of my childhood," he said, smiling at her from across the table.

The party went in three carriages—Papa directing that she and he share the last one. They rode out of Schloss Ehrenburg, rattling over the cobblestones of the narrow, medieval town streets and then into the countryside along a wide, sandy road. Farm fields gave way to forest, and soon heavy trees pressed in on either side, most still full and green, some with flares of yellow leaves. As they approached the lodge, Papa knocked on the box and told the coachman to stop. He wanted to walk the rest of the way along a shortcut he had used as a boy.

Climbing down, Vicky breathed in the rich, moist scent of the woods. A dirt path ahead of them wound away under heavy black tree limbs. Only the occasional chirp and screech of a bird broke the deep quiet—it was a fairy-tale setting, like one imagined by the Brothers Grimm.

"Oh, Papa, so peaceful."

He smiled and held out his arm. "Now, we walk and you tell me all."

As they proceeded, arm in arm, down the path, Vicky attempted to describe the situation in Berlin—cautiously, for she worried Papa would become infuriated, and that couldn't be good for him. Her father had read about the Prince Regent's impasse with parliament, but he'd had no news directly from Fritz's father, and he hadn't understood until Vicky told him that the Prince Regent had refused several compromise proposals. "He wants the whole package, every single measure. He says it's his right. His *Kommandogewalt*," Vicky explained.

Papa shook his head. "He can't dictate to them in every regard. He has to give in on some things. It's their budget to control."

"He says if parliament won't agree, he will dissolve parliament."

"But Fritz advises him not to do this, *nicht wahr?*"

"Papa, Prince Wilhelm barely speaks to Fritz."

"What!" Papa stopped and looked at her, astonished.

"He's got it in his head that Fritz secretly supports his enemies and would be happy to see him pushed aside when the king dies."

Papa shook his head again. "Doesn't he know his own son? Fritz should reassure him. Do they see each other most days?"

"They see each other at weekly Crown Council meetings, during which Fritz is allowed to say nothing, and they never confer."

Papa was silent, contemplative, as they resumed walking.

"Dark days indeed then at the Black Horse Inn," Papa said finally, giving her a sad smile.

She returned the smile but shook her finger, saying: "I told you, you mustn't say that." Last year, when she'd been at Windsor for Bertie's party, Papa had taken to calling the Berlin court "the Black Horse Inn" and her father-in-law "the innkeeper."

"I promise, never in front of Fritz," her father said. To hear Papa making fun of the Prince Regent, and the absurd levels of self-importance in the Hohenzollern court, would be so hurtful to Fritz, who found court formality unremarkable. It had been bred into him, she had come to see.

"Fritz must recognize his father's stance is unacceptable," her father continued.

"Papa, darling Fritz is in a terrible position. You know he reveres his father and is devoted to the army. He desires full funding for the plan and also the three-year term of service for conscripts the king is set on."

"But this can't be at the expense of parliament's authority."

"Fritz doesn't like the standoff. But when I ask him how a compromise could be reached, he says he's not sure."

"I must speak to him today about this," said Papa.

"Don't lecture him, Papa, promise me."

"There's no going backward, Puss. The innkeeper can't reject parliament's decision. It doesn't matter if all those reprobates in the court egg him on."

"Fritz knows this. Still, it's complicated for him. His loyalties are divided."

"The truth isn't negotiable!" Her father's eyes blazed. "You can't believe in a parliamentary government and then not let parliament do its job."

"In Prussia they're just getting started. I understand that better now. How long has there even been a parliament? Twelve years, that's all."

"Which is no excuse. Not only is the king shirking his duty, he is leaving the door open for radicals who would overturn the monarchy entirely," Papa said, insistent.

"I agree with you, of course. But it's impossible for Fritz to condemn his father. Please, Papa, let's not argue at the moment. Let's just enjoy the day, our holiday," she said.

They'd come to a low wooden gate, which Papa opened for her. They entered the park. Ahead of them, across a rolling lawn and up on a small rise, she could see the lodge, painted yellow.

"There it is!" she exclaimed. "Tell me, when was the house first built?" *Best to distract Papa now,* she thought, and waited for his disquisition on the history of the Rosenau.

But instead her father stopped and gripped his stomach.

"*Dieser Schmerz!*" He stooped over and groaned.

"Papa, what is it? Where is your pain?"

He didn't answer at first, and Vicky crouched down to look into his grimacing face.

"I must sit," he said.

She spotted a small iron bench, some twenty yards ahead, perched on the bank of an ornamental pond. "Look, can you reach that seat?" she said, pointing.

He nodded, and slowly they walked toward it. Holding his arm, she could feel her father shaking, and when she sat him down his face was gray and perspiring.

"I'm going to fetch Fritz," she said. "You must wait here."

She hiked up her skirts and ran as quickly as she could up the hill to the house. What a relief to find Fritz, with the rest of their party, still outside, admiring the yellow gables, the Gothic casement windows, and the stepped-up roof. He quickly returned with her to where Papa sat, bent over.

"Here, let me carry you," said Fritz, endeavoring to slip one arm under Papa's knees.

"No, no, I can walk," her father replied.

They each took an arm and carefully hauled Papa to his feet and helped him traverse very slowly up the rise and inside. He lay down on the sofa in the front parlor and closed his eyes.

"Vicky, you have exhausted him!" Mama said accusingly after she and Fritz left Papa to rest and came out into the hall, closing the door behind them.

"Mama, no, it was only a short walk up from where the carriage set us down. He was very content to be walking and then, suddenly, he said he had a terrible pain in his stomach."

"It's infuriating. Dr. Clark told him not to travel if not totally well, and he assured us all he was all better. Clearly not." Her mother scowled at Vicky before clucking discontentedly and going to sit with Uncle Ernest and Aunt Alexandrina on the back terrace.

PAPA WOKE UP after an hour, eager to continue the day as if his "brief attack," as he called it, had never happened. They had luncheon. Papa took them on a tour of the house, pointing out the reading nook in the library, the line of stag's heads mounted in the upstairs hall, the stars painted on the ceiling of the pretty yellow front room. They walked the hilly terrain behind the house and Papa said to Vicky: "Now you see why I love Scotland so particularly. It reminds me of home."

But Vicky felt unnerved by his collapse.

"You saw how much pain he was in? His face sweating? And he was nearly panting as we walked him into the house," she said to Fritz that night as they got ready for bed.

"He is not well, certainly."

"And Mama is quite unsympathetic. As if it's all some plot to inconvenience her!"

"Perhaps she feels a bit responsible. He complained to me yesterday of too much work and not enough good rests in these past months."

"Like your own existence, dear heart."

"But your father lacks his usual vitality. He seems downhearted."

"I agree. He's not himself."

She didn't mention to Fritz how irate Papa had become hearing about the situation in Berlin—nor how his terrible pain had followed directly on after her account.

AT LUNCHEON THE next day Vicky was relieved that instead of discussing Prussian politics Papa turned the conversation to Mama's favorite subject—a bride for Bertie.

Bertie, as heir, couldn't marry a mere English noblewoman. Nor could Catholics be countenanced, which ruled out women from the French, Spanish, and Austrian royal houses. Scandinavians were acceptable. The Dutch too. But a German princess would be ideal, and quite what Mama was used to. She had instructed Vicky and Fritz to be on the lookout.

Papa, too, was preoccupied by Bertie's marital prospects— he didn't want the boy to have time for ill-advised "adventures." Better get him a wife soon, he often declared.

At his eighteenth-birthday party, Bertie had told Vicky he had no intention of marrying immediately and certainly not to any woman he didn't admire. "Mama showed me a picture the other day of the horse-faced Princess Marie of the Netherlands. Plain, but with a lovely figure, she said. I just laughed. Hard to get beyond the face."

Vicky spent many chilly Berlin evenings with Fritz away studying the *Almanach de Gotha*, the hefty directory of European royalty. As it happened, her first discovery had had unforeseen consequences.

The ancestral lands of the Hesses of Darmstadt lay near Frankfurt. The Grand Duke of Hesse and by Rhine, to use his full title, had no children of his own, but his brother Charles, set to inherit, had three sons and a daughter, Anna. Vicky had heard from Marianne that young Anna was vivacious and appealing. She had promptly taken a trip to Darmstadt under the guise of visiting some notable churches in the area. Anna had turned out to be lively, yes, but she had a dumpy figure, a terrible complexion, and worst of all, an eye twitch.

"She shares this unfortunate habit with her father and her second brother, Heinrich," Vicky had written to Mama. Louis, the oldest brother, had no twitch. Tall, with wavy brown hair and a neat mustache, he had excellent manners and seemed kind. Perhaps a potential husband for Alice, Vicky had thought, and urged Mama to invite Louis and Heinrich to England. They had gone for the Ascot races this past June and her parents liked both boys. Better still, Alice and Louis had gotten on marvelously. When it came time for Louis to return home, he'd asked for Alice's photograph. And now the two of them corresponded.

"Of course, Alice is only seventeen. Far too young to get married," Mama said now.

Vicky noticed Fritz smile into his soup.

"Let's go over the other choices for Bertie," Mama demanded. "I heard a good report about Elisabeth of Wied. Said to be sensible and good-humored."

"I met her in Berlin," said Vicky. "She is boisterous and not pretty enough. Bertie won't like her."

"Princess Marie of Leuchtenberg, isn't she one of dear Augusta's cousins?"

"Terrible teeth—almost black," said Fritz.

"What about Prince Hohenzollern's Swabian niece? She's called Stephanie, I think."

"She's twelve, Mama," said Vicky.

"We can't wait that long," said Papa.

"Given all this, we must seriously consider the Danish option," said Vicky.

Fritz groaned.

Papa smiled.

Mama frowned.

After a lightning courtship last year, Wally Hohenthal had married a wealthy British diplomat called Sir Augustus Paget and gone to live in Copenhagen, where Paget was ambassador. There husband and wife had met the Danish royal family, including two beautiful young princesses, Alexandra and her little sister Dagmar. Wally had written to Vicky to say that the charming Alexandra, called Alix, was now sixteen, and was not only tall, slender, and lovely, but she spoke German, French, and English very well, and danced beautifully.

Exactly the sort of woman Bertie would be willing to marry, but unfortunately, particularly from Fritz's point of view, Danish. Denmark controlled the German-speaking duchies of Schleswig and Holstein, causing resentment throughout Germany. Vicky often heard the situation described in Berlin as "the enduring shame." A marital alliance between England and Denmark was bound to offend the Prussians deeply.

"Perhaps it's just a matter of presentation," Papa said now. "The young people could meet and become enraptured with each other; then it's not a political matter but a love match, like your own, Fritz. Who would stand in the way of love?"

"I can think of a few people in Berlin," said Fritz.

Everyone laughed. But Vicky knew it wasn't really a joke.

"Let's show Anna and Elisabeth to Bertie first," said Mama. "Perhaps he will like one of them and then we would be safe. No need for the paragon from Denmark."

As Bertie was away on a North American tour for three months, showings would have to take place later in the year.

DUKE ERNEST HOSTED a large banquet in their honor that evening, during which there were no opportunities for further family discussion. The next day, with Fritz and herself and the children due to return to Potsdam, Vicky was on guard, watching Papa carefully to see what he would say to Fritz. At breakfast her father seemed tired but calm and spoke of nothing important, only a new clock tower going up in the Coburg town square. But at eleven A.M., when they stood in the front hall, packed and ready to leave—Mama had gone out to take a last look at her grandchildren, settled in the first carriage with Mrs. Hobbs—Papa cleared his throat.

"I have heard enough, dear Fritz, from Vicky and from others to understand something of your current difficulties," he said.

Fritz nodded. She sensed he was immediately wary.

"I would like to advise you," Papa continued. "But, of course, in the end, a man must chart his own course, as he thinks best."

"*So ist es,*" Fritz said. That's the truth.

"I would only say, as you have heard me say before, that a monarch truly responsible to the people cannot act in defiance of the people's representatives. Should that occur it would be terrible for Prussia, and in all the places where Prussia is looked upon as a natural leader," Papa said.

"I never forget what you have told me about government," Fritz replied.

"It's worrisome that your father is not open to a path of compromise," Papa said.

"He cannot—" Fritz stopped, reluctant to be drawn into any criticism of the Prince Regent. "It is my duty to support him. In any way I can."

"I understand," said Papa, "but there are larger principles at stake, don't you admit?"

"Certainly," Fritz said with a sigh.

"History has shown that when a monarch fails to find a reasonable way to lead, there is likely to be some violent break, with men on one side or another seizing power," Papa continued. "Should that happen . . . well, then all will be lost. Better to give in on small matters than lose authority totally."

Fritz nodded. They walked through the door, out into the sunny *Schlossplatz,* their carriage waiting. Vicky was relieved.

Papa hadn't chastised Fritz or accused him of falling short of his expectations.

As they drove away, she leaned out the window to wave. Her father appeared small, stooped, and a bit forlorn, standing motionless next to Mama, who, in a white lace dress and blue bonnet, fluttered her white handkerchief in the air to bid them farewell.

16

Berlin and the Isle of Wight, January–July 1861

*O*n a bitterly cold night in January at the Sanssouci Palace in Potsdam, the king breathed his last. With a dozen other members of the family, Vicky and Fritz stood as silent witnesses around a massive oak bed as the candles burned down to their sockets. Queen Elisabeth sat in a chair, beside where her unconscious husband lay. For the final hour she remained motionless, bent over with one arm slipped under his neck, resting her head next to his on the pillow.

Vicky was now Crown princess, while Fritz was now Crown prince, the direct heir to the throne. Their home was no longer called the Königliches Palais, instead the Kronprinzenpalais. Preparations began for King Wilhelm's coronation in the autumn. Fritz, among many, urged his father to hold the ceremony in Berlin, the modern center of government. But the new king wanted to crown himself in the traditional way at the Schlosskirche in Königsberg, just as Friedrich I, the first Hohenzollern king, had done in 1701. This gesture—to take the crown and place it on his own head—signified personal sovereignty, that his authority descended directly from God. The king's ministers advised

that a constitutional monarch in the age of representative government should not follow feudal custom, but he would not be
swayed.

This conflict aside, Fritz and his father got on better in the first
months after the old king's death than they had in a long time.
Her husband came home every night in a happy frame of mind,
delighting always to tell her how much progress he and his father
and Moltke were making, especially with the distribution of the
Dreyse needle gun, a special type of fast-shooting rifle that had
been previously too expensive to issue to the whole army. Now
the Krupp company could manufacture thousands of the necessary cast-steel barrels in a single week. Who would have thought
she'd ever care about guns? But she wanted to share Fritz's interests, even the militaristic ones, and on this matter he reminded
her of Papa, extolling the wonders of modern industry.

Parliament had granted temporary funding to establish a number of new regiments. On February 12, father and son presented
colors to these fresh troops at a jubilant ceremony held in front
of Friedrich the Great's tomb in Potsdam. "All rancor forgotten,
we rode together out onto the field side by side," Fritz told her.
"It was a beautiful occasion. Uplifting. Rank after rank of men
saluting and then cheering wildly."

At the beginning of March, the king dissolved the parliament
and scheduled elections for later in the year, to restart negotiations over the future of the army with a new chamber of deputies.

"Maybe it's for the best," said Vicky when Fritz told her.

"*Bestimmt*. I believe so. My father said today that while he
doesn't think a constitution is necessarily conducive to the well-
being of a nation, having found one, it's his responsibility to conform to it. That's something, don't you think?"

Vicky and Fritz laughed together over that. The new king, aged
sixty-four, might never climb to Papa's heights of liberalism, they
agreed, but feeling duty-bound to follow constitutional precepts
was an acceptable stance to start a new reign.

WHEN VICKY SUGGESTED they go to Osborne with the children for a summer holiday, Fritz at first resisted, fearing to shatter the fragile rapprochement with his father by requesting to take his whole family abroad and into Prince Albert's company. But in June the king suggested the trip himself. He was leaving for Baden, to rest up for the coronation, and he proposed Fritz and Vicky likewise go away.

"Maybe he felt a little guilty, too, for his bad temper previously," Fritz said. On March 16, Grandmamma had died suddenly, and Vicky had departed for London without asking the king's formal permission, assuming that Fritz could just inform him. At Windsor, sitting beside Mama while her mother soaked one handkerchief after another with tears, Vicky received a scathing letter from her father-in-law demanding to know why he had learned in the newspapers she'd left the country. Fritz had apparently not seen him in time. She wrote back immediately, apologizing, and Papa did too, but everyone at court heard the king grumbling about Vicky's transgression until Fritz asked him please to stop, saying his wife had meant no disrespect.

All this behind them now, they were settled happily at Osborne House. And while her mother still mourned copiously, Alice, now engaged to Prince Louis of Hesse, was laughing and rushing around excitedly all day, chatting about her husband-to-be with anyone who would listen.

"Louis worries that because Darmstadt isn't as grand as London, after we marry I will wish myself back, but I won't, Vicky, I know I won't," said Alice during one of their frequent walks. "He is the kindest, most wonderful man imaginable."

Vicky smiled. Lovely to see Alice, usually quite serious, infatuated with her groom-to-be. It reminded Vicky of her own delight when she and Fritz were first engaged.

"Mind you, Papa said the wedding will not take place until next summer at the earliest," said Alice. Her sister had just turned eighteen.

"A year's not that long," Vicky replied, squeezing Alice's hand.

Vicky felt proud of her part in securing her sister's happiness and was spurred on in the search for Bertie's bride. Her brother had spent the past year studying at Oxford and between terms had visited them in Berlin, where he caught sight of Elisabeth of Wied. "Not at all lovely," he declared, and refused to consider her further. Reports of Anna of Hesse's twitch had reached him independently, so he dismissed that possibility also. Back to Alexandra of Denmark. In the spring Vicky had traveled with Fritz to Strelitz when the young princess and her mother were visiting mutual friends. She'd admired Alexandra from the first moment they were introduced. Soft-spoken but assured, the girl was a good deal taller than Vicky, slender, with thick dark hair and a peachy complexion. She carried herself beautifully, having been instructed in ballet, and her large blue eyes looked out on life with such gentleness.

Wally had obtained a photo of Princess Alexandra, and Vicky had brought it to Osborne to show her parents. After it was passed around before supper the first night, Papa declared: "I would marry her immediately!"

Maybe that irritated Mama, because she was still agonized by the thought that the girl wouldn't do. She'd heard rumors that Alexandra's mother had had an affair, and her grand-uncle the current king of Denmark had divorced two previous wives and lived with a third, morganatic, one. "It's a bad family, clearly," Mama said.

Bertie was away in Ireland with the army for the summer. But Fritz had written to him enumerating the girl's charms, and Bertie allowed that Vicky could set up a "chance" meeting with the Danish princess when he came back to Germany in the autumn.

There things stood, although Mama extracted a promise from Vicky that she wouldn't stop looking for other candidates.

PAPA'S FAVORITE, ALFRED Tennyson, had published a new work, *Idylls of the King*, a retelling of the King Arthur legend. On fine afternoons Papa and Vicky sat together on the terrace, taking it in turn to read aloud. Vicky enjoyed the beautiful verses and the romantic stories of the Round Table, and Papa found the epic deeply moving, sometimes putting the book down, overcome.

In general, Papa was in low spirits. He still suffered bouts of intense stomach cramps and feverishness. He complained of aching limbs. He told Vicky that Grandmamma's estate had been left in a shambles, and he was still trying to sort it out. He'd been burdened, also, by Mama's refusal to work or make public appearances. She cried constantly and called herself "a poor, abandoned, orphan child." When she could be persuaded to talk of something else, her attention immediately shifted to Bertie, and she fumed over his failings—idleness, self-indulgence, a taste for unsuitable company.

"But wasn't his year at Oxford a success?" Vicky asked Papa.

"What do you consider success? The tutors say his written work wouldn't pass muster for an ordinary student. His oral presentations achieved a higher standard, but never better than a low pass. He spent all his time with the fast young men of the Bullingdon Club, those types I despise."

Vicky felt sorry for her father, but also for Bertie. When her brother had visited them, his amusing conversation and gracious manners had made him a sensation in the court. "He does so much better than I do, Papa, really, even Crown Princess Olga raved, calling him her *beau idéal*. He won over everybody."

"What does it matter? When you think that at any moment your mother could be carried off and the nation and the empire left in the hands of this feckless boy—for that is what he is still, a boy—the mind rebels."

"Papa, you yourself constantly remark on Mama's good health. She will no doubt live a long life. And should the worst happen, Bertie would still have you."

"I fear your brother would exile me immediately."

"We must stop speaking in this morbid way," scolded Vicky. "We've had too many actual deaths in the family this year. We needn't imagine others."

"Very true." Papa gave her a small smile. "Let's return to Tenny-son. I don't want you to overlook this beautiful passage." He read out: *"When Arthur reached a field-of-battle bright / With pitched pavilions of his foe, the world / Was all so clear about him, that he saw / The smallest rock far on the faintest hill."*

"Arthur's purpose is so apparent," Vicky said.

"Genau," said her father. "He fights to lift up mankind and cre-ate a perfect kingdom."

"Lovely. I must read this later to Fritz."

FRITZ RODE OUT often with Papa, or with her younger brother Arthur, now eleven. And sometimes alone. He relaxed and got browner as their first ten days of holiday passed. Vicky was glad. Her husband, fagged by endless duties in Berlin, had badly needed time off.

Mama bought a pony for William, and Fritz taught the boy to balance on the small saddle and led the animal, Willy astride, around the stable yard. While her son's arm was not better, Vicky wished his character, at least, would improve. William, now two and a half, could be very contrary and so often defied Mrs. Hobbs in the nursery. But he always minded Fritz and was ec-static to be on horseback, learning to ride just as his father did. He also enjoyed following his grandfather around the estate, and how, after meals, Papa would swing him in a large white table napkin.

Later, William claimed that being swung by his grandpapa on the English Isle of Wight was his earliest memory. Vicky won-dered if that was true or if she had described the scene so often to him that he only imagined he remembered. What she never forgot was Papa's quiet pride in his toddling grandson. She kept a well-thumbed image in her mind of the three of them walk-ing single-file along a narrow border path in the walled garden: Willy first, carrying a small rake that Papa had told him they needed that day; Papa next, catching the rake from time to time to steady it as Willy labored to hold it up with his right arm; and

Vicky, last, listening to her father declare: *"Wir müssen uns an die Arbeit machen."*

And long after it was reasonable she kept hoping that her first-born would turn out to be in some way like his valiant grandfather. Enlightened statesman. Wise counselor. Lover of verse.

ON JULY 24 they had just sat down to luncheon when a footman came in and handed Fritz a telegram. He looked up after a minute, grave faced. Someone had shot at King Wilhelm when he was out riding in Baden that morning. Fritz's father had suffered only a grazed neck, but Fritz decided to leave immediately to be with him.

An hour later she kissed her husband goodbye at the door of their bedroom.

"You'll return here?" she asked.

"Not now. Maybe we will all come back next summer. But you must stay as planned. Your parents need you," he said.

William cried bitterly when he realized his father was departing and clung to his legs. "We will ride together again, *mein Junge,* when you are back at home," Fritz told him.

Vicky held the sobbing Willy's hand as they stood under the carriage porch watching Fritz climb into the pony trap that would take him to the pier.

THE NEXT DAY they learned the identity of the would-be assassin: a university student from Leipzig, angry that the king was not doing more to bring about the unification of Germany.

"A bad deed in a good cause," Papa said. He had ceased sending memoranda to Berlin since word had reached him that Wilhelm threw them into the fire, unopened. But after the old king's death he couldn't help himself, and penned a long letter to Fritz's father urging him to actively support and expand the Prussian constitution, thus to serve as a model for the rest of Germany and attract the other German states into a union with Prussia. In such a new nation, Papa told the king, lay the future security of Europe. He'd received no reply.

Papa stayed up late that evening, while the rest of the family went to bed. He asked Vicky to sit with him on the balcony off the library. The night air was heavy, still, and warm. They read for a while and then sat quiet, listening to the burring and chirping of the nightingales.

"Imagine, Vicky, had that young man not missed . . ."

"How terrible that would've been for Fritz," she replied.

"A shock, *ja*. Yet he would have found his feet. And many good men would have rushed to his aid."

"We mustn't talk like this," Vicky said. She couldn't confess that she, too, had conjured up a different future: No Königsberg ceremony, Fritz crowned in Berlin instead, Prussia set on a better path. And her own real life begun, free of the oppressive court and Fritz's parents' demands, sharing her husband's work, doing good. But she felt ashamed to think this way and tried not to.

"God forgive me, it's neither a good or decent desire," said Papa.

They sat in silence for several minutes.

"But I would so like to see it, Fritz and you, king and queen," he said quite softly.

She laughed. "And you will, Papa, someday. Your scheme fulfilled."

"I am a schemer, I suppose. For good, not ill, I pray," he said.

Another long pause.

"You're not sorry, are you?" he asked.

"What do you mean?"

"To have gone to live in Prussia?"

"How can you ask that!" she said, suddenly vehement.

She saw Papa wipe a tear from his cheek.

"Don't cry over me, Papa. You can cry over King Arthur, but not me," she said. "I don't like it!"

"We are in God's hands in any case."

"Not only that," she said, surprised to sound so heated. "We must believe the king is a person of good faith and who means well."

"*Ja*," said Papa. "But he's set against me now; he doesn't want my advice."

"You can send all your thoughts to us."

Her father nodded, rather absently. Then he said: "I've been thinking about something Fritz said the other day, how when his father encounters any opposition to his will, he calls it disloyalty or proof of secret revolutionary intent. His own ministers are so branded and the parliament too. He's suspicious of everyone, keeps the police sniffing out plots. That shows he's weak."

"Let's hope that after he's crowned, he will feel more secure and listen to wise men who serve him honorably," Vicky said.

"But he's also shortsighted," her father continued. "Perhaps he won't overturn the institutions he's sworn to maintain, but they are distasteful to him, and I worry he'll never allow representative government to become strong and well established."

Vicky shook her head. "I don't agree. Too many people in Prussia expect him—and tell him—that he must. Including his wife, and his son and me. Not that he seeks my counsel!"

"But you will always be Fritz's closest adviser."

"Yes," said Vicky, smiling.

"There's that. Only that."

"Bed now?" she asked hopefully. She hated to see her father so pessimistic.

"*Komm, ja,* enough lamenting for one night," Papa answered.

LATER THAT WEEK she and Papa took the children to see the mill on the neighboring Carisbrooke estate. A plodding gray donkey walked in a worn sandy circle to keep the wheel turning. Pointing at the animal, her father asked her: "Don't you think, *Liebchen,* that beast would much rather be munching thistles on the lawn?"

She laughed. "I suppose."

"Small thanks he gets for his labor. That's me! I'm that donkey."

"Papa, don't be silly. Everyone is so grateful for all that you do," she said.

He just shook his head.

As they headed home, Vicky reflected how odd it was, trying to hearten and cheer Papa. He'd always been the one to do that for the rest of them. She wished she knew what caused his joylessness. Was he dispirited because he didn't feel well, or was he out of health because he was overburdened with work and worry?

It pained her terribly to leave him, so ailing and downhearted, when, two weeks later, the servants packed them up to return to Potsdam. She wouldn't have gone at all, but Fritz expected her and the coronation loomed. She couldn't tarry in her old home— her duty lay elsewhere now.

17

Berlin, November and December 1861

At Königsberg Vicky caught a bad cold, and back in Berlin after the exhausting coronation week she suffered with a high fever and ear abscesses that left her temporarily deaf. Her mother-in-law sent frequent notes commanding her to get up for the ceaseless rounds of dinners, receptions, teas, concerts, and opera performances filling these, the frenetic opening weeks of the winter season, the first of the new reign. As ever, Augusta was never content in public unless accompanied by a deferential and uncomplaining Vicky and a full suite of ladies. She was like a slave, captive to Augusta's compulsions, and the queen's morbid restlessness exhausted Vicky and depressed her. Fritz's mother put little of her impressive energy to good use, and since the coronation her need to be out and deferred to by all as the sovereign's wife had reached a high pitch. Vicky supposed it was some compensation for the king's lack of love, but she, Vicky, was relieved to be ill and unable to leave her bed for the moment.

ON THE FIRST afternoon Dr. Wegner allowed her to dress and go downstairs, she still wore a cloth tied around her head. It was

November 5, Guy Fawkes Day. Vicky imagined that at Windsor they must be erecting the huge bonfire always lit on this occasion. She had just sat down to write to Mama and to Alice when a maid interrupted to say the queen had sent word she would call at four. Vicky sighed. Fritz's mother was not losing any time, so eager was she to upbraid her in person.

At least Fritz arrived home early and was with her when Augusta swept into the drawing room as the clock chimed the hour.

"You look quite recovered," the queen said, settling herself in a large armchair opposite the sofa where Vicky sat.

"Mama, don't be ridiculous," said Fritz. "Can't you see she still has her head bound? Wegner insists she can only be up for a few hours."

"But the fever's gone?" the queen asked.

"Yes, thank goodness, though I still have pain," said Vicky.

"Quite a lot of pain!" Fritz said, indignant. "The doctor has Fräulein Stahl pouring oil in her ears both morning and night."

Vicky touched the cotton wrapping gingerly to be sure it hadn't slipped out of place.

"If you're here to see when Vicky can leave the house, to wait on you, it won't be this week, or next," Fritz continued.

"That's not why I've come," replied his mother coldly. "We need to complete plans for the celebration." The queen had announced some time ago that she would host a banquet on November 21, to celebrate Vicky's twenty-first birthday, but as the proposed guest list featured only Augusta's friends, Vicky hadn't looked forward to it.

"No, we will cancel that," said Fritz.

"I will not have the occasion go unmarked," said the queen imperiously.

"We will make no plans until my wife is completely well," answered Fritz.

Mother and son glared at each other. So unlike Fritz to confront the queen. He usually advised "keeping Mama quiet" by doing exactly what she desired. Vicky searched her mind for some distracting topic. Before she could land on one, the queen turned to Vicky and, with a sly smile, said:

"I suppose your parents are very distressed by all the stories."

"Stories?" asked Vicky, mystified.

"Mama, what earthly purpose—" started Fritz.

His mother continued, unheeding. "I wished to write to dear Victoria but wasn't sure if I should. Would sympathy be welcome? So difficult to know. Since dear Fritz never caused such trouble for us."

"What are you referring to, Aunt?" Vicky said.

"Your dear brother, Vicky, and his indiscretion," she said.

Vicky looked over at Fritz. He gave her a small nod and then put in: "Mama, Vicky and I have not discussed this yet."

"*Ach*, I'm sorry. You knew nothing? I hope I did not do wrong by mentioning it," the queen said, clearly not sorry at all.

"Which of my brothers? Bertie?" asked Vicky.

Fritz nodded again, then rose. "Mama, I want Vicky to go back upstairs to bed. I will call on you tomorrow."

"What, no tea?" the queen asked.

"No tea today," Fritz said pointedly, and took his mother's arm to escort her out of the room.

Fritz returned to recount the story as he had heard it. During Bertie's summer in Ireland, fellow officers had introduced him to an actress called Nellie Clifden, and she'd spent several nights in his bed. Nellie, now appearing in a West End revue, had boasted about the liaison, and this delicious gossip was now being feasted upon in the men's clubs of London. The dandies had nicknamed flame-haired Nellie "the Princess of Wales." Accounts had reached the Berlin court a few days ago, and Prince Karl and his cronies were laughing to think of straitlaced Prince Albert, who tediously (in their view) expounded on the importance of virtue in public and private life, shown up by his licentious son.

"Do you think my father knows about this, and my mother?" she asked.

"It's possible no one has dared to tell them yet."

Vicky shook her head to imagine Papa's eventual distress. "Very wrong and silly of my brother," she said.

"I would wager it was only a momentary passion of Bertie's," Fritz said. "And while your parents will be horrified, I can't imagine he meant much harm. It's not like Fritz Karl and the rest of them, married men who openly keep mistresses."

Looking over at her lovely husband, she felt, as ever, so fortunate. "You'll let me know when you take a mistress, won't you, dear heart?" she asked lightly.

"*Aber sicher!* You'll be the first person I tell, *mein Schatz,*" Fritz replied, smiling back at her.

THE VERY NEXT day Vicky heard from her mother that Papa's old friend Lord Torrington had traveled to Windsor earlier in the week to inform Papa personally of his son's misbehavior.

Papa became so distraught that Mama feared he'd completely collapse. Perhaps Nellie had fallen pregnant, or planned to blackmail the family or to publish her own account of the affair in the newspapers. Papa wrote to Vicky: "I am at a very low ebb. Much worry and great sorrow, about which I beg you not to ask questions, have robbed me of sleep during the past fortnight."

Vicky felt anxious about her parents, so far away, but she couldn't leave Berlin to be with them. The elections directly after the coronation had returned a chamber even more liberal than the previous one, and the new parliament had already voiced loud opposition to the king's expensive military reforms, especially extending the mandatory enlistment period. In response Fritz's father had declared he would no longer abide by constitutional rules. What that would mean for the future, no one knew. When two army comrades had invited Fritz to join a hunting trip to the mountains south of Breslau, Vicky had urged her husband to go. He needed an escape from the tension, and she was still weak from her illness. On top of that she woke up every morning very queasy—she suspected she was pregnant again. After Fritz's departure she drifted through several days in an idle, nauseated fog, only rousing herself with the idea of a new project, a set of watercolors illustrating *Idylls of the King*, to give to Papa as a Christmas present.

As she got out her paints and set to work, she thought much about Bertie. Yes, Papa had every reason to fear for his reputation and bewail his bad behavior. And certainly, Bertie needed to take his duties, and his future, more seriously. She'd been annoyed when, after she'd contrived to introduce him to Princess Alexandra back in September at Speyer Cathedral, he'd refused to find an opportunity to get to know her better. Yet Bertie's desire for a bit of fun and freedom, so noxious to Papa and Mama, wasn't so surprising in a young man aged twenty.

She herself was always disparaged by her Prussian family, who believed a princess shouldn't spend endless hours reading, painting, and studying as she did. Were Mama and Papa guilty of similar narrow-mindedness—in a different way, of course—when it came to Bertie? Would they only approve of their heir if he acted exactly like his father? Could they not be persuaded to appreciate Bertie's good points: his warmth, his kindness, his talent with people? She resolved to discuss all of this with Fritz when he came home.

On November 23 Mama wrote that Papa was so irritable and trying. He claimed his body ached and he couldn't sleep at night, but he refused to work less or cancel appointments that Mama deemed far from vital. He had traveled to Sandhurst in the driving rain to inspect construction of new buildings at the Royal Military Academy. He'd twice gone to London in a single week for meetings at the Royal Society, to discuss a new exhibition. And now he'd resolved to visit Cambridge to see the errant Bertie, who was resident at the university there for the current term.

Vicky wrote back immediately, hoping that Bertie and Papa's meeting would go well, with contrition on one side and forgiveness on the other. Mama replied, three days later, that indeed Bertie had expressed his deep regret and vowed never to repeat such an escapade. Papa and Bertie had talked over everything during a long walk in the countryside; it had begun to pour and Bertie had missed the path, so they'd both ended up soaked. And while that had been unfortunate, Mama noted, Bertie *had* agreed to meet Alexandra again in the New Year and consider proposing.

"Despite this fine resolution your dear Papa still complains of being worn out and very unwell," Mama wrote on November 28.

Vicky was certain that Papa would improve now that the rift with Bertie had healed. Fritz, returned from hunting, delighted to hear about her pregnancy, had agreed with her. "Your father is never well at times of family upset," he said. "Advise him to rest over Christmas and come and visit us in the New Year. You can tell him your good news in person." But she put off writing to her father until she could finish her paintings.

On December 1, Mama reported that Papa had a high fever. The doctors had told him to stay in bed, but, preoccupied with a new crisis, he'd resisted. Lord Palmerston, the prime minister, and all the cabinet were outraged that an American ship had stopped a British steamer, the *Trent,* in the Caribbean, and the American captain had, in a blatant violation of international law, removed the two representatives of the rebellious Southern states they discovered on board.

"They are such ruffians," Mama said of the Americans.

The British government sought reparations and the release of the two captives, but meanwhile began readying troops to send to Canada, in case of war with the United States. Vicky shuddered to think of her country lining up on the side of the slaveholding Southerners, even if the incident was an insulting violation of neutral rights. The foreign office had drafted an ultimatum to be sent to Washington, which they had submitted for the queen's signature. Papa had spent a sleepless night amending it. "He showed it to me at breakfast, and while he said he had felt so ill he could barely hold the pen, he moderated the demanding tone," Mama said. "The Americans are given a way out. In the final draft I am said to hope that the American captain did not act under instructions or, if he did, that he misapprehended them."

Lord Palmerston accepted all the alterations and praised them, suggesting that perhaps now war could be averted.

"Papa's perspicacity never fails," said Vicky after reading the letter aloud to Fritz. "He brought the peace!"

"Maybe now he will rest properly," said Fritz.

On December 5 Vicky heard from Alice that Papa had collapsed at his desk, and that he was unable to sleep and moved restlessly from bed to bed in the night. Lord Palmerston had come to Windsor and was shocked by the Prince Consort's appearance. He demanded that other doctors be summoned because Dr. Clark and Dr. Jenner could not agree what was wrong with their patient, calling it a feverish cold one day and gastric fever the next. Yet Mama insisted in her letter of December 6 that while Papa coughed and moaned frequently, he needed only an extended holiday, ideally at Osborne, to recover.

The morning of December 9 brought another report from Alice describing Papa as by turns furious, "a strange wild look in his eyes," and bewildered, only wanting to lie on a sofa pushed up next to the window "so as to watch the clouds sail by."

"We must go," Vicky said to Fritz when she finished reading this letter. "Something is dreadfully wrong."

"A two-day journey and a winter crossing when you are not strong?" Fritz asked. "Do you really think—"

"Should we consult Dr. Wegner?"

In truth, she did feel poorly. And that afternoon, after examining her, the doctor said, "The prince is prepared to undertake the trip with you, Your Highness, although I'm not certain the king will allow it. I believe it too perilous to risk your health and the baby's. What if there is typhoid at Windsor? You must not go."

Vicky began to weep. "I can hardly bear it. Not to be with Papa now, to comfort him and care for him, when he is so ill."

Wegner nodded but added nothing more.

London correspondents for the Berlin newspapers reported

the next day that the Prince Consort's doctors were "alarmed" at the state of his health. The prime minister considered his well-being of "momentous national importance" and was being kept informed by twice-daily bulletins from the castle. Vicky felt too ill to get out of bed, but Fritz telegraphed Sir Charles Phipps, Papa's private secretary, asking why they were not receiving more direct news.

On Wednesday, December 11, a letter came via messenger from Mama, in which she said that while Papa "wandered" at times and did not look like himself, he had passed two "excellent" nights and seemed to be recovering. And a new doctor was attending, a Dr. Watson. Nothing was heard from Phipps, but Vicky felt relieved, and hardy enough to venture to the third floor. She passed the afternoon in the nursery, playing with Willy and Charlotte. Did they remember their grandpapa? He hadn't been well—they must pray for his health. Willy looked so sweet, his face screwed up earnestly, as he beseeched God to "make Grandpapa *gesund*."

On the next day, Thursday, she heard nothing at all. Very bewildering. She behaved like Papa, wandering around from room to room unable to settle anywhere, or read or work or rest. Later Alice recounted how Papa had slept most of that day but woke, confused, in the early evening. "If only nothing happens to Vicky," he had said to Alice. "I no longer trust anyone."

On Friday at noontime, a pale, sorrowful Fritz came into her sitting room, where she lay curled up on the sofa, drowsing. He held a yellow slip of paper, a telegram. "This is from Phipps, *Liebling*," he said, sitting down on the sofa next to her.

She waited, willing Fritz to say nothing dreadful. He sighed and said softly: "Phipps advises I prepare you for bad news."

"What does that mean? Papa still lives, doesn't he?"

"*Doch*, for the moment, but—"

"No," she said, shaking her head and sitting up. "He will not die. He's weak and discouraged and it's all been too much, Bertie's episode and all his work. And he's concerned about us, Fritz.

You understand that? In future we must be more considerate and not worry him. His constitution is not strong. But Mama says the new Dr. Watson is so sensible—good and clever."

After a moment Fritz said, gently: "It may be that even the best doctor can't help him now, Vicky."

"Don't say that," she said, suddenly stern. "I know he will rally."

She asked Marie to bring in her prayer book, and all the rest of the day, she sat or lay on the same sofa, praying and singing Papa's favorite hymns, "Rock of Ages, Cleft for Me" and "To Thee, O Lord, I Yield My Spirit." Alice had written that he had most often, in these days of sickness, asked her to play "Ein feste Burg ist unser Gott," so she favored that one. It was absurd, really, singing the same tunes over and again by herself, but it eased her worry. From time to time, people came in: Marie bearing the newspapers; the maid with a tray of tea and biscuits; finally Mrs. Hobbs brought in little Willy to say good night.

"Why do you sing, Mama?"

"Because it makes me brave, William."

And when she finally got into bed at nine, Fritz came to hold her hand, and they prayed together.

"Tomorrow will bring good news, wait and see," she told him.

Mama's telegram arrived at eleven in the morning. Fritz brought it to her, and she unsealed it with trembling fingers. "'Beloved Papa looks so much better this morning,'" she read aloud. Such a rush of exhilaration. "God has not abandoned us, you see?" she said to Fritz, tears of joy running down her cheeks. "You see?" He hugged her tightly as she sobbed against his shoulder.

A SUNNY AND frigidly cold Sunday, December 15. At nine Fritz departed alone to meet his parents at the Domkirche, and Vicky sat down at the pianoforte in the sitting room to play more hymns, intending to conduct her own, private church service. When she saw the score to Beethoven's Piano Sonata Number 14 on the stand, she recalled how months ago, before the coronation, she had resolved to master it. The entire "Moonlight" sonata

was so lovely, especially the slow, mournful beginning, momen-
tum building while brighter phrases crept in, asking: should we
not believe in the beauty of the world?

Putting the hymn book aside and opening the music, she
started to play. Just as she reached the end of the first movement,
the notes cascading lower, she heard the door open and, glancing
left, saw Fritz slip into the room. What could he have forgotten?
Absorbed by the final passage, she played on to the finish, the
two last chords like a double full stop at the end of a long, lan-
guid, dreamlike sentence.

"What do you think?" she asked as she swiveled around on the
bench. "Not perfect yet, but I am improving."

He stood in the middle of the room, stock-still. Fearful, even.
"*Liebling*, the worst news from Windsor. Your father died last
night."

As Fritz uttered the words, a ghastly image of the death's head
flashed in her mind. *No one, not the noblest among us, is spared.*

He came toward her as she started to weep, but she wished
she had all the strength imaginable to push him and his hideous,
inadmissible pronouncement away.

18

Berlin and Windsor, Winter 1862

How strange that all was the same and yet totally different. She lived in the same palace, slept in the same room, looked at the same furniture. The carriages trundled by out on Unter den Linden, and the days followed, one after another, as though nothing had changed. If the world went on undisturbed without Papa in it, what was the world worth, anyway? Would she feel any differently at Windsor, where everyone shared her suffocating, crushing grief? Maybe there she wouldn't be struck by how shrunken and cold and pointless everything was now. People tried to be kind, and the king had declared a week of official court mourning before departing the capital to spend Christmas in the pump room at Bad Ems, but Vicky felt utterly desolate and even Fritz didn't appreciate that.

He left on the eighteenth to travel to England for the funeral. Vicky wasted no energy begging to accompany him, still she stood mute next to his valet, Streicher, as the man packed Fritz's bags. If by magic she could have shrunk herself and slipped into a portmanteau, she would have.

The day of Papa's funeral she stayed in bed, looking at the

pictures she had of him, one after another, and kissing them, and weeping.

In the early evening Marie came in to tell her that the queen was downstairs. Vicky longed to send Fritz's mother away without receiving her, but she supposed Papa wouldn't have approved of that. Augusta had admired him, as much as she, such a chilly being, could ever venerate and cherish another person.

When Vicky entered the drawing room the queen stood up, which ordinarily she would not have done. She wore all black, including a heavy wool crepe-trimmed cape. "I am so very sorry, my dear."

"Yes."

"The king bade me come on his behalf, to tell you we both mourn with you, and your mother too." She reached out and clasped Vicky's hand.

Vicky nodded. She sat down. Fritz's mother began to speak, but Vicky barely followed. Something about the Prussian ambassador's intending to meet Fritz after the funeral and sending Mama a wreath at Osborne, where she had gone with Alice and the other sisters.

After a few moments Vicky became oddly restless and indignant. "I don't want to sit here and talk about Papa being dead," she said abruptly. "I want it to matter somehow."

Fritz's mother frowned. "What do you mean?"

The queen had such an inhospitable face—high arched brows, tight mouth, haughty expression. Why even spend the effort to be candid? Perhaps only for Papa's sake. And to strengthen her resolve.

"I feel very discouraged," Vicky began. "I am doing my duty here, in this position—Fritz's wife, your daughter. And it is no easy one."

"Do you think mine any easier?" asked the queen, affronted.

"I don't know, Aunt. I imagine not. But I'm speaking of myself now. I've been able to remain determined and make my best efforts because I knew that would satisfy Papa."

The queen glowered.

"And now Papa is gone and I am wondering if I will ever care about anything again," Vicky continued. "I love Fritz and the children. But is there any reason to work here any longer? Perhaps I should retire to the country. You could declare me insane and never think of me again. Would you prefer that?"

"You cannot be well. Why on earth would you say such a thing?"

"I am in earnest." She hadn't realized just how earnest until this minute.

The queen snapped, "No, I don't prefer that."

"In that case I ask that you act toward me in a more equitable way," Vicky said. "For my part I accept there are disagreeable duties that I must perform. Trying, petty things you desire, that are required in my position. And I will do them again, gladly even. In return, I want you to behave more reasonably."

She wouldn't have dared to speak like this before, but doing so enlivened her.

The queen looked angry. "How high-handed you are, sermonizing. If you knew all I put up with, I—"

Vicky interrupted. "Forgive me for sounding high-handed. I mean to ask most seriously and most fervently for your support. We should be true allies and better friends. Otherwise it will all have been in vain, the energy Papa devoted to you, your husband, and your son. And my coming here to Prussia."

"It is you who is duty-bound to support me!" Augusta said.

Vicky let that remark hang, unanswered, for a long moment. Then she said, in a lower, softer voice: "Can we not speak kindly to each other and work in concert? Matters here wear a threatening aspect. I'm sure you agree."

"I do agree, and I spend my time warning the king against the choices others try to push upon him."

"Fritz told me there are generals who propose to break with the law," said Vicky. "Rubbish the constitution, close down the parliament, run the government themselves. Is it true?"

"Not Moltke, but yes, some others."

"That would be monstrous. Don't allow the king to condone it."

The queen raised her eyebrows. "Do you believe this within my power to prevent?"

"Aunt, I think if you remain calm and resolute, and explain that it would be an offense against God, and beneath the king's dignity, to break with legal order, he won't ignore you."

"Perhaps," she said, sounding skeptical. "Last week a number of generals turned up at the palace late in the evening to declare their personal fealty. Like Teutonic knights of old, they are attached to the monarch body and mind, they said, so he has nothing to fear by asserting his will."

"What childish games!" Vicky exclaimed. "Acting as if they live in medieval times. Don't tell me the king embraced them?"

The queen shook her head. "No, he suspects they're fanatics."

"So, it's clear, you and he occupy common ground."

"On occasion."

"Then build on this! We mustn't be passive and sit to the side. When I feel stronger, I will be more determined than ever to see that what Papa envisioned comes to pass."

"I never opposed your father's ideas, Vicky, but his approach could be presumptuous."

Vicky shook her head. "Not true. The king has had the benefit of Papa's counsel since he first visited England. And we must never forget the courage and rectitude and good sense my father always demonstrated."

The queen sighed. "I won't forget, but many in court will be content never to think of him again."

"I would be content if you and I could be more in harmony," Vicky said. "Don't we both want the same things for this country?"

The queen pursed her lips, indignant still. And suddenly Vicky felt very tired. She stood and said, "You will forgive me, Aunt, if I go back to bed."

The queen stood as well, and she peered at Vicky's face closely for a moment, as if hunting for proof of insubordination and evil intent. Eventually she nodded. "Good night. I will pray for your father's soul."

"Good night," said Vicky. She leaned forward and kissed her mother-in-law's heavily powdered cheek. Maybe her pleas would come to nothing. However, she had spoken her mind, and the truth, and that had lightened her grieving spirit.

FRITZ RETURNED FOUR days later and recounted the details of the funeral at Windsor. She cried so hard that she could barely catch her breath. Fritz stayed at home in the quiet days running up to New Year, and they spent the afternoons lying together for hours, Fritz stroking her, and holding her, and making love to her, gingerly, as he didn't want to disturb the baby. She appreciated, in a deeper way now, how Fritz had been given to her by Papa.

She hoped the new baby was a boy, and that she could name him Albert.

In January Fritz went back to work and the weather turned bitterly cold. Vicky felt lethargic. She couldn't summon up again the blazing resolve she had felt that one evening with the queen. She hardly read and stopped following the news. From time to time she asked her husband if the political situation had improved, but he always shook his head no. She went to the nursery every afternoon to play with the children, but she seldom enjoyed it. They screeched, or quarreled over a toy, and she ended up scolding them. A sense of dread and purposelessness weighed down upon her constantly.

Marianne came often to see her and very patiently listened to her talk about Papa. Vicky also had her cousin Adelheid now living nearby. The daughter of Mama's half sister Princess Feodora of Hohenlohe-Langenburg, Adie had recently moved to Berlin with her husband, Friedrich, the Duke of Augustenburg, who was called, inevitably, Fritz. This Fritz had grown up with Vicky's Fritz, and the two men were firm friends. Adie was a serious matron, extremely devout, with a broad face and placid blue eyes, but warmhearted. Together they could recall former times at Windsor, when Adie's family had visited. One morning when her cousin called, Vicky stirred herself to get down a copy of the play she had written years ago for Bertie and Adie and Alice to act out one Christmas. She pulled over a chair to reach the correct box of papers stored high in a cupboard, but when she clambered up, the small chair immediately teetered beneath her—unable to bear her weight—and she quickly jumped back down. *That's my existence now*, Vicky thought. *I don't have the proper underpinning, I am no longer supported adequately now that Papa is gone.* She felt so bereft she struggled to speak further to kind Adie and was relieved when her cousin departed.

ON JANUARY 27, Willy's third birthday, Vicky rose out of bed trying to remember if she'd ordered the cream cake he liked, and enough meringues. Marianne and her three girls were joining them at teatime to celebrate. She thought she would send a message inviting Cousin Adie as well, and her young daughters Calma and Dona. Only little ladies would surround Willy on his special day, no small gentlemen at all, but Fritz would attend, and that mattered most to her son.

Vicky was fully dressed before she realized something odd—for the first time since Papa's death she had not awoken to experience the sickening crush of grief all over again. She sat down on the edge of the bed, trying to take that in. How distressing to be growing accustomed to living without him. Disloyal and very unfeeling of her.

ANOTHER FORTNIGHT PASSED and Vicky had to concede that while she still felt shattered, the overwhelming waves of grief came less frequently and endured for shorter periods. Mama, on the other hand, never stopped weeping, and according to Alice she blamed Bertie for Papa's fatal decline. In daily letters to Vicky—long recitations of her despair and loneliness—her mother confessed that she felt unable to continue with her "utterly extinguished life."

Vicky wrote that Papa's death must be God's will and he, a most perfect being, lived in heaven now, at peace. Vicky did find that thought comforting, but Mama was not consoled. Nor did she agree when Vicky suggested they try to carry on together for his sake, doing good and being good. And Mama completely ignored her pleas to forgive Bertie.

Her brother wrote Vicky his own sad letters. Mama was demanding he leave England and take the long trip to the Near East that Papa had planned as the capstone of his education. He preferred to stay home and help her, but Mama rejected all his kind efforts. "I suppose I must go, and make the best of it," her brother wrote. When he returned he would meet Alexandra of Denmark again, because that was whom Mama insisted he marry, as Papa had wished it so.

FRITZ ARRIVED HOME one evening in mid-February very low, having spent the afternoon in the Wilhelmstrasse with the king, recently returned from Bad Ems.

"My father says it's all the fault of the 'New Era' ministry," Fritz said. "The increased liberal and progressive showing in the last election would not have happened without them in place."

"If the Prussian people want progress, it's hardly the ministers' doing," said Vicky.

"He's looking for strong-minded men who will bring the deputies to heel and compel them to fund the army reorganization."

"He'd change the whole ministry?"

"Anyone who is not a military man or a conservative has to go, he says, and a new premier should be appointed. He may bring Manteuffel back or install his cousin, General Edwin von Manteuffel, or Roon's choice—Bismarck."

"Not your mother's nemesis, surely! And Bismarck is so . . ." She searched for the right word. "So extreme."

"*Das ist er.*" He is that.

"Your mother must be distraught at the very thought," Vicky

said. She'd never confessed to Fritz that she found Bismarck's vigor rather appealing—it was a great shame he had all the wrong ideas.

"Apparently Mama tells Father every night he has reached a historic crossroads and God is watching him, so he must not turn toward absolutism or be led astray by evil men." Fritz smiled. "She stays calm but she keeps repeating, 'God's eyes are upon you.'"

Vicky smiled too, pleased to think that her mother-in-law was doing as she had advised.

"Did you reason with him yourself?" she asked Fritz.

"I tried. But when I spoke up for the ministers, and their difficult position, he opened his desk drawer and pulled out a copy of the *Norddeutsche allgemeine Zeitung*. There's a new story alleging some opposition on my part, saying that I privately back parliament on military reform."

"But you have publicly declared the opposite. On many occasions!"

"The editors wish it to be true, so they write it."

"Terrible."

"*Ja*, and then my father asked why he should listen to me, as I am actually a liberal."

"You are a liberal, if that means wishing constitutional government to function!" Vicky declared.

"Most of all I'm a son who doesn't want to be thought his father's enemy," said Fritz.

He looked so mournful that Vicky crossed the room to curl up next to him on the sofa. "A hint of disapproval from Papa always made me miserable," she said. "So I imagine how distressed you must feel."

He looked down at her and stroked her hair. Vicky continued: "One day you will be able to resurrect the notion of the New Era in the fullest sense. And in the meantime, I am very proud of you."

He gave her a tight smile, but he wasn't consoled, she could tell. Nothing upset her dear, loyal husband more than his father's animosity. How reprehensible that the king—flailing, trying to hold back the tide of history—would in his rage lash out at his son. If only Fritz had a bit of Herr Bismarck's audacity—he might insist his father had no right to hurl such accusations and discover the king would cease making them. Perhaps she should suggest this. But tonight Fritz looked so glum, she found no opening.

At last, in March, Dr. Wegner allowed her to travel to England. But she made little difference at Windsor. Her mother still cried for hours and slept with Papa's coat over her like a blanket. All of Papa's things were left as they had been the day he died. Her mother would not see ministers, read papers, or go out in public. She refused even to choose new clothes.

Alice scolded Mama and told her she remained sovereign and must do her duty. But Vicky found it difficult to condemn their mother. How sad to know you would go to bed alone, and get up alone, for the rest of your life. Vicky couldn't imagine it. She resolved that when she returned to Prussia she would ask Fritz to come home every night, no matter how late, and not sleep some nights during the week at the barracks, as had become his habit. Perhaps, too, they could resume a program of study in the evenings. Papa wasn't living any longer, but he'd taught them how to live. And she remembered the stories Papa had told of his youthful tour of Italy—the architecture, the art, and the landscapes he had seen there. She would ask Fritz if they could go to Italy together. There: that was something to look forward to. Her life was not over.

VICKY WAS STILL at Windsor when the new Prussian parliament voted down funding for the army reorganization and the irate king dissolved the chamber. New elections, the third in two years, were scheduled for late May. At the same time, Fritz's father dismissed all his ministers, excepting Roon and two other conservatives, and announced that he sought a new minister-president to bring order out of chaos. The short-lived New Era was officially at an end. "Bismarck came from St. Petersburg for an interview with my father, as Roon advised," Fritz wrote. "But it didn't go well. Bismarck demands a free hand not only in domestic matters, but foreign too, and my father says he's like a schoolboy with his obsession over the Austrians and his insistence they be driven out of German affairs."

Vicky recalled Bismarck's fulminating against Austria on both occasions they had met—not the way a schoolboy might, but as a zealot did, unrelenting and belligerent. How would he mediate the domestic dispute between the king and the deputies? He'd never struck her as judicious. It was all very concerning. Vicky already found it hard to explain, here in England, why the Prussian government had broken down so dramatically. And when her mother had asked what would happen next, she could only say that with God's help this would be the final struggle to establish reasonable politics in Prussia. Things couldn't continue as they were.

19

Berlin and Potsdam, Spring and Summer 1862

A few days after the parliamentary elections on May 23, in which the progressives and liberals once again won an increased number of seats, Vicky came down to breakfast to find her husband studying a sheaf of papers.

"You can't imagine what this is!" he exclaimed, waving the pages in the air, white faced and nearly shouting.

"What?"

"A military plan to subjugate Berlin street by street when revolution breaks out."

"But there's no revolution—the election has just taken place, peacefully," said Vicky.

"General Manteuffel and his cabal have informed my father he has no choice now, he must abolish the constitution and rule by fiat. When the people object, the army will be brought in to take control in the capital."

"This cannot happen! Don't tell me the king agrees?"

"My father sent the plan to me with a note. He's opposed in theory, but he hopes now I understand the pressure he faces."

Vicky sat down and stared at Fritz, hardly comprehending that all the disputing and debating and uncertainty had brought them to this dreadful pass. A repudiation of progress! A return to absolutism! She thought longingly of Papa, his calm and focused way of speaking, his clear, principled mind. If only he were here. What would he advise? What should they do? Fritz looked drawn and sick. Ghastly. How offhandedly people used that description, but now she saw before her a living, breathing illustration of the word.

"You must go and speak directly to your father," she said.

Fritz nodded.

"Those men are madmen. And playing off his worst fears," she added.

"But if the alternative is submitting to the will of parliament, he might just choose this," Fritz said, shaking the papers again. "It's possible."

"Tell him he mustn't. Passions are running so high, but his responsibility is to stay calm and take a long view—think things through."

Fritz looked rueful. "I'm not sure my father will want to hear that from me."

"Which makes no difference at all!" she replied vehemently. Fritz could not quail now. "Your duty is clear—steer him away from catastrophe. Be the voice of reason and insist that he listen to you."

A pained spasm passed over Fritz's face.

"Darling, it won't help if you tiptoe around him," she said, softening her tone. "Speak clearly and definitively. This"—she pointed at the papers—"cannot be permitted."

Fritz groaned and buried his head in his hands. A lifetime habit of obedience wasn't serving her husband well. Were she in his position, there was no doubt of what she would say and how she would act.

"Don't despair, darling. You are strong; be strong now," she urged. Wasn't that something Papa had told her once?

After a long moment, Fritz dropped his hands and, sighing, rose out of his chair. "I will do what I can."

FRITZ WAS GONE that whole day, and she was about to order supper on a tray when he came in through the door. One glimpse at his face and she felt reassured.

He threw himself down on the sofa. "So, I spent two hours with my father, and several more each with Roon and Moltke. No one wants a repeat of the bloodshed of '48. No troops will occupy Berlin. But my father still will not yield on army reform."

"At what cost?" Vicky asked, indignant. "Does he mean to endlessly exasperate the parliament?"

"I don't know, *Liebling*," he said, sounding spent. "For the moment I believe the worst has been avoided. Roon still pushes for Bismarck to head the ministry, because he won't listen to any parliamentary bullies."

"Bullies! Bismarck will be the biggest bully of all, and run roughshod over everyone! It's nonsense. Roon and his reactionary friends believe Bismarck can magically reverse the natural course of progress. Maybe there won't be blood running in the streets, but neither will there be proper democratic government."

Fritz nodded, weary.

"Bismarck's undoubtedly clever and energetic," Vicky continued. "But I can't imagine where he would steer the king and the country—being, as you and your mother know, false and dangerous."

Fritz looked defeated. "Can we eat? I've had nothing since breakfast."

They shared a sad, quiet meal. Vicky longed to discuss the situation further. If Bismarck did become minister-president, how would he cope with the military? He'd trained as a lawyer and had never been an army man, she knew. But her husband had had enough. In bed, he soon fell asleep, while Vicky lay awake into the small hours, staring wide-eyed at the ceiling, trying to imagine the future, and calculating what Fritz might do or say next.

THEY LIVED, FOR several weeks, as if under enormous, threatening storm clouds that never blew away, nor did they break. She and

Fritz moved with the children to Potsdam for the summer, and the king and queen took up residence at Babelsberg. Fritz traveled to the Wilhelmstrasse most days, to talk to Moltke, the ministers, and some deputies, seeking a way out of the impasse. A compromise emerged—the parliamentarians had proposed to drop all other objections to the king's plan if the conscription period for soldiers could be cut from three years to two, which was acceptable to Moltke. Fritz urged his father to agree. Still the king resisted, unwilling, he declared, to show "inconsistency" to the world.

Vicky, pregnant and restless, spent her days nervously wandering around the Neues Palais and soon became fixated on Willy's head. It drooped to the right in an odd way now, as if his neck couldn't support the weight of his growing skull. Fritz strained to see what she was describing. "Don't torment yourself over this. He's fine," he told her one evening as they walked out of the nursery.

Fritz did agree that the boy, now three and a half, was too often naughty—pulling the tablecloths off set tables; rushing, when ladies stood up, to crawl under their hoop skirts; and flying into a rage when told it was time for bed. When Vicky or Mrs. Hobbs paid Charlotte any attention, Willy liked to pinch his little sister and make her cry. Vicky read aloud to him, her favorite English books, but he was frequently too restless to listen. And when she took him into the garden to work alongside her, he'd quickly lose interest and run away. All very dispiriting.

Willy's grandparents adored him and never found fault. Even now the king often dropped in at the Neues Palais to see the boy—full of smiles for him, barely acknowledging Vicky. One afternoon in late June, Vicky came upon her father-in-law sitting in a large rattan chair in the garden room with Willy on his lap. The king looked so benign that Vicky suddenly took heart. Roused, she crossed the room intending to declare to her father-in-law: "Those of a different opinion are not trying to destroy your army or limit your power, only collaborate in government for the good of the nation. Be brave! Rule in the manner that is now the order of the day."

But the king glanced up and, as if reading her intention on her face, reared back. The fond grandfather expression turned into a stern, forbidding stare that dared her to defy him. So she just smiled weakly and said, "Willy very much looks forward to your visits."

How spineless and cowardly she was. Did she think he'd shout at her? He'd done that before and she'd lived. Did she fear he'd dislike her more than he already did? She had no true need for his affection. No, she concluded, it was that she couldn't bear to be dismissed—she hated to be told how little her opinion mattered.

JUNE GAVE WAY to July, and the days became much hotter. Her pregnancy far advanced, Vicky felt very uncomfortable, constantly perspiring and fearful of the ordeal ahead. Fritz's mother came to the Neues Palais every day, to visit the children, but also, she said, "to see how you are getting on, Vicky dear." Papa's death and the political crisis had surely softened the queen, for she had never before expressed such concern. Vicky had believed her mother-in-law deplored her closely spaced pregnancies and what they revealed about how intimate she and Fritz remained. The queen liked to say that by providing her husband with two offspring, seven years apart, she had more than done her duty to the dynasty.

But in these sweltering days Augusta was both solicitous and confiding. She told Vicky she stayed constantly vigilant, urging the king not to go in a reactionary direction and thus endanger the crown. As they strolled together in the garden one morning the queen reported: "I say to him: Think of Fritz! And how can you forget darling little Willy? You want him to inherit one day, don't you? Years from now? Then you must find a way to work with the parliament and the ministers."

Vicky smiled and linked her arm with the queen's. "You are a good wife, a good mother, and a lovely grandmother. Thank you."

The queen squeezed her arm. "Let's pray that he listens. Not for our sake, even, as much as for the country."

On July 16 Fritz left for three days in Königsberg to open a new university building there. Early on July 17 Vicky was still in bed when a maid came in with a scribbled note from her mother-in-law: "There's been a great scene. I was out with the king yesterday and he told me of his definite intention of taking the bête noire into the ministry. I will come later to discuss with you."

"A most alarming conversation," Aunt Prussia began as soon as she had settled on the yellow sofa in the drawing room. "The king and I have been enjoying the sunny weather, and you know the path out of the library doors that goes down to the river? Yesterday in the late afternoon I suggested we walk it, not intending to speak of anything serious. In fact, I was just chatting about dear Charlotte's sweet little expressions, and suddenly he stopped and stood quite still in the middle of the path. And he said, 'I must tell you something.' And then he explained that the ministers were pressing him to make a decision on the matter of the new premier and that he had decided only one man could master the situation, namely Herr Bismarck-Schönhausen, who was fully behind the military program and would defend the government skillfully and eloquently. I immediately told him how greatly saddened and astonished I was to hear him speak so and that I had always hoped he would refrain from making such an extreme choice, which could only inspire mistrust and worry in me. And then he said—"

Her mother-in-law's voice broke. Vicky, startled, realized she'd never before seen Fritz's mother in tears. But the queen swiftly wiped her eyes with her handkerchief, sniffed, and continued.

"He then said that only his own opinion mattered on this question. And when I replied—and I did so quite calmly, Vicky, I want you to know, I was very upset but I did not fly at him, I was composed, and I replied to say that the appointment would give a very unfavorable impression of Prussia, first of all in Germany, and then also in England. This seemed to make no difference to him. He said, 'If I can't have Bismarck, then I should have to leave it all to my son.'"

"What, he's thinking of abdication?" Vicky asked, shock and amazement running through her. How wonderful if the king would step aside!

But the queen frowned and shook her head. Had she noticed Vicky's immediate euphoria?

"He only brought that up to frighten me and show me he's in earnest," the queen said. "And when I pointed out that Bismarck would terrorize and dominate everyone, including the king himself, and that the people of Prussia would be the ones to suffer the most, he wouldn't agree. He said, interrupting and nearly shouting, that the private views of me, his wife, were of absolutely no concern to him. No concern at all. And then he broke off the conversation, turned, and went back up the hill, leaving me standing there."

Since the coronation, Fritz's father and mother had gotten on better, and it was said that he no longer pursued other women. The queen had taken charge of several important charities, and the king often praised her work. And while he hadn't agreed to follow her political advice in recent months, he hadn't dismissed it either. Until today. To think of this proud woman valiantly facing down her husband on a vital issue, and then being treated with complete disdain, was hideous. How aggrieved and distraught the queen must have been to confess it all to her! A surge of sympathy propelled Vicky out of her chair and over to embrace her mother-in-law.

"I am so very dismayed to hear of this," Vicky said.

Her mother-in-law was stiff at her touch and immediately shook off Vicky's arms. "You needn't feel sorry for me. I will still be queen," she replied. "But you should be sorry for the world if that terrible adventurer rises and rules!"

Vicky straightened up. The queen scowled at her, her face blotchy and her rouge smeared. Another wave of pity broke over Vicky, and her own eyes filled with tears.

WHEN FRITZ RETURNED the next day and Vicky told him the whole of the queen's account, he said, "It's as if my father is putting the noose over his own neck."

"Might your father abdicate?" Vicky asked. "If he finds his duties so onerous, maybe it would be for the best." She had thought of little else since the queen's visit, imagining how Fritz as king would compromise with parliament, appoint a liberal as minister-president, and end the constitutional crisis in the best possible way. And then, a new life for them all!

"No, he'll never do that," Fritz said. "He's the faithful soldier of the Fatherland for life. And it would not be for the best. It would be awful."

20

Coburg and Potsdam, August and September 1862

When on August 14 Vicky gave birth to a son, Fritz said it would be "too provocative" to call him Albert, so they settled instead on Albert Wilhelm Heinrich, to be known as Henry. She was grateful that the labor was short and the baby healthy. Henry lay in her arms, a tranquil sleeping cherub, and she marveled that her grief and anxiety during the last nine months seemed not to have touched him at all.

Mama grumbled over the name, even after Vicky said the baby could be known simply as Albert in England. But her mother's true preoccupation, besides preserving her late husband's memory, remained arranging Bertie's marriage. She had invited the Danish princess Alexandra and her parents to meet her and Bertie at Laeken, Uncle Leopold's palace in Brussels, during the first week of September. There, she could personally inspect and possibly approve of the girl. Her mother planned to travel on to Coburg, to visit Uncle Ernest and his wife, and she insisted Vicky and Fritz join her there.

"You mustn't abandon me the way Alice has done," Mama wrote. Vicky's loyal sister, who had so attentively nursed Papa in his last days and then comforted Mama for months after his death, had gone ahead with her marriage to Louis of Hesse on July 1. The wedding had taken place in the dining room at Osborne, and Lenchen had reported that every woman attending wore black except the bride.

"Alice has forgotten her mother," complained Mama. "I feel very let down."

THERE WAS ONE piece of good news before their departure for Coburg. Fritz spoke to the king and found, to his relief, that his father had now changed his mind about Bismarck. Not because Fritz and the queen vehemently opposed the man's appointment, but because the king had concluded the Junker champion was quite unstable. Bismarck had been serving during the last few months as ambassador in Paris, and word had trickled back to Berlin that he'd become friends with Emperor Napoléon and declared to everyone that Prussia and France must be allies. "My father is infuriated. Some things about the world baffle him, but he knows *that* can't be correct," Fritz told Vicky. As a boy the king had witnessed the Prussian humiliation at the hands of the first Napoléon's armies—to his mind, France would always be his country's dire foe.

"I should thank Bismarck for his pro-French remarks—I used them to disparage the terrible fellow in a most satisfactory way," Fritz reported, grinning.

At the baby's christening on September 5, the queen appeared tired and mirthless, standing next to the king at the font. But she, too, had been reassured by the king's promise to eschew Bismarck. "He agrees now," she whispered to Vicky. "Bismarck can't be trusted." The queen departed for a visit to her old home in Weimar the next day, while Vicky and Fritz took the train to Coburg.

"YOU'RE LOOKING SO well!" exclaimed Vicky as she embraced Mama in the front hall of Schloss Ehrenburg. Her mother wore black, naturally, and a large black bonnet with floor-length crepe veiling attached. But, peering out from amid her widow's weeds, her mother's doll-like, pink-and-white face looked smooth and rested, and her eyes bright.

"I'm not feeling well at all," her mother replied.

"It wasn't a success in Brussels?" Vicky asked anxiously.

"Dreadful to meet the Danes without dearest Papa at my side. However . . ." Mama paused dramatically and then beamed. "It has all been settled!"

"They are engaged? Tell me." Vicky escorted her mother into the drawing room while Fritz remained outside with Uncle Ernest, speaking with the Coburg mayor and other local worthies.

Mama perched on a small gold chair and began to recount how she had received the princess and her parents in the red salon on the first floor of the Laeken palace, with Bertie of course. Mama had warmed immediately to Alix, who had turned up in a black dress—so tactful—and appeared to be very quiet and dignified, altogether more distinguished than her rather common family. Such was Mama's state of nervous exhaustion and great sorrow that she found it hard to converse, but she did manage to tell the Danes about beloved Papa and a good bit about Windsor and the family. The girl had listened closely and sat quietly, demonstrating excellent posture. When she spoke her voice was low and soft, not grating at all, so Mama felt glad and very relieved.

"Yes, but then what happened? Did Bertie propose? That very day?" Vicky asked.

Mama looked puzzled. To her this was clearly a side matter. "Two days later, I believe, in the garden," Mama said. "In any case, he told me at luncheon it was done, and we can announce it next week."

Poor Bertie. Vicky hoped he wasn't marrying now solely for duty's sake. He must feel some real affection for the princess, mustn't he? Vicky wrote immediately asking her brother for his account of the Laeken meeting, but he added few details. "I asked her, and she accepted. Then afterward I asked her if she liked me, and she said she did, so there we are."

DESPITE FRITZ'S URGING, the king still refused to amend the length-of-service provision and thus despoil the crown of its rights. On Wednesday, September 17, when the new budget came up in the parliament with the monarch's whole plan attached, it was voted down 308 to 11. Roon and the other ministers declared they could not go on without an approved budget. The government ground to a halt.

"Your father is being extremely foolish," said Mama when Fritz read out the news to them just before dinner. Fritz nodded grimly. The king had ordered his immediate return to Berlin, and a special train had been arranged to take him at midnight.

As they walked toward the dining room, Vicky whispered to Mama that she thought it best she accompany Fritz. "He will need me."

"No, Vicky, I've barely seen you, and the children, you can't go," Mama whispered furiously back.

"I will leave the children. They can follow with Mrs. Hobbs in a few days. In any case I can't possibly have things all packed up in time to take everyone tonight," she said.

Her mother sniffed. "I am astonished that you would leave me here alone."

Vicky sighed. It didn't matter that Uncle Ernest and Aunt Alexandrine danced in attendance; her still-grieving mother had expectations, which Vicky felt compelled to meet.

"All right then, Mama, I will stay until Saturday," she said.

WHEN NEXT VICKY saw Fritz, he was in the library at the Neues Palais, slumped in an armchair, his long legs stretched out in front of him, his face pale and exhausted. She shut the door behind her, and he said, without preamble: "My father wants to abdicate."

She felt an odd, giddy sensation of relief flow through her. A kind of loosening, in her arms and legs, and behind her eyes. But Fritz's expression, his posture, the tone of his voice, all telegraphed his extreme distress. She had to proceed delicately.

"He's not ill?" she asked as she bent down to kiss his cheek.

"No, it's not illness," Fritz said, brusque.

She sat on the chair next to him and waited. A long, fraught interval. The clock on the chimney piece ticked loudly and she heard the rattle of a wheelbarrow as one of the gardeners passed by under the open window. It was late in the afternoon but the air was still heavy and close.

Eventually Fritz said, in a strained voice, "He believes he must lay down his crown. Because everyone in the ministry opposes him. And his conscience won't allow him to go on if he must sacrifice the reorganization of the army. He'd always resolved to defend the army unto death and now he's unable to. He showed me the deed of abdication, all complete. It requires only his signature."

How strange, Vicky thought. *The king prepared a document to wave in front of Fritz without signing it; why? To test his son in some way?*

She asked only: "You were shocked?"

"I'm still shocked," said Fritz, shaking his head. "My poor father. He feels completely let down by the ministers. Roon insists a legal budget must be passed."

"As indeed it must," said Vicky.

Fritz winced.

"Darling, what did you say to the king?" she asked in a soothing voice.

"I told him not to do this awful thing. No one wants him to go. Least of all me. It would be damaging to the dynasty, and to the whole country."

With all the force of her being she longed to shout, "Fritz, you are mistaken," but she couldn't say that; she had to coax him.

"He replied?" she asked.

"He had no reply. He looked defeated—in tears!"

This also struck Vicky as odd. Her father-in-law never conceded defeat on anything.

"And you're certain he's serious?" she asked.

"Completely serious. I told him he'd be setting a terrible precedent, allowing parliament to unmake a king. Anyone who reveres the crown can see how dangerous that would be!" He stared at her pointedly.

"And so how did you leave it?"

"I begged for time to find another solution. He shrugged and said he thought it was too late but if I wanted to see Roon, I should go ahead. I'm supposed to meet the minister at six."

How to get Fritz to see this in a different light? She quickly arranged the points in her head and began, gingerly: "Don't you believe, darling, that it's all happened like this—with this endless wrangling and constant back-and-forth arguments, with new parliaments and new votes—because your father, although well intentioned, can't manage?"

Fritz scowled.

She continued: "He can't change his views, being what they are, yet he's holding on to something that he must give up on, given his duty."

"Which is why he's in agony!" Fritz said loudly. "He knows he can't break the promise he took to uphold the constitution, as dubious as he finds constitutions."

"Good, because otherwise General Manteuffel might already have the troops in the streets," Vicky replied.

Fritz nodded. He was rubbing his temples in a worried, nervous way.

"But the constitution demands certain flexibility from the crown," Vicky continued. "And don't you agree, the king cannot provide it?"

"Does that mean I must displace him? Cast him aside?" Fritz asked bitterly. "I can't. And I won't."

Vicky felt a grip of impatience in her chest, but commanded herself again to stay steady. "You don't believe you'd be better equipped to manage the situation?"

"I don't want to assume the throne under the shadow of his ouster."

"Fritz, that's a different question. Your loyalty to your father will blind you if—"

"Imagine if this were your father! You would never want to injure him in any way," Fritz said, interrupting, his voice rising again.

"Taking up your father's wishes is not injuring him," she answered. "And Papa would never have allowed things to continue so long in a such a disgraceful condition of uncertainty."

Fritz's eyes blazed. "Father has been in a very difficult situation. You saw, you were there, for so much of it. The frustration we all felt three summers ago, when nothing worked, the mobilization a shambles."

"I appreciate that your father has always believed the army should be entirely under the control of the crown."

"As do I!"

Vicky nodded. "Still, compromise with the deputies is necessary, and your father continues to resist. What confuses me is why he didn't just summon you and hand over the abdication deed, signed and done. Perhaps he hoped you would react in this way? To feel sympathy? To talk him out of it?"

"You would feel sympathy too, if you'd seen him yesterday. He looked so pathetic and broken."

"Your father is typically furious, not broken, Fritz darling, you know that. He may be bluffing or playing up in some way."

Fritz didn't seem to register this. "I'm not sure I could do the job better," he said.

"Darling, of course you could! You've already embraced the length-of-service compromise. That's all the deputies ask for."

Fritz shook his head. "Nothing would change the fact that my father would be making a disastrous decision in a moment of despair—I couldn't live with myself if I took advantage."

"The circumstances require you to agree to take up the task he feels unequal to," she replied. "You must go back and see him and tell him you accept."

"I can't imagine ever uttering those words."

"At this moment your country needs you," she insisted. "If you don't answer the call you're putting your personal feelings before your duty."

He started to shake his head violently. "No, no, no!" he exclaimed. "There must be some other way—I will discuss it with Roon."

He got up out of the chair and strode toward the door. She called out: "Please, Fritz, think about what I'm saying." But he didn't answer.

SHE WENT OUT and found a shady corner in the garden and sat down to ponder. She was in no doubt that Fritz should accept the crown—but was it actually being offered? The king might have been making this gesture as a feint, to put additional pressure on the ministers, threatening them with the prospect of working with his more liberal son to spur them to extreme measures. Or it might suit him to be able to say he'd tried to abdicate but couldn't because his son wouldn't give him a way out. Perhaps then he'd feel free to break with the law? In any case the consequences could be disastrous—vast public discontentment resulting in riots, or the overthrow of the monarchy, or a crackdown on opposition that would end in military rule in Prussia.

For a moment, she wished the queen were here with her to discuss the situation, but no, she amended silently, Augusta would not welcome the abdication, nor the prospect of being supplanted by Vicky, under any circumstances.

Later, upstairs changing for dinner, she heard Fritz in his dressing room speaking with his valet. She was very eager to hear what he'd learned, but she thought it better to wait until they were alone. She'd chosen a dress she knew he liked, a teal blue gown trimmed with ecru lace. She smiled encouragingly at him as he sat down at the head of the table, she at his right hand. No guests joined them, since they had been scheduled to be in Coburg.

The servants served out the food and withdrew.

Noting his tense expression, she started gently: "How did you find Roon?"

"Fed up and quite despairing. My father's furious at him and the other ministers because they won't ignore the deputies. Or defy them."

"Which is quite unjust, since under the law—"

Fritz interrupted. "The way Roon put it was, 'I can offer the king no solution, but another might.'"

"What does he mean?"

"I immediately took it to mean that Bismarck would be willing to ignore parliament."

"Your father has said he won't have Bismarck."

"*Richtig.* And I reminded Roon of that, but he just shrugged."

Vicky narrowed her eyes at Fritz, perplexed. Was Herr Bismarck still a possibility? She'd been convinced her father-in-law had come to distrust the man too much to ever work with him, but perhaps not. She shook her head slightly. How difficult to give advice with imperfect information at hand.

"Is Roon aware that the king threatens to abdicate?" she asked.

"Most definitely, and he abhors it. He agrees with me that an abdication would be extremely damaging to the monarchy. Perhaps fatally so. I must not allow my father to do it, he says."

"Then General Roon and I disagree—not for the first time, or the last, I would imagine," she said lightly.

Fritz did not look up. He was cutting his meat with undue vigor.

"I've been thinking, darling," Vicky continued. "Should your father be able to say he has no choice, that you refused the throne, he may use that as an excuse to do things that you could never approve of."

"This is no bluff—Roon believes that too."

"Hmm, I wonder why the minister asserts this," Vicky mused aloud.

"Because the king is serious! Why won't you believe this? You are searching around for hidden motives where there are none."

Stung, Vicky didn't reply for a long moment. Finally, she said: "Fritz, do you remember how dismayed your mother was when your father told her that the opinions of his wife didn't matter to him?"

He gave her an irritated glance. "And so?"

"I begin to feel that you—"

He cut her off. "Don't do this. Don't tell me that is what I am doing."

"But you are, rather," she said, trembling a little now.

Fritz put down his knife and fork and pushed back a few inches from the table. The chair legs scraped against the floor. "I need you to understand that what the king is proposing is not something I want. Or can accept. Do you see that?"

"I do see that. But, Fritz, your father is not up to the job. You are. You should take this opportunity."

"This is not the way I desire it to be," said Fritz, pronouncing every word distinctly. "And I expect you to support my decision."

She laughed. "You expect me to endorse something that I think wrong and ill considered? I can't."

"Very disloyal of you," he said curtly.

"Not at all. The essence of loyalty. You must not let down yourself and your family and hundreds of thousands of people you don't even know by shirking your responsibilities in the name of some narrow sense of duty to a father who has never respected you, who frequently insults and derides you."

"I will not allow you to speak of my father in this way," Fritz said.

"I'm a freeborn Englishwoman and I can say what I like," she answered vehemently.

"Not when I order you not to." He was shouting now.

"I'm not under your command, Fritz, and I've had enough of staying silent. You father is a poor leader and a hazard to the country."

"Stop! I refuse to listen to you a minute more!"

Vicky stared at him, at first stunned—as if the air been knocked out of her—then she began to shake with rage and found the breath to hiss: "Which proves to me that you're a fool, and that I've been a fool to have confidence in you."

The room turned without warning into a cold and remote polar space, although the evening was warm and the windows open to the garden. Fritz's face was frozen, horror-struck, and she wondered if she'd shattered something between them that could never be repaired. She found herself missing Papa as she hadn't for months and months. Keenly, freshly, like a rip inside her. She was alone in the world and had no one.

She looked away from Fritz, to the right, at the blue and silver wallpaper on the far wall. She sensed her husband standing up. He said, in an odd, strangled voice, *"Du hast mich verlassen."* You've forsaken me.

She heard the tapping of his boots as he walked away, and the sound of the dining room door opening and closing, but she kept her gaze focused on the far wall. The pattern had become infinitely complex and interesting, and now her eyes began to follow the swirls of silver up and then down again, as if with careful concentration she would find they led her to some place of comfort, far away.

AFTER TEN MINUTES Vicky got up from the table, tossed her napkin down beside the plate of uneaten food, and went upstairs. She took the seat at her dressing table and looked in the glass at her pale, shocked face. Then she rang for Dawes, her dresser, to help her. She went through all the motions of getting ready for bed woodenly, automatically. The cool, smooth sheets were a relief when she slipped in between them, and she thought maybe she could relax and even sleep. There was no sign of Fritz.

What sleep she did get was brief, fitful, and confused. She woke every hour or so, and at one point went over to the window and pulled the curtains apart to see if the sky had begun to lighten. Not yet; still pitch-black. She returned to bed, but she left the curtains open to watch for the dawn.

The birds had started their morning chorus and the sky glowed pink above the trees when the door to the bedroom opened and she heard Fritz padding in. She was lying on her side facing the window. The bed creaked underneath him when he got in next to her, and she pretended to be asleep. He seemed to be waiting to see if she would turn or say anything to him. But she lay motionless, and then, eventually, he was turning on his side, curling away from her, and after several long moments she heard his breathing become steady and regular. She cried quietly for a short while.

THE ROOM WAS bright with sunlight when she awoke. Fritz had gone. She dressed and went downstairs. On the stairs she was startled to hear Willy's high, excited voice, coming from the dining room. Entering, she found Fritz sitting in his place, with Willy, red faced and sweaty, standing near him, holding his hobbyhorse between his legs.

"*Guten Morgen, Liebling,*" said Fritz mildly. She didn't look him full in the face. "Willy wanted to join me to say *Guten Morgen* to his lovely mama."

"Watch me, Mama," said Willy. "I am riding so very fast." He started speeding around the table. The dining room wasn't the place for running and horseplay, but she said nothing reproving as she slipped into her seat.

"I see you, Willy, you look strong," she called to him, her voice a bit shaky.

She picked up her napkin and spread it in her lap. Only then did she look properly at Fritz.

He appeared tired but not angry. His eyes—attentive and grave—met hers. Then he said in a soft, even voice, "I have been thinking that I must consider your opinion in this matter."

Hope flooded her chest, and the sense of lightening again as she'd experienced the day before. But at the same time, she felt suspicious. Was he just trying to humor her? She nodded, on guard.

"I need some peace and quiet to think, so let's make today a family day and just enjoy each other's company. It's Sunday, after all. And we needn't go to church, we'll stay home."

She nodded again and then managed to reply, "Yes, let's do that."

They sat in silence together, only the sounds of Willy's pelting around the room intruding. She supposed she should offer up something conciliatory. But she felt no true desire to do so.

Fritz cleared his throat. "Willy, shall you and I go upstairs and find your ball and the cricket bat? Mama's going to watch us play after she has something to eat."

THEY SPENT MUCH of the day in the garden. They were very polite to each other. She didn't ask Fritz if he'd decided to see the king or what he would say to him, although she longed to know. She was impatient for him to act as he ought, to release them from this precarious limbo, and end the trepidation she felt for the family and for all the country. She recalled Fritz at Balmoral, during his first visit, and the vision of liberalism and constitutionalism he had shared with Papa: Prussia could be a leader in the world, an exemplar in Europe. And here they had arrived at the hinge moment, so much hanging in the balance. Would Fritz turn his back on those dreams? Fail to live up to his ideals? She could not bear to voice these questions aloud, but they filled her head as the afternoon wore on.

At four a footman came out to the sunny glade where they were sitting with the children, baby Henry on Vicky's lap. The servant said Baron Stockmar had arrived and was waiting to speak with them in the library.

"I am sorry to disturb," her private secretary said, rising as they entered. "But I've learned something I thought you'd want to know. It appears Herr Bismarck has returned to Berlin, for what reason, no one knows."

Vicky and Fritz locked eyes, and as he gazed at her she saw in his expression a kind of stricken guilt, a sharp, self-reproachful disappointment.

Oh, my love, she thought. *My poor dear love.*

After a long moment Fritz said: "I must speak to my father immediately. Baron, will you send a messenger over to Babelsberg requesting an audience?"

No reply came from the king that evening and nothing the next morning either. Fritz paced around his study, unsure what to do.

"I could just ride over there," he said.

"To Babelsberg?" Vicky asked.

"*Ja,* but he has perhaps gone into town."

Vicky wasn't sure what to suggest. Was it wise for Fritz to chase after the king? Or, having sent his request, was it better to wait to be summoned? "Why don't you see if he sends for you this afternoon? With this lovely weather, he's most likely staying in the country, and if you hear nothing it's easy enough to reach Babelsberg quickly from here before day's end."

The first part of the afternoon passed with no word. At three they decided to take tea on the terrace. They had just sat down at the table when Vicky glanced up and saw her private secretary walking toward them. Stockmar came right to the point. "The king has decided to elevate Bismarck. Only Roon is happy. It will be announced in the papers tomorrow."

Fritz threw his head back, staring up at the sky for a long minute, and then, turning to Vicky, said: "My father will suffer greatly at the hands of this dishonest character."

21

Berlin and Italy, Autumn 1862

*F*ritz went to see the king the next day and returned, white with rage, after little more than an hour. When he told his father he felt terribly betrayed, the king just laughed and said: "You were no help. You neither wanted the throne nor could you break the impasse."

Apparently, Roon had instructed Bismarck to come from Paris and then persuaded the king to meet with him. Bismarck proclaimed that monarchial rule remained the basis of all authority in Prussia, and he cared not a whit for the opinions of the deputies. Bismarck said: "I would rather perish with Your Majesty than abandon you in the contest with parliamentary government."

"In other words," said Vicky, "the man told your father exactly what he wanted to hear."

"*Ja,* and when I said this is madness, no one in Prussia will tolerate defiance of parliament, my father merely laughed again," said Fritz. "He told me there's been too much wearisome talk about principles and laws and doctrines when what the people desire is efficient administration, a powerful army, and the king presiding from his rightful throne."

"What about Germany? The efforts to unite the nation?" Vicky asked.

"Bismarck's theory is that Germans don't look to Prussia for liberalism but for strength," said Fritz.

"And the king agrees?"

"My father appears like a man transformed," Fritz said. "Doing God's work, defending the Fatherland against evildoers. Bismarck has convinced him he needn't concern himself with anyone else's opinion but his own."

VICKY SUPPOSED THE king had found a personally satisfying way out of his dilemma. He hadn't broken his vow to respect the constitution—instead he was allowing Bismarck to break it for him. The new minister-president, simultaneously appointed foreign minister, let it be known that for "reasons of state" the deputies' opposition to the expansion and reorganization of the army could not be recognized, and the plans must go forward as written. Vicky imagined that if this happened in London or Paris, angry citizens would promptly erect barricades in the streets. Yet in Berlin, even in parliament, the response was oddly muted. The most prominent men in Prussia, who had feared worse—martial law—grumbled a bit but then sat back to watch where the audacious Junker would take them. When on September 30 Bismarck rose to address the deputies, the afternoon papers published his maiden speech in full, and Vicky prepared herself to despise every word.

Bismarck described how the borders imposed on Prussia at the Congress of Vienna, which had divided the country in two, were not favorable to a healthy economy. He said that several opportune moments for Prussia to found a united Germany had already been missed and the next must not be squandered. The constant seeking of majority resolutions in parliament bogged down efficient administration and could not bring about the desired new nation. Only iron and blood would do that, he said.

Fritz had gone to the barracks, and she was alone in the library when she finished reading. She marveled. Bismarck, for so long branded too irresponsible and too violent to occupy high office, had not changed. Yet for the moment he held the future of Prussia in his hands, the king having left it to him, and now he was spelling out his intentions in clear, if deplorable, terms.

In the days since Bismarck's appointment Vicky had been careful to neither blame Fritz nor chastise him. Instead she told him that while she believed he should have immediately agreed to take the throne, even had he done so, the king might have balked. The abdication threat was just that, a threat, not a firm resolution, and it protected the king from claims he had too readily resorted to Bismarck. Roon, she saw now, had cleared the way for his friend, and both these gentlemen understood the king better than his own son did. Would Vicky condemn Fritz forever for this? No, she thought, she mustn't, for that would be to crave power more than the well-being of the man she loved. And she loved Fritz. She desired nothing as much as to be proud of him again, with her whole heart. But she also seethed. She hated that Roon and Bismarck had outflanked her—or, rather, both her and her husband—and she fervently hoped Fritz would be better prepared in future to face down his father and these reactionary ministers.

THE QUEEN, RETURNED from Weimar to the reality of her enemy in place, fell into a kind of constant, raging bitterness that made her very uncongenial company. She and the king barely spoke, except to insult each other. Vicky felt very sorry for her mother-in-law, but when she called on her to commiserate and point out that Bismarck's day couldn't last forever, the queen just lectured, in her old imperious way, warning that high-minded principles and liberal sentiments would count for nothing now that Prussia was run by a cynical and unscrupulous reprobate.

Fritz's father announced to the whole court that he would not tolerate "sermonizing" from his son and his English wife, in public or private. At a Crown Council meeting in early October, the king accused Fritz of grimacing in an insubordinate manner when the minister-president was speaking.

Fritz, recounting this to Vicky, paused and grinned: "So afterwards I challenged the king."

"You did what?" Vicky asked, startled.

"I said, if you don't want me around, let me take my wife on a trip to Italy."

"What did he say?"

"He immediately agreed. He said that as both of us are so unreasonable and unhelpful to the new ministry, we should leave."

Vicky shook her head, incredulous. "I suppose there's no reason to stay in Berlin to be in turn tortured and ignored."

The next day she wrote to Mama to ask to use the royal yacht *Osborne*. It was agreed they would meet the boat at Marseilles and then cruise around the Italian peninsula, making frequent stops. Only later did it occur to Vicky that perhaps Bismarck preferred them to be out of the country as he picked up the reins of government. Could he have urged the king to send them off?

But by the time Vicky realized that they had likely played right into the shrewd man's hands, they were sailing toward Naples, with Bertie as their sole companion.

As FRITZ HAD predicted, the news of Bertie's engagement to a Danish princess had infuriated many in Berlin. Prince Karl publicly denounced Fritz, saying the upcoming marriage was the most recent proof that the Crown prince was perpetually confused in his allegiances, since otherwise he would have prevented the match. How exactly Fritz was supposed to have blocked the Prince of Wales's choice of bride remained obscure, and her husband dismissed his uncle's condemnation as just another family unpleasantness. Still, Vicky thought it very generous of Fritz to risk more disapproval and include Bertie, eager to undertake one final overseas excursion as a bachelor, along on their Italian trip.

She studied Italian in the evenings and liked to retire early, while Fritz and Bertie sat up together telling stories in the main salon. She didn't approve of all their smoking and drinking but she was glad to see Fritz relax and enjoy himself. And Bertie's company was as ever a great pleasure to her. Her brother, about to turn twenty-two, had lost his youthful pudginess, and his once-spotty skin had cleared—he looked so debonair and handsome, it was astonishing. When he told an off-color joke in her company, she would frown, but then he'd rib her for being starchy and Mama-like, and she'd end up laughing. On one afternoon when they were alone Vicky confessed how distressing she found it to watch her father-in-law behave so cravenly, neither seeking a democratic compromise with parliament nor abdicating in Fritz's favor as he should have done.

Bertie shook his head. "This chap Bismarck's a loose cannon," he said. "The king won't like all the trouble he riles up. By next year he'll be gone, Puss, mark my words."

Perhaps Bertie was right. She hoped so.

When they anchored in the Bay of Naples, Vicky spent days exploring the ruins and painted the vistas completely incognito. In Rome they visited the Vatican and met Pope Pius IX. Vicky found him a jocose old gentleman who smiled a great deal but had enormous dignity. Sometime later Mama wrote to report how His Holiness had told Odo Russell, British ambassador to the Vatican, "that in the whole course of a long life he had rarely been as impressed by anyone as by her Royal Highness the Crown Princess of Prussia." And Mama was so proud, only wishing Papa were alive to hear it.

For the last week they settled in entrancing Florence. At the small Hotel Paoli on the Lungarno, they were registered as the Count and Countess von Preussen, accompanied by their English cousin, the Baron of Renfew. The other guests—British, French, Swiss, a smattering of Americans—eyed them curiously, and Vicky supposed no one was fooled. But only a single English lady—a tall, stylish brunette wearing a chic navy coat over a matching dress of navy stripes—approached her directly one morning as she waited for Fritz in the front parlor.

"It's the Princess Royal, is it not, Your Highness?" said the woman in a low voice, making a small curtsy.

"Yes," said Vicky, smiling.

"I am Lady Helen Fairfax; my uncle is Henry Cole, who worked with the Prince Consort on the exhibition. I saw you once long ago, when you were a child, at the exhibition opening."

What a great pleasure to speak about that happy day with someone who had witnessed it too. And when Vicky asked the woman what brought her to Florence, Lady Fairfax explained that she had, in the last year, been widowed. Her much older husband had died, and they had had no children. Left with a small income, she had decided to fulfill a long-cherished dream and move to Italy to study sculpture. She had let a small villa in the hills outside the city for two years and would be moving in next week.

While out sightseeing with Fritz and Bertie that morning, Vicky found her mind drifting, imagining a different fate for herself. What if she had been born into another family? And had never married or become a mother? She pictured herself, like Lady Fairfax, a well-bred but obscure English lady with a little money of her own, come to live among artists and intellectuals here in Florence. Would she have been happier with that existence? She didn't know. She found it nearly impossible to envision herself not the daughter of Queen Victoria. But she envied Lady Fairfax the freedom to live in this cosmopolitan milieu, unshackled from official duties and removed from public notice. And she wondered how she, Vicky, would compare to others as an artist and a thinker if she appeared in the world without family antecedents. Could she have been distinguished on her own merits? She wasn't sure, and she suddenly felt sad to realize that she would never know.

That afternoon they visited the Uffizi. She quickly lost track of Fritz and Bertie, who were striding through the galleries intent on seeing everything, while she was content to examine Leonardo's drawings in a quiet room on the second floor.

After an hour she felt a touch at her elbow, and she turned around to find her husband smiling at her, a glint of mischief in his eye.

"*Mein Schatz*, let me show you the best picture of all," he said, and taking her by the hand Fritz led her to stand in front of Titian's *Venus of Urbino*, a pale, reclining nude, holding her hand decorously between her thighs.

"See this beauty? She looks just like you," he said, and he winked at her. The lighthearted Fritz of old.

"I'm nothing like that," Vicky said, peering around anxiously. Had anyone overheard?

Fritz leaned over and whispered in her ear: "Tonight, I hope to feast my eyes on such a beautiful sight again. How fortunate am I?"

She felt her cheeks get hot, and she told him to hush. But his ardor secretly pleased her and she reflected that had she been just a little-known British lady with artistic pretensions, no handsome prince would have sought her hand. Fritz's loyal heart and sterling spirit shone forth every day, and she must remain undaunted in her defense of him when they returned to Prussia and the great disturbance that Herr Bismarck, with all his dangerous ideas, had created.

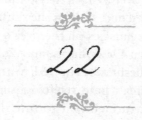

22

Berlin and Windsor, Winter 1863

$\mathcal{T}$hey arrived back at the Kronprinzenpalais on a Tuesday afternoon the week before Christmas, and Fritz and she ran up the stairs together, Vicky nearly vibrating with excitement to see the children again after almost two months. Baby Henry didn't know her but sat placid and deliciously roly-poly on the knee of his wet nurse, Frau Höffer. Two-year-old Charlotte had missed her mama, Mrs. Hobbs said, but when Vicky knelt down to greet the girl, she pretended she didn't care and wouldn't give either of her parents a kiss. Up in the third-floor playroom they found Willy building with blocks. He shouted happily and came barreling toward them as soon as they crossed the threshold. Vicky noticed immediately that his head was even more droopy, and later, when they were alone, Fritz confessed he saw this now too. "Let's get Langenbeck to take a look at him," he said.

Dr. Langenbeck diagnosed torticollis, an imbalance in the strength of Willy's neck muscles, and urged prompt surgery to correct it. But, to Vicky's vast relief, Dr. Wegner argued the prince was much too young for an operation, and he recommended a brace be devised to straighten his head. Fritz asked his favorite saddle maker to work with the doctor. The final contraption had a belt that buckled around Willy's waist affixed at the back to an iron bar. The bar led up to something that resembled a horse's bridle, which slipped over Willy's head, and then a screw on the top of the bar was tightened, to turn the skull to the left and hold it there, stretching the muscles on the neck's right side.

Willy laughed when Dr. Wegner and Fräulein Stahl put the brace on him for the first time, but Vicky turned away so no one could see her tears. The "head-stretching machine," as Wegner dubbed it, looked like a medieval torture device. Fritz clapped the doctor on the back. "Could be a very good thing," he said. With Wegner ordering that Willy spend two hours each day in the brace, the boy soon came to hate it, crying and hitting Fräulein Stahl when she attempted to buckle him in. Often Fritz had to be called to calm Willy and persuade him to don the device. Meanwhile, Dr. Langenbeck advised that to truly strengthen the nerves and muscles, electromagnetic current should be applied regularly to the boy's neck. He came one cold morning in February with a little machine, and held up a loose wire to the side of Willy's throat and shocked him. Willy screamed in pain. Vicky, standing alongside, shrieked at the doctor to stop immediately.

That night at bedtime Vicky went to the nursery and lay down next to Willy in his bed. "I'm sorry, sweetheart, that the doctor hurt you today," she said.

"Nasty, naughty doctor," said Willy.

"I know, he is, but he's trying to help you."

"You must smack the doctor and tell him *nein*."

"I did tell him no. When I saw you had so much pain."

"I will smack him."

"No, Willichen, you mustn't smack him. I won't let him do it again. He's just hoping to make your neck and your arm and all of you grow strong."

"I am strong. Later I will smack him."

"It's true, you are strong, but if you want to be like Papa and ride big horses and do everything Papa does, it takes even more strength."

Willy didn't answer. He slipped two fingers of his right hand into his mouth and started to suck on them. A terrible habit in a child already four, and usually she'd snatch his hand away. But this time she let him be.

"William, sweetheart, you know your uncle Bertie is getting married, in England?" she asked. "Would you like to go with me to the wedding?"

"On a boat?" Willy loved boats.

"First a train and then a boat."

"Papa *kommt mit*?"

"Papa might follow us."

"I want to go."

"In England you'll see Grandmamma again, and Auntie Beatrice, and your uncles. They are big boys but you can play with them."

"We go *morgen*?"

"Not tomorrow, but soon," she said, standing up. She tucked the blanket in more tightly, and thought how unfair it was, all that her little boy had to cope with. He couldn't be left alone to just grow up. A trip together could be a lovely thing.

BUT THEN THERE was the problem of Mama. Her mother told Vicky that in her weak and nervous state the prospect of the wedding exhausted her, and Vicky must come at least two weeks beforehand to take charge of all the entertaining and last-minute arrangements for the ceremony set for March 10. And she definitely could not bring her children. "We shall not have a hole to spare in the castle," her mother wrote. "It is already a fearful squeeze."

Now Vicky wrote to say that while she would come early to help, as the king had agreed, she was loath to leave Willy behind because she'd been away so recently in Italy. Couldn't she have Willy there with her?

To her relief, in her next letter Mama allowed Willy, but described her total despair about the forthcoming event. "It's for me far worse than a funeral to witness," she wrote.

"I almost laughed," Vicky said after she read this passage aloud to Fritz. "Mama sees things in an intensely personal way."

"Which has always been the case," said Fritz, reaching for his pipe. They were sitting together in front of the stove in the upstairs sitting room.

"She doesn't understand why I am happy and excited about Bertie's wedding, since I loved Papa too."

Fritz gave a sad smile. "Your father only died a year ago—it's still fresh in her mind."

"It's been fifteen months. And she seems absolutely determined not to enjoy any part of this!"

"She imagined for years your father would be with her, to see their son and heir married."

"Yes, I know, and to be denied that is very cruel," she conceded.

Here was Fritz, home before nine on a Wednesday evening, and they could sit companionably together. Mama would never enjoy such cozy intimacy again—and some people never had it at all.

"So, what do you think, darling, will you be permitted to come?" she asked.

Fritz sighed. "I'm still not sure."

Fritz had resumed attending the council meetings, but father and son rarely spoke. While the king seemed content with Herr Bismarck's conduct, the minister's actions constantly offended her husband. During their time in Italy the minister-president had demanded that all members of the Prussian civil service take a loyalty oath, swearing fidelity to the crown. Judges, university professors, teachers, and state employees were also banned from promoting any political movement deemed contrary to the views and the will of the government. And Bismarck constantly lectured parliament that they did not live in England, where the ministry answered to the majority in parliament, but in Prussia, where to contest the decisions of the king's ministers was to attack the crown itself. In a speech on January 27 he had declared: "The Prussian monarchy has not yet fulfilled its mission, it is not yet ready to serve as a

mere ornamental feature of your constitutional edifice or to become a superfluous cog in the machinery of government."

Fritz joked. "How will you feel in future if you're married to a
superfluous cog, *mein Schatz*?"

But Vicky didn't find it funny. "I'm looking forward to a future
in which Herr Bismarck is superfluous and gone from our lives,"
she retorted.

Given all the bad feeling about Bertie's marriage in Prussia,
Fritz had, at first, reluctantly resolved to skip the wedding, as
much as he hated to let down his dear brother-in-law and Mama.
But then the baron advised against that, predicting Fritz's absence would create fresh comment in Berlin and in England. Fritz
knew he must approach his father for leave to go but dreaded the
unpleasant conversation he was certain would ensue, and the
possibility of being told no.

"I'm waiting for the right moment," he told Vicky.

In the end, Mama wrote a beseeching letter directly to the king.
Affie had come down with gastric fever and could not act as
Bertie's "supporter" on the day, and the groom requested Fritz in-
stead. Even then, the king consulted Bismarck before agreeing.
They heard the minister told him: "It little matters if the Crown
Prince goes or doesn't go, as everyone knows he's completely in
thrall to his wife's English family." Fritz was permitted a trip of
five days' duration.

"As you said before," Fritz added, "we are by turns insulted and
ignored. We have no real influence or importance now."

"Yes, and that's hard to bear. But it won't last forever."

"Certainly not."

"And you're happy you will be with me on Bertie's wedding
day?" she asked.

"Very happy for that, *Liebling*," he said.

Vicky went on ahead with Willy via Düsseldorf and Belgium to
England. Mama had sent the Scotch dress, complete with little

kilt and silver ornaments, for Willy to wear for the wedding. At first her son didn't want to try on the skirt—he was a boy, he explained to his mother solemnly—but Vicky told him Uncle Arthur and Uncle Leopold would wear theirs. And Willy loved the dirk, the small dagger, attached to his special Highland stockings. He brandished it at Charlotte in the nursery, so Vicky had to confiscate it until the big day.

At the hotel in Düsseldorf, he was thrilled that a small bed for him was pushed right up next to her large one. And for every mile of the train journey he sat on Vicky's lap, watching the unfurling countryside and counting all the white horses they spotted along the way. She had never enjoyed him more. Every time the train stopped he'd ask her anxiously: "*Wir nichts* go home now? *Wir* go on? Mama and me?" And she could hug him and say: "Yes, we are going on together."

They boarded the *Osborne* at Antwerp, and Willy explored every inch of the boat with a pair of kind midshipmen as guides. He'd return to fetch Vicky from time to time, so he could show her the huge wheel, or the line of special brass-rimmed weather gauges, or the impressive piles of ropes and chains, neatly rolled on the deck. The grinning sailors seemed to follow his mixture of German and English words. Only Vicky's vow that they would return to the yacht, to cross back to Belgium with Papa in a few weeks' time, kept him from weeping as they disembarked.

When Vicky, lying in bed at Windsor that night, recalled Willy's wide eyes shining with excitement as he took her around the boat, a wave of love rolled over her, catching her by surprise. Most of the time the guilt and fear about his poor arm acted like a dark, cold undertow on Vicky's feelings—she'd look at Willy and all she could see was what she didn't like about him, not his bright, happy spirit. Which was very wrong, she knew, and she must try to do better.

But then Willy misbehaved and caused a scene at the wedding. Bored by the long ceremony, and sitting far away from his parents, who stood near the bridal pair, he first scratched Leopold's bare legs to get his uncle's attention. Told off for that, he angrily threw his sporran, the Scottish purse, into the aisle, and finally poked Arthur with his dirk. Fritz scolded him afterward, as did Vicky, and the boy cried copiously.

Vicky was sure everyone saw her son as proof of boorish Prussian combativeness and was silently disparaging her for not raising him better. She'd been so mortified she hadn't enjoyed the wedding breakfast at all.

Later she learned that Queen Victoria's grandson Prince Wilhelm of Prussia's "creating a commotion" was even mentioned in the *Sunday Times*'s account of the wedding. But Mama waved off the upset. "William's just a naughty little boy. He'll grow up soon enough," she said.

Of course, some boys remain naughty, Vicky reflected as she watched Bertie and Princess Alexandra ride away for their honeymoon at Osborne. She hoped Bertie would find happiness—the kind that kept a grown man out of trouble—with his beautiful young bride.

23

Berlin and Danzig, Spring 1863

*W*hy not spend half the year at Osborne? Vicky nearly blurted out to Fritz as they were docking at Antwerp. No one in Berlin wanted them, Mama would have Vicky's support close at hand, and they could raise their children in peace on the Isle of Wight. She had this brilliant notion on the tip of her tongue, before acknowledging that her husband would never willingly sacrifice his regimental command, nor would the king permit his grand-children to be constantly in the company of Vicky's family. She was following Fritz to the top of the yacht's narrow gangway—on this cold and misty morning, just past dawn. Willy, who'd been roused from a deep sleep, rested his head on his father's shoulder while Fritz, having hoisted him up with one arm, stretched out the other to grasp the rope handrail. Stepping carefully down behind him through the gray damp, Vicky felt as though they were forsaking safety and light to return to a dark realm of frustration and strife. Then she shook her head impatiently. She herself hadn't slept much, it was always difficult to say goodbye to England, and they had a long day's train ride ahead. What would Papa say? That the times demanded steadfastness and courage, and she could not be knocked under so easily.

TWO DAYS AFTER their return, a friend of Fritz's from his Bonn days, a lawyer named Heinrich Geffcken, asked to meet at the Kronprinzenpalais.

Her husband had come home early from work so as to receive Geffcken informally in the library, before he and Vicky were to depart for a state dinner at the Berliner Schloss. Fritz reported that the lawyer had particularly asked if Vicky might join them.

First the two men studied a daguerreotype that Fritz had unearthed of their Bonn student debating society. "Here I am front and center," Fritz said, tapping on the picture. "Although I never said much, while you, my dear Geffcken, were the noisiest among us, and you're obscured in the back!"

"I was considered overly disputatious, don't you remember? I believe other members pushed me to the rear," Geffcken laughed.

Then they all sat down and the man turned to Vicky: "Has the Crown Prince told you the latest? The minister-president has declared that false reports in the press are dangerous and may derail the proper functioning of government."

Vicky nodded. "He mentioned something of the kind. Also, my secretary saved cuttings for me—I'm afraid I have not yet read them all." The pile of newsprint on her desk towered several inches high. As the baron had often remarked, it was a curious fact about politically backward Prussia that fully five times as many liberal newspapers and magazines were published as conservative ones. Over a million citizens read dailies that criticized the autocratic methods of the new government.

"Bismarck's livid, and he's now dug up some obscure regulations that date back to the Manteuffel era and fined a number of editors for publishing lies. Or stories he considers false reports. And several radical publications and two Catholic weeklies have been closed down altogether," Geffcken said.

"Shameful!" said Vicky.

The lawyer turned to Fritz: " I've come to ask, Prince, that you speak out before these suppressive measures go any farther."

Fritz looked perturbed, his forehead furrowed. "I worry, dear Geffcken, that this is not my role, although I agree it's disgraceful."

Geffcken raised his eyebrows. "I beg your pardon, but you are mistaken. Everyone would heed your words, including the king. I think His Majesty may be ignorant of the insidious nature of what's going on. Bismarck allows no one else to approach him."

"The minister is certainly dogged in his attention, hovering constantly. I never see my father alone any longer," Fritz said with a small smile.

"Princess, what is your opinion?" asked Geffcken. Here's why he'd asked for her—to bolster his case.

Vicky glanced over at Fritz. How to be candid in front of his friend without undercutting him? "I think the prince should carefully consider the demands of his conscience, and if he finds it necessary to speak out in this matter, determine a suitable occasion to do so."

"Just so," said Geffcken, nodding vigorously. "You need to give people hope, Prince, that their freedom will not be curtailed."

"And aren't you obligated to disclaim any part in illegal acts, which these are, I imagine?" Vicky added.

Geffcken nodded. "To restrict the press is contrary to the constitution."

Fritz rubbed his temple nervously. "Let me think it over, and let's see what happens in the next few weeks. Perhaps pressure from the deputies will force Bismarck to reverse course," he said.

Vicky felt deflated, but at least Fritz hadn't ruled out public opposition. "In the meantime you could take the chance to speak to the king privately," she suggested.

Fritz nodded, still perturbed.

After the lawyer left, Fritz said to her: "I mustn't be used as a tool by any faction. And to make a public statement on this—that will enrage my father."

Vicky felt a flash of annoyance. "Can you really stay silent?" she asked.

Fritz frowned but did not answer her then.

THE ANNUAL DIPLOMATIC reception at the Berliner Schloss was held the next week. Crossing the echoing entrance hall on Fritz's arm, Vicky could hear the low roar of dozens of conversations already under way in the Weisser Saal. As soon as they entered, Herr von Beust, the Saxon envoy, a heavyset, voluble gentleman, button-holed Fritz, and Vicky took the opportunity to carefully scan the cavernous room looking for her object—the minister-president. There, she spotted him, tall and pale, standing by the king's side. Since Bismarck had assumed high office, she'd encountered him twice, but at public ceremonies during which they'd had no chance to speak. Both times he'd been elaborately polite, bowing obsequiously to her, acting out a conspicuous reverence—which she took as a taunt. It was high time they had a proper conversation.

On this evening Bismarck wore a black suit and black cravat, which exaggerated his pallor, and he had, balanced on his nose, a pair of black-rimmed spectacles, attached on both sides to a long black ribbon that hung around his neck. He stood a good half a foot taller than the king, and in the dim candlelight he appeared Mephistophelian—his clothes, his coloring, the way his large body was held up by short legs and small feet. Even the shiny dome of his balding head looked sinister to her, as if he were about to sprout horns. Well, she would tell this devil exactly what she thought of his conduct of government.

She glided away from Fritz, and skirting the crowd directly in front of the king, came around on Bismarck's left and looked fixedly over at him. He must have sensed her gaze, for he turned his head, met her eyes and bowed. She nodded, and waited for him to take the necessary steps toward her. He hesitated, then approached.

"Princess, good evening," he said, in English. He looked uneasy, and ignored the hand she stretched out to be kissed, merely bowing again.

"Good evening, Herr Bismarck."

"Congratulations are in order," he said with a vague smile. "Your Highnesses have gained a beautiful sister."

"Yes, we have," said Vicky. "Bride and groom seem very happy together."

"A shame the Danish princess comes with so much political complexity."

"This does not concern us," she answered curtly. "Princess Alexandra is a member of our family now."

Bismarck raised his eyebrows. "I always wonder, Princess, why you do not choose to be more protective of your husband."

Already he was trying to knock her off balance—she refused to allow it.

"Sir, I seek you out not to discuss my family but to tell you how disappointed I am in you. I had prayed you might prove an honorable statesman despite all that was said and rumored beforehand. Now my hopes are dashed. With your unprincipled and misguided policies, you are setting back the country's progress by decades."

Bismarck laughed. "Princess, you are always—what is the English expression? Like a breath of the spring air. So lively, and even your stern disapproval on this occasion cannot dim that pleasure for me."

She frowned, but he continued: "Perhaps you could start a fashion for vivaciousness and persuade more German women to attempt it. In that way you might actually do some good for your adopted country."

"Do not stray from the topic, sir," she said, trying to sound like Mama at her sternest.

He smiled again, the wretched man. "Our topic is politics then?"

"Indeed, and matters of state."

"In that arena you are an amateur, Your Highness, and I beg you to leave it to others."

"Not when I see so clearly how your administration ignores the constitution, denies the press its rights, and encourages bellicosity."

"Goodness," said Bismarck. "So much to answer for!"

"I would like to hear you justify it all," she retorted.

"Where to start? What will satisfy you? Let me think—first

principles, I suppose. In the case of a conflict between the crown and parliament, the residual powers remain with the monarch; this is how our law has it. And as the king's first minister I am obligated to operate his government as he desires. I am undertaking to do exactly that." He smiled jauntily, but his eyes remained watchful, waiting to see how she'd call him out.

"Nonsense," she replied. "Parliament was assigned taxing and spending prerogatives by the constitution. And freedom of the press is sacrosanct."

He raised his eyebrows. "Your Highness, let's address your true concern. I ask you: why do we in Prussia have to be like other countries? We're not England. Why start now?"

"Because there's no need to turn your back on the English model, it's an extremely good one. You are reluctant to adopt it, sir, because you prefer to exercise power unfettered."

"How can you call me unfettered, when I serve at the pleasure of His Majesty the king?"

"At the moment you have taken advantage of the king's preoccupation with army reform to cut corners and pursue your agenda extra-legally. That's reprehensible."

For a moment he looked a bit abashed. Was she imagining it?

"I regret, Princess, that I do not enjoy your confidence. I had hoped that you would appreciate, as so many others do now, that the stalemate between the crown and the deputies could not continue. It made Prussia a laughingstock and was impeding progress in many important ways."

"The situation was not so dire as to require the sweeping away of free expression and your imposing all sorts of loyalty oaths and the like."

He looked at her curiously. "You see no problem with ceaseless attacks on the government in the press? Or the constant pitched battles in the parliament and on the bench? This was beneficial to the country in your opinion?"

"The free exchange of ideas is vital to an open society."

Again that curious look. "Open, is that the goal? Which might

suit you and other intellectuals, but would it be good for the common man?"

"Of course. Fundamental civil liberties are the basis of a sound
justice system."

He smiled. "I believe in justice as much as the next man, but
what we require now in Prussia is a strong executive and an assertive foreign policy. You can't concede this, Princess? Even a
small bit?"

It sounded like an appeal, but looking him straight in the eye
she couldn't be sure. His expression was opaque. Was he simply
condescending to her? Or perhaps waiting for her to capitulate to
him on some point so he could crow about that to others?

"What you're doing is in no way acceptable," she said.

"And yet you enjoy a position of great privilege in the state that
I fight to preserve," he replied, his tone queerly light for all the
portent it carried.

"My position has nothing to do with it. Although the king's
does. His moral role remains vital." No point in conceding the
monarch had played his part inadequately in recent months.

"I had hoped you'd grown," Bismarck countered sharply. "But
you continue to echo your father's views, insist on the peculiar
constitutional system that flowers in the damp clime of Britain,
without understanding how here, in Prussia, a deep, traditional
conservatism must contend with forces unleashed by the revolution and constant pressures—the huge number of immigrants
from Poland, the demands of new industry, the desire for a
proper nation-state of the Germans—all of this." He paused and
then added: "Moving the country forward requires . . . what is the
English word for *Geschicklichkeit*?"

"I suppose dexterity," she said, frowning. "But—"

"I use dexterity, as I attempt to preserve and expand Prussia."

She wasn't quite sure what he meant, beyond elaborate self-
justification, and she couldn't bear to hear Papa maligned. "My
father would never agree that opportunistic maneuvering should

supersede the concepts of right and wrong," she said, her voice rising.

She heard Bismarck sigh. "I suppose I waste my time trying to reason with a dead man," he said shortly.

"You are reasoning with me, sir, and I have my own views. Of the duty ministers have to conduct honorable government and to answer to the people's representatives."

He shook his head impatiently and said, "My point is lost on you."

This infuriated her. "I suppose you don't believe a woman can follow?"

Now he laughed. "I never doubt your intelligence, or your influence, Princess."

"What influence?"

"I believe your influence over your husband is very pronounced."

"And you wish that otherwise?"

He gazed down at her for a long moment. "My hope is that you appreciate the responsibility you take on when you exercise your persuasive powers." He smiled—a small, nasty smile. "And don't be so certain that the paths you choose for the prince are the right and safe ones."

She opened her mouth to ask what exactly he meant by that, but a footman had come up behind Bismarck and tapped him on the shoulder. The servant whispered something in his ear, and then the minister said: "I am being summoned back into the king's presence. Good evening." He departed with just a nod of his head.

How vexing to watch Bismarck slip away, having enjoyed the last word. In what way were the paths she picked for Fritz unsafe? Was he implying her judgment was poor? She drifted to the side of the room to remain undisturbed as she went over the whole conversation. She'd done adequately well and scored important points, she was sure. She may not have persuaded him of much, but she had sensed that he was bestirred, and that pleased her too.

Both Lady Buchanan, the wife of the British ambassador, and a friend called Mathilde Siemens had recently complained that, in society, Bismarck's conversation was banal and perfunctory, and he never took any notice of their remarks. But with her he'd been interested, engaged, even seeking, she sensed, some approbation. Which was odd considering she could never endorse his repressive measures. He must know that. So why did he even venture an overture? For that was what it was, an overture, she was quite sure.

Later she confessed to Fritz that she had taken Bismarck to task, and how he'd been uncontrite and claimed he was running the government the way the king wanted it run.

"I'm not sure that man is sincere about anything," Fritz said. "It suits him to play my father's devoted servant at the moment."

Vicky nodded. "Is there no one to convince your father of how dangerous Bismarck is? The king mustn't like the uproar over the press restrictions."

"Didn't I tell you? I approached my father the other day to tell him I oppose what's happening. First, he laughed, and said the journalists deserve to be jabbed at—they pretend they speak for the people but they only speak for themselves. And then he forbade me from making any public comment."

Vicky sighed. "So you're supposed to act as a kind of mute puppet? While Bismarck holds the puppet strings?"

Fritz flinched. "I don't like to regard myself that way."

"I'm sorry, darling, I know you're in a difficult position."

He looked very cast down for the rest of the evening, and Vicky silently castigated herself for not being more sensitive. But really, how insufferable to live as passive witnesses to the outrageous actions taken by Bismarck in the king's name. She despised it.

ONE DAY EARLY in May, Fritz returned home unexpectedly when she still sat at luncheon with cousin Adie. He motioned for her to come out in the hall to speak privately with him.

"I've been ordered to undertake an inspection tour of forts in the eastern provinces," he told her, very aggrieved. "I'm leaving tomorrow, apparently. For a month."

Her suspicions aroused, Vicky asked quickly: "Did your father tell you this directly?"

Fritz shook his head, a mutinous look on his face. "No, he had Roon do it. At today's Crown Council there was a long discussion about imposing additional press restrictions. Bismarck is still irate about the journalists, arguing they publish slander and hatred day after day. He proposed a new statute that would ban any publication that takes a general attitude dangerous to the public welfare."

Vicky scoffed. "Which is ridiculous. Who would make the judgment? Bismarck himself?"

"The ministers seemed ready to accede to it all. I sat there in a rage, saying nothing, as that's what my father prefers."

"So the king, too, agrees?"

"I could tell that he has his doubts. But Bismarck is making progress with him. Getting him preoccupied over the corruption of soldiers, who are naïve and have no knowledge of politics. The minister tells him revolutionaries with evil intent could use the press to turn the troops against the crown." Fritz rolled his eyes.

"What nonsense."

"*Genau,* so afterward I informed my father I would in no way support such a law."

"Then he ordered you on tour?" Vicky asked.

"He told me I shouldn't get so exercised about it. But when I continued to argue, he summoned Roon, and the minister came into my father's office with an itinerary, which he then went over with me. It's all written out here. They must have set it up beforehand." Fritz pulled a piece of paper out of his coat pocket.

Now Vicky understood. "They believe if you are absent you can't, or you won't, object," she said.

"Exactly. And I resent it," he replied, his eyebrows pulled down, scowling.

Vicky's heart leapt—Fritz was showing his mettle at last. "I suppose you can't simply refuse to go?" she asked.

"Defy a direct order? No."

"What about telling your father that your absence will not make any difference? That you would still object, publicly, should a ban be imposed."

Fritz waggled his head, assessing. "*Ja*. Maybe that."

"Let's think carefully. Best to put it in writing. Before you leave, send a letter to the king, and another to Bismarck, laying out your position. Then they can't claim they didn't know how you'd react," Vicky said.

Fritz nodded. "Will you help me draft these?"

"Yes. And if the ban goes forward you will have to find a place to declare that you do not approve of it—or any of the other auto-cratic methods of this government."

Fritz nodded again. "If it comes to that, I will have no choice."

Vicky had a gleeful thought: perhaps this would be the way Herr Bismarck's goose got cooked.

FRITZ WROTE TO his father stating that should the king consent to the unconstitutional measure his minister-president proposed, Fritz, as Crown Prince, would have the "unhappy" duty to protest in public. He wrote another, similar letter to Bismarck. Vicky copied out both in her own hand to keep as a record.

Fritz left the next morning. Two weeks passed and nothing happened. The king must have decided he wanted no public row with his son and instructed the minister-president not to go for-ward. Finally, they were doing good, exerting the proper influ-ence. Fritz wrote from Breslau to say he too assumed the matter closed. He asked Vicky to meet him on June 4 in Danzig, where they would preside together over a parade and military review and then have a short holiday before returning home to Potsdam.

On the afternoon of June 3, as Vicky and Dawes were stand-ing in front of the open wardrobe choosing which gowns to take, a maid came in to say the king's messenger had arrived and was asking to see her downstairs. "His Majesty requests you put this into the Crown Prince's hand tomorrow," the man said, passing her a large white envelope with Fritz's initials—FW—written on the front in the dark brown ink the king favored.

Vicky couldn't sleep that night in the train carriage to Danzig, she felt so apprehensive. From time to time she took the letter out of the pocket of her cloak and stared at it, wishing she knew exactly what message was contained inside. She was tempted to open it, to be better prepared to advise Fritz when he read the contents, but stopped herself. She mustn't stoop to unseemly behavior, even at this volatile moment.

She met Fritz at the city hall, in the office of the mayor of Danzig, Leopold von Winter, another of his friends from Bonn. Winter, an energetic gentleman with a bushy black mustache, had dined with them several times in Berlin. The morning newspapers were spread out on the large wooden desk.

"Can I guess? Has the worst happened?" Vicky asked as she shrugged off her cloak and untied her bonnet.

"*Ja*, the government has gone forward with the ban," said Fritz shortly. "The list of newspapers and magazines that will be closed immediately is even longer than I expected."

Then Fritz took his father's letter from Vicky and tore it open. After a minute he said: "The king orders me to accept the new regulation and say nothing against it."

"No thanks for the tact and discretion you have shown so far?" Vicky asked facetiously.

"None," Fritz said with a short rueful laugh. "He only reproaches me for my previous letter."

"People here will find this decree enraging," Mayor von Winter said to Fritz. "You can't ignore it when you speak today."

Fritz nodded and looked at Vicky. "You agree, *Liebling*?"

"Yes, because if you don't declare that you abhor the ban, and explain that you had no part in devising it, everyone will believe you support it. You could lose as much as your father by staying silent."

"And the consequences?" he said.

"Of speaking out?" she asked.

Fritz nodded. "The Prussian officer's code of conduct applies to me as well. The king could strike me off the army list and strip me of my command. And, think, he might be persuaded . . ."

Fritz paused. He abruptly got up from the wooden chair he had been sitting in and, pointing at the door, said "Excuse us, Winter, do you think you might step out while I speak with my wife?"

Fritz watched the heavy door close behind his friend and then nodded to himself, grim. He turned to her and said in a soft voice: "It would cost him something, but my father might be persuaded that Fritz Karl is, after all, the proper heir. And he could rely on Bismarck's help in whatever machinations would be required to push me aside."

Vicky felt so mournful for him—her husband was never happy at odds with his father, and yet he'd rarely enjoyed his deep affection. And now he was forced to concede that the king would be willing to choose another man's son to be his heir. But it had been ever thus, this lamentable family dissonance, and weren't there higher stakes now than personal ones? Not just the freedom of the press, but a duty to call out the new government for its high-handed approach? If Fritz said nothing now, how much worse might things get? Vicky was resolved.

"We shall have to live with what comes," she said. "Bismarck is the author of this mischief. The king may change course if you publicly declare your opposition."

"I doubt it. There's nothing my father hates more than insubordination."

"Your choice is to remain passive or to speak out and refuse to be party to illegality."

"And you advise speaking out, come what may?"

"I do," she said fiercely.

Fritz gazed at her for a long minute, the way he so often used to, as if trying to absorb her face's every detail. And then he smiled. "How can I deny you? My clever, courageous wife."

"So you'll do it? Today?" Vicky felt a surge of exhilaration, so strange, since they might be taking the first steps toward being disowned. But at least Fritz—and she—would no longer be mute. And who knew? The country might very well rally around the Crown Prince, demand the ministry reform or be dismissed, perhaps even force an abdication. She felt ablaze with energy.

"I will," he said.

IT REQUIRED SOME negotiation on Vicky's part, brokering between what Mayor von Winter longed for Fritz to assert and what Fritz, as Crown Prince, was willing to say. The mayor hoped Fritz would take the opportunity of today's parade to deliver a total condemnation of Bismarck's government.

"I would be inserting myself too far into the political sphere if I did that," Fritz said.

"But you are obligated to explain clearly what concerns you about this situation," Vicky said.

"I regret that Bismarck and his disastrous measures have put such distance between the people and the king," Fritz said stoutly.

"Start there," advised Vicky. "And then explain briefly why the press decree is illegal and disastrous."

Fritz nodded.

"And you can end by assuring people of the noble, fatherly, and magnanimous intentions of the king." Not that she believed her father-in-law practiced any of these virtues.

"*Gut*, let's write that," said Fritz. Together they composed the short speech.

It was a glorious, sunny afternoon. People had filled the town square, a large cobblestoned space lined with tall, narrow stone houses—painted pink and yellow and red—topped with orange-tiled roofs. Vicky admired how each house had some unique detail: quaint embellished gables, or a gilded clock, or a set of three poles on the roof flying the golden lion banner of the city, the red-and-white striped flag of the Hanseatic League and the black eagle of Prussia. The crowd faced the reviewing stand, set up next to the

Junkerhof, the merchants' headquarters, directly opposite the huge town fountain, which featured an iron statue of the god Neptune.

Vicky thought Fritz himself looked godlike as he stood at the podium, his head thrown back, the medals on his chest glinting, his words rolling out over the rapt crowd. In his respectful, reasonable, and soldierly way he declared to the world that some principles were inviolable. He remained loyal to his father, even as he rejected the corrupting influence of the king's first minister. Vicky, exulting, imagined Bismarck reading the speech and fuming. This public condemnation of the minister's unconstitutional behavior from the Crown Prince would resonate all over Germany.

Cheers afterward rose to nearly deafening levels, echoing off the stone houses. The police had to clear a path for them to walk the short distance from the reviewing stand to the hotel. Vicky held tight to Fritz's left arm, and as they passed, men and women with joyful faces reached out from between the officers standing on either side to touch them. The mood was delirious, and for a moment Vicky reflected on how quickly people's passion could be aroused. There was vast energy that lurked in big crowds, which could be stirred up by a speaker's words. Today the citizens of Danzig had been eager to hear the Crown Prince defend liberty, but could not the same excitement be incited by less rational opinions? It wasn't a privilege to be played with lightly—this adulation one could elicit from large public gatherings. Another reason to adore Fritz, she thought, squeezing his arm. He used his influence judiciously.

As people called out, "Long life to the Crown Prince," Fritz beamed and nodded, acknowledging everyone. *"Danke, danke,"* he murmured, and declared frequently, "Long life to the king."

TWO HOURS LATER, in their hotel room, Fritz read aloud a telegram from his father. He was ordered to immediately retract his remarks, return to Potsdam, and confine himself to the Neues Palais and its grounds.

For a fearful moment, Vicky worried that Fritz regretted the speech, and she flashed back to Bismarck's asking her why she was not more protective of her husband. Had she pushed Fritz too far?

Fritz tossed the telegram down on the desk and looked over at her. "So, there we are, *mein Schatz,* as we expected," he said, and shrugged. He sat down on the foot of the bed and started to take off his boots.

"You're not retracting?"

"No. I said what needed to be said."

"I am so very proud, Fritz. I can hardly express it."

He smiled at her, but his eyes were pensive.

"Maybe we should go and live in England for a while," Vicky said.

"I know you would like that," Fritz said. His boots in hand, he stood up and placed them neatly under the desk.

"You would miss the army," she said.

"So much. And my country. I cannot imagine abandoning Prussia, even at this moment when my father despises me." He walked, in his stocking feet, to stand in front of the open window and gaze down at the square below, where many people still lingered. Vicky could hear excited chatter and, coming from farther away, the brassy clanging of a band.

She stood up and went to Fritz. She embraced him from behind, resting her cheek for many minutes on the warm expanse of his back. Perhaps they would now be exiles, not sure of their position, living day to day. Would Fritz hire himself out as a mercenary? Would they be forced to live on the charity of her family? She had her dowry money, but that would not pay for the kind of life they lived now. She suddenly pictured them, herself and Fritz and the children, huddled around a fire in a small cottage like the ones on the Balmoral estate. It wouldn't come to that, surely. Plenty of men would recognize that what Fritz had said today was correct. Reason would prevail. Wouldn't it?

ONCE HOME IN Potsdam, Fritz wrote a long letter to his father to say he regretted that they remained divided on this issue and volunteering to resign all his official roles, even his army commission, if it so pleased the sovereign. The king was not mollified. Moltke came the next evening to tell Fritz he faced arrest, court-martial, and confinement in a military prison.

Fritz recounted this to Vicky in the upstairs sitting room after Moltke had left. He spoke in a matter-of-fact tone—she sensed he was almost relieved to know what they were facing. She, on the other hand, felt deeply unnerved.

"General von Manteuffel has convinced my father that the punishment for disobeying a commanding officer must apply no less to the heir to the throne than to the most obscure ensign," Fritz said. "And naturally Uncle Karl is loudly agreeing."

"Fritz Karl, too?"

"My cousin sent me a note to say that he is going to Baden to visit his mother, but he wishes me well."

"No help at all!"

"At least he's staying out of it."

Vicky struggled to comprehend it: the Prussian military machine, brutal and unforgiving, would destroy a popular and gallant prince? The heir to the throne? This would have been absurd, were it not so frightening. Yet Fritz was calm.

"What now?" she asked, straining to keep her voice steady.

"Moltke intends to go back and reason with my father, but he doesn't promise success. Listen, *Liebling*, he and I talked it over and we've decided. He'll know if I'm going to be arrested and he will come to take you and the children out of the country. You will leave immediately, no heavy luggage, only what you can carry. The English servants, Mrs. Hobbs and your dresser and the maids, can accompany you, but that's all. Osborne's best. If it's a year or more before I can join you, borrow money from your mother and rent some suitable estate nearby. I will not impose on the queen's hospitality indefinitely, and I think she will understand that I will find a way to repay her, somehow, someday." He looked at her steadily. This might have been the worst moment in all his life, but, the die cast, he remained resolute and collected.

"Oh, Fritz," she said, beginning to sob. "I can't go. They can lock me up as well. I don't care. I won't leave you here."

"Absolutely not," he said, suddenly stern. "You must promise me that you'll do exactly what I say."

"But when they put you on trial? I want to be here, to support—"

"No, let my mother cope. She'll be loud and unrelenting in my defense. Her cherished only son, attacked unjustly by the forces of reaction! Imagine how she'll enjoy it!" He laughed shortly. "I want you and our children to be safe and unmolested, out, away from all this madness."

Because he was so composed she couldn't scream. Still, she wanted to, and to weep and tear at her clothes. It all seemed unthinkable, but at the same time, sickeningly real. Had Fritz's speech really been so incendiary? The king's wrath was disproportionate—Bismarck must have been orchestrating this. Perhaps the minister had been warning her when they met and she had missed it, so busy had she been scolding him. Vile man. Now he was taking his revenge.

"No tears, no regrets," Fritz said, voice lightening. "If this is a rebel army, I'm the commander. Those are my orders."

She wiped her eyes with a handkerchief and tried to pull herself together. "Fritz, I didn't expect—"

He shook his head. "We can't grieve, *Liebling*. We did what we had to do, and the king will do what he wants to do."

Fritz slept that night holding her tightly against him. But he fell asleep before she did, and slept soundly, while she lay awake for hours, full of dread, wondering what would become of them.

GENERAL VON MOLTKE returned the next morning just before noon, and Fritz and Vicky received him together in the drawing room. She was shaking as she held on to Fritz's arm.

"I've come with good news," he said after bowing.

Vicky's heart leapt. The king must have seen sense and forgiven Fritz.

"The court-martial will not go forward," said the general, "and while a formal reprimand will be issued, it will not be made public."

"That's something," said Fritz cautiously.

"That's so much!" exclaimed Vicky. "Does the king accept now that Fritz has done nothing wrong? That he was perfectly right to say what he did?"

The general smiled. "No, Your Highness, I'm afraid not."

"What then?" she asked.

"Herr Bismarck opposes any further action being taken in this matter," Moltke said.

Fritz shook his head. "Incredible."

"I don't understand. Bismarck is supporting Fritz?" asked Vicky.

"Only because it suits him," Fritz said.

"Exactly right," said Moltke. "The minister-president has advised the king not to make a liberal martyr of his son. And the king has accepted that advice."

Vicky struggled to take this in.

"I retain my command?" asked Fritz.

"*Ja*, and you will still sit on the council. Bismarck orders no change in your official status. However—"

"Ah, the catch!" said Fritz.

"It's not a particularly punitive one. Bismarck suggested, and the king agrees, that it is better that you and the Crown Princess leave Berlin for the time being."

"To go to England?" asked Vicky, her spirits rising.

"No, to live somewhere out of the way, here in Prussia. An acquaintance of Bismarck's has been persuaded to lend you a house on the island of Rügen, in the Baltic Sea."

"How convenient," said Fritz.

"Isn't it?" answered the general.

Looking down at Vicky, Fritz said, "I hear Rügen is beautiful, *Liebling*. Quite wild, not neat and tidy, like the Isle of Wight."

Vicky's head was a whirl of questions: How long would this banishment last? What would the public explanation be? Was the king contemplating making Fritz Karl heir? But as Fritz's manner remained unruffled she thought she must be too. "I'm sure I will enjoy it, if we can be together there, along with the children, yes?" she asked.

"*Jawohl*," said the general. "The whole family goes. For two or three months. Until this episode is forgotten."

OF COURSE, VICKY was relieved that Fritz was spared a trial, prison, exile, and any further punishment. But she was incensed that the king's leniency had been engineered by Bismarck—and how the minister so clearly had the upper hand. He probably considered them in his debt and believed he needn't worry about them further, that they'd have to stay *stumm*. Well, they weren't completely without recourse.

Before departing Potsdam, she copied out and assembled three complete sets of Fritz's correspondence with his father—all letters sent and received—concerning the press ban. Vicky sent one set to Mama and gave another to the baron for safekeeping, and a third set she sent to a new friend, the political attaché at the British embassy, a man called Robert Morier. In her accompanying note to Morier she wrote that should anyone ask, he could feel free to inform them fully of Fritz's position.

When a number of these letters leaked out and appeared in the London *Times* and in the magazine *Europe*, published in the free city of Frankfurt, Vicky was glad. Because of Bismarck's press edicts, none of the Prussian newspapers dared to support the Crown Prince or commend his Danzig speech.

Fritz asked her nothing about where the leaks might have come from. She sensed he preferred not to know.

ON RÜGEN, THEY saw no one. The long, empty weeks passed slowly but not unpleasantly. Many mornings they ventured out in a small boat to look at the seals and to fish. Fritz and she would don two battered, broad-brimmed straw hats they'd found hanging near the back door and march down to the dock, Willy in tow. They'd seat him in the prow wearing the cork buoyancy vest that Affie, now an officer in the British navy, had sent for him. And they'd set out, Fritz at the oars. Willy loved to watch the white-tailed eagles soaring above them, wheeling and swooping, and coming to perch on ledges on the chalk cliffs above the sea. Other times the boy would lean over to drag his fingers in the water. And always he wanted to direct his father on where to steer. They spent many happy hours together. Vicky was content.

24

Berlin, Windsor, and Berlin Again, Fall–Spring 1863–1864

In late September Vicky and Fritz returned to Berlin, and the king and queen invited them for dinner. Danzig was not mentioned once. Fritz's father spoke politely to them, but remotely, the way he might greet strangers. When Fritz pointed out that Vicky's mother missed her Prussian grandchildren, the king looked puzzled, as if he hadn't any part in preventing them from traveling abroad. So her dear husband announced they would go to England for a month before Christmas, and the king did not object.

Fritz's mother called at the Kronprinzenpalais the next day. After Mama's unhappiness had been mentioned at dinner, the queen had chimed in, citing her own grief at being separated from the children while they lived on Rügen. Now her mother-in-law sat in the nursery, holding baby Henry on her lap, beaming at Willy and Charlotte, who were sitting at a little wooden table across the room gobbling up some sweets she'd brought for them.

Vicky felt annoyed. It was ten in the morning, not an appropriate time for anyone to eat chocolate. But the queen seemed less embittered than earlier in the year, and now that Vicky had returned home perhaps they could recapture the fellow feeling they'd shared before Bismarck's appointment.

"Thank you for your letters, Aunt. Fritz was very grateful for your steadfast support throughout," Vicky said.

The queen said nothing, just raised her eyebrows. Which surprised Vicky. "You don't believe you were steadfast?" she asked.

The queen sighed and motioned for the nursemaid to come and take Henry from her.

"My dear, what exactly did you and Fritz hope to accomplish with that public proclamation?" she asked. "Did you think it would put Bismarck in his place?"

"I might not express it quite like that, but the speech made a lot of difference. All the liberals know now that Fritz is on their side, and he had a chance, for once, to express his deep resentment—the resentment we all feel to have the country co-opted in this disgraceful way."

"But what has changed?"

"What do you mean?"

"The ban remains in force. Bismarck is undisturbed in his exercise of office. What advantage has been gained by Fritz's petulant show of disobedience?"

Vicky frowned. Why was the queen being dismissive? Bismarck was her enemy, too. "Nothing immediate, but your son said what had to be said," she answered stoutly.

The queen shook her head. "Of course, a court-martial would have been ludicrous, and Fritz is not a traitor. But making such a display was foolhardy on his part."

"I don't agree," said Vicky. "Fritz could not remain silent."

The queen pursed her lips. "By openly opposing the chief minister you brought unwelcome attention to yourselves, Vicky, and Bismarck will be unstinting now in his efforts to isolate Fritz. And you are already derided in the Wilhelmstrasse as the interfering little minx who put him up to it."

Vicky felt shocked and strangely hurt by her mother-in-law's scorn. She took a moment to recover but then she drew herself up on her chair and lifted her chin. "I—or rather we—cannot take any notice of the craven persons who do nothing to oppose this terrible man and are content to insult us," she said.

"You can never help yourself, can you, my dear?"

"Help myself how?"

"You're so sure you're right, you rush forward, saying things without considering carefully the consequences. You encouraged this outburst of Fritz's and now he's defeated and held up to ridicule as a man who does what his wife directs even when it's not sensible."

Vicky longed to leap up and order the queen out of the palace. Her right arm quivered to point the way. At the same time, in a cooler part of her brain, she wondered if the queen wasn't correct. Could they have misjudged matters? No, she refused to repent—or to be cowed. She took a deep breath. "If I devoted my time to listening to all the unkind gossip about me in Berlin, I would have no time left for anything else. And Fritz says he has no regrets for what has occurred. That's all that matters to me."

The queen gave her a long, assessing look. "Very well, my dear, if that is how you choose to look at it, I suppose I cannot dissuade you. But I advise that you think more carefully in future. It's folly to take on that devious man with artless public display and childish gestures."

IN THE WAKE of the queen's visit Vicky felt alternately maligned, humiliated, and defiant. She turned over the matter endlessly in her head, before remembering Papa's saying once that to do something because it is right, even if painful, is to score a moral victory. The speech at Danzig represented such a victory, however much Junkers sneered, the king raged, and the minister-president dismissed them. Fritz was more than ever lauded as the great hope of the future, the modern prince who stood up for principle. Hundreds of men from all over Germany had written to him, thanking and praising him. Cousin Adie's husband, Fritz, Duke of Augustenburg, had penned one of the most effusive missives.

Her Fritz had folded this letter into a small square and carried it around with him until the paper softened and began to fray.

Now that they had returned to the capital, Vicky invited Adie and Fritz Augustenburg to dine frequently. In fact, their friends had troubles of their own. By rights, Augustenburg should have ruled in the disputed duchies of Schleswig and Holstein—he'd descended directly from the sixteenth-century ruler of those lands, which straddled German-speaking and Danish-speaking territory. But the duchies had been assigned decades ago to the Danish crown, to be the personal property of the Danish king. This settlement infuriated German nationalists everywhere, and especially in German-speaking Holstein, which lay just beyond the outskirts of Hamburg and included the strategic deep-water port of Kiel on the Baltic Sea. In Holstein men considered the Duke of Augustenburg their rightful ruler, and they resented that the Danish-speaking minority in Schleswig clung to another.

During the previous spring the king of Denmark, Frederick VII, had declared that to end the eternal divisiveness, a new national constitution would be drafted recognizing the duchies as properly part of Denmark. From all over Germany came the outcry: the Danes had to surrender the territory they had no right to, the Duke of Augustenburg had to be restored, and Schleswig-Holstein had to become a member state of the German Confederation. The Frankfurt Diet called for the seizure of the duchies by force of arms.

Now this provocative Danish king had died. Bertie's father-in-law, Alix's father, was set to be crowned Christian IX. The Copenhagen parliament insisted he sign the new constitution before the coronation. And it appeared he would do so.

When Fritz Augustenburg asked them if he had their support for his claim, despite their family connection to the new Danish king, Fritz said yes immediately. And Vicky nodded, too, although she worried. Would Bertie and Alix understand that as Crown Princess of Germany's largest state, Vicky was duty-bound to be a German patriot? And might they see that Adie and Fritz Augustenburg were also part of the family and valuable allies in the struggle for a more liberal Prussia? Vicky couldn't be sure. It was a muddle. And the timing distressed her—she hoped this looming matter would not intrude on their English holiday.

No such luck. At breakfast on December 4, when Fritz and Vicky had already been resident at Windsor for two weeks, they learned that Alix's father had signed the new constitution. She and Fritz sat with Mama at the table, strewn with the morning's papers. Bertie and his wife had come two days before to join them here at the castle, but, typically late arrivers at breakfast, they had not yet appeared.

"My position today is quite dreadful," Mama announced. "My natural sympathies are with my nephew Fritz Augustenburg. And dear Papa said before he died that Holstein in particular belongs to Germany. But Alix will see it differently."

Vicky nodded sadly.

"Oh why, oh why, must Bertie's wife be a Dane?" moaned Mama. She had previously confided to Vicky that while she did not find Alix particularly clever or interesting, the girl and Bertie got on well. The young couple lived a fast life, with many late-night London parties, raucous country weekends, and a band of rather risqué friends. Still the new Princess of Wales expected a baby in March—and that pleased everyone.

Ten minutes later Bertie came in, leading Alix by the hand. Her brother shot Vicky a warning look across the table and she resolved to say nothing. As soon as Alix sat down, she began to sob. "The duchies belong to Papa—to no one else," she said.

"The citizens of Schleswig and Holstein disagree," said Fritz calmly. "In both duchies, the local assemblies voted this week once again to support the Augustenburg claim."

"Not the moment for any comment from you, Fritz," Bertie snapped.

"These are just facts," Fritz said. Vicky could tell her husband was trying to be helpful.

"That scoundrel Bismarck will hide behind such facts, and parrot your and Vicky's liberal sentiments about German self-determination. But watch, Prussian support for Fritz Augustenburg will have one aim, the aggrandizement of Prussia," her brother declared.

Fritz scowled.

"That's so unfair!" Vicky said heatedly. "Not all Prussians think as Bismarck does, Bertie."

"We shall soon see."

"I have already shown by my own actions—" Fritz began.

"Feeble as they were," said Bertie.

"Don't you dare say that!" said Vicky. "Fritz opposed Bismarck publicly, and paid a stiff price for it."

"What price was that exactly?" asked Bertie scornfully.

"Children, stop this quarreling at once. I cannot stand it," shrieked Mama.

Vicky ignored her. "Bertie, Fritz won't forsake his old friend and the desires of the German nation, just because King Christian has decided he'd like to take territory not rightfully his own."

"And you can't help but insult my wife and her family right here in our home."

"It's still Mama's home and I am not insulting—" said Vicky.

"You are, and behaving in your usual overbearing, bossy way."

"Now you're insulting me!" she shouted at Bertie.

Mama began weeping loudly, joining in with Alix's sobs, and she demanded that Fritz and Vicky leave the room.

It took the whole day and a long walk alone before Vicky saw she had no desire to fall out with either Bertie or Alix over this. Although why Bertie wasn't more loyal to his first family, instead of the rather parvenu one he'd married into, she couldn't think. And how nasty he'd been to Fritz. Still, before tea, she sought out her brother and his wife. They were sitting together in the conservatory, the only place at Windsor where Mama permitted Bertie to smoke.

"I came to apologize, Alix. I know your father is an honorable man."

Alix nodded, saying nothing.

"Bertie, I beg your pardon too. I had hoped to avoid politics entirely during our holiday."

"The whole matter is very tedious," said her brother. "The sooner it's over, the better."

"Bertie, you're not saying Papa has to give in?" asked Alix in her thin, high voice.

"No, I'm not saying that." Bertie patted her hand.

Vicky imagined that the Danish king would soon be forced to give in, one way or another, but she didn't argue. Mama had banned any further discussion of the duchies under her roof.

However, before they departed a week later, her mother took Fritz and Vicky aside to say that while she couldn't tell this to Bertie, she favored the Duke of Augustenburg's claim and had written to the prime minister to inform him he must follow suit.

BACK IN BERLIN, Vicky heard many unkind remarks about the Danes and their clueless new king, and repeated a few herself, which wasn't properly loyal, but she couldn't resist. The consensus was simple: to recover Schleswig-Holstein for the German nation, Germans everywhere must march immediately to the aid of their brothers to the north.

Fritz worried that Bismarck—who some months ago had dismissed the desires of the Holstein Germans as being of little concern to Prussia—would drag his feet coming to their defense. But no, the minister-president immediately reached out to the Austrians, and on January 16 the two German-speaking powers, along with the rest of the Confederation, demanded Denmark give up any plan to absorb the duchies. Copenhagen refused. War was declared. Fritz was thrilled—he and the reorganized Prussian army would finally be going into action.

Why hadn't those silly Danes realized they had no choice but to back down? How many would die because of their foolish pride? Vicky felt exasperated. But at least Prussia would now advance the cause of German self-determination—a birthright already enjoyed by the English. And the French.

And this time she resolved to be brave for Fritz. She packed his trunks, she helped him select the horses to take, and on his last night at home a week later she had the servants set a small table for supper in front of the sitting room fire. As they ate, they talked about future trips they would make: maybe Switzerland, maybe Malta, and why not the Holy Land? They toasted the success of Fritz's command. Vicky, tipsy on all the Rhenish wine they drank, got up before they'd properly finished and stretched out her hand to Fritz. "We must spend the rest of the evening in bed."

Once in their room, they quickly got out of their clothes. Fritz was as ardent as ever, but on this night he went too fast for Vicky. And after he rolled off of her, he immediately fell asleep. Vicky let him doze for a short while, lying on his back beside her, but then she climbed on top of him and whispered in his ear, "*Männchen,* time for second helpings." She could tell he was surprised—she never took the lead this way. But in a heady new world, where she was toasting her warrior husband going off to battle, some other things could change as well.

THE KING EXPRESSED his lingering resentment toward Fritz by appointing Fritz Karl commander of the Prussian forces. Her husband was made first deputy to Field Marshal von Wrangel, he of the meringue-covered backside, whom Vicky had met on her maiden trip to Berlin. The troops called this hero of Prussia's struggle against Napoléon, now eighty years old, "Papa Wrangel," and he held the title of supreme commander of the combined forces of Austria and Prussia. But the old man couldn't keep anything straight, and soon Fritz issued the orders and determined all the strategy.

During the first weeks of the war, the Danish army retreated out of Holstein into Schleswig, pursued by the much larger force fielded by Austria and Prussia. At the end of March the Danes were entrenched in a fort at Düppel, on the border of Jutland, their historic homeland. Fritz Karl and Fritz encircled the fort and awaited the order from Berlin to take it.

The queen chose this moment to summon Vicky to the Wilhelmstrasse for an audience with the king.

She arrived at the king's office at four in the afternoon to find Fritz's parents glowering at each other. A maid was pouring out tea. As soon as she left the room the queen said: "Vicky, now the real fighting will begin, so I am insisting that Fritz be pulled out."

"Oh no," Vicky said at once.

"What?" the queen snapped.

"That would be terrible for Fritz," said Vicky.

"The heir's life cannot be hazarded," said the queen.

"Fritz is a soldier. He's waited so long for this," said Vicky. "I know the danger—"

"I called you here expecting your agreement," the queen said.

Vicky turned to the king: "Please, don't deny Fritz this chance."

"I am his mother," said Augusta.

"But I am his wife," said Vicky. "And I know his heart."

"I have no time for any of this," said the king, sounding very annoyed.

"Vicky! I am astounded! You'd be happy to see Fritz dead in a ditch in Denmark?" asked the queen.

Vicky hesitated for a moment. She'd pictured it so many times: Fritz's body crumpled on the ground, his blue coat stiff with blood, his silver spiked helmet, dented, lying next to him. A vision unbearable to dwell on. But neither could she deny Fritz's most fervent wishes. "I would be heartbroken. I'm not sure I would be able to live any longer myself," she said quietly. "Yet Fritz deserves the opportunity to excel at what he loves."

She prayed God would forgive her and that she hadn't tempted providence with her words.

"What a lot of nonsense. You're a ridiculous girl," the queen said, glaring.

"I'm not listening to another word of this," said the king in a loud voice. "Go away, both of you. I have much to contend with. I'll think about Fritz later."

The next morning Vicky got up early and went right back to the Wilhelmstrasse.

The chief clerk at first would not admit her, but through the open door she saw the king sitting at his desk. He waved her in.

"I've already decided to leave Fritz where he is," he said.

"Thank goodness."

"I wished to say this yesterday, but there would have been a tremendous scene," said the king. "And still might be." He raised his eyebrows and shook his head slightly. But then he caught her eye and smiled. She was amazed. Had he ever looked affectionately at her before, in all the years they had known each other? She thought not.

She was prompted to ask: "Aren't you proud of Fritz?"

"Sure I am, very," he said.

How strange and unnatural, she thought en route home: Hohenzollern father and son had been at war in peacetime, but now, hostilities begun, they were the closest of allies.

FOR THE STORMING of Düppel on April 18, Fritz designed the plan of attack and was in the thick of the fighting. Prussia and Austria emerged victorious but many lives were lost: 1,700 Danes and nearly 1,000 Prussians and Austrians. Vicky, light-headed with relief that Fritz was safe, wrote him an ecstatic letter. But his return note to her was subdued. "I am happy that our army fought so well," he wrote. "Still, it was a dreadful, bloody scene, and I felt sick when I surveyed the aftermath. And what of the Princess of Wales? I thought about writing her today, but I fear she will not want to hear from me."

Vicky's own letters to Bertie remained unanswered. Her new nephew, Prince Albert Victor of Wales, had been born in January, eight weeks premature. Mary Bulteel, now called Mary Ponsonby, told her that Alix's baby weighed only four pounds at birth, and that in England people said stress over the war in Denmark had brought on early labor. How very sad. Vicky hated to think the rift with Bertie and Alix might continue. She had always imagined that her children and Bertie's would grow up together, and spend every summer *en famille* at Osborne.

IT HAD BEEN fifty years since the last Prussian victory at arms, and wild excitement erupted in Berlin. The king and queen appeared on the balcony of the Berliner Schloss to greet the cheering crowds on the evening of the nineteenth. But Vicky, not feeling well, chose to stay home. For several weeks she had been privately celebrating something else—she wrote to Mama that night to confide her secret: she expected her fourth child.

"I little needed this additional anxiety in my present sorrow and worry. Your pregnancies are too frequent," her mother replied. Still, Vicky savored the feeling of the baby growing inside her, perhaps another boy, a son for brave Fritz, who so enjoyed playing and riding with his children. She kept the news to tell him in person.

25

*F*ritz returned from war a happier and more confident man. He'd grown a full, bushy beard and was very brown from the weeks he had spent living outdoors. His former stiff-backed public persona had relaxed. He never lacked dignity, but now with strangers he was the man he'd always been at home—at ease in his skin, strong and limber, like a sure-footed, noble cat. Upon his entering a drawing room, Vicky saw how women gazed at her husband with glowing eyes and would cluster around him, fluttering their fans like preening birds inviting his attention. Men addressed him now with a sincere, honest regard that went beyond courteous deference.

A temporary armistice was declared, and in Frankfurt and Berlin, the ultimate fate of the duchies was now debated endlessly. Bismarck announced that the Duke of Augustenburg was not the only claimant—another son of ancient lineage, the Duke of Oldenburg, had come forward, and Bismarck desired to explore Oldenburg's rights before granting Prussia's full support to Augustenburg. Vicky and Fritz doubted that the minister-president gave a fig for the Duke of Oldenburg, but even his machinations could not dim their gladness that the fighting was over and their joy in expecting a new member of the family by summer's end.

During one of the numerous gala banquets put on to celebrate the victory, General von Moltke took her aside. "I imagine the prince has not described to you just how impressive he is in command?"

"He's told me the barest details and never brags about his own performance," said Vicky.

The general smiled. "The Crown Prince is an excellent tactician, but he possesses another talent, quite rare, and very valuable. He avoids interfering unnecessarily with his subordinates in their own sphere, while always managing to keep the general course of action under his own control."

"He tells me his subordinates are all splendid men."

"*Jawohl.* But it is he who directs them so skillfully. His cousin, I fear, lacks this light touch on the reins. And no one rivals the Crown Prince for remarkable composure in battle."

Vicky felt tears smart her eyes.

"Your husband is immensely popular, not only with the officers, but with the soldiers of the line."

"To whom he is devoted," said Vicky.

"Yes, and they return that devotion. They've taken to calling him '*unser* Fritz.'" Our Fritz.

That ordinary men should regard Fritz not as a remote, privileged son, but as one of their own, was the best possible recognition. She was witnessing him calling upon his God-given gifts to carve his own place in the world. She knew the burdens that an inherited role imposed—how it left you questioning your own abilities, separate from family and position. So Fritz's success made her particularly jubilant.

Fritz spent his days now visiting the wounded in the hospital and organizing pensions for the families of those killed. He requested Vicky paint a series of pictures of soldiers in uniform, to be sold at auction to benefit the pension fund. When she asked what more she could do, he described how wounded and dying men had been left suffering on the Düppel battlefield for days. Prussia needed an army nursing corps like England's—perhaps she could start one? Vicky remembered meeting Florence Nightingale at Windsor as a child and wrote to her now for advice. She contacted doctors and hospital wardens in Berlin, inviting them to come and discuss how to get the corps started. Few people turned down a chance to meet Vicky and Fritz and to see the inside of the Kronprinzenpalais, and now she capitalized on that curiosity. Even dreary public events became worthwhile when she could ask people for contributions to her nurses' corps fund. Every morning at her desk—reading over her lists, checking off tasks, writing to potential patrons—she felt the thrilling sense of purpose that up until now only study had provided.

CONSIDERING HOW OUTNUMBERED the Danes had been, the self-congratulatory air in Berlin quite soon became distasteful. Fritz agreed. Strange to see members of parliament drop their constant carping at Bismarck for taxing and spending without proper authority. A few liberal newspapers had been allowed to publish again, but the criticisms of the minister-president from their side—from all sides—were much milder now. Most journalists, it seemed, were impressed with Herr Bismarck and hoped he might further improve on Prussia's standing in Europe.

The shameless minister even tried to endear himself to Fritz. Bismarck wrote him several letters, praising his battlefield skills and claiming that he was currently in desperate need of the Crown Prince's guidance as the king was indecisive and lacked his son's vigor. Should the Prussian army, still in place in Schleswig, invade Jutland and occupy Denmark?

"That sly fox," said Fritz. "He's trying to get me to make a statement that later he'll derive some advantage from."

"It's almost laughable, the confiding tone, feigning his devotion to you," said Vicky.

"I'd ignore his letters, but then he'd use my silence against me. Help me compose a response."

The short letter back began with Fritz's amazement at being consulted: "Up to the present I had no reason to suppose that you attached any value to my judgment." Then Fritz asserted that an occupation of Denmark was not necessary, nor could it be justified.

"You don't think he really imagines he can absorb Denmark into Prussia, do you?" Fritz asked Vicky.

"On what pretense?" Vicky replied. "France and England would surely go to war over that."

"He must have another motive for writing," said Fritz.

"Beyond a general desire to manipulate you? I think he's exploring possibilities. Maybe he leaves Denmark but swallows up the duchies," said Vicky. "Bertie said something like that in the beginning, remember?"

"I do. But my father won't want to deny Augustenburg his rights, or refuse to give Austria and the German Confederation what they expect."

"Maybe that's the delay: Bismarck, laying siege to your father's conscience."

Fritz shook his head. "The king must resist—it would be shameful to do otherwise."

A few days later Fritz returned from the Wilhelmstrasse with news. "As you surmised, *Liebling*, Bismarck has been giving my father stern lectures daily. He insists that Prussian soldiers did not fight and die for Fritz Augustenburg."

"Yet Fritz has agreed to give Bismarck everything he wants, including a Prussian naval base at Kiel. Hasn't that been the dream for decades?"

"*Ja*, but now my father has the idea that the Austrians would never allow that, and that perhaps Fritz is only proposing that to enrage them." Fritz rolled his eyes.

"What nonsense! If Bismarck told the king the sky was falling, he'd believe it."

Fritz nodded. "The devious fellow dominates him completely."

When the final armistice was announced, it satisfied no one, which, Vicky supposed, was the minister-president's design. The Danes gave up Schleswig and Holstein forever. Prussia continued to occupy Schleswig. The Austrians, alarmed at Bismarck's constantly shifting demands, insisted that they would control Holstein. The Duke of Augustenburg got nothing.

WAN AND SO often fractious, Willy had had a hard winter, with his father away for months. The relentless physical program to fix his poor arm continued. He spent two hours a day attached to the head-stretching machine and then was confined for an additional hour every afternoon in an uncomfortable brace designed to increase the length of his left arm, which wasn't growing as fast as the right. There were regular animal baths. And once a week Dr. Langenbeck would apply electric shocks to the left shoulder and upper arm to galvanize the dead muscles. This treatment still frightened her son, but he'd been persuaded to tolerate it for a few minutes at a time by Fritz, who told him he was thus doing his duty as the youngest soldier in the army of the king.

Yet Willy's short left arm remained useless, it was perpetually cold, and the small purplish fingers on that hand curled inward like a claw. The arm's muscles seemed stiffer than they had been, and it could only be stretched out completely at the elbow with effort. His head still lolled to the right, despite all the bracing, and Dr. Langenbeck warned that unless this markedly improved by his sixth birthday next January, the operation to correct the droop must be undertaken.

Sometimes Vicky's nagging worries about Willy's future consumed her and she'd weep—would he ever be able to cut his own food? Dance elegantly? Drive a carriage? And she hated to see him so peaky. One day in June it occurred to her she should send him to Osborne for the summer. She couldn't go, pregnant and busy with her nursing corps work. And Fritz couldn't take him as he was about to depart for many weeks in Pomerania, to assume an additional command, of the Second Army Corps, based there. But the boy had a sweet new governess, Fräulein Dobeneck, who was teaching him to read and write. She could escort Willy, and once there he'd have seven-year-old aunt Beatrice and his younger uncles to play with, and Mama to look after him. He needed a holiday from arm treatments, and the sea air and bathing at Osborne would be a tonic.

Baron Stockmar and Max Duncker, Fritz's new private secretary, immediately recommended against this plan. Lord Palmerston had loudly condemned Prussian aggression against the Danes, despite Mama's favoring of Augustenburg, and now the English prime minister accused Bismarck of bullying the Austrians. With anti-British sentiment resurgent in Berlin, it wasn't a good moment to send Willy to England.

Still, Vicky wanted to ask the king's permission, and Fritz supported her.

At first her father-in-law said no. And then, a week later, while Vicky was still pondering if she should ask Mama to write directly to the king, she heard from the Wilhelmstrasse that her request had been granted.

Two days after an excited Willy had departed, several nasty stories about her appeared in the conservative papers. She was derided for preferring all things English to anything Prussian—the heir's trip being just the most recent example. She wondered if the king's reversal had been the doing of Bismarck—looking for some mud to throw at her. Not that she really cared. Fritz and she must always protect and provide the best for the children, especially Willy.

Mama reported that the weather was splendid and Vicky's brothers and sister played happily with their Prussian nephew. Vicky felt a bit homesick, reading this, but she had her nursing work to get on with and the long-planned improvement of the Neues Palais grounds to undertake. She reminded herself of Papa in the old days, out every morning early to talk to the gardeners and direct new plantings. She had been determined to revive the eighteenth-century gardens, and at her direction flowers and trees were brought in from all corners of Germany so the palace grounds properly represented and reflected the glorious beauty of the nation.

In the late afternoons she would sit on the back terrace and rest, while her little children played nearby. Charlotte, four now, and Henry almost two, were more peaceful characters than their unruly older brother. And she loved them. But they were both far more attached to Mrs. Hobbs than they were to her. And she wondered exactly how this had happened. She'd borne three children before her twenty-second birthday. Was that too young to have so many? And Willy so constantly preoccupied her—maybe she'd deprived the others. Most likely it was her fierce desire to advise and protect Fritz in the last years that had absorbed undue energy, leaving, perhaps, not enough for any of her children.

Vicky resolved to do better this time. The coming baby would live in her room at first and she would get up in the night when needed. She would nurse for at least three months and take on as much of the daily care as possible. God had granted her another chance to be a mother, and she would embrace it the way Fritz embraced being a soldier.

HER HUSBAND RETURNED in time for the baby's birth, on September 15. A beautiful boy. Vicky suggested that, as a gesture of reconciliation, they ask the king to name his grandson. The king chose the name Sigismund, which meant "protection through victory" in honor of the events of the year. Vicky liked the inevitable shortening: Siggy.

She held firm to her intention to feed the baby herself. Mama's anger radiated off the pages of her letters from Balmoral as she berated Vicky, a refined woman of rank, for acting like a cow. Her mother-in-law came in a rage and when Vicky refused to leave off nursing, the queen shrieked hysterically that this was it—Vicky was finally, fatally, and forever dishonoring the entire family. Even the king wrote a stern note instructing her to hire a wet nurse.

"I think you can safely ignore that, *Liebling*," said Fritz when she showed it to him. "It reads like something my mother told him to write."

"You don't think your father cares one way or the other?"

"He only cares not to have to listen to her go on and on about it."

At two months, the dear little boy weighed fifteen pounds, looked pink with health, and slept like a top. Vicky nursed Siggy five times a day and then once again at midnight. She washed and dressed the baby herself and had his crib placed in the dressing area ten feet from her bed.

During one nighttime feeding she realized that she had never been quite so content as this, even in her most passionate moments with Fritz. These days, with her precious son tethered to her, were so fulfilling. He relied on her completely, and she could meet all his needs. She adored the pull of his little toothless mouth on her nipple, his tiny hand resting on her breast, the soft grunting he made as he fed. She'd never felt such a connection with her other three children, and she wondered, with a pang, if it was too late to make it up to them.

PART IV

Mother

26

Berlin, Winter 1865

*I*n the New Year, the king ordered Vicky to detach herself from Siggy and resume all royal engagements. As ever, she found the formal evenings endless, and the receiving rooms suffocating and hot. She struggled to stay awake and knew herself to be a poor dinner partner when the meal started after eight. Perhaps she had so few friends in Berlin, now seven years after first arriving, not only because she was a suspect Englishwoman but because her own internal rhythms didn't fit court life. She liked to get up early, work hard during the day, and go to bed at nine.

The triviality of ceremonial encounters constantly irritated her. Over three days in January she met two hundred young daughters of Prussian noble families, and their mothers, as part of the traditional "coming out" ritual. But, as she wrote to Mama, only a handful of these women spoke about anything beyond the weather, or the flowers in the room, or the current fashion for bonnets and gowns. She'd have to reimagine these dull occasions when she became queen.

What a relief, amid the season's social inanities, to finally welcome her sister Alice and Prince Louis of Hesse to Berlin. Louis, a loving husband, was not a rich man. After marrying he and

Alice had lived in a dark town house that opened directly on the main square of Darmstadt, the capital of the tiny state of Hesse, two hundred miles away. Alice subsequently spent much time in England, and her first child, a daughter called Victoria, had been born at Windsor. But Mama had paid for a new castle, and now Alice was settled more comfortably in Germany. Over the past summer when Vicky had expected Siggy, her sister, too, had been pregnant again, and when her second daughter, Ella, was born eight weeks after Siggy, Alice followed Vicky's example and chose to feed the baby herself.

Now the sisters sat together for hours nursing and discussing all that had happened in the family and the world since they'd last seen each other at Bertie's wedding. Alice was growing lovelier with age—Vicky admired her thoughtful face, eloquent blue eyes, and contained smile, and appreciated the intent way she listened. From time to time, they traded babies. Alice's milk supply was not as copious as Vicky's, and Ella was a delicate little thing who needed to eat more. Mama never heard any of this, of course. She remained furious at them for nursing at all.

"What I don't understand," said Alice one afternoon in Vicky's sitting room in the Kronprinzenpalais, "is the game Bismarck plays at. The war has been over for a year yet Augustenburg still doesn't rule in the duchies."

Vicky sighed. "I think he's keeping everyone off balance, back and forth, first extracting promises from the Austrians and then demanding different ones from Augustenburg, looking for the settlement he most prefers."

"Stalling long enough so no one will notice when Prussia simply absorbs Schleswig?"

"I suspect."

"Such underhandedness! Why doesn't anyone here object?"

"Fritz does, but his father pays little heed. That devil is so skillful at weaving a net of untruths, the king gets more and more entangled."

"Louis worries that once Bismarck has Schleswig, he'll move on to gobble up Holstein," said Alice. "That'll set off the Austrians for certain, and enrage the Confederation."

"Yes, and Prussia will be completely isolated and all the other German states will attack us." It pained Vicky to state this aloud—but it could not be denied.

"Does the king understand this?"

"Fritz describes how his father stumps around declaring he can't wait to be rid of the whole business. But then Bismarck meets with him privately and speaks of how he owes it to the Prussian people to expand the borders of the Fatherland like all the Hohenzollern kings before him."

"And he's persuaded?"

"Apparently. You know what the deputies say? They call Bismarck the king's last mistress. Because only such a creature could wield so magic a power over an old man!"

They both laughed. "But really, what would Papa say?" asked Alice.

"He'd be rendered speechless," said Vicky. "I don't think he ever imagined Wilhelm turning into a spineless creature, led astray by a reckless adventurer."

"Dreadful," said Alice, shaking her head.

DR. LANGENBECK REMAINED insistent: he must perform surgery on Willy's neck, a prospect that distressed Vicky no end. The physician pointed out that not only could the boy not hold his head straight, the skewed position of his neck had begun to impact how his face was developing. The features on the left side were flatter and smaller than those on the other side, and his left eye not nearly as big as his right. To Alice, Vicky confessed how anguished she was—about the surgery, but also about Willy's looks. He'd never be beautiful like Fritz and Papa.

"He's just six, you goose!" Alice exclaimed. "It's too early to predict what Willy will be like grown."

"You've seen him. He'll always be a bit lopsided and funny looking, with the poor lame arm hanging down. How terrible in a man who will be forever on public display!"

"Now you sound like Mama, intent on finding fault with your children," Alice scolded.

Vicky put a hand over her eyes. "It's not only Willy. I begin to think Charlotte has a sullen temperament, and Henry seems slow."

"Henry is not yet three."

"What if he turns out to be stupid?"

"Vicky!"

"I only tell these things to you, Alice dear. Fritz dismisses my worries, and the king and queen are especially smitten with Willy. Because he's heir. They spoil him outrageously and he's clever enough to wheedle endless treats out of them."

"Evidence of a great mind! You have nothing to fear—Willy will be an intellectual paragon."

"Don't mock me."

"I'm not mocking. I'm telling you something other people won't—don't burden your children unduly, Vicky. You were constantly held up as perfect in our family. And I'd watch you toe the mark, whatever mark Papa put down. Wasn't that burdensome?"

"I didn't find it so," she said. "And you exaggerate."

"No, I don't think I do. Not that I don't applaud you, dear admirable mark-toeing sister, always striving to be good. But your expectations can be punishingly high."

Vicky felt suddenly enraged. "Think if my expectations were lower! Think if my children were to grow up motherless in this prideful court, where title and position mean more than character, where the only virtues extolled are military ones. Imagine that! How can you say I shouldn't worry or bother or expect much of them?"

Alice absorbed her anger without comment. After a pause she said softly, "I didn't mean to upset you, dearest. Even in England it's difficult bringing up children in a royal court. Mama and

Papa did quite well, for all that Mama could be critical and self-ish, and Papa overly demanding."

"You found him so? I didn't see any fault."

"Of course not," Alice said, smiling. "But remember how harsh he was, with Bertie, in particular? And even you, so much the favorite—he was constantly after you to learn this, read that, believe as he believed. I began to feel sorry for how he thought of you as a means, a way to advance his political agenda."

"Nonsense! Papa always wanted the best for me! For all of us!"

Alice shrugged. "Perhaps. I think it was difficult to be Papa be-cause some of his most cherished ambitions he could only pursue indirectly. Through his children. In any case, I tried, you know, after you were gone, to take your place in Papa's affections. But I couldn't manage it."

"Don't be silly, Alice, Papa was so very fond of you."

Alice raised her eyebrows, skeptical. Then she continued: "Back to Willy. What he needs is a good tutor, to encourage him to be sensible, honorable, and a staunch believer. That's your aim, yes?"

"Most of all I long for him to be independent—impervious to flatterers at court and the machinations of devious politicians. Not to be drawn into all this—this disrepute," she said, and waved her hand in the air.

Alice smiled again. "Nothing like the king then? In Papa's image?"

"Yes."

"Well, a lame arm doesn't keep one from becoming that kind of man," her sister said.

ONE MORNING NOT long after Alice and Louis had gone home to Darmstadt, Vicky went to call on her cousin Adie, who was despairing over her husband's uncertain future. She returned to the Kronprinzenpalais before noon to find that, in her absence, Fritz had allowed Langenbeck to perform the operation, severing a tendon at the base of the boy's neck near where it attached to the collarbone. The skin was well numbed, the cut not deep, and it was all over quickly, Fritz reported. "I thought it better and less distressing for you not to be present," he added. "And Willy behaved very quietly and without complaint, only weeping a little afterward."

But when Vicky went upstairs to the nursery to see her son, he looked so strained and pale. A bulky, thick white bandage wrapped around his neck. She held open her arms, and he immediately ran over to sit on her lap, nestling his head between her shoulder and neck. "The doctor did this," he said, making a sharp, horizontal flick with his hand, and he shivered. She squeezed him and rocked a little. "You were so brave," she said. Willy, very unusually, stayed quiet in her arms for a long while.

Still, the boy could hold his head upright now, and that was a blessing. From behind he appeared completely normal. It was Willy's face that was lopsided, chin twisted to the left and the left eye's lid not totally open. The doctor suggested another operation would be required when he was older to align the chin, but for the moment, this particular torture—surgery—was done.

MAMA HAD COMPLAINED that at Osborne last summer the lovely boy had shown signs of that "terrible Prussian pride and ambition, which grieved Papa so much." Now Vicky asked her mother's advice on Willy's education, and Mama suggested they employ an Englishman as tutor, Major John Cornell, who had transformed brother Affie from a callow lad into a well-spoken and dignified young naval officer.

Vicky asked Fritz if they could invite Major Cornell to Berlin to meet him.

"Why? We'd never hire him," said Fritz.

"But he's a military man," said Vicky. "I thought he would please you, and your parents."

"My parents will never accept an Englishman—not appropriate for a prince of Prussia. It is coming up time to find Willy a military governor. I had one from age seven. Roon mentioned to me the other day he had someone to suggest."

"That reprehensible minister mustn't have any say in Willy's upbringing! And a military governor won't be a teacher," Vicky exclaimed.

Fritz looked at her forbearingly. "My father will want a superior officer in that post, approved by himself. And then other men, Prussians, can be brought in to tutor him in mathematics, history, science, religion."

"Just a whole array of different men?"

"Make inquiries—perhaps ask dear Professor S," said Fritz, smiling. He often teased her about her unwavering faith in Professor Schellbach's perspicacity.

"I don't think the professor knows much about the education of young children. And in any case, don't you believe it would be better to have one excellent man take charge of Willy's education? The way Alice and I had Tilla, and Affie had Major Cornell." No point in mentioning ineffectual Mr. Birch, Bertie's tutor.

"First, the military governor must be appointed. At the moment Fräulein Dobeneck is sufficient for teaching. Willy and Charlotte read and write, don't they?"

She admitted they did, and dropped the matter for that evening. But she was sure the model of one tutor was best—it came down to finding the perfect person. Vicky asked the baron if he could begin searching, quietly and discreetly of course, for candidates. And she wrote to Robert Morier at the British embassy for suggestions—he knew so many liberal people in Prussia. If the heir's tutor could not *be* English, Vicky wanted someone who thought as Papa did, and who would keep Willy's feet planted firmly on the earth.

Morier wrote back immediately to say he was on the lookout for an excellent man.

27

Berlin and Potsdam, February–June 1866

*F*ar longer than Vicky did, Fritz clung to the belief that the matter of the duchies would be settled peacefully, and in Fritz Augustenburg's favor. The horses convinced him otherwise.

The first step in any mobilization plan, Fritz explained, was the large-scale purchase of horses—for the Danish War, the Prussian army had acquired twenty thousand in total. When Fritz heard Roon was requisitioning up to ten thousand horses per week, he tracked down the minister and demanded to know why.

"He immediately asked me if I did not find the administration of Holstein by Austrian authorities intolerable, as the king certainly does," Fritz said. Large public demonstrations calling for the restoration of the Duke of Augustenburg occurred regularly in the duchy—in defiance of Austria's obligation, under the armistice agreement, to keep order. And hostile articles attacking Prussia appeared constantly in the Holstein press, much to the consternation of everyone in Berlin. Vicky felt certain Bismarck was drumming up such "outrages," but she hadn't any proof.

On this wet and dreary Friday evening at the end of February, Fritz and Vicky sat together discussing the horses in the library of the Kronprinzenpalais. Because Vicky was pregnant again, due in May, they had an excuse to skip the vacuous entertainments held in the court during these, the Carnival days, running up to the start of Lent. No need to venture out in the darkness. They could instead stay at home and contemplate a true nightmare—a German civil war.

Bismarck had been elevated to Count von Bismarck over the summer, confirming to Vicky's mind that the king remained entirely under his sway. She was convinced that eventually, in defiance of everything rational, decent, and humane, the minister-president would make war against Austria and the German Confederation. His ostensible reason would be the dispute over the duchies, but his true purpose would be to establish Prussian domination north of the Main River. How long had he aspired to banish the Austrians from Germany? Join up eastern and western Prussia? Decades. And now he appeared on the verge of achieving his dream—at vast cost in human blood.

"So the horses mean war is certain?" she asked.

"It means hostilities are far more likely than not. Roon told me he aims to obtain a hundred thousand, maybe a bit more, this time."

"In time for a spring campaign?"

Her husband nodded and looked glumly into the fire. He still wore the full bushy beard he'd grown while in Denmark. He looked a bit like an apostle—as if John or Matthew had come back as a kindly Teutonic warrior. He gave a heavy sigh. "Bismarck's greatest skill might be to take the old gentleman, my father, to places he never meant to go—by sheer force of his will."

VICKY HAD TAKEN to ruminating on tyrants of the past: Caligula, Robespierre, Oliver Cromwell. Maybe Bismarck wasn't a regicidal revolutionary like Cromwell, but he had the same dictatorial predisposition, and where would it all end? That made her muse on *Macbeth*—which she'd studied closely with Tilla. Would the minister-president become a version of Shakespeare's Scottish king, brought low by guilt after his wicked pursuit of power?

What would remorse look like in Bismarck's case? She had trouble picturing him ever contrite and repentant.

To ease her anxiety, in the afternoons Vicky often went to the corner room on the top floor of the Kronprinzenpalais, where she had set up her easel and installed a small writing desk. Sometimes she'd ask Fräulein Dobeneck to send Willy up for an hour before tea. Her son liked to sit cross-legged on the floor with one of his illustrated animal books open in his lap, describing to her at length the ferocity of the white tiger and the strange features of the Australian kangaroo. But when she told him it was time for poetry, he'd listen quite contentedly as she recited English verse. One afternoon she began: "'Tomorrow, and tomorrow, and tomorrow,'" and Willy chimed in: "'Creeps in this petty pace from day to day . . .'"

"You know this?" she asked, astonished, putting down the brush and swiveling on her stool to face him.

"You always say that poem, Mama."

"It's a speech from Shakespeare, William, but no matter. What comes next?" she challenged him.

Willy thought for a minute and recited: "To the last silly bill of corded time."

"Close," she exclaimed. "That's so well done!"

He beamed up at her. She slipped off the stool and went over to give him a hug. "You are my very good boy."

"I am," he said, and burrowed his head into her shoulder.

How sweet he could be. After she went back to sit in front of her painting, she stared at the canvas for a long moment without seeing it. What would become of Prussia? What would be left for Fritz—for Willy—to inherit? Part of her longed to think she was a hysteric. Everything could still be resolved in a peaceful, reasonable manner—so many people desired exactly that. Why didn't she have more faith?

Alone with Fritz that evening, she described how Willy had recognized the speech from *Macbeth*. "He has an excellent memory—don't you find?"

Fritz smiled. "I do, and I am happy to hear you praising him."

She frowned. "You think I don't do that enough?"

"He's most often a worry to you, I know."

"It's such huge responsibility to bring up the heir! Above and apart from his distressing handicap!"

Fritz nodded.

"And nowadays I wonder if the pride and devotion for his country which William will need to have, as a foundation for all his work, will be possible," she continued vehemently.

"*Liebling*, it's not as bad as all that. Prussia is not embodied by one man. And Bismarck will not be eternal."

"Few tyrants are, but they wreak havoc while they rule," she told him.

WHEN, TWO WEEKS later, a dinner was planned at the British embassy, to welcome new ambassador Sir Augustus Loftus and his wife, Vicky persuaded Fritz they must attend. She would wear a heavy velvet cloak to better conceal her condition. Count Bismarck, whom she had not seen in over a year, would surely be there, and she looked forward to confronting him. She imagined no one else in the capital was quite as brave as she—willing to condemn the man to his face. But on the morning of the dinner, Robert Morier wrote to say the minister-president had sent regrets, claiming to be ill. Vicky at once concluded that he'd opted to avoid her, since protocol demanded that on this occasion, he sit on one side of her, with Loftus on the other.

The new ambassador met them at the door. A taciturn man with a mane of white hair and a solemn air, Loftus struck Vicky as reliable but unimaginative. He bowed and then gave her a small, sad smile.

"Smells of powder here in Berlin, Your Royal Highness."

"Indeed," she replied, as Fritz had stepped on to greet Morier.

"I asked Count Bismarck again yesterday to reveal his intentions," the ambassador said.

"And?"

"The Austrians must make concessions in Holstein, stop arming and encouraging the rebellion, or there will be war, he told me."

"Bismarck makes all these claims, but my husband and the Duke of Augustenburg and everyone sensible knows it's a ridiculous diversion. The Austrians are not provoking us—quite the opposite."

"And the king? He's content to let this war happen?" asked the ambassador.

"The queen and Fritz urge him to oppose it, but he's in Bismarck's hands now."

"Have you thought, Princess, that your own mother could do some good?"

"I don't see how. The queen's government has already warned Bismarck against any violent annexation of the duchies."

"A personal appeal, perhaps, from one monarch to another?"

Vicky and Fritz decided to take Loftus's suggestion, and they telegraphed Mama, urging her to plead with the king. "Dear Brother," Mama wrote, "You are deceived, you are made to believe that you are to be attacked, and I, your true friend and sister, hear your honored name abused for the faults and recklessness of others—or rather more, *one* man." She begged the king to think deeply before permitting so fearful an act as the commencement of war.

Fritz's father responded by sending Mama a list of the perfidious misdeeds of Austria. In the postscript he wrote: "I am not under the influence of my minister-president."

THE APPROACH OF war felt like a hideous monster coming to devour all her happiness. Once full mobilization began, in the first days of April, she walked the rooms of the Kronprinzenpalais aimlessly, too disturbed in mind to concentrate any longer on painting, reading, charity work, even a letter. In her blackest moments, she once again took to picturing Fritz lying dead on a muddy battlefield. When she was a widow, she wouldn't want to remain in Berlin, amid the ruins of her and Fritz's hopes. But would she be welcome back in England, with her Hohenzollern children, after Prussia had set off an orgy of killing in Germany?

On the morning of April 12 she awoke to some cramping and wondered if the baby had decided to appear early. Fritz sent for Dr. Wegner, but the pains were gone by the time he arrived. Still, Fritz thought it better to move to the Neues Palais, so she could wait for the birth out of the tense city. Leaving Mrs. Hobbs and the housekeepers to pack the luggage and organize the children, Vicky and Fritz traveled at noon to the station with Dr. Wegner and boarded a private compartment on the train. They were under way when her pains returned and began coming in regular waves.

"Goodness me, I think the baby might be born right here," she said.

Fritz stared at her, stunned. "If that happens I think we can manage together, can't we, doctor?" he said, a slight quaver in his voice.

Dr. Wegner shook his head, alarmed. "Princess, are you certain? Do you want to lie down?"

"Not just yet, I think, but soon." She bent over as another contraction began.

"We are nearly at Potsdam," she heard Fritz say.

When the train stopped, Fritz carried her out, hurrying down to the far end of the platform, where their coach waited. Ten minutes later they arrived at the Neues Palais. Fritz, still cradling her, mounted the shallow stairs two at a time, rushing toward their bed. The pains were deep and long now. She heard Dr. Wegner calling for help, for hot water, and for clean linens and towels. A chambermaid darted down the passageway ahead of them and Vicky saw a large white sheet billow above and settle gently atop the velvet bedcovers just before Fritz placed her down. A few moments later she was overcome with the urge to push. Knees up, with Dr. Wegner still shouting for water, she could feel the baby's head crowning. "It's now," she said to the amazed Fritz, who gazed down at her, wide-eyed.

Two pushes and her beautiful daughter was born, caught by the doctor. Such a surge of exhilaration. The chambermaid found an old petticoat of Vicky's to wrap the baby in and presented her to Vicky.

"I think she's Victoria," said Vicky, tears of joy running down her cheeks.

"*Jawohl*," said Fritz. "She already knows how to make an entrance."

"And perhaps her christening can be on Mama's birthday, May twenty-fourth."

"As long as the action has not yet begun," Fritz replied.

THERE WAS AN inexplicable slowdown in the mobilization in the days after the baby's birth. Later Fritz discovered that Bismarck took that time to make a secret alliance with Italy, so the Austrians would have to fight on two fronts. Vicky was grateful that her husband remained at home as she recovered. She nursed and the baby quickly gained weight. All four of her older children found their tiny sister entrancing—even Siggy took a turn holding her. Mama was pleased that finally a child of Vicky's bore the name of one of her parents. For a brief interlude before the cataclysm, Vicky felt at peace.

The baby was six weeks old when Fritz returned from the Wilhelmstrasse to say that the formal declaration of war against Austria and the Confederation states supporting her was imminent. General von Moltke had divided the army into three corps, the largest of which, nearly 120,000 men, would fight under Fritz's command in Bohemia. General von Blumenthal, Fritz's good friend and a skilled tactician, would be his deputy. The two men now expected the order to travel east any day. And on June 5, it came.

Vicky struggled to stay composed, anxious that the children not notice her distress. The next morning, she lined them up in the main hall of the Neues Palais from largest to smallest, baby Victoria in Mrs. Hobbs's arms, to say goodbye. William begged to go along to war, stamping his foot and weeping in frustration when told no. But Fritz got them laughing by describing how he and General von Blumenthal would be catering to the horses, feeding them special "strengthening" straw and the "magic" carrots they were bringing along as treats. Vicky could hardly bear the sight of the children's small faces turned up to their papa's so trustingly, innocent of the mortal perils he would face, not understanding they might never see him again. His last kiss. His last glance. His last words to her: "Be brave." And he was gone.

TWO DAYS LATER Siggy was so fretful and cross. "Must be teething," said Mrs. Hobbs. And Vicky agreed. Siggy, nearly twenty-one months old now, had a very sunny temperament and was never out of sorts. A good night's sleep would remedy him, and some ice to apply to his gums.

The next day he had a fever and rolled about in his crib in obvious discomfort. "If he's not better tomorrow we need to call the doctor," said Vicky. But all the doctors, including Dr. Wegner, had gone to the front. She asked Fräulein Dobeneck to discover if a junior practitioner remained in the town of Potsdam.

A Dr. Schmidt turned up the following afternoon. He looked younger than Affie, and was very nervous and overly deferential to Vicky, repeating over and over, "If I can be of service to Your Highness," "It would be an honor, Your Highness," "Blessings be on your whole house, Princess." In between all this bowing and fawning, he had nothing useful to say about Siggy.

"His Royal Highness is young. So many young children fall ill this time of year," the doctor said.

"In June? Are many other children in the area ill?"

"Here in Potsdam? None, that I know of."

"Why did you say that, about many others?" she asked sharply. He looked at her fearfully.

"What do you think is causing the prince's fever?" she said, trying to keep her voice steady.

"It's not certain."

"You're not certain? Or it could be many things?"

"Both." Again, that fearful look.

"Please come back tomorrow. Let us pray the prince improves overnight."

Vicky worried that she would catch whatever Siggy had, and then the baby would have it too. With her darling son now wailing in pain hour after hour, she told Mrs. Hobbs to send to Berlin for a wet nurse. When the woman arrived that afternoon, Vicky promptly handed over tiny Victoria.

She moved Siggy's crib into her room and for the next five days spent all her time holding him or kneeling by his crib. Soon Siggy could no longer stand by himself and would neither eat nor drink. In the middle of one night, she was awakened from a doze by strange mewling from his crib. Her hand shook as she turned up the lamp, and she saw him jerking, stiff and odd, like a body possessed. Another convulsion followed before dawn, and this time Siggy's little eyes rolled back in his head and the grotesque jerking went on for five minutes. She held him in her arms but she couldn't soothe him. Dr. Schmidt looked horrified when she described the episodes. Finally, when she pressed and pressed, he conceded that the prince most likely had meningitis.

Vicky heard herself ask: "And can he recover?" The doctor said nothing—his stricken face gave the answer.

As Vicky watched her son's torment—his piteous cries and his violent spasms—she asked herself: Was God punishing her for loving Siggy more than her other children? Did God abhor her vanity in believing this son so clever and good he would be Papa reincarnated? If she asked Him to spare Siggy, as she did over and over again, what price would she be willing to pay? *Just let him live and I will die,* she thought. *I will write my instructions.* Fritz might marry Louise, and bring her to live in Potsdam, and her sister would bring up the children in a sensible English way. She felt a deep pain for all the things she'd never do, never see, and a dread at the thought of falling out of bright life, the cycle of the seasons, into fathomless darkness. She wanted to believe in heaven, for the chance of seeing Papa again, but she feared there was nothing after death. Still, she appealed to God and told Him she was ready to die if her son could live.

Nothing came of this, so in the small hours of the next morning she made a different request—more shameful. She would sacrifice Fritz if she could keep Siggy. Her husband might be killed anyway, at any time, but this was the crucible moment for Siggy—should he survive it she knew he would grow into a beautiful man, strong and good. She could see him before her eyes, the adult Prince Sigismund.

But, of course, there was no bargaining, no pleading, no escape. She was forced to look on in agony as her heart's treasure suffered grievously, hour after hour, burning with fever, his little face twisted in pain. The queen had come immediately when she learned Siggy was ill. Fritz's mother loved the little boy and she watched over him for an hour or two whenever Vicky tried to sleep.

On the last morning the queen sat beside her on her sofa as she cuddled the now unconscious Siggy. Together they witnessed him struggle for breath and then fall still. Vicky saw his skin turn waxy and blue, and she knew she'd never be whole again.

She clung to the dead boy, who belonged, after all, to her. The queen, hollow eyed and shattered, held out her arms to take him away. "Come, Vicky dear, you must rest now. Give him to me."

"No, I won't," she said, shaking her head and sliding along the sofa, away from the queen.

Fritz's mother didn't insist. After ten minutes of silent vigil she rose and went to fetch Mrs. Hobbs.

That kind lady drew up a chair and sat down in front of Vicky. She began murmuring in English: "You took very good care of him, Princess, but God has taken him now to Himself and Siggy will be safe and happy, you needn't worry. But you mustn't try to keep him here where he doesn't belong. Please give him to me now and I can wrap him up and then he will be warm on his journey and you can be sure that he's comforted."

Listening to the up-and-down hum of Mrs. Hobbs's voice,

Vicky thought, numbly, how English was so much softer a language than German. Yet the words were no balm. The nurse reached over eventually and removed Siggy from her arms. She could not fight to hold on to him—exhaustion had overtaken her.

The nurse left the room. "You need to be in bed now," the queen said, and helped her stand up. "It's been days since you've had proper sleep."

"But what about Fritz? Who will tell Fritz?"

"I will travel to Silesia and tell Fritz myself," the queen said as she led Vicky by the arm down the corridor. "And we'll come back together, for the funeral."

Vicky spent the next two days sleeping or simply lying, stupefied, in her bed. Mrs. Hobbs endeavored to keep the children away. Still, on the second afternoon, when Vicky lay curled on her side in the darkened bedroom, looking at the wall, she heard the door crack open, then Mrs. Hobbs whispering something and a child's light step. Willy came to kneel down next to the bed so his face was level with hers.

"Will you die and go to heaven, like Siggy, Mama?" he said very quietly.

"No, darling, not now, I'm just resting."

He started to cry, and he put his good right arm around her shoulder and cuddled up closer. "I don't want a different mama," he said.

"No, no, you'll have no other mama," she told him. "Don't worry." And she stroked the back of his head. She was going through the motions of being herself, but, in truth, she felt she had swallowed stones and become numb and removed from everyone.

It was a strange relief to experience a conflagration of fury when the queen returned and told her that Fritz would not be coming home. The king had given him permission, yet he refused to leave his troops. He had said to his mother: "I am in the service of the Fatherland. I would never forgive myself if we were attacked when I was absent." As the queen stood next to her bed, recounting this, Vicky shook her head in angry disbelief.

Her husband, at his post, about to fight a war he had neither supported nor believed in, could not spare three days to travel back and forth and be with her while they committed their most cherished son to the earth? That struck her as preposterous as well as hard-hearted. What was love of country in comparison to love of wife and family?

"He told me you would understand," said the queen.

"I don't understand, and have no desire to do so," she said. She struggled to sit up. When she could see her mother-in-law's face more clearly, she felt a bit ashamed. The queen looked strained but stoic, as if she was, with great effort, fencing in her own grief to support Vicky—she didn't deserve to be raged at. The person Vicky really needed now was Mama, and even more, she longed for Alice. There was nothing she couldn't confess to Alice. But neither of them could come to her now, with the war on. She must manage somehow, on her own.

THE QUEEN HAD brought a letter for her from Fritz, which Vicky put in the drawer of her desk without opening. She felt so angry and disappointed in him she couldn't bear to read his words of sympathy. Also, she had a final duty to perform for Siggy. The king had decreed that he was to be entombed in the crypt in the side chapel in the Friedenskirche in Potsdam. Vicky wanted his funeral to be beautiful, to properly honor his precious soul. She asked for masses of white flowers, and arranged them in every corner and around where the tiny white coffin would sit for the funeral service. She displayed a painting she had done of him. She vowed to greet the assembled company with dignity. The queen stood beside her as the two dozen guests filed in. Papa Wrangel represented all the military men who could not attend, and he wept. Augustus Loftus came at Mama's behest, and he gazed at her sorrowfully. "England mourns with you, Your Highness," the ambassador said. Vicky doubted this—her countrymen surely disdained all bellicose Prussians—but it was good of him to aver it. She struggled to recall herself, the innocent English bride—that poor girl had had no idea of all of the different griefs the world could dish out. Robert Morier's face looked gray and crestfallen, his usual liveliness drained away. He murmured, "I have no words, Princess."

Fritz wrote every day, sometimes twice. She'd open the letters and then put them down without reading them through. Finally, she knew she must respond, so she wrote a short note. "In you, of course, the soldier is uppermost," she told him. She signed it without sending love.

SHE HAD SNAFFLED Siggy's bedclothes from his cot, and they still smelled of him. It was a comfort to sleep with them next to her face. She carefully rolled them up each morning and hid them under the bed for the day. But one morning she neglected to put the small sheets and light blanket away immediately and some heedless maid came to change the linens, bearing everything away to wash. Realizing this, Vicky wept as if her little boy had died a second time.

When she told the queen that the floor frequently swayed under her as she walked across it, and that sometimes dark puffy clouds gathered in the high corners of the bedroom, her mother-in-law told her she must go to a clinic in the country for a rest. She shrieked that she would not be separated from her other children. After that she kept her peculiar sensations a secret, and she ordered herself to sit at her desk every morning and read. But she couldn't concentrate on any book, and instead stared out the window at the grounds, cursing the sunny summer weather—cold, bitter winter would have better matched her state of mind.

ON JUNE 28, the baron came to the Neues Palais without an appointment. Vicky supposed he was anxious that she attend to her correspondence—the hundreds of letters of sympathy she'd received. But as she had, just two days previously, sent word to him that she could not yet cope with work, she felt very annoyed when he was announced.

"I have news you should hear immediately, Princess," he began. Her heart leapt in alarm. Fritz, dead? No, it couldn't be—surely a member of the family would come to tell her this?

The baron read the fear on her face. "I should amend. I have brought good news. Word reached Berlin late last night of a tremendous battle against the Austrians at Nachod."

She nodded. The war; she hardly cared.

"The Crown Prince has been triumphant. His army dominated from the first hours. It seems the decisive advantage is Prussian equipment—the fast-firing breech-loading needle gun shoots four bullets to the Austrian muzzle-loader's one," said the baron. "I remember the prince explaining to you, to all of us, the potential of that weapon. It seems to have more than delivered on its promise."

"Yes, yes," she said impatiently. A former version of herself might have taken an interest, but now she felt aggrieved by the whole martial enterprise.

"And the scale of the victory is such that—"

She cut him off. "Does it ever occur to you, baron, that this war, any war, is a kind of arrogant folly? Men insisting on bringing more violence into a world already full of suffering and grief?"

He looked at her pityingly. She supposed she did sound unhinged. But how ghastly to be talking about the effectiveness of needle guns when so many mothers would now be burying their sons. As she had just done.

"You may be correct, Princess, but the Crown Prince's victory—"

"I refuse to celebrate what is actually a kind of giant, barbaric egotism. My husband is corrupting himself by even being involved."

The baron said nothing for a long moment, then began, gently, as if reasoning with a hysterical child, to speak. "Whatever judgment one may cast on the ethical responsibilities of professional soldiers making war on behalf of legitimate national interest, I am certain, Princess, that you will soon appreciate the prodigious skill and leadership demonstrated by the Crown Prince. All Prussians are in his debt."

"Yes, fine, I understand. And thank you for coming." She stood up abruptly to signal the meeting was over. He kissed her hand and departed.

The next day she received a letter from Fritz, enclosing a cornflower he had picked for her on the battlefield. He prayed for her, and for Siggy's soul, morning and night, he wrote. By return post she replied to say she abhorred the fighting and that he must beseech God every day, as she did, for the war's immediate end.

SHE STARTED TO believe that she would never recover in Potsdam with Siggy's things—his favorite ball, his shoes, his high chair— always in front of her eyes. She wouldn't be allowed Osborne, she knew. But when she told the queen she thought to return to Rügen, her mother-in-law suggested the children might like better Heringsdorf, a little town on the Baltic, known for excellent bathing. So on July 2, she gathered them all up and left.

28

Heringsdorf, August 1866

*T*he children did love the beach at Heringsdorf, stretching long, wide, and white in both directions. But Vicky preferred the pine forest behind the sand dunes and the winding paths through the trees that she followed alone in the cool breezy mornings, passing through ever-shifting shafts of sunlight, watching birds flit between branches, feeling the soft crunch of the needles underfoot. *I've entered one of God's natural churches,* she thought as she inhaled the crisp, elevating scent of pine and closed her eyes to better hear the separate strands of birdsong.

When, after a week, she began to feel a bit less wretched, she wrote to Mama to say so. Her mother wrote back commending her for elastic spirits and predicting she would soon be quite gay again. Vicky seethed: *this* from a woman who made a virtual religion of her own grief and demanded everyone in the family accede to it! But after a long, restless night and a morning session communing with the pines, she resolved to stop invidious comparisons. Vicky was not a queen, to whom everyone deferred, and she still had four very young children to raise. Guilty already for neglecting little Victoria—a dear, pretty thing who laughed now and had begun to sit up—she made a vow to attempt to reconcile herself to what had happened. In that spirit, she reread Mama's letter, and took it as encouragement to be strong and move on from her misfortune.

But when Mama next wrote, "Think, *what* is a child in comparison to a husband," Vicky fell into a gloom for several days—at a moment when everyone assumed her to be rejoicing. Not only had Fritz survived Nachod, and a number of subsequent bloody skirmishes, but during the ultimate battle, at Königgrätz, Fritz Karl had extended his troops too far, too quickly, and only her husband's steely nerves and swift maneuvering of his men into place had secured the decisive victory for Prussia. The king had embraced Fritz on the battlefield and awarded him the country's highest honor, the order Pour le Mérite.

The trounced Austrians sued for peace, but the bloodshed was appalling—nearly ten thousand Prussian casualties and forty-four thousand Austrians killed or wounded.

Vicky waited warily for Fritz's account. Would his amazing success leave him gloating and prideful? She thought not, so ingrained was his modesty. But on the street ecstatic men and women came up to her in tears to commend her husband's bravery and thank God for preserving his life, which they prayed would be a long one. The newspapers published pictures of Fritz each day alongside lengthy reports of his valiant exploits. At night, from her bed, she heard men singing patriotic songs as they staggered out of the beer hall down the road. Even Willy and Charlotte caught wind of Fritz's triumph and they marched around singing "Papa beat them all" and "Hail to the fatherland." One morning she heard them in the garden shouting, "All the Austrian dogs lie dead," and she flew out of the house to slap their hands, both of them.

"We do not say such things," Vicky said.

The children cried, and William looked at her in a rage, eyes afire. "I hate you, Mama," he said. "I'll tell Papa when he comes home to send you away!"

Vicky dragged Willy to the nursery and locked him in.

Then she scolded Mrs. Hobbs and asked where on earth the children had heard such things.

The patient English nurse, whom she had relied on for years, never so much as recently, looked at her, incredulous, and said: "Do you believe, Your Royal Highness, that I could keep the children from witnessing what is happening here? Perhaps you would prefer they never go out, but did we not bring them to the seaside for the fresh air?"

"No, of course, they must go out. But I never thought they'd pick up such ugly sayings."

"One hears these things constantly now."

Vicky sighed. She supposed the children couldn't remain immune to the euphoria. At least she had had a letter from Fritz that morning. He'd described the Königgrätz battle as frightful, like all the battles before it. In the aftermath, he and Bismarck had toured the scene and the minister had become sobered and depressed to envision his own son, Herbert, still in school in Berlin, among the dead young bodies lying festering in the sun. Together Fritz and Bismarck had then, with enormous difficulty, persuaded the king to make peace with the Austrians, without further fighting. The warlord monarch longed to march on Vienna and directly annex Austrian territory rather than lay down arms. But Fritz had supported Bismarck's view—the war's goal had been to insist that Austria stay out of German affairs and clear the way for a new nation led by Prussia. That accomplished, there was no need to further humiliate Emperor Franz Joseph and his people, who in future could be valuable allies.

Bismarck felt indebted to the Crown Prince for his help, and at the moment the two men were in uneasy alliance, although the king resented Fritz's role in forcing him to "bite into this sour apple and accept a disgraceful peace."

The final line of Fritz's letter read: "You think that I am completely absorbed in my military career. As far as my duty demands it, yes. Certainly I am. But I pray this is the last war we will experience."

FRITZ PLANNED TO join them in Heringsdorf as soon as the armistice was finalized. She felt shy to see him and wondered how they would find equilibrium together again—their treasured child snatched away, he elevated to the status of national icon, she still sorrowful and embittered.

After Fritz's return was fixed for August 5, the village mayor announced he would host a short welcome ceremony outside their rented house. Vicky couldn't bear the thought of meeting her husband again for the first time in such a setting, but Kurt von Normann, one of Fritz's secretaries, who had arrived ahead of him from Berlin, advised that she must not refuse the gesture. So she sent a note to Fritz asking him to approach Heringsdorf via the quiet lane that passed through the pine forest. She left the baby at home and took the three other children to her favorite glade and sat them all down on a fallen log to wait.

When she first caught sight of him riding toward them accompanied by four officers, she recognized, with a sharp stab of shame, that Fritz, too, had suffered intensely in these past weeks. He looked thinner and harder. All traces of the Hamlet-like youth wiped away, her husband was a handsome but weathered man now. As he swung off his horse and came to embrace her, she saw the creases on his sunburned face had deepened, especially across his forehead and on either side of his mouth, and his tired eyes were sunk back in their sockets. He gazed down at her sadly, acknowledging in silence the blow that had hewn them both. The children, unmindful, jumped up and down with glee until Fritz crouched down to hug each in turn. They walked the rest of the way back to the house as a family, Fritz carrying Charlotte, his two surviving sons skipping along on either side of him.

Following the welcome ceremony came a dinner hosted by the mayor and attended by local worthies and the handful of officers who had arrived with Fritz. Vicky felt impatient to have him to herself. He seemed to feel the same and begged off after the main course and several toasts. "I am exhausted, gentlemen, and must retire. I look forward to seeing everyone in the morning."

Upstairs, Fritz seemed so hulking and male, there in the white bedroom, where she'd spent so many nights alone. Undressed, his body looked sinewy, his shoulders knobby, his stomach taut. He made love to her with such tender gravity that she wept.

"Please, Vicky, *mein Schatz*, don't cry," he said. "We can have another son, don't you believe that?"

"All I want is Siggy returned. Just him. Perfect, beautiful, lovely him. I am like one of your soldiers, shot through the middle and still bleeding."

They lay facing each other and he was stroking her arm.

"Or maybe I'm bled out," she said, "and there's nothing left inside me but grief. I'm hollow with it."

He gathered her to him and for a long time they lay still, entwined.

"It was terrible to go through it alone, without you," she said finally.

"*Ich weiss.*" He knew.

"How could you possibly remain away?"

"I had to choose. You are strong. I knew you could endure it, as hard as it might be. And to return to you would have required leaving thousands of other women's sons unprotected, having called them to do battle."

She supposed a better person would have forgiven him, right then, but not her. She wasn't ready to let go of the resentment lurking inside her. Yet she found it comforting to lie in his arms, and she hoped he felt some peace, too. He shifted onto his back and she laid her head on his warm chest. He smelled pleasantly of the outdoors, and of leather and tobacco. Here they were, so close to each other once more, and yet his experiences in the last weeks were entirely apart from her, and she could never share in them. She struggled to imagine the rush and clamor and yelling in battle. She wondered about the mental strain of command, the necessity of staying composed and clear when all about you men were fighting and bleeding and dying. How was that for Fritz, really? She wished she could comprehend it, even in part.

"It was unspeakable. Butchery," he said, as if following the train of her thoughts. "That's what war turns out to be. Thousands of slaughtered men. Each a tragedy in himself, individual. Think, five or ten other people who loved each man and needed him. The frightful scale of it—it's impossible to take in."

"But still you're proud of the outcome, aren't you? Everyone here is giddy, drunk with joy."

He didn't reply for a long minute. She listened to his heart beating steadily beneath her cheek. "In that hour, at Königgrätz, when I saw we would be victorious, I got down off my horse onto my knees to thank God for delivering us. We were very fortunate. It could easily have been otherwise."

29

Berlin, Autumn 1866

fter ten days she and Fritz took the children back to Berlin and then traveled on to Silesia to work in the field hospitals there. The army corps nurses taught her elementary care—how to change bandages, wash and tend wounds. She was proud she had a strong stomach and deft enough hands for the work. But she devoted much of her time going from bed to bed speaking to injured men as so many wanted to meet her. While the majority were Prussian soldiers, a fair number came from Italy. She carried a small Italian dictionary in her apron pocket to supplement her basic knowledge of that language.

One day she sat down next to an Italian soldier—Alberto, he said his name was.

"Like my papa," she told him. *Come il mio padre.*

He'd lost a leg and two fingers. Yet his brown eyes shone out quite merrily from under a cap of luxuriant curly hair, and he described how he planned to return to his home in Ferrara, where his father had a small shop of hardware and general merchandise. He held up his maimed, bandaged right hand, index finger pointing skyward, the two smaller fingers shot away, and he declared with a humorous flourish: *"Sarò il capo adesso!"* Now I will be boss.

She paged quickly through the dictionary.

"*E tutte le donne ti ammireranno, come io,*" she replied. And all women will admire you as I do.

He laughed and rested his left hand on her sleeve for a moment. "*Grazie, Principessa, lei e molto gentile.*"

She never forgot him. One afternoon two decades later, passing through Ferrara on a dusty summer's afternoon, she wished to get down from the train and scout out Alberto and his shop. But then she'd have had to tell the story to everyone with her, and it would have sounded so trivial, because she couldn't confess that the light touch of that youth's hand, and his simple words, had reminded her how wondrously worthwhile life was, even as she still ached over Siggy's loss. People needed her, and there remained so much to learn and much to do.

WHEN FRITZ'S ARMY in the east had been busy with the Austrians, Prussian troops had invaded those German states in the west that had backed Austria. Hanover fell immediately, and Mama's cousin, blind King George, was deposed. He fled to Vienna, and the whole of his kingdom became part of Prussia. The Duke of Nassau and the Elector of Hesse-Kassel were likewise toppled off their thrones, and their lands were seized. The free city of Frankfurt put up no resistance yet was occupied, and annexed, and huge reparations were levied on its citizens. Fierce fighting had gone on in Hesse-Darmstadt—right in the streets of the capital— but because of Fritz's intercession, the sovereign grand duke, Louis's uncle, was allowed to keep his dukedom, after sacrificing one-third of it to the conquerors.

With these spoils Bismarck established a new entity, the North German Confederation, of which he was chancellor and the king president. German kingdoms and dukedoms south of the Main River, including the rump Hesse-Darmstadt, remained nominally independent but bound into a tight military alliance with Prussia.

The French watched the dramatic developments on their eastern flank with mounting alarm—the British, too. Lord Stanley, the new British foreign secretary, got up in the Commons to de-nounce Bismarck as the enemy of European peace.

Bertie had sent such a kind note of sympathy at the time of Siggy's death, and since then he and Vicky had corresponded regularly again. Now her brother raged against Bismarck for his horrid treatment of poor King George, and bewailed, too, Alice's bleak time—nursing shattered young Hessian soldiers until the day before she gave birth to her third daughter, Irène, named for the goddess of peace. Prussian occupiers had turned Alice and Louis out of their castle home to use it as army headquarters, and Louis's family struggled to raise the hefty taxes demanded by Berlin. Alice's notes to Vicky arrived irregularly—all short and angry.

At least Uncle Ernest, Papa's brother, Duke of Saxe-Coburg and Gotha, had flipped his allegiance from Austria to Prussia at the very last minute, so he retained his title and all his lands and had a place of honor in the victory parade in late September, rid-ing through the Brandenburger Tor at the head of his battalion.

On that day Vicky felt strangely touched as she watched line after line of Prussian soldiers—their faces beaming, their helmets flashing in the sun—march down Unter den Linden. It couldn't be denied: the Kingdom of Prussia and its army had done more for German national unity than all the reformers and revolution-aries of the last fifty years. And while the people revered the king and Bismarck, they adored the Crown Prince. Her husband was mobbed wherever he went.

FRITZ AND SHE had been invited to travel to St. Petersburg for the wedding of the Russian czarevitch, Alexander, to Alix's younger sister Princess Dagmar of Denmark. They debated for several weeks whether to go. The king would attend, because the czar was his nephew and the groom his grandnephew. Many of Fritz's family, including Fritz Karl and Marianne, intended to accom-pany him. But Vicky hated to leave the children after a month-long absence in the field hospitals, and she dreaded the inevitable scenes between resentful Danish and English guests, on the one hand, and her gloating Prussian relations on the other.

Mama had a different preoccupation. Alix, who had given birth to a second son, Georgie, over a year ago, was now pregnant for the third time and could not travel. Bertie proposed to go to the wedding alone, since Mama had no desire to visit barbarous Russia. An unescorted Bertie would be lured into some scrape or another, Mama was sure. Vicky must go to keep an eye on him. She was about to agree, reluctantly, when Fritz offered to attend solo and look after Bertie, allowing her to stay home and enjoy the relative quiet in Berlin.

The royal party was gone for eight days and when they returned Fritz, in typical male fashion, claimed to remember few details of the lavish affair, mentioning only that there had been no unpleasantries over the wars or Bismarckian perfidy. Also, Bertie had behaved. Vicky invited Marianne to come to the Kronprinzenpalais for tea so she could hear a fuller report. When they settled in front of the warm stove in her sitting room, Vicky immediately asked if it was true—politics hadn't intruded?

"Thanks to your husband," Marianne said with a smile. "Fritz managed it all beautifully. As soon as we arrived, he sought out the bride to ask if she felt distressed that we were attending her wedding."

"How did she reply?" Vicky asked, astonished that Fritz hadn't mentioned this.

"She looked very surprised. But she thanked him for his candor and graciously welcomed us all," said Marianne. "I noticed she often sought him out afterward."

"To converse with?"

"To talk with, and also to dance. He partnered her on several occasions."

Vicky shook her head—hard to imagine a younger Fritz demonstrating such aplomb. "I suppose he thought it best to confront the matter right away. It was bold. She might have rebuffed him completely."

"It was, very bold, and poor little Dagmar rather leaned on Fritz, and on your charming brother Bertie, throughout. She doesn't seem very taken with her groom."

Dagmar had originally been engaged to Alexander's very attractive older brother, Nicholas, called Nixa, who had died suddenly of meningitis the year before. Dagmar's mother had prevailed upon her to take on the unappealing, lumpish Alexander instead, even after the young man declared he had no interest in his older brother's forlorn fiancée. The czarevitch's objections were swept aside by both sets of parents, who were eager for the match between the pretty Dane and the heir to the Russian throne.

"Sad to think of a young's woman life sold and sacrificed quite like that," said Vicky.

"True," said Marianne with a rueful smile. "I sympathize very much."

Vicky flushed. What a thoughtless remark—given Marianne's uneasy marriage. "But you and Fritz Karl seem to get on better these days," she said, stumbling to recover.

Marianne nodded. "I'm more favored now that I have produced an heir." Her fifth child, the longed-for boy, Prince Friedrich Leopold, had been born almost a year ago. "And my husband has been more content in general since the victories, as so many men here are, don't you find?"

Vicky nodded, gazing at her kindhearted friend. By any measure Marianne was a woman a husband could be proud of. Tall, graceful, an excellent musician—although somewhat hard of hearing, whether because of her injury at Fritz Karl's hands no one quite knew—Marianne had exquisite manners and a tinkling laugh, and was very good-looking. Such a shame she had suffered so. Vicky thought in a flash of her own daughters—no loveless royal marriages for them, she resolved.

That evening, when she and Fritz rode together in the carriage toward the theater, she asked him about his encounter with the Danish princess.

"You went right up to her immediately?"

"*Ja,* to apologize for our company if she found it distasteful," he said.

"But Marianne reports she was very gracious, and then, in particular, kept seeking you out—you and Bertie."

"So many women enjoy your brother's company. As for me . . ." Fritz reached out and picked up her hand. "I think she liked that I told her all about you, and how I hoped her marriage would turn out as happy as my own." He brought her fingers to his lips and kissed them, looking into her face with smiling eyes.

She laughed. Maybe the public, looking at her life from the outside, still thought of her as a woman of charmed fortune. But she knew different. She'd been deprived first of Papa and now, agonizingly, of Siggy—and the course of political events had revealed that she bobbed upon a sea of uncontrollable currents as much as anyone else. Still, her girlhood dream of love had been fulfilled, a hundredfold. She hadn't realized how infatuation would deepen into mutual, sustaining devotion. In court it might have been disparaged as *bürgerlich*—like middle-class folk—to pursue and relish a happy family life, but she and Fritz had been married nine years, had been tested terribly, and their intimacy had only grown. He was the true golden ticket she'd been given by a benevolent God. Some compensation, she supposed, for living in a strange land of soldiers where she never felt truly at home.

AN ELEGANT YOUNG man with neat black whiskers and mustache, Captain Gustav von Schrötter of the Field Artillery Regiment of Guards had joined their household in July as Willy's military governor. Unusual for a Prussian officer, Schrötter wrote poetry and loved music, and he was a calm, upstanding presence. Willy happily spent hours with him every day, riding, walking, and being taken to play with the sons of noble families of Fritz and Vicky's acquaintance.

Over the summer Fräulein Dobeneck left to get married. In her parting words to Vicky she complained that Willy, although bright, was frequently impertinent in the schoolroom and thought a great deal of his own importance. Vicky fretted over this, and the way William so frequently prattled on and on, without expressing any particular idea, just eager for the sound of his own voice. Captain von Schrötter in place, Fritz now agreed they could employ a suitable civilian tutor.

The baron immediately proposed Herr Gustav Willert, a man of forty, educated at the University of Königsberg, in East Prussia, who worked for the wealthy Siemens family. Werner Siemens owned the most advanced and successful technical company in Europe, and he and his wife, Mathilde, presided over a salon of journalists, academics, and artists at their mansion in Jägerstrasse, where Stockmar had encountered the family tutor. Now the Siemenses generously, if reluctantly, agreed to give Herr Willert up if the Crown Prince and Crown Princess thought him the best teacher for the young heir. Over luncheon at the Kronprinzenpalais, Mathilde Siemens described Herr Willert as truly a friend to her two boys. "He's unlocked their natural curiosity and taught them an enormous amount without resorting to stern lectures or corporal punishment," she confided to Vicky. That worried Vicky—Willy needed a firm hand. Still, she had the baron invite the teacher for an interview with her and Fritz on a blustery day in October.

Herr Willert turned out to be a large man, rather lumbering in his movements, and dressed in a baggy brown suit. His twinkly blue eyes looked out at her over small gold spectacles worn on the tip of his nose. He seemed benevolent and good humored, if a bit shy. He spoke no English and only rudimentary French. When Vicky asked how a program for Willy and eventually Henry, too, might be structured, he said he would pursue various activities and inquiries that interested them, and have them work directly with tools, paint and brushes, paper and scissors, so as to harness their enthusiasm. This approach sounded far too casual to Vicky—what of serious training in the classics, and instruction in science, literature, history, and modern languages? The teacher nodded while she spoke but responded: "All in good time. It's best to let young children direct themselves to start."

Such an odd idea, and she would have delved in deeper, but she could tell Herr Willert did not appeal to Fritz.

"What an ugly East Prussian accent that man has," said Fritz afterward. "And his rumpled jacket! It must have been ten years old."

"Yes, he doesn't dress smartly. But he's kind and sensitive, as Mathilde Siemens described," said Vicky.

"Perhaps suitable for the Siemens household, but not for a court appointment," pronounced Fritz.

"So, no?"

"Definitely no," he replied.

Given her own concerns about Willert's laxness, Vicky accepted this and wrote him to say that she and the Crown Prince could not deprive the Siemenses of his excellent service.

It was fortunate Robert Morier had recently encountered someone he thought perfect for the job. In a letter she received while still in Silesia, Morier asked: could the royal couple meet Dr. Georg Hinzpeter when they returned to Berlin?

Although the same age as Herr Willert, Dr. Hinzpeter was completely different in character: tall, thin, and acerbic. Employed currently as the tutor to the family of Count Gortz, a friend of Morier's, who lived in a tiny East Hessian town called Schlitz, Dr. Hinzpeter appeared sober, neat, and very sure of himself. He sat down on the drawing room sofa and immediately began speaking in English. His diction was like Papa's—he spoke precisely, but with Germanic constructions and a scholar's erudition. Soon their discussion turned to quite abstract matters, so Fritz requested they switch to German so he could follow.

"What would be your goals for our son as his teacher?" Vicky asked.

"An exceptional effort must be made to ensure that the young prince attains the highest possible degree of development," the doctor replied.

"Perhaps you have heard, sir, that the prince has some physical limitations, and frankly I am not sure how naturally intellectual he is," Vicky said. Fritz flinched—he'd never have confessed such a thing to an outsider. But she wanted to be candid with the man who might direct Willy.

"The aim must be, nevertheless, to take the student as far as possible," the doctor said.

"I agree," said Vicky. And Fritz nodded.

"This process will take time and great commitment. The prince must be shielded from distraction, from anything that will waste time and energy. There is too much to accomplish to lose focus," said Hinzpeter.

"He does ride and exercise every day with Captain von Schröt-ter," said Fritz.

"Of course, to be expected, but every other hour must be de-voted to study. The power of cognition takes much discipline to form."

Vicky nodded. "In that regard do you think mathematics and sci-ences are more important than grammar and classical languages?"

"It will change at different moments, as I look for the best ways to enhance the boy's intellect."

"What qualities of mind do you feel essential in a future king?" she asked.

"An ability to distinguish good from evil and between truth and falsehood. And, naturally, independence of judgment."

"Just so!" said Vicky, pleased to hear her own thoughts so well articulated. "Of course, mental attributes are but one part of a man's abilities. What of his soul?"

"Only the Christian feeling of the need for salvation and trust in God's domination in the world can grant the sovereign the strength to rule," Hinzpeter replied.

"You are a Calvinist, then, doctor?"

"I am, Princess."

"What you say is a bit heavy for a small boy. Do you mean that you will always keep right and wrong in clear sight in the school-room?" she asked.

"Yes, Your Highness," said the doctor with a thin smile. "And as your son grows older, and as you and your husband continue to live the life of rectitude and service you are known for, he too, with proper instruction, will discover the rewards and necessary abnegation required to fight for truth."

This sounded exactly right. She looked over at Fritz and smiled. How extraordinary to find a man who could echo—no, improve upon—her own notions on how Willy should be educated.

Their conversation lasted another hour and Vicky found it completely absorbing. The doctor's political views seemed in harmony with their own—Bismarck's methods were distasteful and the war hideous, but now Prussia could foster economic and social advancement throughout Germany. Liberal reforms would inevitably follow, as they had in England with the expansion of industry and empire.

She'd have offered Dr. Hinzpeter the job on the spot, but Fritz would have found that undignified. As the doctor got up to leave, he made a final point: "In order for a tutor to succeed, there are two things he needs. The first: to be in agreement with the parents about the meaning of an educated and developed mind."

"I think we are in agreement there," said Vicky quickly.

Hinzpeter held up a finger: "But the tutor must also be allowed to gain real influence over the pupil's mind and soul, and that requires freedom to act as he sees fit, without interference."

"The Crown Princess and I will consider further," said Fritz. "Thank you for coming."

WHILE IT WAS true that the baron had strongly advocated for Herr Willert, Vicky felt confident her adviser would see the wisdom of appointing Dr. Hinzpeter instead. She asked Stockmar to spend a few hours with the doctor and then come to talk with her. At her desk, writing letters, when a footman came in to announce the baron, Vicky rose from her seat in pleasant anticipation of a happy discussion.

"A very superior man, don't you think?" Vicky asked as she settled on the sofa across from the baron.

"Certainly, Princess, a serious scholar, and an idealist who has lofty goals for the young prince."

"Just the person we require then."

She saw Stockmar's face crease as he pondered his answer, and her heart sank a bit. "I fear he lacks warmth and is too much of a Spartan thinker to engage successfully with your son," he said finally.

"I disagree. Especially now, with all that's gone on, we need a moral man to take charge of Willy," she answered sharply. "Someone who emphasizes doing one's duty, making sacrifices for others, behaving with integrity and decency. The doctor will teach him that."

"Will a young boy learn that directly? Can such things can be taught explicitly?"

"Of course they can! And you see how obstreperous the prince is. The doctor will keep him well in line and insist he do excellent work."

"He will be very stern, that is true."

"When we met with the doctor both my husband and I were taken with his seriousness of purpose."

Stockmar nodded, still unconvinced, she sensed, reluctant to let go of his own candidate.

"In any case, Captain von Schrötter will remain his governor," Vicky continued.

"I observe that the young prince adores the captain."

"Yes, which is pleasing, but it is time Willy's real education starts."

The baron's eyes skittered about the room for a moment as if looking for inspiration from the furniture. "I know what a high value you place on education, Princess," he said eventually. "And you were yourself such an able student. My father would come home from Windsor to praise you fulsomely."

Vicky smiled. "The old baron was very kind to me, to all of us."

"I caution that your son is—well, let me put it this way: I believe Prince Wilhelm requires particular sensitivity in a teacher, not only because his talents may not be as evident as yours were at an early age, but because of the other challenges he faces."

"You think I can't concede that my son is not a natural scholar?"

"I only wonder if Your Highness appreciates the various pressures—"

She interrupted. "Having grown up in a court myself I know well the pressures on royal children, baron! And if you imagine I'm ignoring Willy's handicap, pretending that I don't see it, quite the opposite—I have trouble forgetting about it."

Her secretary nodded, watchful, waiting.

"And I can do nothing to remedy that," she continued heatedly. "Nor can the doctors, it seems, despite all that they keep trying. I—I mean the Crown Prince and I—can still bring William up to be a good man—upright, conscientious, and sound. You don't have to be a genius to become that sort of person." Hadn't Alice once said that? she thought, suddenly pained. When would she see her sister again?

"That is true," the baron conceded.

"Particularly in Berlin's triumphal atmosphere, my husband and I are more committed than ever to protecting Willy from influences that will corrupt him."

"Of course, and this is a parental decision, not a political one, but I advise—" started the baron.

"I am quite settled on him, as is the Crown Prince," she interrupted.

The baron tightened his mouth, as if with effort he was keeping himself from saying more. And she was glad because she didn't want to hear more. After a moment he continued: "If that is your choice, you must watch to see how the prince reacts to what will be a very strict regime."

"The prince requires skilled supervision immediately, and to be compelled to work hard and prepare for his future role," she countered.

Stockmar nodded and got up from his chair. "Shall I write to the doctor and offer him the post?"

"Yes, thank you, Baron," she said crisply. She felt very let down. She supposed all Stockmar cared about was having his friend in the household to commune with. Her secretary should have better understood what was required and put his own desires to the side in service of Willy's interest. She turned her back on him and returned to her desk without a further word.

DR. HINZPETER ACCEPTED the post, and arrived at the Kronprinzenpalais at the end of November. To supervise Charlotte, Vicky had found, through Cousin Adie, a French governess, Mademoiselle Octavie Darcourt. The two teachers immediately got on. Vicky spied them walking together in the halls of the palace in the late afternoons, while Willy was out riding with Captain von Schrötter and Charlotte had her tea. They always looked very serious and—did she imagined it?—disgruntled.

After three weeks the doctor asked to meet formally with Vicky to discuss his student's progress, and he insisted Mademoiselle Darcourt attend as well to talk about Charlotte.

"Both children are difficult to manage," the doctor began, glancing at the Frenchwoman, who nodded her agreement. "Often inattentive, restless, and noisy. They lack discipline."

Vicky was eager to explain. "I've been the only one who ever scolds them," she said. "The servants indulge them, even Mrs. Hobbs. I fear they are quite spoiled. Not to mention their grandparents! The king and queen like to summon the children to attend on them at a moment's notice, or they arrive here unannounced. The other day the king came with a half dozen gentlemen to show Prince William a medieval armored breastplate someone had recently dug up in the Thuringian Forest. Imagine! They spent an hour together examining it."

The two teachers remained stone-faced, uncharmed by this account.

"And the Crown Prince?" asked the doctor.

"The children will obey their father, although I notice my husband has a soft spot for Charlotte, which she cleverly exploits."

Again, no indulgent smiles or nods of recognition.

"The Crown Prince often travels, as you understand," Vicky continued quickly. "He is rarely in Berlin during the week and I have been forced to be the sole policeman in the house, responsible for keeping the children in order. Now that you two are here, I hope you will take over the effort and I will back you up."

Dr. Hinzpeter frowned. "It's unfortunate that the children do not live in a more sober atmosphere."

"As you and mademoiselle are here now, we will make it so," Vicky said.

The doctor still looked unhappy as he departed the room, which maddened her. He clearly did not approve of the way their household was run. Didn't he realize that a royal palace in the center of Berlin could never be the same as an isolated country estate near Schlitz, and there would always be distractions for children who were public favorites and had very possessive grandparents? She should simply dismiss the doctor's discontent, but it bothered her that she didn't measure up in the tutor's keen eye. And how dreadful it would be if this estimable character quit his post, for she was sure Willy needed him, his strong moral influence. She must do better to regulate matters here so the doctor could work effectively.

WILLY WAS SOON a better, faster reader and improved in math and French. Best of all, he was quieter and more polite in the house and at the table with Dr. Hinzpeter's stern eyes upon him. Charlotte had to be dragged through her lessons, and finally Mademoiselle Darcourt suggested that it would be best to teach Charlotte and Henry, now four, together, as competing with her little brother might spur on the girl. Vicky found it hard to believe that Charlotte, six, couldn't learn—she'd already asked Vicky if Dr. Hinzpeter and Mademoiselle Darcourt would get married one day, and played up winningly to her father and the king and queen. Vicky suspected that Charlotte was just very stubborn and unwilling to do what other people expected.

Captain von Schrötter expressed much dissatisfaction with the new arrangements. He complained to Fritz that Dr. Hinzpeter punished Willy too frequently, rapping his knuckles painfully when he gave the wrong answer and keeping him inside too many hours of the day when he should have been outside riding or playing.

Vicky had no patience with this. "The captain knows nothing about the demands of an excellent education," she told Fritz. "Our son cannot be trained to be a mere Guards officer like Schrötter."

"Still, it's a pity they don't get on—he and the doctor."

"Did he say that—that they don't get on?" asked Vicky sharply.

"It's quite clear the captain does not approve of the doctor's methods."

"Which should be no concern to us. Willy is making good progress."

"I like Schrötter. I'd be very sorry to lose him," said Fritz.

"You know dozens of other excellent officers who would be pleased to supervise Willy."

"True, true enough." Fritz got up from the sofa in her sitting room and went looking for his pipe. It was a Saturday afternoon and they had three receptions to attend that evening. He no doubt wanted a nice, quiet smoke in his study before going out. Further discussion of their household could wait.

ONE MORE EVENT of that extraordinary year, 1866, was to live in Vicky's memory forever. At a dinner at the Berliner Schloss in December in honor of General von Moltke she was seated next to Otto von Bismarck. The queen had planned the tables, and Vicky imagined Fritz's mother had deliberately sought to make the minister uncomfortable. And he looked leery as he approached the table, where she already stood behind her assigned place.

He didn't realize that Vicky had already decided to calibrate her manner toward him. She'd aired her fears to Robert Morier that should she continue to act as she had in the past—being forthright with Bismarck, taking issue with his methods, and expressing scorn for the paths he was leading Prussia down—she would only hurt Fritz. How ironic to finally see the wisdom in Bismarck's suggestion to be more protective of her husband. But now she knew the chancellor was no temporary royal favorite, and his ministry wasn't a phase they simply had to endure. He had "reset the table" of the country, of all of Europe, was how Morier had expressed it. Time for a different approach, especially as Fritz, although ever mistrustful of Bismarck, did appreciate the man's accomplishments.

"As matters stand Bismarck can too easily blame you for the Crown Prince's relative diffidence toward him," Morier said.

"Relative to his cousin or his uncles, you mean?" she answered, smiling. All the other Hohenzollern princes were unceasing and obnoxious in their praise for the king's first minister.

"Yes, I understand from friends in the ministry that Bismarck struggles to take the measure of your unassuming husband. Although they have been allies on several important occasions, the chancellor believes the Crown Prince's reserve hides a rank dislike for himself—an antipathy that you have planted permanently in his soul—and he fears the heir is his implacable foe. With the king nearly seventy now, that's disturbing to him."

"It's not that I dislike the man; I've always been impressed by his cleverness, his energy, and his charm, even," she said. "It's just that I can't revere him the way everyone else in Berlin does."

She flashed back to Bismarck's teasing her long ago in that sparkling Versailles ballroom. She'd had no clue then of their entanglements to come—how could she have had? She sighed at the memory, and then continued: "I am willing to salute, too, his particular genius—he sees opportunities where other men only see dilemmas. But he's willing to do anything, say anything, lie, cheat, scheme to get what he wants. How can anyone extol such a devious person?"

"His talent has garnered him enormous power—and made Prussia great."

"Yes, and I must adapt myself to that."

So, resolved on this occasion to be affable, she smiled back over her shoulder at Bismarck as he drew out the chair for her, chirping in English: "Thank you, sir."

He frowned. After he sat down and shook open his napkin to place on his lap, he said immediately: "Your Highness blames me for King George's fate."

"Blames you? Why would I? I understood that Hanover was always allied with Austria, and because of that an enemy of ours."

His mouth twisted into a tight, scornful smile. "'Ours'?"

"Why do you always have difficulty, Count, accepting that I am as loyal as the next Prussian?"

He raised his jutting brow. "What of your sister and brother-in-law in Darmstadt?" he asked.

"Yes, I regret conditions in Darmstadt and I worry for them, especially my tiny nieces. But I enjoy all the praise my uncle garners these days. Sincere admiration expressed in Berlin for a man from Coburg! It's radical!"

He gave a low, good-humored snort. "Fine, fine," he said. "I wonder what your father would think of that."

"I have difficulty imagining what my father would think about so many things," she said, laughing.

He had the good grace to smile, and she congratulated herself for getting the conversation off on the right foot.

"The consequences of the war are certainly far-reaching," she continued. "I understand you yourself, Count, have received a large estate—the gift of a grateful king and parliament."

"*Ja*, at Varzin in Pomerania," Bismarck said tersely.

"And since the war you always appear in your uniform, I notice. You're quite the military man now."

"Unlike the Crown Prince, I don't care much for clothes, but I have decided that a shabby uniform looks better than a shabby tailcoat."

"What do you say of my husband? That he cares too much for clothes?"

"He always looks splendid and—" Bismarck reached for his glass and took a sip of wine. "And now that I have seen his tailors' bills I understand why."

Vicky stared at him. What did he know of Fritz's expenses?

"You were not aware? All of your household bills are now reviewed by me. The king requested it," Bismarck said, smug that one of his shots had landed.

Fritz would be furious to learn this. But she mustn't rage or get knocked off balance.

"Of course, you don't see my accounts," she parried. "So fortunate that my dear father set up my income to be separate from Hohenzollern funds."

Bismarck nodded gravely, as if he agreed with her father's wisdom, but she felt confident he wasn't happy that her money was beyond his scrutiny and control.

"Tell me, Count. Clothes, bills, the rest of it," she said, resuming her bantering tone. "How can any of this be interesting to a great man like yourself? What of you at this time of triumph? You are the author of our many successes: don't you wish you were king? Think, then you might never have to bother with any of us, my husband, me, our children, the queen?"

"Oh no, I couldn't stand to be the king, or a prince, always on display."

"Always wearing expensive, well-tailored clothes?"

"It wouldn't suit me."

"What about becoming president, then, in your own right? You'd be like Mr. Lincoln was, or the current American president—is it a Mr. Johnson?"

"I could never live in a republic. You must know me well enough to realize that, Princess."

"Even if you were at the very top? All-powerful?"

"No, I haven't the background. It's not the way I'm built. Prussians don't make natural republicans."

"I suppose I should be glad of that—for my husband's sake and our son's."

And then they both laughed, surprising each other, she felt. They couldn't be friends now, never that, but they could enjoy a moment of mutual recognition. And that pleased her, in an obscure way.

Seeking safer waters, she pushed the conversation to the topic of gardening, and specifically the trees that would grow well in Pomerania. She discussed the new plantings she'd chosen for the Neues Palais gardens. She even promised, at the end of the dinner, to send to the Countess von Bismarck some cuttings from the best flowering shrubs she'd grown, which she felt sure would flourish in the new gardens at Varzin.

As THE CARRIAGE rolled toward home she reflected how it might be her duty, on occasions like this evening, to engage in a reasonable conversation with the man—and to curb her tongue when tempted to criticize him in public. Bismarck's achievements were so exhilarating for most Prussians that they didn't question his methods any longer. Even Fritz had made a resigned peace with him. Yet she was enough of an Englishwoman, still, to find that nothing he said or did, even as it brought greater glory to the Hohenzollern throne, could ever bridge the gulf between her and Bismarck. She'd forever stand in opposition, on principle. She could never glorify him, nor embrace him. To echo what he'd said at dinner, it wasn't the way she was built.

30

Paris and Potsdam, June 1867

As the spring weeks unspooled and the weather warmed, Vicky once again dwelled obsessively on Siggy. Last year he had still been with them when the trees went from bare branched to lacy yellow-green to fully leafed. Fritz would nod resignedly when she mentioned this and then change the subject. She described her renewed grief in letters to Mama and Alice, and while her sister sympathized, her mother declared that repining did no good and would only distract her from her many responsibilities and the needs of her large family. A childish, angry stubbornness welled up in her upon reading this—no one, not even Mama, should tell her how to feel.

Still, she was not deaf to her mother's words, and when Fritz asked her to accompany him and his father on a state visit to Paris, she thought she couldn't refuse, even though the trip was slated to last ten days, encompassing the dreaded one-year anniversary of the boy's death, June 18. She hoped a change of scene would make her more cheerful, and perhaps in the city she'd loved at age fourteen she would once again feel enchanted by life.

From the minute they arrived, she loathed it, the whole hot, packed metropolis—the pavements so crowded that they could hardly move along; their rooms in the hotel Le Meurice, stuffy and overfurnished; the carriage's shuddering stops and jerky turns in the heavy traffic; the dirt; the soot; the sour smell of garbage and manure; and the relentless sun always beating down. How shocking to see bevies of garishly made-up women, clearly prostitutes, surrounding the entrances of hotels, shops, even the Louvre. Every evening she and Fritz were obligated to attend some noisy entertainment. She never felt a cool breeze, and the constant chatter of French in her ears irritated her.

The occasion was the opening of the Exposition Universelle d'Art et d'Industrie, Emperor Napoléon's answer to Papa's exhibition—a show intended, as the French leader never ceased proclaiming, to herald a glorious new era of European peace. What a load of bosh. Since the Austrian war had ended last summer, the tensions between Bismarck and the French had been continual. She understood from Fritz, and Robert Morier, that in exchange for staying neutral in the German conflict, France expected some territorial compensation—to absorb the Palatinate or Luxembourg perhaps. But Bismarck stalled and sent mixed messages and avoided definite commitments to any proposal, infuriating Count Benedetti, the French ambassador in Berlin. Now Emperor Napoléon strove to reassert the preeminence of France another way—via a grand celebration of industry and art—and he'd invited the German royals to come and enjoy Paris *en fête*.

On the first evening, at the state banquet held at the Tuileries in their honor, Napoléon and Eugénie spoke to her affectionately. They recalled together her visit with Mama and Papa, who, the emperor said, was the most distinguished and remarkable man he had ever known. But the lavish seven-course meal—starting with pâté and cream soup, progressing through fatty meats in heavy sauces, and culminating in gooey cheese and mountains of pastry laden with spun sugar—made Vicky feel ill.

She had looked forward to spending time with Bertie and Affie, in attendance representing Mama, but her brothers were always rushing off to the races or going to see some show. On the one occasion they did come to tea at the hotel, they spent the whole hour describing the glorious beauty of Hortense Schneider, a famous soprano appearing at the Théâtre des Variétés. Fritz beamed and chuckled—but she was disgusted. Her mood soured further at the exposition itself. She felt proud of the beautiful contribution from England—an array of Staffordshire china and delicate Coventry glass. But she was horrified by the North German Confederation's display: three huge fifty-foot cannons manufactured by Krupp, along with some smaller firearms, including an updated breech-loading rifle.

That night in the hotel room she raged at Fritz.

"Who designed the exhibit? Who decided that Prussia, or, rather, its proxy, the Confederation, should exhibit instruments of war at a fair dedicated to the promise of peace?"

Fritz shrugged. "I'm not sure. I wasn't consulted."

"I can't believe it was Bismarck's idea. He'd never be that dense—allowing the worst clichés about Prussian militarism to be reinforced."

"Likely Roon, then," said Fritz.

"Which just confirms what I have always suspected. The minister of war is a blind, narrow-minded reactionary, and the whole bureaucracy at the Wilhelmstrasse does not include a single man with a talent for publicity. Or any sense of what Germany's place in the world is! They could have sent musical instruments, works of art, or even other, more benign industrial marvels, like locomotives. But no, it had to be guns and cannons—that's their favored calling card. Ridiculous!"

Fritz nodded along in a mild sort of way, but then, maddeningly, he asked her: "Are you sure you are quite well, *Liebe*? You seem out of sorts."

"The food here doesn't agree with my tummy, but otherwise I am fine," she answered curtly. "I find so much about Paris appalling—not just the cannon exhibit."

"Just as well you live in staid old Berlin then," he said lightly.

She supposed he meant to be teasing, as she so often disparaged the Prussian capital, but this remark irked her as well.

"Everything's so vulgar, and it's clearly infectious—look at my brothers, enthralled by a cheap singer, gallivanting around in a most unbecoming way, drinking far too much champagne!"

Fritz smiled. "Hasn't Bertie always had a passion for Paris? He told me he fell in love with it when you came here with your parents."

"Paris was much less dissolute then. Don't tell me you like it?"

"I do rather, and it's nice to see Father enjoying the trip. As ever, he's much more relaxed without Mama in attendance." The queen, wary of the political tensions, had stayed home.

"Your father is behaving like a schoolboy on a holiday," said Vicky reprovingly. "Did you catch sight of him when we were leaving the banquet the other night? He had one of Eugénie's ladies sitting on his knee!"

Fritz laughed. "He claimed to me later they were demonstrating some French children's game to him. Anyway, he is in fine humor, and that's unusual."

She scowled. Her husband, her brothers, and her father-in-law might all have been having a marvelous time, but she was out of step with them, in a foul temper, and, even amid the festivities, grieving Siggy. So disheartening to feel ill on top of everything else.

Her mood lifted when Alice arrived the next day. Vicky knew Alice had never truly condemned *her* for Prussian brutality during the war—but it had taken time for the two of them to get back on intimate terms. The frost had started melting at Christmastime, when Alice's letters grew longer and more frequent. Now they had a chance to be in each other's company for the first time in nearly two years.

Alice and Louis moved in downstairs from them at the Le Meurice hotel, and on the first afternoon Vicky sat with her sister in her suite, beside two large windows open to the clamor of Rue de Rivoli below. "The museums are marvelous and the shops are full of lovely things, but otherwise Paris is awful," she told Alice.

"I'm happy to see you in such good looks, dearest, but it's a shame you are not at all merry," said Alice.

"It's completely disappointing! I had wonderful memories and was looking forward to returning here, and now it's completely fallen flat."

Alice smiled. "Yes. But I imagine other things are upsetting you as well. What's the date?"

"The twelfth of June."

"And last year this time?"

"Last year Fritz had left, and Siggy fell ill, and I was frantic, and then—"

Looking into Alice's caring face, she found the tears she worked so hard to hold back all the time burst out of her.

"Everyone wants me to forget Siggy! Mama, especially, and even Fritz," she said as she wept. "And I have been trying. But I still miss him every day, and I fear that the other children, dear as they are, they are not as . . . they just can't take his place."

"Of course not," said Alice soothingly. "How could they? Each being uniquely him- or herself. And I don't believe Mama wishes you to forget Siggy. She's distressed because she knows you still mourn and she should like you not to be sad. Why's that surprising? She loves you, Vicky."

In her current cast-down state, Vicky was tempted to take issue—Mama's love was so often conditional. But what she really needed was Alice's reassurance.

"Tell me, do you think I have dwelled too long on Siggy's death? Tell me the truth."

"No, I don't, Vicky. In any case, is there some requirement to recover on schedule? Some prescribed plan of study one can march through, mourning someone? You adored Siggy, and you will always miss him."

Vicky nodded. "Yes, that's right. And when I'm working it's not as bad. This winter often I got so caught up in the nursing school, I'd go hours and hours, almost a whole day, without thinking about him. But it lurks beneath, and I get pulled down into gloom, especially when Bismarck's conniving is thrust in my face, or when the people around me act foolishly. As they do here, now! Wait until you see the king capering about. It's disgraceful!"

Alice, who was sitting beside her on the sofa, leaned into her in a companionable way. "I'm sorry that you are not in harmony with your family and I imagine that neither Fritz nor the king appreciates quite how you feel. But I've never been here before, you remember, too young for your long-ago trip. Can't you put aside your abhorrence of Paris for just a few days and show me around a bit?"

"I suppose I could do that," Vicky conceded, smiling.

FOR SEVERAL DAYS it was pleasant. She and Alice explored the shops and Vicky splurged on some beautiful undergarments and the sweetest little white boater hat—chicer than anything you would ever see in Berlin. She paid for Alice to have a new gown of dove-gray velvet made up—the fabric set off her sister's soft complexion and soulful blue eyes beautifully. They had a day out in Fontainebleau. The empress invited them for luncheon at St. Cloud, and Vicky took Alice to the room where she had stayed in '55, and together they stood on the magical balcony that overlooked the city.

Alice and Louis came along with her and Fritz and the king to see the antics of the famous aerialist Blondin, who tied shooting Roman candles and Catherine wheels to his body and then teetered across a tightrope stretched high across a sandy circus ring. The greasy smell of frying potatoes in that stuffy tent made Vicky's stomach turn, and with no water closet or privy to retreat to, she stood shaking, willing herself not to be sick in public, taking large gasps of air and gripping her hands together for much of the show. She was lucky to get through it without vomiting, but she couldn't share in the enthusiasm the others felt at the spectacle.

And the next day there was a terrible scene—two, indeed. The Prussian ambassador in Paris, Count Robert von Goltz, called on them at Le Meurice at eleven in the morning to report that Napoléon and Eugénie had decided to expand the dinner planned for the next night, the seventeenth, at the Hôtel de Ville and make it a proper ball, inviting the whole of the diplomatic corps and many notable figures who had flocked to Paris for the exposition. "I hear the English novelist Charles Dickens will be attending, Princess," the ambassador said to her. "And some flamboyant American writer called Mark Twain." He pronounced the name "twine."

The king of Prussia was to be the guest of honor of the whole affair, because, Goltz explained, the emperor, having witnessed how much the Prussian king was enjoying the French capital, was now hoping to press his advantage. At the ball or afterward, Napoléon would likely ask Fritz's father directly for the territorial concessions he felt he was owed in the wake of Prussian triumphs.

"The king is very pleased to be so fêted, but the chancellor is worried. He is traveling from Varzin to be here for the ball, and make certain—" Goltz paused.

"To ensure my father doesn't make any promises that Bismarck won't want to keep," said Fritz with a short laugh.

"Exactly."

"Still, it's a great honor, and I'm sure my father will enjoy the evening immensely. Bismarck, less so, as he will be required to remain ever vigilant!" said Fritz. The two men laughed together.

Vicky frowned. "I will not be attending this ludicrous affair," she announced.

Fritz looked startled, the ambassador confused.

"I will not be dancing, and laughing and participating in diplomatic shenanigans, on this night when a year ago . . ." She took a huge gulp of breath, half gasp, half-sob. "When a year ago I suffered my great sorrow."

The ambassador, now alarmed and embarrassed, got immediately to his feet. He bowed. "I will see Your Highnesses tonight for dinner at the Austrian embassy."

Goltz departed, and Fritz came over and sat beside her on the sofa. She was crying in earnest now, deep, stuttering sobs. What a fool she'd been to ever agree to come here. Dance into the night, and right into the morning of the day Siggy had died? She would not do it—she absolutely refused.

She looked up and met Fritz's eyes. He seemed pitying but also resigned. "I fear you will have to soldier through, *Liebling,* for my father's sake. He will expect you."

She shook her head violently. "I won't, I can't. Imagine the clock strikes midnight and I'm standing there pretending to be happy and gay, flattering our hosts, but not too much, as I will be under the direction of the abominable Bismarck, used as a decorative royal pawn in his chess match with the emperor. All I will be able to think about is that poor lost boy whom I failed, whom we failed! Don't you ever consider that, Fritz? Don't you ever think that had Bismarck not schemed and plotted and caused the war, which meant that all the doctors were gone, leaving behind only some young fool to care for Siggy—if not for that he might still live? Doesn't that ever occur to you?" Her voice was high-pitched and tearful.

"Vicky, this is all the past now, the painful past, and I don't like to dwell on what might have been. I don't blame you for mourning Siggy. But we must do our duty and go on bravely, and think about our country and about our children who still live."

Horrid Fritz to preach to her. She felt very hard done by. She stood up and declared: "This occasion is out of the question for me. I'm going home. If you insist I will stay for tonight's dinner, but no longer."

He shook his head. "I don't think that's best, Vicky. And in any case, you can't leave without consulting my father."

She didn't even bother answering. For too long she'd submitted to the king's directives. Not now. She went into the bedroom and called for Dawes to start packing.

Fritz came in after a quarter of an hour and looked at her, exasperated. "You are being unreasonable. I'm going out to acquire the new dinner jacket you insist upon"—she had told Fritz he couldn't dine with the Austrians, so recently vanquished, wearing one of his uniforms—"and I hope you will be calmer when I return."

She simply tightened her mouth and shook her head at him.

Next, she summoned the concierge and asked him to look into train tickets for late this evening. The man returned after an hour to report the only first-class berth available was departing the Gare de l'Est at seven P.M., for a connection at Cologne in the morning for the train to Berlin. "I will go at seven then," she told him. Why stay for the dinner? She was finished with Paris.

When Alice joined her for luncheon in her suite, she attempted to persuade her not to go. The ball was an important occasion. It would look very unseemly if she did not attend. It would cause comment in the press. Think how miffed their hosts, the emperor and Empress Eugénie, would be. Could she not stay until Sunday morning?

"And spend the anniversary in the train? No, I won't," she told her sister.

She returned to the bedroom for a nap. When she woke up at four she thought she heard Baron Stockmar's voice next door in the parlor, speaking with Fritz. She emerged. Fritz, looking grim, was sitting, his legs crossed, in an armchair in front of the ugly, bulbous mirror on the left-hand side of the room. Alice stood by the window, the baron near the door.

"Good afternoon, Baron," Vicky said.

"Your Highness," he said with a kind smile. "I understand you may be departing."

"Yes, on the seven o'clock train. Dawes will accompany me. You need not return to Berlin now if you prefer to remain here in Paris."

"The baron will stay," said Fritz sharply.

"Of course, darling," said Vicky, "as you wish."

"I went to inquire and the king does not desire you to leave.

He expects to see you at all of our remaining engagements here in Paris, including the ball," Fritz said pointedly.

"When you see him tonight you can tell him I am unwell and chose to return home," she replied, just as pointed.

Fritz sighed, dropped his head, and then rubbed his temples with his hands.

"I think it very unfortunate and disappointing," he said. "And my father will be enraged. At least your gracious sister has agreed to sit in your place at the table tonight if you are absent, and I suppose she and Louis can appear tomorrow at the ball with me, but I must say—"

"Thank you, dearest," she said, interrupting Fritz, directing her smile at Alice. Her sister nodded back sadly.

Vicky turned to Fritz. "I have come to the limit of what I can endure."

Fritz raised his eyebrows. "A ball is not a battle. And you might return to the hotel before midnight if you feel—"

"No, I can't stand any of it, all this carrying on, elaborate courtesies and feigned friendships when in the end Bismarck will manipulate the situation to his own liking."

"Leave the chancellor out of it."

"I'm leaving myself out of it."

"And letting me down completely, leaving me scrambling to make excuses." Fritz glared at her.

"Perhaps if your father actually enjoyed my company I might reconsider, but he doesn't, he never has, and I'm not willing to play along on this occasion," she snapped.

"I'm astonished you would behave in this very selfish way," he said, and rose to his feet. "I am due at the tailors now for the final fitting of that damn jacket." He stalked out of the room.

Fritz hadn't returned by the time she departed the hotel at six, but she left him a note. "Dearest, I would stay if I could, but I can't, and you know the real reason. I will see you at home. I hope it all goes brilliantly."

She was disappointed to find Alice out when she went down-stairs to say goodbye but ordered flowers for her sister's room, to thank her for her help. She felt a wonderful glow of freedom and de-fiance as she climbed into the carriage for the ride to the Gare l'Est.

THE NEUES PALAIS, vast and ceremonial, was by no means a cozy retreat, but as Vicky rode up the drive from the station the next afternoon it struck her as an oasis of peace and tranquility. Her stomach still felt queasy, after twenty hours in transit, but now that she was home she'd soon feel better. Her children in the nursery had never seemed so winning. She distributed the pres-ents she had brought, and she cuddled little Victoria on her lap for a long time. Fritz had nicknamed the baby, now fourteen months old, "Moretta" because of her almond-shaped "Moorish" eyes. Vicky sang a nonsense song to her. "Victoria Moretta is queen of the May, a pretty, clever, most darling pussetta."

She hugged and rocked the baby, breathing in her lovely sweet smell, and told Mrs. Hobbs she'd put her to sleep in her cot be-fore heading downstairs for supper.

Being alone like this, especially after days in frenetic Paris, felt like taking a long, cool drink of water. The whole of her re-laxed and rejoiced as she lingered over her meal in the empty dining room, the midsummer evening sun slanting in through the tall windows and setting the space aglow with unearthly or-ange light. After eating she went to the library. She picked up her copy of *Emma* and began reading again Austen's tart descriptions of her young heroine, and was instantly transported to a benign English village. How incredible to live in such a charming place as that! When she began to feel sleepy at nine thirty she got up and climbed the stairs slowly. It was still not dark out, and she thought how faraway in Paris the ball must now be under way. How fortunate she was nowhere near, instead at ease here in her comfortable, silent home. Tomorrow, on the anniversary, she would spend the morning at the Friedenskirche, praying next to

Siggy's tomb, and go back in the afternoon with armfuls of flowers from the palace gardens. That would be a sad but very restorative and proper way to honor the occasion.

She thought to take a bath. The bedroom she and Fritz shared now had a large bathroom adjoining, where there had once been a dressing room. Tonight, she admired anew the stately copper bath she had had installed two years before when the remodeling took place. Turning on the brass taps to the cheerful roar and splash of the running water, she looked around for the soap and the flannels. Everything had been put away in their absence. She walked in and out between the rooms several times, taking off her dress, putting down her necklace on her dressing table, coming back to test the water's temperature. Stripped down to her chemise, she walked over and opened the small mahogany cupboard opposite the bath where the flannels were kept, still humming the silly Moretta song. As she reached up for a flannel, she saw on the same shelf the pile of white cloths she kept for her monthly courses, ones she'd fold and button into her drawers.

The pile was high, untouched for a number of weeks, and she gasped. In a rush of violent, heart-stopping amazement she thought, *I'm pregnant, that's why I have been feeling ill.* She'd been so preoccupied with grief and resentment, she'd forgotten to count the days, and then she'd blamed French food, Parisian vulgarity, the company, the exertion of travel, for her symptoms.

She sat down on the edge of the tub, the water still pouring in behind her, taking in her joy, yes, but also a sudden sad recollection of those happy weeks right after the Danish war when she'd felt just like this, frequently nauseated but so excited about the baby growing inside her. This one might be another boy, but he could never replace Siggy. She would allow no one to say that or try to compel her to believe it! Not even Fritz. For a moment she pictured Fritz's face and the gleeful way he'd look upon hearing the news. She wished she could tell him right this minute and erase some of the anger he must have been feeling toward her tonight. She sighed. She feared he would not be happy with her for some time to come, and as she contemplated that, she felt the heat of the rising water on her backside and stood to turn off the taps.

HER HUSBAND RETURNED from Paris four days later, cheerful enough, but definitely preoccupied. She wondered, guiltily, if he had compiled an inventory in his mind of all her worst traits, and from time to time reviewed it. He chose to sleep in his dressing room for the first few nights; he said he was still adjusting to a proper schedule after late hours in France.

When she'd told him she suspected a new baby was coming, his face did light up with the almost boyish delight she'd expected. He added, a touch complacently: "I knew you were not completely well." She attempted to say she was sorry for not being better tempered in Paris, but he waved her off. Which was odd—he'd been furious with her when she'd left.

She quizzed him: Had there been some nasty scene between Napoléon and the king? Had the ball not gone well? Was Bismarck tormenting him? No, no, nothing like that, Fritz said. The emperor had tried to corner the king at the ball, but Fritz's father had laughed and said political matters could be considered at a later, more serious, moment.

One evening, nearly a week after his return, Fritz suggested a walk after dinner in the gardens. Something about the way he said it made her think this wasn't a spontaneous notion. She examined his face. He looked calm but solemn. What could be on his mind? She tried to ignore the nervous fluttering in her stomach and tucked her hand in Fritz's crooked elbow as they set out. It was nearly nine but they would have a short opportunity to view the plantings in good light. She chatted to him about the Jacqueminot roses in the far corner. "The pink ones were slow to bloom but now they are riotous and the fragrance heavenly. I want you to smell."

They were halfway there, passing by the large circular beds of purple and chrome-yellow heartsease, when he said, "I must tell you something that I fear you won't like."

Vicky felt immediately on alert, and, again, strangely nervous. Fritz's tone was not exactly confessional but certainly intimate.

"Yes?" she asked, letting go of his arm, taking a long sidelong look at him as they continued to stroll leisurely. He was gazing down, and he'd rolled his bottom lip under the top as he thought over his next words.

"On that night in Paris after you left . . . ," he began.

"Which night? You and your father stayed on for several more nights."

"I am speaking of the night of the ball."

Her stomach lurched—had something regrettable happened because she wasn't there?

"When I returned to the room at the hotel that night, I met a woman there. The actress Clementine du Rossier."

He paused and Vicky stopped walking to gape at him. Ever since the Danish War, when he'd become a star, he'd had plenty of opportunities to take up with other women. Before that too, probably, but afterward, definitely. She imagined ladies, noble and otherwise, must regularly have offered themselves, perhaps with just a suggestive look, a word or two, maybe a soft tap of a fan on his wrist—promising novelty, a secret stolen time no one else need ever know about. But she'd always felt smug, confident that he was impervious to such blandishments. And the gossip mill in Berlin had agreed. The Crown Prince was a remarkably handsome man with an odd, incomprehensible loyalty to his diminutive English wife. But perhaps no longer.

"You know this woman? She came because you asked her?"

"No, I didn't ask her. We saw her, don't you remember, in the Offenbach show at the Tuileries?"

"I don't remember—she was someone you admired in the show?"

"*Ja*, she's beautiful, but, *Liebling*, I thought nothing more about her until I found her there, sitting on the sofa in the hotel room."

"Was she wearing clothes?"

"Of course she was wearing clothes, evening clothes."

"But she hadn't come to drink tea, or champagne, or whatever else one serves to actresses in hotel rooms, had she?" she asked vehemently.

He reached out to pat her shoulder. "Shh, now, let me tell you the rest of the story."

Hugely relieved that he'd hardly be describing it this way if he'd actually gone to bed with Clementine du What's-her-name, she still felt very affronted.

"I sat down to speak with her and she admitted that she'd been sent by a dear friend of mine, for the evening, for mutual pleasure." He laughed a little then, recounting. "'Ah, so,' I said. 'The pleasures will be mutual, but the payment individual? As in, only one of us will be paid?'"

Vicky scowled up at him. Why had he even spoken with this hussy? Why hadn't he immediately ordered her out of the room?

Fritz continued. "I needn't worry, she told me, because payment had already been taken care of by my dear friend, *un homme d'une grande importance*, she explained, who had persuaded her for this one night to resume the profession that she had left behind many years previously when she had first become an actress, you see." He looked down at her, eyes twinkling.

"I see," she said. "And what lured her back into her former line of work? Was it because the promised payment was so large, or because it was you she would get to meet?"

"We didn't discuss details," he said, waving his hand nonchalantly. "But I imagine the size of the payment was the inducement, and she assured me she would keep the money even if I turned down her services. Then I told her she was very beautiful, but that as I am very content with my wife I have no need for anyone else."

"That's all? Then she left?"

"She told me my wife must be a lovely woman, and also very fortunate. When I escorted her to the door, she gave me a kiss on the cheek." He patted the spot. "And she called me *un prince de la plus haute noblesse.*"

He looked rather pleased with himself, but also on guard, awaiting her reaction.

Vicky found the account stunning, as if the world had been slightly reordered, but she sensed he had told her the whole truth, and she mustn't get too hysterical.

She sighed. "Darling, you are *haute noblesse*, always, and while I can't say that I am at all happy to have been the subject of a conversation between you and a Parisian courtesan, I appreciate that . . . well, I know that your loyalty is always . . ." She found herself tearing up, overwhelmed and unable to say how much it meant to her, his devotion, and his enduring love through all her griefs, her dissatisfactions, her harangues.

He reached out and stroked her cheek.

She found a balled-up handkerchief in her pocket and blew her nose. "Do you believe it was an attempt to blackmail you? Bismarck's most likely?"

"No, no." He shook his head. "I suspected immediately that it was a gesture from someone on high in Paris. I had Normann make some inquiries."

He paused. He looked away for a moment, considering exactly how to go on. "It seems that the lady Rossier was the gift of Napoléon. A personal gift. Perhaps to make me feel more kindly disposed to him, to the French cause . . . who knows his exact intentions."

Now Vicky really was furious and stamped her foot in rage. "He sends a woman to seduce my husband? And yet he pretends to be my friend! He goes on about Papa being the most honorable man he ever met. It's disgusting!"

Fritz reached out and put his hands on her shoulders. "Calm now, *Liebling*, you need to look at this clearly."

Vicky had a strange sense of dislocation—it was usually she who was pleading with him to be coolheaded. She glowered. "And why is that?"

He sighed. "Let me ask you something. Do you believe that everyone thinks like you do?"

"Of course not, I know they don't."

"Do you think that it's possible to convince others to behave as you would like? My father, the emperor, men such as that," he said.

"No, certainly not, I have no influence, although—"

He'd cocked his head, looking down expectantly.

"Although I wish I had more!" she said heatedly.

He shook his head slightly. "Wishing doesn't make it so, and standing in judgment . . ." He trailed off.

"So my objecting to these things is futile?" she asked him.

He sighed. "I think in these days you are still so distressed about Siggy, which makes you impatient with everybody. However, it's always been your nature to remonstrate when you disapprove, and that is not always constructive. Especially in your position."

She scowled.

"*Liebling,* do I not remain in compliance with your high standards?" he asked, raising his eyebrows, questioning. "I am endeavoring to do my best."

She couldn't help but laugh a little. He was so sweet really, the way he was admonishing her without grinding down the point.

"Your recent behavior does indicate that you continue to meet my expectations, yes," she replied in a matching, slightly facetious tone.

He smiled. "I am glad to hear you laugh. I debated for a long time whether to tell you about this incident, since I didn't look forward to listening to you explode."

She thought, *Am I really so unreasonable?* But gazing up at his dear face, she let him continue without disputing.

"Then I thought, no, I must tell you, because I am sure it's being gossiped about and I didn't want you to hear it from someone else," he said. "Also, there should be no secrets between us."

The sun was fast disappearing, and they should be heading

back, without visiting the fragrant roses. He looked especially handsome in the dim, golden light, her gallant soldier prince.

"No secrets," she agreed, and she slipped her hand into his. "Shall we return inside?"

They walked in companionable silence back to the palace. How, she wondered, did other women manage, who could not be sure of their husbands' faithful hearts?

31

Cannes, Autumn 1869

Vicky walked along the seafront, her arm linked with Alice's, while the children ran, skipping and prancing, ahead of them in the sunshine. On this, the second day of their holiday, they were on an expedition to visit a grove of exotic parasol pines just outside of town, and there to have a picnic.

Mild air, sparkling water, the cawing of gulls, and the creaking of fishing boats straining on rope moorings—the scene enchanted her.

"A heavenly afternoon," she said.

"And to think, the end of October," her sister replied.

"With luck the weather will continue like this for weeks and weeks," Vicky said.

Alice called out, "Victoria, not so far. Wait for the others."

Vicky saw her eldest niece, way out in front, stop short, while Alice's other two little girls—Ella and Irène—hurried up behind her. Victoria of Hesse was tall for her age, nearly seven, and blessed with long, thick, flaxen hair. The Hesse girls were all beautiful—in particular five-year-old Ella, with saucer-like blue eyes and an angelic expression—and Vicky felt a pang for Charlotte, nine now. Her daughter, skinny and wan, had mousy brown hair so scant it had to be cropped short and Vicky insisted she wear gloves since she bit her nails down to the quick. At least little Moretta, trotting beside Charlotte, was a vigorous child, who already rode a pony at age three. Moretta liked to point to the picture of St. George on the nursery wall and declare that one day she too would fight dragons. Charlotte scoffed and said there was no such thing as dragons, but her younger daughter paid no notice. Moretta had very fierce intentions.

Now strolling behind the five girls, and absorbed in some private conference, were her two sons—William had thrown his good, right arm around Henry's shoulders and was nattering at him as they ambled along. Poor Henry. At seven he seemed doomed to act as ten-year-old Willy's acolyte, parroting whatever his boisterous older brother said. Would he ever get out from under Willy's domination? This was one of Vicky's perpetual worries. Of the many resolutions she had made for their stay here, foremost was her plan to spend time with Henry—and with William and with Charlotte—alone. In Berlin Vicky didn't have much individual time for her older children, occupied as she was with endless public appearances, her charity work, and the care of Moretta, and little Waldemar, conceived just before the Paris Exhibition. The sweet baby was eighteen months old now and as she had predicted Fritz, Mama, and the king and queen all considered him a replacement for Siggy. And while she adored Waldy, Vicky never forgot Siggy—and she didn't want to.

Raising her eyes to scan the soft, undulating profile of the mountains in the distance, she sent a silent message of thanks to Fritz. Her husband knew how much she disliked Berlin without him, so when Bismarck and the king ordered him to travel to Egypt for the opening of the new canal there he proposed that Vicky spend the time abroad, somewhere warm. She chose this picturesque French seaside town after Mama told her many English people came here to escape the damp winters at home. To provide her company, Fritz invited Prince Louis of Hesse to accompany him to the Near East, leaving Alice and her children free to join Vicky. Alice confessed that she and Louis were very poor now and constantly had to ask Mama for money, but their three daughters flourished and a year ago she'd given birth to a son, Ernest Louis. Now Vicky could look forward to weeks and weeks with Alice.

The tutor, Dr. Hinzpeter, had come with them to Cannes, and a new military governor, Lieutenant August O'Danne. Earlier in the year, Captain von Schrötter had finally resigned, complaining that Dr. Hinzpeter did not recognize his authority and often punished the young heir without consulting him. Also, as the captain told Fritz, he did not like how Hinzpeter never praised William, and frequently detained him inside for extra lessons. The king had raged that "the damn doctor" had too much influence over both his grandsons, and demanded that a new military governor be appointed and have final say over Willy and Henry's daily life. But Vicky resisted. Every candidate the king's military cabinet put forward she found an excuse to reject. She insisted on someone under forty, who spoke good English, and who had artistic interests. She secretly hoped that if months and months went by with no appointment, the search would be abandoned and Dr Hinzpeter would have sole oversight of the two princes.

In the end Fritz landed on O'Danne, who had grown up in Mecklenburg with his German mother after his Irish father had died, and served as an officer in the Second Army under Fritz. The king grumbled that the man was not first-rate, but acceded to O'Danne on the condition that he and the queen spent every Friday afternoon with the two boys, to take proper measure of their progress. William and Henry inevitably came back from their afternoons at the Berliner Schloss all swelled up. One day Henry announced: "As a prince of Prussia I will need to command other men. Grandmamma says I will find my place in our navy."

Vicky laughed. "The Prussian navy is nothing, Henry! A dinky collection of ships that could dock on the Havel River in Potsdam."

Both her sons looked at her, hurt.

"It's Britannia that rules the waves, darlings," she explained.

"Not forever. Prussia can build up its navy," Willy retorted.

"Perhaps, but it can never catch up with England."

It was important for them—especially now—to understand that the world did not revolve around Prussia.

THEY HAD REACHED the grove of palms. Bright sun filtered down between the trees but the sea breeze kept the air pleasantly cool. Two maids laid down blankets to sit on, and the butler, Herr Kimmerling, was opening the wicker hamper to hand out cakes. Alice and Vicky settled themselves on the soft ground covering, and Vicky immediately reached for her work bag. Henry and Mary Ponsonby had had a second son, and asked her and Fritz to stand as godparents. As they had not been able to travel to England earlier in the year for the christening, she hoped to quickly finish off a cream-colored jacket as a gift for the baby, Frederick Edward, to be known as Fritz.

The children set out to explore, happier, it appeared, to be at liberty than eat anything. The two little girls, Irène and Moretta, were soon crouched next to one big trunk and plucking at the grass. Next Vicky heard Willy call out. "No, Ella, don't go that way, the game is that you follow Henry, and Victoria follows me."

"What if I don't like to follow you?" shouted Victoria.

"You must. We are racing that way," Willy replied.

"Willy always wants to set the rules," said Charlotte. "Let's forget about him and go make little houses out of all these funny cones."

Charlotte bent down to pick up two cones, and then all three older girls headed to join Irène and Moretta. Willy stood still, his arms crossed, a furious look on his face, glaring at his retreating sister and cousins.

"Get back, we haven't finished the race!" he yelled.

"Maybe later," answered Ella, saucily.

Willy made a sudden lurch forward, as if planning to charge at

Ella. But Henry grabbed his right arm and whispered something in his ear. Then Willy called out, "You'll be sorry, you sillies. We'll come and smash your houses."

"Willy, stop it! Don't say things like that to the girls," Vicky exclaimed.

Both boys looked startled by her sudden interference and frowned. After a minute Willy said: "Come on, Henry." And she watched them go off at speed, weaving between the trees. Willy's running gait was unsteady and his body pitched awkwardly to the right, while his left arm hung down in its strange, inert way as if pinned onto the shoulder. Vicky sighed. Her eldest son exhibited not a trace of his father's remarkable physical grace, which constantly pained her, and shamed her. She sighed again.

"What, dearest, William's upset you?" asked Alice in a light tone.

"I hate his overbearing way of speaking."

"He's the oldest of them, he thinks it's his right," her sister answered.

"And I just wish, I always wish . . ." she said, trailing off.

"You mourn his arm," Alice replied.

Vicky put down the knitting needles to look directly at her sister. "And do you blame me? It's a mutilation. If it were Henry it wouldn't matter."

"But it isn't Henry. It's Willy, and I notice while he complains about the stretching exercises, he's never too concerned about this lameness."

"Part of his monstrous pride."

Alice gave a sharp tut. "Can he never please you? Perhaps his character needs improvement. But, Vicky, as a child you too were very bossy and prideful like Willy."

"Not like Willy at all!" How could Alice say that? She had felt the responsibility of being the eldest in the family, but she didn't bully the others as Willy so often did.

Her sister smiled. "Perhaps you were kinder, dearest. Still commanding, as I remember!"

Vicky scowled at Alice and picked up her knitting again.

"Won't you admit that William's domineering qualities are not all bad, especially in someone who has to lead?" Alice asked. "And it's wonderful he's so interested in things. This morning he showed me a smoky topaz stone he discovered in the garden and explained at length why it's a wonderful find."

"At length? You mean he blathered on about it?"

"I like his passion. And he can be instructed to curb his egoism. The good doctor, I'm sure, will be tireless in that regard."

Vicky sighed. "I wish Willy were cleverer, but failing that, if only he could have common sense and good judgment. And be less impulsive!"

"Does Fritz worry as you do?" Alice asked.

"Sometimes. Mostly he wishes he would be nicer to his sisters and more generous. When he's at home, Fritz tries to spend time with all the children. But William whines that his father should play only with him and Henry. They're the boys, they're most important. Then Fritz cuffs him and he sulks."

"Goodness me."

"The king and queen reinforce this idea that he is foremost in the family. The king, in particular, always takes a special interest in Willy."

"He represents the future."

"I suppose," said Vicky.

"And, needless to say, none of that will last. Once Fritz is king, so many things will be different," Alice said.

The girls came running over seeking cakes and the time for private talk ended, but Alice's last remark lingered in her mind. When after two hours, the sun slanting down in the sky, the servants packed up the picnic things, and they all began walking back into town, Vicky found she only half listened to Alice chatting to the children. Instead she was thinking how wonderful it would be if only Fritz's father would die. She longed for this, which she couldn't confess to anyone, not even Alice. But next year she would turn thirty and her husband was already thirty-eight, and they had so little say over their own lives. Fritz was obligated to travel all around at Bismarck's direction, and the king doled out their allowance grudgingly, always carping that they were rich off Vicky's English income and didn't really need as much as he gave them. And, worst of all, was how much influence Fritz's parents exerted on the minds of the children. This needed to end before they got much older.

She loved to picture it: the king's funeral and then Fritz's coronation, her at his side. She imagined how the whole court would be reorganized and certain reprobates—starting with the loathsome Prince Karl—pushed aside. And what would become of Bismarck? She doubted now that Fritz would banish him, he was too effective and too popular. But eventually he'd skulk off to Varzin and Fritz could appoint his own man. Someone Vicky admired and trusted too, and the whole atmosphere in Berlin would be different—more open, more modern, and more progressive. She and Fritz would be at the center of it, setting the tone, casting off the old stiff hierarchies, and promoting the public good. So exhilarating to contemplate this! But at the moment of peak excitement, she brought her thoughts smashing back to earth again, rebuking herself: Fritz never stopped honoring his father and mother, she must seek to do likewise, whatever her frustrations. To yearn for the death of another person—that was truly wicked, an offense against God. And then she vowed, as she had many times before, to stop.

They had reached the last steps of the walk home—the gate of their rented villa only a few yards ahead. She watched a footman push it open, heard the iron hinges groan—an unpleasant, croaky sound that jabbed at her soul. How much longer would they live in the cage of their circumscribed existence? Fritz would be such a marvelous king now, tested by battle, and not yet old. And what about her? After a dozen years in Prussia she had a keen sense of its strengths—and its weaknesses. Her apprenticeship was complete. She itched to assume the role she had prepared for for so long.

THE NEXT DAY, Vicky took Henry out on his own to look at the large ships docked at Port de Cannes. Away from his older brother, her second son was very sweet, if only he were more interesting to converse with. When she asked where in the world he hoped to sail if he became a naval man, he had no answer beyond "every place." On the following Monday she took Charlotte to luncheon at the Grand Hotel. After they had taken their seats at a corner table, Charlotte asked her, "Do you think everyone here knows who we are?"

Vicky laughed. "Some people do, probably. Our stay here has been written about in the newspapers. But I hope we are left in peace to enjoy our meal incognito."

"I would like everyone to recognize us, and come up and bow," Charlotte said.

Vicky tried to distract the girl by talking about the ancient world. Ruins of a Roman town had been discovered nearby during the construction of a new railway line. But Charlotte remained preoccupied by who might be looking at them, and she sat in her chair in an odd, self-conscious, mannered way which greatly annoyed Vicky.

At least Willy had plenty of time for her stories about the Romans, particularly the rise and fall of Julius Caesar—they discussed it for an hour after supper the next night. She woke up in the morning searching her mind for something else she and Willy could enjoy together here in Cannes. He did have some artistic talent, maybe hire an art master for them both? She made inquiries and early the next week a painter named Gadiou called at the villa. He set up a bowl of fruit on a table in the front room and she and Willy, each with a sketch pad, sat down side by side to draw. At first, Willy was very enthusiastic, moving his pencil rapidly across the paper, his face twisted with concentration. But,

having produced his drawing, he barely listened to the French-
man's corrections, started moving restlessly in his chair, and finally, after he asked several times to be excused, she dismissed
him, and he ran off to look for the other children.

"It was completely maddening. He's so inattentive and careless
about his work," Vicky said to her sister later.

"Perhaps too much to ask of him to sit for an hour and do
nothing but draw a single picture," Alice said.

Vicky frowned. "You and I did such things with Mama when
we were younger than Willy is now."

"We lived in a different world, at a different time."

"But one reason to come here was to have Willy in a simpler,
better place—no soldiers marching by, no constant talk of war
and battles. And, best of all, away from his grandparents who
continually encourage his terrible complacency, the sense that
he's so special he doesn't have to try at anything!"

Alice smiled. "Be patient, dear Vicky, we have not even been
here a fortnight. Willy's still adjusting."

But Alice's three girls seemed well settled. They did their lessons in the morning with Alice, and in the afternoons played contentedly in the garden. Lieutenant O'Danne was teaching Willy
tennis and he sometimes took Victoria along to the courts. He
remarked she had an excellent stroke. Willy overheard this, and
insisted that his playing was better, but the lieutenant told Alice
and Vicky later that Victoria surpassed him. "She's a fine natural
sportswoman, Princess," he said to Alice.

Vicky couldn't help but feel envious—of the grace and beauty
of Alice's daughters—and other circumstances of her sister's life.
She knew this to be so ungenerous. And perhaps no one else
would even understand. Vicky had made the far better match, to
a famous and wealthy husband, poised to be king of a powerful
nation. A retinue of fourteen had accompanied her to Cannes.
Alice was married to a minor prince, heir to a bankrupt grand
duke, and she could afford only a baby nurse and a lady's maid,
which was why she taught her children herself. All her dresses

and hats had seen better days. But, at home in Darmstadt, Alice had far more freedom than Vicky did, and much more time with her husband. In Berlin, Vicky did have her nursing corps work and now, with help from dear Professor S, she was starting a school for young women. Still, too many days were bleak with Fritz away, and too many hours taken up with meaningless social occasions where everyone talked constantly of rank, title, and precedence. She hated it now more than ever—and she dreaded her return to Prussia after Christmas. In the last few winters she'd suffered from neuralgia, sharp pain in her face and legs, which she supposed was her body's response to the soul-crushing atmosphere at court.

DURING THE THIRD week of their stay a family from Paris moved into the villa next door to theirs. A Monsieur Cazanouve and his much younger wife, with their two children, an older girl, perhaps aged twelve, and a little boy, maybe six. Vicky and Alice met them in the road and exchanged polite bows but no further intercourse between the households ensued. Except that Willy was fascinated by the girl. In the afternoons, before tea, he took to standing by the low wall that separated the back gardens, and waiting for the French children to emerge. When they did, Vicky would watch him talking animatedly to the girl, who listened quite passively on her side of the wall. Sometimes he'd throw his ball up with his right arm and catch it, as if demonstrating a trick. One evening, when they all ate supper together, he told them about Véronique, as the French girl was called. She liked dancing, she didn't ride, and she only spoke a little English and no German.

"I think she's very pretty," Willy said.

Henry nodded solemnly. "She is."

"And I told her about our home in Berlin and how Prussia is now the most important country in Europe, no longer France," Willy continued.

"How did she answer to that?" asked Alice, with a smile.

"She said she didn't believe it. Still, I can tell she admires me."

"And your physique?" snapped Vicky, irked by her son's boastful tone.

Alice glared at her from across the table, and gave a tight, stern shake of the head.

"Any girl knows a prince like me is worthy of great esteem," said Willy, in a somewhat airy voice. But his cheeks flushed red, as if she had slapped him.

"Do you think our French neighbors avoid us because of Bismarck's saber-rattling?" Vicky asked her sister one afternoon as they walked into town.

"Very likely. Who in France has ever applauded his ascendance? Or the phenomenal success of the armies he controls," said Alice.

"Not that it's any of their concern," said Vicky.

"How do you mean?" asked Alice sharply.

"It suited the French when Germany was divided and weak. Now that Prussia's made her strong and united, I'm glad Napoléon is up nights worrying about what Bismarck will do next," Vicky said.

"We aren't going to quarrel about this, are we?" asked Alice.

"No, certainly not. You know I'm no mindless disciple of the hateful man," Vicky exclaimed.

"Between hotheaded Napoléon on the one hand, and scheming Bismarck on the other, it can't end well," Alice said.

"When war with France comes, as dreadful and calamitous as that would be, the unity of Germany would come about at once. Fritz says it, and the Baron too," Vicky said.

"I hope we will be better prepared in Darmstadt if there's another war." Alice sighed.

Vicky reached out for her sister's hand and squeezed it. "At least this time we will be on the same side."

FRITZ AND LOUIS arrived in Cannes on December 17, full of stories of their marvelous travels. They spent the week of Christmas all together, enjoying the bright weather—cooler now than previously, but still warmer than Berlin. Vicky gloried in having both Alice and Fritz close at hand, all the children around them, her in-laws far away. She met twice with Gadiou, the art master, to improve her watercolor technique, and she produced several paintings of the beautiful sea that pleased her. Dr. Hinzpeter asked to be allowed to stay behind with William and Henry for three additional months—arguing the boys required this quiet atmosphere to make real progress in their studies. Fritz thought it a good notion, so they told the doctor yes.

Vicky saved until Christmas Eve some special news for her husband. She expected a baby in June. Here in lovely Cannes her typical nausea had barely bothered her.

Fritz grinned. "So tell me, *Liebling*, do you intend to exceed your mother in this regard and have ten?"

"Perhaps," she replied. "Little babies are so precious. It's much harder to manage older ones."

"But all the children have thrived in Cannes, I think."

"Yes, it's been lovely. I am only sorry to have to go back to Berlin and to leave the boys."

"It will do them good," said her husband.

On December 27 they boarded the train for Berlin—along with Louis and Alice, and their children, who would accompany them as far as Frankfurt. Willy and Henry had come to the station to say goodbye, with Dr Hinzpeter as escort. Henry wept, and clung to Vicky. "I wish you wouldn't go," he sobbed.

But Willy did not cry. He just jumped up and down in an excitable way for the ten minutes the boys stood on the platform.

When the train had pulled away Vicky said to Fritz: "Willy is so hard-hearted. He was completely unperturbed about our departure. He doesn't care about his poor mother."

Fritz scoffed. "I think he was just cold. I noticed he had no jacket, he must have left it behind in the carriage."

As the swaying cars gained speed, and they were swept alongside the glistening water, Vicky pictured the two boys heading back to the villa, Willy filling the carriage with his talk, about some game or some other interest of his own—tennis, or boats, or stones. If only he was less garrulous, more considerate of others, no longer so complacent and full of himself. He wasn't like other boys—he couldn't be allowed to be. Not with all that faced him in the future. Often she wished to shake him and shout at him to make him see. But right now, staring out the train window, she began to feel that the overwhelming responsibility of ensuring he became a man equal to his destiny would crush her—that she couldn't bear it, she wasn't equal to it. With a screech of iron wheels, the train turned into a narrow mountain pass, the slate-gray rockface pressing in on the edge of the tracks, and her heart constricted. She might do everything she could for William, and still fail. The train rushed into a tunnel, the lamps flickered and the compartment was cast momentarily into darkness. Moretta squealed: "Mama, it's nighttime!" and then the cars burst out the other side and into a wide, sunny vista of terraced lavender fields and olive groves. Shades of green, rows of purple, and patches of yellowy brown flashed by her eyes. So pretty. But in her gnawing preoccupation she felt removed, unable to fully take in the scene, because she was elsewhere, trapped in a tunnel of her own fear.

32

Potsdam, Spring 1870

*B*ack in Berlin the winter dragged on endlessly, and everyone suffered bad throats, running noses. In March, during a long spell of especially low temperatures, the pipes froze and then burst in the Kronprinzenpalais, and water flooded down from the ceilings into the nurseries and the bedroom she and Fritz shared. They decamped for Potsdam and Vicky, while upset by the expense of repairs and new furniture, was happy to have an excuse to miss many evening court events—she lived too far from town to attend.

Fritz still went to the Wilhelmstrasse every day when he was not traveling. He returned one evening with surprising news. His cousin, their old friend and the onetime minister-president Prince Charles Anton of Hohenzollern-Sigmaringen, was coming to the Neues Palais to discuss a sudden proposal from Madrid. The Spanish prime minister, Marshal Prim, had offered the prince's eldest son, Prince Leopold, the throne of Spain, to replace Queen Isabella, whose debauched behavior had so offended her cabinet that they had ousted her. She lived now in exile in Paris and young Leopold had this wonderful opportunity in the offing.

"Your Royal Highness, I am sorry to arrive with so little notice," said Prince Charles, kissing Vicky's hand a mere hour later.

"In any circumstance I am delighted to see you, Prince," said Vicky.

"Your husband has told you of the choice now facing us?"

"He has," Vicky said, smiling at Fritz, "but he has not told me his own opinion—or yours."

"Both Prince Charles and I want to know what you think, *Liebling*," said Fritz, reaching for his pipe.

"It's a great honor, and I am sure Leopold would fill the role admirably. A German Catholic sitting on an ancient throne! That would certainly be an astonishing sight," she said.

Prince Charles nodded, his face lit up with excitement and pleasure.

"But the French won't tolerate it, I fear," Vicky added. "They will feel themselves encircled by Hohenzollerns—in resurgent Prussia across the Rhine, and then in the nation on their southern border."

"*Ja*, but why should the French decide the matter?" asked Prince Charles sharply. "This is a Spanish affair."

"Maybe so, but at the moment, the French are particularly sensitive to expanding Prussian influence. You don't agree?" asked Vicky.

"I agree—but I don't believe that reason enough for my son to refuse the offer."

"Then you, and we, must be prepared for the consequences of accepting." Vicky glanced over at Fritz to see if he concurred.

Smoking his pipe, her husband appeared deep in thought. After a moment he said: "French attitudes shouldn't restrict German actions."

"But this could set off the powder keg of ill feeling," Vicky replied.

"Moltke and I were discussing it the other day. War with France may be inevitable—we can only hope to have time to prepare sufficiently," said Fritz. "No, what bothers me about this proposal is how it looks."

"Looks?" asked Prince Charles.

"I'm not sure a Hohenzollern should accept a throne after the previous monarch has been forcibly removed," Fritz said.

"The Spanish give us all sorts of assurances that they were very sorry to have been forced to take extreme action. It was only because the queen attempted to elevate one of her paramours, a drunk and a commoner, to minister of state," said Prince Charles.

"Still, it's undignified," said Fritz. "You must ask my father, of course, but I imagine he will say the same."

"I will speak with His Majesty tomorrow, if I am able," said Prince Charles.

"And consult with the minister-president as well," said Fritz.

Vicky frowned. "Is that necessary? The king is the head of the family, not Bismarck."

"You set out the diplomatic objections yourself, Vicky," said Fritz. "Prussia's chief diplomat can't be excluded from the discussion. In any case, my father will insist."

"I will start with the king," said Prince Charles.

THEY HEARD NOTHING more about the Spanish question before Fritz departed the next week for Bavaria and then Württemberg. If the French attacked across the Rhine, armies of the independent south German states would need to work together with the North German Confederation forces, and the king had already assigned Fritz the difficult task of commanding the non-Prussian troops in a coordinated defense.

"Are you certain there's going to be a war?" Vicky asked Fritz when he returned.

"Not certain, but as you have seen—" He looked at her, rueful. "Once war talk heats up, war itself tends to follow quickly on."

"And do you feel ready?"

Fritz shrugged. "While Moltke's quite confident, the French army is large and fast moving. You remember the speed of their mobilization in '59? They might be across the Rhine before we can get sufficient troops there. Our German allies are willing enough but not well trained. Those Bavarian officers looked fat and lazy to me. And they march as if they have peas in their shoes."

"What does the king think?"

"He agrees that the enemy will be formidable. He hopes war can be put off."

"And Bismarck?"

"Bismarck confides to me he doesn't want war. Yet Napoléon may bring it to our doorstep, he told me, and we can't duck the fight. The Prussian people won't stand for it."

"He's calm?"

"*Sehr ruhig.*" Very composed.

Vicky turned this over in her mind. She'd watched the minister operate for eight years. A mild and seemingly confiding Bismarck was a Bismarck who felt he was master of the situation. He became angry and hysterical only when circumstances spun out of his control. If he wasn't worried now, did that mean the French were unlikely to attack?

She wished she knew. But she was glad when, the next week, one potential provocation evaporated. The king persuaded his kinsmen to turn down the Spanish crown—it came with too many liabilities, including an unstable political situation in Spain. And he agreed with Fritz: it was beneath the dignity of a Hohenzollern to take up a throne vacated by a deposed monarch.

A BEAUTIFUL SPRING emerged by inches in Potsdam, and on April 1 Willy and Henry came back from Cannes. Both had grown taller, and they looked so healthy and handsome as they bounded into the Neues Palais. No one was more thrilled than little Waldy, who had been asking continually in his lisping voice for "Hensy *und* Willy." The little boy screamed delightedly, and hugged first Willy and then Henry about the legs.

William struck Vicky as much improved. Of course, his withered arm still hung down in its odd, unnatural way, and now his claw-like left hand appeared more purple than ever. She must have Dr. Langenbeck examine it. But at the supper table, Willy had them all laughing imitating the French proprietor of the sweet shop in Cannes who would roar at the boys when they spent too much time choosing their purchases. Willy glowed with pride when Fritz clapped him on the back. "You're a terrific mimic, *mein Junge.*"

After the meal, Willy came up to her sitting room with his portfolio and cuddled down next to her on the sofa. She noticed he had spots on both his cheeks, like the ones that formerly plagued Bertie, but she admired the concentrated look in his large blue eyes as he carefully opened the folder and took out three drawings in colored pencil. "I did these with the master after you left," he said.

Two were of the French garrison soldiers on parade near the park, and another, quite beautiful, was the view of the mountains from behind their villa.

"Willichen, these are really lovely," she told him.

"I made them for you, Mama," he said, sounding very proud.

"I'm going to frame this mountain scene and hang it on the wall."

He beamed at her, very pleased.

"I was so sad here without you and your brother," she told him. "I constantly wondered what you were doing and hoped you were well."

He nodded, but now he began glancing around the room, as if uninterested in what she was saying.

"Look at me when I am speaking," she said sharply. As soon as the words left her mouth, she regretted them. His body stiffened and his face fell. "I am looking," he said.

She tried to recapture the tenderness between them. "It's important that I can talk to you and know that you hear me. You are my boy, my special big boy. Aren't you?"

He gave a small smile, and then nodded. "Yes, Mama," he said. But she sensed some shift away from her. Maddening. Nothing to do but go on. "Now that you have returned we can discuss all that you are studying together. And I hope you will begin to work harder, Willy. The doctor wrote to me to say you are very intermittent in your attention."

"Pardon?" he said. They were speaking English. Maybe Willy didn't know all those words.

"You must work hard every day at your studies," she said.

He nodded. "I do, Mama. I do."

"I am not sure you do. It's not enough to simply sit at the desk and listen to what the doctor says, you must put your whole effort into it. Strive to reach the highest standard. This can be very satisfying! It was for me at your age."

Again he looked at her rather blankly. Aggravating boy. He wasn't listening, despite her appeal.

"Can I go now?" he asked.

Vicky sighed. "Yes, but you need to be better, William."

ONE EVENING IN the following week Vicky invited the American ambassador to dine with them at the Neues Palais. George Bancroft was a historian by training and had been secretary of the navy during the American war in Mexico. Fritz found him interesting company, and Vicky liked his wife, Elizabeth, a rather austere woman, but well educated, from Boston, who presented herself with the appealing straightforwardness of the American bluestocking. The Bancrofts brought along their houseguests, a Mr. John Bigelow, the American consul general in Paris, and his wife, Jane.

Over the meal the Bigelows disclosed that they had come to Prussia to install their fourteen-year-old son in the Potsdam home of Herr Professor Dr. Lahnemann, head teacher of Latin and Greek at the local gymnasium. "Paris is very frenetic and distracting," explained Mrs. Bigelow, in her soft drawl—she hailed from Baltimore. "And we intend for him to be well prepared to attend Yale College in a few years' time."

Her husband cut in. "I've lived all over Europe for two decades, and I believe the scholarship in Germany surpasses anywhere else—if you will excuse me, Princess, even England."

"You needn't persuade me. I am the proud daughter of a Bonn scholar and the happy wife of another," she said, smiling at Fritz.

"This Dr. Lahnemann, he will instruct your son for a year?" asked Fritz.

"For two years, we imagine. I hope the boy won't be too homesick or miss his brothers and sisters. But he's a stalwart lad, our Poultney. And the capable Frau Dr. Lahnemann, mother of six little ones herself, promises to take good care of him," Mr. Bigelow said.

Mrs. Bigelow looked quite cast down. She was a fair-haired woman, with very white, nearly blue-toned skin and sparse, pale eyelashes. Vicky felt for her. "I was heartsick to have my sons away recently, so I understand how much you will miss—is it Paulty?" Vicky asked.

"He's called Poultney. That was my name before I married. But his friends call him Poe," the boy's mother said.

Vicky smiled. "We shall ask Poe to come here to play with Prince William and Prince Henry. They are fascinated by America, especially Indians. I have been reading aloud to them from *The Last of the Mohicans*."

"Poe's favorite! And all *The Leatherstocking Tales*, too. He even brought along to Berlin the bow and quiver of blunted arrows we bought him at Niagara last year," said Mrs. Bigelow.

"This is not the landscape that Fenimore Cooper envisioned," said Minister Bancroft, gesturing with his hand at the large, ornate baroque dining room in which they sat. "But I imagine very satisfactory games could be acted out here." Everyone around the table laughed.

"The attics are very big," Fritz told the Bigelows. "When I was a boy, when it rained, I played up there for hours. Making battles. Your son must come and do this with our boys."

ON THE NEXT Saturday Vicky sent a carriage to fetch Poe Bigelow from the Lahnemanns' house in a small street in the town of Potsdam. Very fair like his mother, Poe was a lanky boy, not particularly tall but conspicuously and unself-consciously American. When he held out his hand to shake hers when they met, Dr. Hinzpeter, standing nearby, hissed, "You must bow, boy." Poe bent awkwardly from the waist, but with a small smile, as if to say, "Isn't this quaint?"

From the start, Willy and Henry were entranced by Poe and all that he could tell them of the life and practices of the red man. He'd brought along the fabled bow and arrows, and they immediately headed out into the park and engaged in long, elaborate games of running, chasing, and hunting each other. And on subsequent Saturdays, when it rained, they took Fritz's suggestion and headed for the attics. Fritz told Vicky they were obligated to invite other boys from time to time for these Saturday sessions, the sons of important officials or high-ranking officers. But the native youngsters had clearly been drilled beforehand on the stiff orthodoxies of Prussian etiquette and could not be natural in the princes' company, nor hers. These young Prussians spoke only when spoken to, waited to be told where to run, and turned up in their best clothes, which they seemed reluctant to get mussed. Willy dismissed them all as hopelessly uninteresting, good only in the role of the captives, to be caught and tied to trees. But he asked for Poe Bigelow every week.

That poor lad. Vicky didn't think he was fed properly at the Lahnemanns', although he never complained, telling them that the family was kind and the doctor an excellent teacher. But at Saturday supper, which Vicky liked to serve to the children at five, before Poe returned home, he regularly devoured two or three helpings of beef and vegetables, sopping up every drop of gravy with bread. Because the kitchen staff could never master English nursery dishes to her satisfaction, when Vicky had time she preferred to cook for the children herself. One evening when she'd made rice pudding, Willy's favorite, Poe said, "This is very delicious, thank you, ma'am."

"My mother makes the best puddings in the world," said Willy complacently.

"As I said, it is very good," Poe replied. "Still, I am sure my mother could make a rice pudding just as good, maybe better."

Willy scowled, but Vicky laughed.

"Do you like German food, Poe?" she asked him.

"It's all right, ma'am. Very sour, though."

"All that potato salad and salty sausage?"

"Yes, ma'am," he said, wrinkling his nose. "I can't really get accustomed to it."

She smiled at him. "Next week I think we'll have leg of lamb, and green beans and raisin cake. How does that sound?"

"That sounds wonderful, ma'am."

What a good influence Poe Bigelow was. Challenging Willy rather than deferring. If only she could find a half dozen like him, she'd start a little grammar school here in the Neues Palais for Willy and Henry. That was what their education lacked: the company and competition of normal children, with sensible parents, who wanted their sons to grow up to be sober, responsible, and well-educated men. In other words—not the children of the Prussian officer class. She sighed. What a terrible fuss there would be if she started such an academy and excluded all the best-connected youth. She'd have to think of a different solution. Perhaps the school could be restricted to English and American boys? She laughed out loud. That would certainly never be allowed.

As MAY TURNED to June she began to feel very apprehensive. It didn't matter that this was her seventh child—no birth was without risk. Fritz stayed home every day to be close to her, and sometimes in the afternoons he took the children to visit the farm they owned at Bornstedt, two miles distant, where he'd set up a playground with swings, a seesaw, and a small field for cricket and football. One of the dachshunds at the farm had a litter of puppies, and the children came home with rapturous descriptions of the little dogs. She would sit on the terrace, too great with child to move around much, and wait for them to return for supper. She'd hear Fritz leading them back singing together, even Waldy, riding on Fritz's shoulders: *"Alle Vögel sind schon da, alle Vögel, alle!"* The happy sight brought tears to her eyes, and she promised God that if He would protect the whole family, guide her through the ordeal ahead, and present her with a healthy new baby, she'd be content and no longer wish impatiently for the king's death and a freer, more productive life for her and Fritz.

DR. HINZPETER FROWNED continually over these afternoon expeditions that absented the princes from the schoolroom for many hours. Vicky finally told the tutor to go on holiday. "I need the children to spend time with their father," she said. "Who knows what will happen this summer?"

"But I hear you plan to visit England in August with the children."

"Yes, if it is possible. Fritz and I have not decided."

Another Hinzpeter frown.

"Doctor, let us see how events unfold. So much uncertainty in the air now. And I am distracted with personal concerns at the moment."

She was very relieved when the baby, a girl, arrived safely on the morning of June 14 after a painful, but relatively short, labor.

"Are you disappointed not to have another boy, a playmate for Waldy?" Vicky asked Fritz.

"No, *Liebe*," said Fritz, gazing down at the girl they had decided to name Sophie. "I'm pleased, and I hope she grows up to be as clever and as good as her mother."

TWO DAYS LATER she was nursing the baby when Fritz burst into the room. "Prince Leopold has announced he will accept the throne of Spain," he said.

"What? I don't understand. Didn't you tell me he and his father sent a telegram to Madrid refusing? Weeks ago."

"Apparently Marshal Prim just ignored it. Because Bismarck told him to."

"Bismarck? But why would he do that? When was he communicating with Prim? Isn't he in Varzin?"

"He's recently returned. And he sought me out to tell me that it's in Germany's interest for members of the house of Hohenzollern to have more influence in Europe."

"And your father agrees?"

"I have been away from the Wilhelmstrasse of late, so I don't know all the details. But yes, the king has been persuaded. He told Prince Charles that if his son wanted to accept, he would not stand in the way."

"So, they've gone ahead?"

"*Ja,* and it was supposed to stay a secret until the Spanish parliament met again after the summer, but the news leaked. The French are incensed—the Foreign Office in Paris has already declared that the Spanish have no right to make this offer."

"As we predicted. And what does Bismarck say to that?"

"He denies that he or anyone in the Prussian government has any control over a private agreement between the Spanish ministers and Prince Leopold of Hohenzollern."

Vicky sat staring at Fritz. Bismarck was a master of secret dealings, but it seemed inconceivable that he would orchestrate so blatantly an offensive action against the French now. Didn't he worry, as Fritz and the king did, that Prussia wasn't ready for war?

"The king never consulted you on any of this, ostensibly a family matter?" she asked.

"Bismarck insisted that the English must not catch wind of it before Prince Leopold made up his mind."

"The English?"

Fritz looked at her resignedly.

"Oh, I see," she said. "Bismarck thought if you knew, you would tell me, and I would tell Mama, and it would reach the prime minister. And Mr. Gladstone and the Foreign Office in London would be against it."

Fritz nodded.

"I just don't know what to think," she said, sighing. Perhaps her mind would be sharper if she hadn't so recently given birth. As it was, she felt muddled and anxious. How hateful that Fritz was always kept out of things because of the minister's distrust of her. More than that, she sensed Bismarck was playing some frightening new game, which she didn't understand.

ANXIOUS DAYS OF rumor, fear, and contradicting newspaper reports followed. She tried to shut out most of it—newborn Sophie deserved her full attention, and the other children as well. The bits of news they did hear alarmed them. "The French army might march on us? They will come to Potsdam? And shoot people?" asked Henry.

"Not to worry, darling, Papa and the other generals have things well in hand."

Willy was listening, and he shook his head. "I think it will be a very difficult fight."

The French ambassador in Berlin, Count Benedetti, went to the Wilhelmstrasse to see the king and demanded the monarch compel his cousin to withdraw his acceptance of the Spanish throne.

"My father refused," Fritz reported. "But he sent Roon to talk with the Hohenzollerns at Sigmaringen to discover if they really mean to continue."

"I hope they regret the decision. Look at all the trouble it's caused," said Vicky.

The French next called upon the British government to demand that this action be blocked and a Hohenzollern never assume the throne of Spain. There were long reports in the Berlin papers of how the French were conniving to get the queen's government to side with them.

"Why should Britain be dragged into an affair of the Spanish nation?" she wrote to Mama. But before she had a reply, Fritz reported that the new British foreign minister, Lord Granville, had written directly to the Prussian king to say that, given the violent reaction of the French, Prince Leopold must withdraw.

And in the end, on July 11, he did.

"Although I was against the idea from the start," Fritz said to her that evening, "I am not pleased that a German, a Hohenzollern, has been forced to bow to French demands."

"The French have been even more belligerent than I thought they'd be," Vicky agreed.

"You see? They still consider themselves preeminent in Europe, able to dictate to us, treat us as vassals, as they did in the first Napoléon's time! This is what will bring on war eventually," Fritz said vehemently.

She hated to hear this. "But the crisis has passed?" she asked.

"*Ja*, it has."

The next day Vicky spent in the nursery, feeding the baby every few hours. She also had the nursemaids take out of the cupboards all the children's summer clothes, so she could decide what pieces needed altering for the younger ones, which items should be given away or torn up for rags, and how many new garments needed to be ordered. Nothing like an organizational project to calm the mind. She told Mrs. Hobbs to have sailor suits made for Moretta and Waldy—they'd need them if they were going to Osborne in August. And that reminded Vicky of something—she needed Fritz to write to his father and ask permission for the trip. The king had already departed Berlin to take the summer cure at Bad Ems.

33

Potsdam, July 1870

At first, Vicky failed to recognize Bismarck's masterstroke.

She only knew what Fritz told her. On July 13 the French ambassador approached the king at Bad Ems when he was walking in the public garden. Count Benedetti asked that the king guarantee "for all time" that no member of his family would ever be a candidate for the Spanish throne. The king refused this presumptuous demand—"Which he was quite correct to do," said Fritz. And then he dismissed the ambassador—"There was no reason for further discussion," Fritz explained. When a report of this encounter, written by the king's secretary and sent by telegram to the Wilhelmstrasse, was leaked to the newspapers, everyone in France—from the poorest laborers to the parliamentarians to the emperor himself—was enraged by the Prussian king's arrogant rejection of the French ambassador's request. War now seemed certain.

"They lash out at us in anger, but what they truly seek is to smash us, and to stop Germany from being a nation equal to France," Fritz said to her in their room that night as she wept. Maybe that was right, but it broke her heart—all the killing beginning again. Would Fritz really survive a third war? Against the indomitable French army?

France mobilized. Prussia mobilized. France declared war. The king returned from Bad Ems and was greeted at every station along the way by huge, cheering crowds. Fritz came back from a meeting of the Crown Council to say that General von Moltke's most recent report reassured him. Prussian troop call-ups were under way, excellent transport and supply plans had been finalized, and the new Krupp guns had been tested and were operational. When the king addressed the North German Reichstag the next day, he recalled how Germans had been forced to endure incursions on their soil and their honor for many centuries, but those days were past. "We must unite in this struggle for our freedom and our rights against the brutality of foreign conquerors," he declared.

The leaders of Bavaria, Württemberg, Hesse-Darmstadt, and Baden—all the South German states—pledged themselves unreservedly to the cause.

FRITZ AND VICKY decided to hold Sophie's christening a week later, on July 25. In tribute to the alliance now sealed in the face of implacable French enmity, at the king's suggestion they asked the kings of Bavaria and Württemberg to stand as godfathers.

His father's departure fast approaching, Willy became apprehensive, very unlike his usual blustery, boasting self.

"Mama, do you remember those soldiers at the garrison at Cannes?"

"Yes, certainly, they looked very smart. I admired the drawings you did of them."

"Imagine thousands of these men marching across the Rhine. How will Papa and General von Moltke hold them back?" Willy asked her, his eyes large and alarmed.

"Darling, please don't worry. Papa says the German armies are well prepared for battle."

Vicky did not add that Fritz predicted the war would be long and bloody—nothing like the short campaigns against the Danes and the Austrians. It might take months to expel the French from Germany.

She pleaded with Alice to leave Darmstadt, so far in the west, and bring her children to join them in the relative safety of Potsdam. "My place is here," wrote Alice. "We have already begun preparations. Our castle will become one of three field hospitals and we have moved the children to the summer house at Kranichstein. There, I pray, they will be away from the fighting."

Adding to Vicky's strain were the constant denouncements, in the Berlin papers, of England, for standing aloof from the quarrel, and in that way condoning French conduct. Robert Morier traveled to Potsdam to confer with her in person on July 22.

"Bismarck must have known how distasteful Prince Leopold's candidacy would be, and yet he promoted it," Morier said.

"The minister has been ill and living in Varzin for most of the past few months, so I'm not sure how much influence he had. Yes, he urged the Spanish to keep asking. But in the end, it was the Hohenzollerns' choice, and they eventually refused."

"I find it hard to believe that events escalated in this unfortunate manner of their own accord," Morier said. "My mole at the Wilhelmstrasse says Bismarck edited the text of the telegram from Ems. He must have changed it to be more provocative to the French."

"I suppose that's possible—but why would he deliberately bring on the war?"

Morier shook his head. "I don't understand it either, and meanwhile he points his finger elsewhere. He summoned Lord Loftus to his office yesterday evening and lectured him that Great Britain should have forbidden France to declare war. She was in a position to do so, Bismarck says, and all Europe expected it."

"Goodness! So, it's England he blames?"

"And the foreign secretary specifically. He charges Lord Granville with dereliction of his duties."

Vicky covered her eyes with her hands—even worse than she had imagined.

"Perhaps, Princess, you should bring this up with the chancellor directly. If you could persuade him to show less antagonism toward London, everyone else in Berlin will follow suit, including the newspapers."

IT WAS PROBABLY a mistake to confront Bismarck on the day of Sophie's christening. She felt exhausted and miserable, the consequence of caring for an infant, and soothing five nervous older children, while anticipating Fritz's imminent departure for a war more sizable than any they had previously known. She wished to wait and be steadier. But Bismarck, along with Fritz and the king, and nearly every other gentleman in attendance, planned to leave for the front soon after the ceremony. She must take her only chance.

Fritz's father and mother hosted, as was their right, but unlike at baptisms past, the king did not hold his new grandchild at the font. He felt too nervous and shaky for the task, he said, and passed the baby to the queen. Fritz's father looked drained and fearful—maybe his bold words in the Reichstag had been all for show.

Bismarck, wearing his uniform as a major in the dragoons, appeared calm and cheerful. When, afterward, she asked him to step into an adjoining parlor for a private conversation, he smiled knowingly, as if he'd expected her invitation.

"Congratulations, Your Highness, on the birth of your daughter," he said, and bowed.

"Thank you, Count," she answered. "But you no doubt appreciate how the first weeks of my daughter's life have been completely overshadowed by my terror of the coming war and my horror at all the suffering it will bring."

He nodded but said nothing—waiting, watching. She felt suddenly as if he were a circling bird of prey, a hawk or an eagle, and she a little gray field mouse below.

"The brutality of the French soldiers should they invade Germany is certainly my greatest concern," she continued, determined not to betray the nervousness she felt inside.

"Natürlich."

"But I've been in despair about how my own country—"

Bismarck raised an eyebrow.

"I mean how Great Britain, and her foreign minister, Lord Granville, have been besmirched in irresponsible German newspapers and everywhere in Berlin, including at your own ministry. It's as if British neutrality is a crime equal to French aggression."

"Lord Granville is a friend of yours, Princess?"

"He was a close associate of the Prince Consort's. He served on the exhibition committee, and they worked together on the proposed sequel. My father thought very highly of him."

"Ah, the endorsement of the sainted Prince Consort. How impossible for you to ever dare question that."

"A comment beneath you, sir," she said sharply.

But he merely smiled and replied evenly: "The bonds of past friendship can distort one's views, I find. And in this case your favorable disposition toward Granville is blinding you."

"I don't think so."

Bismarck shrugged. "Perhaps you don't want to believe it, or maybe you don't care, but your friend Lord Granville is no friend of Prussia's."

"What evidence do you have of that?"

"His own actions prove it," said the chancellor. "He did not block the declaration of war."

"He does not rule in France," she countered.

"A firm reprimand from him—or threat of action—may well have stopped them."

"You cannot be certain."

"The French would not fight against us if they had no access to England's continued supply of horses, coal, and cartridges."

"How do you mean?"

"As long as Granville does not forbid English merchants to trade with France, he enables our enemies."

"But English trade will not be decisive," she said.

Bismarck looked at her with surprise, feigned, she sensed. "I thought even you would condemn this, Princess."

"I'm just not sure it matters."

"Of course it matters. How else could France contemplate this campaign? Every loyal Prussian recognizes this."

"I am as committed as anyone here," she said frostily. "My own sacrifices and those of my husband demonstrate just how much."

"But you can't help defending an old friend of your father's."

"No, but he is not the issue."

"I fear you are like so many in your homeland, Your Highness, people who never believed that sandy, shabby Prussia, that backward nation of farmers and soldiers, would ever amount to anything, and certainly did not believe it could ever rival Britain."

"I think no such thing."

"And now, as we stand on the threshold of a great struggle, you doubt us. Have you infected the Crown Prince with your defeatist attitudes?"

"My husband, a true patriot, is steeled for the ordeal ahead."

"But will he return—if he returns—to a wife who will celebrate the accomplishments of Prussia? Or one who pines away, wishing for a nation made along Prince Albert's pious liberal lines?"

Vicky, shaking with rage, sensed the hawk Bismarck swooping down, beak open, about to devour her. No! He would not finish her off so easily. She looked down for a moment to collect herself and then with a surge of resolution, she turned her eyes up to look directly into the face of the king's first minister and admonish him.

There she saw—with a start of recognition—amused contentedness. Bismarck wasn't like a hawk but a monstrous, sated grizzly bear, licking his chops and enjoying her distress. He welcomed this war. He had brought it into being somehow, lying and scheming, twiddling telegrams, inciting all the players. Now he was tipping them all—thousands upon thousands of men and women in Germany and in France—into a boiling cauldron of violence and hate. And it pleased him.

"I support the Crown Prince wholeheartedly," she said slowly, jarred by the arrogance and depravity she was witnessing. "His courage and determination, along with that of his comrades, will keep Prussia free, I fervently hope and pray."

Bismarck smiled a nasty, carnivorous smile, showing his teeth. Horrible. How had she ever believed he was sane? Or could be reasoned with? Just then the door opened and Henry poked his head in. "Mama, Papa is searching for you."

Bismarck bowed. "We Prussians gratefully accept the hopes and prayers you deign to bestow upon us, Your Highness."

He walked over to the door, opened it fully, and bowed again as she walked through, still trembling.

SHE COULD NOT bear to burden preoccupied Fritz with her distress over this encounter, and it was difficult to put into words how much she loathed the man and the dreadful fate that he had brought down upon them. Two days later, at five thirty in the morning, while she slept, Fritz slipped out of their bed and departed the Neues Palais, bound for the Rhineland. He left a note. "I chose to spare us both the pain of parting once again, my love. When I close my eyes all I see before me is you and our children. No man has been a happier husband than I."

34

Bad Homburg, August–November 1870

$\mathcal{T}$he French never made it across the Rhine. The German armies—disciplined, tactical, and well equipped—prevailed from the war's first skirmishes, and France enjoyed not a single victory. At the border town of Weissenburg on August 4, Fritz quickly outmaneuvered opposing troops with a bold double-pronged attack coordinating Bavarian and Prussian soldiers. A mere two days later, deep into French territory, his cobbled-together army engaged the enemy again at Wörth and emerged victorious after a fierce fight that left twenty thousand men dead. He might have marched directly on to Paris then, but instead he headed north to reinforce troops commanded by the Crown Prince of Saxony. On September 1, at the small garrison town of Sedan on the river Meuse, German forces surrounded and defeated a French army of one hundred twenty thousand men. Fritz watched hordes of gaudily dressed French soldiers running away as soon as the shooting began. In the captured fortress, hung with white flags, Fritz's men discovered the mortified Napoléon III, who had a final request—to hand over his sword personally to the king of Prussia. Two days later, revolutionaries in Paris toppled the government; declared an end to the venal Second Empire, with its frivolous and extravagant court; and established a republic. Empress Eugénie narrowly escaped arrest, fleeing to England and finding refuge there. Bismarck called it proof of British bias, but Vicky commended Mama for her support of their old friend.

Vicky herself had gone from paralyzing terror to grateful relief to sheer astonishment. If only Papa were alive to see this victory, an endorsement of the German character—the stern discipline and sober commitment Fritz embodied. Vicky thought of Paris three years ago, of how Bertie, and Affie too, had teased them about dull and provincial Berlin, which contrasted so poorly with the sophisticated French capital. Now the truth was revealed. She hoped all of Europe recognized how rotten the fearful extravagance and luxury in France had been, and understood that the German nation, more principled and more efficient, was truly the land of the future.

LIEUTENANT O'DANNE HAD, like most of the other men, gone off to war with Fritz. Potsdam now resembled a large convent of anxious, excitable women. Dr. Hinzpeter, in sole charge of Willy and Henry, struggled to keep their minds on their studies. Willy followed the miraculous course of events in France with exceptional zeal—each morning changing the position of colored pins representing various German armies and the shrinking presence of the French. His grasp of this complex, shifting situation was impressive, but Vicky hated how he prattled on in a grating, grandiose way about the humiliation of France, the total number of prisoners captured, and the various feats of Prussia's generals. When she chided him that it was nonsense to think of the king sitting on the throne of France, or Fritz marching all the way to the Atlantic, Willy looked at her, indignant, and said: "You know nothing about this. You are not at headquarters." He scoffed when she told him to emulate Fritz's modesty, tempering his legitimate pride with prayers for all the victims of this terrible war.

These exchanges troubled Vicky enough for her to bring them up with Dr. Hinzpeter.

"It's true, Princess, while the prince's outward behavior improves, the development of his mind and heart lags," he said. "And the wild excitement here is not helping, although he's hardly alone in his violent Prussian patriotism."

Vicky sighed and shook her head. "I wish more people saw this for what it is—a true German achievement."

In the wake of the stunning victories, the king was giving out medals and promotions pell-mell. Fritz had been made a field marshal; Fritz Karl, too. But most every award went to a Prussian. Her husband told her he had to beg for proper recognition of Bavarian officers, and those from Hesse-Darmstadt, Saxony, Baden. The project of pan-German fellow feeling had a long way to go.

THE QUEEN NOW oversaw a daily assembly at the Berlin city hall, where women met to cut and roll bandages for field hospitals and pack other supplies to ship west. Vicky asked everyone she could think of to join in, including all the soldiers' wives she had met as honorary commander of the Second Regiment of Hussars. She was pleased when two dozen of these wives turned up. But Countess Bismarck, the minister's wife, refused to mix with such lowly ladies, and she had a particular request when it came to the bandages she produced.

"Nothing for the French from me, Princess," she called out one afternoon as Vicky passed the table where the minister's wife sat in exclusively noble company. Cold eyes, tight sneering face, snippy voice—Vicky deeply disliked the countess. And to think she was known for her religious piety!

"Can't we agree that a wounded man is not an enemy, only a suffering child of God?" Vicky asked pointedly.

"I would be happy to see all the French shot and stabbed, down to the little babies," the countess said.

The queen shook her head when Vicky repeated this exchange. "Let's resolve we will both avoid that dreadful woman in future."

VICKY DECIDED TO leave Berlin. The children would fare better away from the feverish capital, and she wished to be nearer Alice, who struggled in Darmstadt, which had been inundated with wounded men. More hospitals were desperately needed in that area and Vicky resolved to set up her own at the *Schloss* at Bad Homburg, twenty miles from Darmstadt. It was a drafty old wreck of a place, but a Prussian possession since the last war, and on the grounds sat two empty barracks buildings that could be put to use. Fritz persuaded the king to allow her to move there, and she telegraphed to Miss Nightingale in London to send out a senior nurse get the hospital started.

As she waited for Florence Lees, Miss Nightingale's colleague, to arrive, she made a quick inspection tour of nearby hospitals, taking along only a nursemaid and baby Sophie, whom she was still feeding. Most of the facilities she visited were truly pitiful. In fetid, overflowing wards, too few doctors ministered to the wounded, many lying on the floor with no blankets to cover them, still wearing the uniforms they had been shot in. Numerous of these men ended up dying of infections, gangrene, or dysentery. The pathetic sights and hideous smell of rotting flesh appalled her, and she appealed to the queen in Berlin to send more nurses from her corps, but all the trained women had already been assigned elsewhere.

On the third evening of her tour, as she hurried back to the hotel at Mainz, where the nursemaid and Sophie waited, her breasts full and aching because she'd gone too many hours between feedings, a heavy rain began to fall. Heaven was crying. Germany might have been winning the war, but her wounded sons died in droves, in squalor.

HOW SATISFYING TO immediately step in and show everyone how to do things better. She paid a team of workmen to convert the empty barracks at Bad Homburg into two wards of thirty-six beds each, complete with sizable storerooms and a pantry attached. Miss Lees preached the importance of good ventilation, and large doors were installed on both sides of the structures and kept open in fine weather, allowing the air to flow through from end to end. Vicky had the walls painted bright yellow, and she found evergreen shrubs to place in the corners. All this— plus white crockery, new wool blankets, and regularly scrubbed floors—made the wards cheerful and bright. Two military doctors came from France with a train full of wounded men as soon as the hospital was ready on September 15.

The injured continued to arrive for weeks afterward. Despite the early, decisive victories, the French republicans didn't sue for peace. Instead, deputies in Paris formed the Government of National Defense and announced they would fight until every single German soldier had been driven off French land. In response, the German armies surrounded Paris and dug in, intending to starve the capital into submission. But they had to contend with the *francs-tireurs*, bands of irregular French soldiers who blew up bridges and trains and launched guerrilla attacks on German patrols.

Journalists came to visit her hospital and interview her and Miss Lees. Vicky typically avoided press attention and never spoke to journalists, but she hoped that by advertising how at Bad Homburg the death rates were half of what they were in Mainz, Frankfurt, and Koblenz, wealthy Germans would be inspired to donate monies to improve wards elsewhere.

Fritz cheered the stories that were written about her and said men teased him at headquarters about his famous wife—she was the true royal star now. "I tell them I prefer it this way, *mein Schatz*."

AT THE START of November Vicky received a castigating letter from the king: she and the children had been too long away from home and needed to return to Berlin to resume proper family life. She telegraphed Fritz to ask what on earth had prompted this order— everything was going so well. He telegraphed back cryptically: "Q *Nase* jnt."

Fritz's English was not fluent, but he'd picked up nursery sayings she used with the children. She understood immediately: Fritz's mother had her nose out of joint because of the attention Vicky was receiving.

She appealed to the king with a lengthy letter, arguing that the children were happy and healthy in Homburg, and worked harder at their studies away from the distractions of the capital. And while she was occupied all day, caring for the nation's soldiers, she spent time with her children in the early evening. By return post, he simply restated his command that she go back.

She walked the floors of her bedroom in the *Schloss* that evening, fuming and weeping. Why did the king waste time with these domestic rivalries? Fritz reported that at the Versailles headquarters—where the king lived alongside his son, the other top generals, and Bismarck—no one could agree on how to cope with the French. Besieged Paris refused to surrender, and Bismarck pressed the military men to fire on the city to force a capitulation. The rules of military engagement outlawed sustained attacks on civilian centers, but the minister didn't care. Fritz was relieved that General von Moltke and General von Blumenthal argued they hadn't enough guns and ammunition to guarantee immediate success—and a premature and ill-prepared bombardment would increase German losses once they tried to take the city. This convinced the king, who, for the moment, rebuffed the increasingly frantic Bismarck.

Still, the atmosphere was volatile—both at Versailles and in England, where, Mama reported, the people, having started out being "very German" and deploring French aggression, were now dismayed by the speed of the German victories and the lengthy siege. "I sent a telegram to the king," Mama wrote. "I implored him to conclude peace swiftly and with generosity."

Vicky began to think that the longer the war went on, the better it was for the French. The Germans looked like arrogant conquerors now, willing to rain down ruin and sow resentment. If a united Germany were coming into being finally, thanks to recent victories, the new nation would not be loved or respected by its neighbors—Bismarck had made Germany powerful, but also hated and feared.

35

*V*icky dawdled for a week and then finally returned to Berlin on November 20, the day before her thirtieth birthday, after the king declared it her duty to receive at home those who wanted to congratulate her. In the end, no one but the queen visited her that day. Fritz was furious. Yet once settled back at the Kronprinzenpalais, Vicky found a satisfying routine of working at the Charité hospital in the morning and devoting the afternoons to the children. She'd dine with the three eldest at night to improve their English conversation and monitor their table manners. War talk was banned—books, art, and music were the only permitted topics.

THE VICTORIES OF the German armies under Prussian command had ignited a feverish enthusiasm in those independent states to join an imperial Germany, with the Prussian king as emperor, or kaiser, the German title from the days of the Holy Roman Empire. Bismarck supported this too, but Fritz's father—who preferred his Prussian title to any other—resisted several such appeals during the Christmas season, shouting that he wouldn't supplant his birthright as King of Prussia and head of the house

of Hohenzollern to become something like a common, everyday
"president." He accused Fritz of backing the change because he
liked the fancy sound of "kaiser" and had romantic notions of
ruling over a second *Reich*. As for Bismarck, the king suspected
the wily Junker of some perfidious power grab he didn't fully
comprehend.

Fritz's father rarely bucked his minister's directives, but in this
case, for many weeks, he did. Only a long letter from King Lud-
wig of Bavaria (actually penned by Bismarck), requesting that
the king reestablish German imperial dignity, finally convinced
Fritz's father to comply, as he was unwilling to refuse a passionate request from the second-most powerful monarch in Germany.

The proclamation ceremony took place on January 18 in La
Galerie des Glaces at Versailles, where Vicky had, so long ago,
danced with Napoléon and first met Bismarck. Fritz planned it as
a glorious pageant, with the new German emperor to sit proudly
on the dais with the flag of Prussia and the flags of all the princes
arrayed behind him. But when his father stalked into the hall
with Bismarck trailing behind, he saw the flags and demanded
that they all be removed. He muttered to Fritz that he regretted
already bidding goodbye forever to old Prussia. Bismarck, also
in a foul temper, read out the proclamation in a gloomy voice,
and the disgruntled new kaiser marched out afterward without
acknowledging any congratulations. He did not embrace the new
nation's destiny, but his son and heir did. And in future it would
be Fritz's to direct.

GERMAN SOLDIERS LIVED outdoors in the wet and icy fields around
Paris, and tuberculosis and other diseases ran rampant among
them. Hundreds lost fingers, toes, or whole feet to frostbite. The
supply lines reaching back into Germany strained under the constant demand for winter uniforms, better boots, proper tents,
and warmer blankets, along with food for the massive army. Fritz
fought with bureaucrats to better equip the troops. But, to Bismarck's mind, the real villains were the intransigent republican

leaders of France, who, holed up in government buildings in the city center, eating their pets and slaughtered animals from the Paris zoo, refused to surrender. In the first week of January the king allowed shelling of the city every night, and four hundred people were killed. When the French still refused to give up, the new kaiser bowed to Bismarck's demands, and the large-caliber Krupp siege guns began bombarding around the clock. The city surrendered three days later.

Vicky heard the news at Charité hospital. As she hurried into the front courtyard looking for her carriage, intending to return home immediately, the bells of the chapel were pealing exuberantly, loud and insistent in her ears. As she crossed the city, the sound of one set of bells died away only to be replaced by that of another. Berlin vibrated with ringing, noisy celebration, the clangor drowning out her thoughts, leaving her discombobulated but also light-headed with relief. Now that the French were beaten, Fritz would come home. She hadn't realized how much she'd feared he would never return alive, until this moment when their long separation was nearing an end.

She discovered the Kronprinzenpalais in an uproar. Someone had draped Prussian flags out of the second-floor windows, singing came from the kitchens, the maids were weeping and hugging each other in the passageways, and on her way to the schoolroom she encountered the *Hofmarschall,* a man named Bauer, who bowed deeply and said, "The royal princes have inspired everyone with their glorious, spontaneous display." She looked at him uncomprehendingly until he described how Willy and Henry had unearthed a French tricolor flag and had taken it outside to the small garden. Summoning all the servants to watch, they had spit on the flag, stomped on it, and finally burned it.

"I could not stop them, Princess," said Dr. Hinzpeter when she found him sitting alone in the empty schoolroom. "As soon as the *Hofmarschall* came in to announce the surrender, they were out the door, screaming and shouting, joining in the general hysteria."

"And where are they now?" she asked.

He shrugged and gave her a sour look, blaming her, clearly, for spawning such uncontrollable creatures.

It took a quarter of an hour to discover the boys—and Charlotte—in the stables. Willy was flailing his right arm in the air, talking with wild excitement about the stupendous victory, and nearly a dozen coachmen and grooms had gathered around him listening, rapt. His sister and brother perched on some hay bales nearby.

All the stablemen bowed low as she entered. "*Unser* Fritz never fails his men," said one groom, holding his brown wool cap over his heart. "I was with him at Königgrätz, Your Highness, and I worship him, and his father, our new kaiser, too. God bless you, Princess." Then he got down on his knees. The other men knelt down also. She had to wipe away a tear at the sight. She musn't doubt it: the course of history had brought them all to a most affecting and uplifting moment, unlike any before in Germany.

"Thank you all. I am going to take the children inside now, but I will be sending out hot ale for every man," she said. "We must toast this triumph, and thank God that soon our soldiers will return home."

She reached out for Henry's hand, Charlotte and Willy following. The children were silent, expecting her to scold them for abandoning their lessons and burning the flag. She searched for the correct thing to say amid all her own contradictory emotions. Finally, on the upstairs landing she stopped, turned, and addressed them, particularly Willy. "This is a wonderful day, and I don't think any of us will ever forget it. But Papa and all the other generals regret that it took this long, and so much suffering, and so many dead and wounded, for the war to end. And I think we should feel sorry for all the hungry people in Paris."

Henry nodded solemnly. Charlotte appeared skeptical. Willy smiled. "*Ja*, Mama, I am sorry for them. But very, very happy for us!"

And all three children began laughing uproariously and jumping up and down. Dr. Hinzpeter stood in the doorway of the schoolroom staring out, a disgusted look on his face.

BISMARCK, CONDUCTING THE peace negotiations, was not in a forgiving mood. He demanded that the French Republic give up all of Alsace and most of Lorraine, the two provinces of France bordering Germany, where many people spoke German dialects. All over the new *Reich* there was a tremendous enthusiasm for absorbing this territory. Vicky worried that the loss of such rich lands would be forever resented by the French. Fritz agreed the decision was provocative, but he was pleased that the large military fortresses at Strasbourg in Alsace and Metz in Lorraine would now be within the borders of Germany.

On top of this Bismarck imposed a five-million-franc indemnity on France and declared that a German army of occupation would remain in France until the debt was paid.

Fritz wrote to confess he was appalled—and across Europe the peace terms were condemned.

"The feeling here toward Prussia is as bitter as bitter can be," wrote Mama. "And to see the enmity growing up between our two nations, which I am bound to say began first in Prussia, and was fomented and encouraged by Bismarck, is a great sorrow and anxiety to me."

Vicky begged Fritz to appeal to his father—the kaiser could order Bismarck, now made a prince and appointed chancellor of the *Reich,* to soften his stance. But Fritz reported it was no use: the kaiser agreed that these spoils belonged to Germany. "I will no longer be able to show my face in England now that we Germans are so despised," Fritz wrote.

36

Berlin and Potsdam, Spring 1871

When her husband returned from France on March 17, Vicky despaired at his ashen, drawn face and his low spirits. In front of the children, Fritz told amusing stories about his months in France, but he confessed to her privately that since the siege began he'd felt very downhearted. Prince Bismarck, happy to forget Fritz's support for the founding of the empire, had threatened him that if he didn't distance himself from his English family and also the liberal Reichstag deputies who regarded the Crown Prince as their champion, he'd be thrown off the Crown Council. Only at Bingen, crossing the Rhine, had his mood lightened briefly. From the train window, looking down at the stately flow of the water, he remembered how worried he'd been last year that the river would fall into French hands. Now both the Rhine and Germany were secure—safe from incursion and invasion forever.

Baby Sophie didn't know him—and wailed when he picked her up. But the other children hardly left his side. They followed him from room to room all day long, and Vicky had him to herself only at night. Yet, that made everything easier. She sailed out every day into the choppy waters of living sure of a safe harbor to which to return, and his physical presence—the smell, the bulk, the musculature of him—was both revelatory and achingly familiar, a touchstone, a comfort, her enduring pleasure.

A new equestrian statue of Friedrich Wilhelm III, Fritz's grandfather, was due to be unveiled in the Lustgarten, on Spree Island, opposite the Berliner Schloss. When Bismarck proposed combining that ceremony with a grand, triumphant return of the army to the capital, Fritz spoke out against. Perhaps they should forgo the traditional victory parade this time, given the outrage over the punitive peace terms abroad, he argued.

"Bismarck told me I fail to understand things," a gloomy Fritz recounted. "This is our way of announcing to the world that we have become a great European power and can no longer be ignored or belittled."

"Which is such nonsense! Everyone knows what has happened," said Vicky.

She read in *The Times* how, on April 10, Benjamin Disraeli got up in the Commons and declared the establishment of the German Empire the most significant political event of modern time, outstripping even the French Revolution. Europe would never be the same, Disraeli predicted.

Vicky struggled to make sense of it all. Like Fritz, she had longed for Germany to be united and victorious, and the German virtues brought to the fore. Now their success—so great and so fast—was tainted by an unstinting admiration for power and those who exercised it. How long would it take for a nation birthed at a moment of chauvinistic fervor to shake off that character? Prince Bismarck would not be eternal, and the king, now kaiser, would die, and then it would be up to Fritz, with her help, to pick new leaders for Germany. But what would be lost in the meantime?

IN THE FIRST week of May Dr. Hinzpeter declared that he must speak to the Crown Prince and Crown Princess most urgently. Vicky had noticed that the tutor's thunderous looks were more frequent these days and he seemed constantly out of sorts.

They sat down together in Fritz's study in the Neues Palais at the end of a beautiful sunny, cloudless day. Working in the gardens that afternoon, Vicky had begun to wonder if the tutor planned to resign, and she fervently prayed this was not the case. For all his crankiness and ill humor, Hinzpeter was essential to molding Willy into a strong, sensible, and independent young man.

Once they were settled—Fritz and Vicky sitting beside each other on a sofa facing the doctor—he began: "As we discussed at the end of last year, Princess, now that the prince is twelve, I revised the curriculum, making it more advanced, with many more hours each week dedicated to history, philosophy, advanced mathematics, along with Latin and Greek."

Vicky said to Fritz, "Do you remember, I wrote to you about this?"

Her husband nodded.

The doctor drew in a long breath and then let it out again slowly before continuing: "I've followed this program for two months and I conclude that I—that we, may be demanding too much of the prince."

Vicky felt immediately irked. "How can you say so after such a short time?"

"It's an enormous effort to keep the prince's attention on his books," said the tutor.

"I will speak sternly to him," said Fritz.

"The prince has badly missed his father's presence in the last year and has become very cocky and offhand about schoolwork; I notice that too," Vicky said.

Hinzpeter frowned. "While he does often expend less effort than what he is capable of, Princess, this is not the real problem."

"What do you mean?"

"As we all witnessed during the war, when current events capture his interest the prince can ably follow and expound on them. Perhaps even too enthusiastically."

Vicky sighed. The inexhaustible torrent of words that came out of Willy's mouth always annoyed her.

"But when he must study more abstract topics or learn the classic languages, which require careful, cumulative effort, he flags. I've come to believe that by constantly placing such high demands on the prince, we may be doing him harm," the doctor continued.

"But you recommended this plan!" exclaimed Vicky.

"I did, and it is in itself a fine plan, and were the prince's abilities adequate to meet it, we could go forward."

"Doctor, I fear that my son may be something like I was as a boy. I had no interest in lessons, I was remarkably lazy," said Fritz.

Hinzpeter gave a brief bow of his head. "I imagine Your Highness is overstating this. But, in any case, you were not being educated in quite the same way as Prince Wilhelm."

"I spent more time than Prince Wilhelm does on military training," Fritz admitted. "But what classical studies I did undertake I did not excel at."

Vicky shook her head. "My husband's experience is not relevant. Prince William may not be a superior scholar but he is alert and animated. He has a vivid imagination. I overheard him the other day speaking with Poe Bigelow about building the mast of a frigate with some wood they found in the park. Poe is being prepared to attend a top university in America and the prince keeps up with him!"

Hinzpeter nodded. "The prince enjoys young Bigelow because, I believe, the boy being a bit older and athletic, the prince admires him."

"That's fine. Poe is a nice lad. But I still don't understand why you want to curtail our son's education and let him escape the rigorous training that you promised to provide."

She felt Fritz put his hand down on top of hers. Perhaps she was being too vehement

"Tell us, doctor, if you continue with the curriculum you devised, how can that harm him?" Fritz asked.

"If the goal is for the prince to be a happy and useful man, perhaps he should not be constantly reminded of his limitations."

Now Vicky laughed. "But we all agree his self-regard is too high."

The doctor looked pained. Then he said quietly, "Do you never imagine that the prince's outward expression of pride, his boastfulness, disguises an inner fear?"

"Never. My boy is not fearful," Fritz said immediately. "I often must caution him to be less daring when we are swimming or climbing down near the river."

Vicky felt impatient with the tutor's speculations. "Doctor, you have often complained that the prince can be hard to manage and indeed frustrating to supervise. I experience that myself. But we require him to have an excellent education and be fully prepared for his duties in the years ahead. Now that my husband has returned he can demand William work hard and be obedient."

Fritz nodded. "I plan to spend much time with the boy in the next few months."

"We as his father and mother are the ones who bear the responsibility for the future, for ensuring the prince becomes an upright and wise man, dedicated to his country's welfare. You joined us wholeheartedly in that effort four years ago, and to give up on it now would be a dereliction of your duty," she said.

Dr. Hinzpeter regarded her in silence, an odd, unreadable expression on his face.

Perhaps she'd gone too far. She added, in a more mollifying tone: "Won't you endeavor to continue on the present course? It's only been a few months."

The tutor shot a glance at Fritz, who nodded and said, "I agree. Let's give Prince Wilhelm a chance to achieve the standard you expect, doctor."

Now the tutor got to his feet. He still looked rather cryptic. Was there something he wasn't saying? "If this is your wish, Highnesses, I will go on." He bowed to them both, and left the room.

"That man can be so irritating," she told Fritz once they were alone. "Quite superior in his attitude toward me, and like most German men not truly comfortable with direction from a woman.

If I didn't think him such a skilled tutor I'd be content to see the back of him."

"Not the easiest of characters, and his remarks about Willy's cowardice absurd. But he is conscientious," Fritz said.

"Yes, and in that way a good model for both Willy and Henry," Vicky replied.

Still, the look on Dr. Hinzpeter's face when he was leaving troubled Vicky. Was it contemptuousness she saw there? It looked more like regret. Did he feel sorry he had taken the job? He had no right to self-pity. They'd granted him an important position and a generous salary. He should just get on with it, she thought impatiently.

IN THE WEEKS after this encounter, Vicky began to wonder if, instead of working alone with the doctor at home, William and Henry should go to a proper German gymnasium when they got older. Willy was a social boy who would enjoy the companionship of others, and he was competitive, so the prowess of his peers in the schoolroom would spur him on to do better. Yes, this was a fine idea. Would Fritz help her persuade the kaiser to allow it? Perhaps the best choice would be a school out of Berlin, out of Prussia, elsewhere in Germany, where William could study alongside his future subjects in a more relaxed atmosphere. Dr. Hinzpeter could be retained as an extra support and live with the boys during the term.

She didn't dare mention this plan at the moment, with Fritz so tired and distracted, but she saved it up in her mind and loved to ruminate on it in quiet moments when she was falling asleep or deadheading roses in the garden. Sometimes she'd go further: She'd picture William as an Oxford man. Imagine her son strolling those streets of warm yellow stone, wearing a mortar board and academic gown, which would flap out a bit behind him as he chatted and laughed with his many friends. For of course he'd be popular—the gregarious German prince, the queen's grandson, a lover of games, of boats, and of male fellowship. And, even better, beneath those famous dreaming spires, he'd become a proper European, with a foot in both countries, his father's and his mother's, and be forever a champion of the friendship between Britain and Germany. She wanted this so much for him, and for herself, that it almost hurt.

Of course, Fritz's father would hate the very notion, but it was hard to imagine the new kaiser living six or eight more years. Her father-in-law had returned from France looking pale and run-down, his mood fractious. He upbraided the servants for serving food that was too rich and too plentiful. He hated to show himself and smile when crowds assembled outside the *Schloss* to cheer His Imperial Majesty, and he grumbled if he had to change into formal clothes—he liked to stomp around in his favorite old mess jacket, the buttons undone, at all hours.

Vicky sighed to think how this feeble old man could in no way check the all-powerful Bismarck. They lived, for the moment, in a brand-new nation that was dominated by the loathsome, dictatorial chancellor. She and Fritz must endeavor to carve out for their children a sphere apart, where reason and the finer virtues prevailed.

37

Berlin, June 16, 1871

*T*he thunder of cannon fire woke them at six on that famous morning.

"They set up howitzers in the Tiergarten. They are doing forty rounds now, and again at noon, and for the last time at six tonight, as part of the celebration," said Fritz. Weary and pale, he had swung himself up and sat now on the edge of their bed, rubbing his face with his hands. Vicky felt sorry for him. They'd returned home at midnight from a banquet at the Berliner Schloss, and now he faced a long day ahead, most of it to be spent on horseback, under the broiling June sun for hours.

The victorious Prussian army, forty thousand strong, had camped outside the city. The kaiser would ride from the Berliner Schloss to meet them at the Brandenburger Tor and escort them back three miles down Unter den Linden to the Lustgarten for the statue's unveiling. As Crown Prince, Fritz would be directly behind his father, and he'd asked his brother-in-law Fritz, Grand Duke of Baden, to ride alongside him, while Bismarck, Moltke, and Roon followed in the third rank. But when the kaiser heard this plan he said no, it must be young Prince Wilhelm, the other heir, next to his father.

Vicky had immediately objected, and had written to her father-in-law arguing that Willy was too young to take part. She worked constantly to pour cold water on William's feverish excitement over the defeat of the French—if only his grandfather would do likewise. Not only had the kaiser ignored her letter, he had personally searched out a beautiful dappled horse for William to ride, and, presenting the animal to him, told the boy that, his mother's objections notwithstanding, he had every right to play a prominent role in this grand occasion.

FOR DAYS BERLIN had echoed with the banging of hammers as carpenters constructed ascending, tiered, wooden platforms the length of Unter den Linden. Thousands of seats, carefully numbered, were placed on the platforms, and sold by ticket to the hordes who had come from all over Prussia—all over Germany—for the celebration. The streets were festooned with evergreen and the smell of pine filled the air. Many homes were completely covered by fragrant branches, and some householders had added flags, or flowers, or colorful, draped rugs to their festive displays. Scores of enemy artillery guns lined the parade route. On each was painted in white lettering the name of the place where it had been captured—Metz, Sedan, Paris—and every one was wreathed in evergreen. Returning from the Charité hospital the previous afternoon she had spotted from her carriage window a gang of little boys straddling some guns, whooping and hollering, while their fathers stood in a drunken group behind bellowing "The Watch on the Rhine." The mood in the packed city was unsettled, but the precise reason for the prickling apprehensiveness she felt eluded her.

Fritz left now to don his uniform, numerous decorations, sword, and side arms, and Dawes came to help her into a lilac linen gown—with luck it would keep her cool during the three hours she'd sit in the front row of the reviewing stand near the Brandenburger Tor. She tapped her foot impatiently while the dresser braided her hair and began to coil it into an elaborate top knot.

Were the children up? Waldy and baby Sophie would stay home, but Henry, Charlotte, and Moretta would sit in the reviewing stand, too, a few rows behind her.

What a relief to find good Mrs. Hobbs already had the girls and Henry fed and dressed by the time Vicky reached the nursery. Henry had asked to wear a sailor suit with neckerchief and short pants, in which he looked darling. The girls had on matching white dresses and red sashes. When she asked for her eldest, Mrs. Hobbs said Willy was down the hall, where Streicher, Fritz's valet, was helping him get ready in one of the extra bedrooms.

Vicky gasped when she came through the door and saw him there. He stood tall, resplendent in the dark-blue, double-breasted, brass-buttoned uniform coat of the Prussian Royal Guards, complete with blue trousers, white-and-blue brimmed cap, and white gloves, with a silver sword in its scabbard hanging from his waist. Streicher was kneeling beside him giving a last polish to his shoes.

"William, you look wonderful," Vicky exclaimed. She could hardly believe how grown-up he appeared—even the unfortunate spots on his chin and cheeks less noticeable today. He rested his left hand on the hilt of the sword, and in this position his two arms looked no different from each other. His shoulders were square, his back straight, his gaze direct—he was an entirely elegant young man, prepared for duty.

"*Danke, Mama*," he said, his voice a bit tremulous. She thought suddenly he must be nervous, and her heart went out to him. How often had she secretly feared she was not impressive enough, nor attractive enough, to appear beside Fritz. Just last year she'd overheard a bevy of women in the opera house cloakroom comparing Marianne's splendid looks to her own—one exclaiming, "If only Princess Friedrich Karl were Crown Princess, the one we have is very plain"—and she'd felt a piercing stab of shame. And, unlike Willy, Vicky had no lame arm to contend with.

She reached out to embrace her son, to reassure him. He refused, however, to raise his arms to embrace her in return. She sensed he felt so pleased with his martial stance that he desired not to disturb it. When she stepped back, she saw he'd cocked his head, questioningly.

"What is it Willy?"

"Now you think it's fine? That I am riding in the procession? You didn't before."

His tone was so discourteous. She was about to scold him, when she thought this pressured moment demanded calm. So, careful to keep her voice even, she answered: "I did not approve, that's true. But now it is a fait accompli, I pray it will go smoothly. It will be very hot out in the sun. Have you eaten enough breakfast?"

"I had plenty."

"You don't want to faint."

He glowered, unwilling to be challenged by her in any way. She felt again the desire to rebuke him. Resisting that, she said: "I will be watching from the stand, be sure to give me your best salute!" And she left the room, trying to ignore her simmering uneasiness.

Two hours later, sitting at her place in the reviewing stand, Vicky could sense, physically, a restless energy emanating from the crowd. The teeming droves of onlookers appeared to have imbibed an intoxicating potion of patriotism, pride, and truculence. And more disconcerting still were the soldiers. Vicky recalled how gleeful the young Prussian troops had seemed to her when the victory over Austria had been celebrated nearly five years previously. The tone of that day had been lighthearted in comparison with this moment. She studied the men in the front ranks, at attention, waiting for the kaiser, and to her they looked arrogant and ruthless, as if by vanquishing the hated French they had cast themselves high above the normal race of men and deserved to dominate.

She pursed her lips and shook her head slightly. What was happening to her? Was she becoming an eccentric, a shrew, disparaging everyone and everything around her? She didn't want to be like that, and yet she constantly felt an urge to push back against the prevailing atmosphere. At a dinner party they had attended two weeks previously she had posed a question for general debate: Is every war a crime, a failure of leadership by self-serving and brutal men? Not one person around the table would affirm this. Most were quick to take offense at the implied criticism of Prussia and Bismarck. The more reasonable guests tried to parse out the definition of a justified war. Fritz laughed at her on the way home. "I know you like that Riesling wine they served, *mein Schatz*. Does that explain your rash declaration?" She smiled at him forbearingly. It was late in the evening—better to let him think she was tipsy than to remind him that what she had put forward wasn't a question to her mind—it was the truth.

The new kaiserin sat next to her, her large white lace parasol abutting her own lilac one. Vicky guessed her mother-in-law shared her discomfort with the air of hedonic, over-the-top triumphalism, but she made no reference to it. "I am waiting to see the lovely boy," she whispered to Vicky, and just then they could see the kaiser approaching along the wide boulevard, with his kinsmen and ministers about him. Cheers of adulation rose to a deafening volume. The kaiser reached their stand and he halted his horse and gravely bowed his head to them both, in turn. Fritz, coming up behind, wheeled his massive white horse around to directly face Vicky and his mother and he drew his sword and held it high in front of his face in formal salute. But Willy, on the far side, continued to face front, not acknowledging anyone, sitting proudly in his saddle, exuding an air of self-importance. She willed him to look toward her but he did not. He seemed to have fixed his eyes on the top of the Brandenburger Tor, at the Quadriga statue there—the goddess of victory in a chariot driven by four horses. Fritz's mother murmured: "He looks very dignified. So sweet and so serious." The kaiser and his entourage now turned to go back up Unter den Linden, and rank upon rank of blue-uniformed soldiers began to follow, fifty abreast, their marching boots slapping rhythmically on the cobblestones. At the sound of a cannon blast, this mass of men, as one, raised their weapons. The road became a gleaming sea of spiked helmets, bayonets, and upright swords, set off by the rolling white foam of thousands of handkerchiefs waved from balconies and windows. The soldiers formed a huge, inundating tide, human and yet impersonal, relentless and implacable.

AT THE RECEPTION afterward at the Weisser Saal, Vicky stood in a receiving line for more than an hour greeting a "swarm of greats" as she described them later to Mama—princes, potentates, bishops, ambassadors, high officials of state. Her smile soon began to feel tight and strained. Finally, the last dignitaries moved past, and she looked around for the children. She caught a glimpse of Willy, exultant, pink-cheeked, the high braided collar of his uniform coat still tight around his neck. He was chatting and gesticulating to an officer a short distance away.

She whispered to Fritz that she must speak with their son. She weaved around guests to approach William and his companion, a tall, pale young man. "William, come here," she said sharply.

William bounced over to her, words tumbling out of his mouth. "Mama, it was tremendous!"

"You didn't salute!"

He looked puzzled.

"Grandmamma and I were waiting, in the stands, for your salute."

He laughed. "I acknowledged no one. So many people called out to me. One man called out, 'Wilhelmkin, Wilhelmkin, long life to you!' I just laughed to myself—and I rode on."

She stared at it him, skeptical. "What? You didn't nod?"

"No, of course not. Such tributes are my due."

She snorted. "That's ridiculous."

He looked at her, his eyes blazing. "Not at all—the people love me."

"Still, you can't ignore—"

He cut her off. "Just because you don't idolize me, Mama, doesn't mean that others don't. To them I am perfect," he said, glaring. His look shocked her, so reminiscent was it of the icy way Fritz's father too often regarded her. Before she could re-cover, William turned away and darted through the crowd, seek-ing more worshipful attentions than hers.

Amid the chatter and smoke of that crowded room the anxiet-ies of the past hours, the recent days, gathered into an ache of trepidation with one focus—her eldest son. The enmity she had seen in his eyes was really quite dreadful. And her head reeled to think what hopes she, and so many others, had riding on the boy. With his flawed body, his difficult, impressionable nature—how could he ever be equal to what his duty would require?

The young officer who had been speaking with William still hovered nearby. Surfacing out of her preoccupied haze, she looked at him properly and he immediately stepped up and bowed low. "Your Royal Highness, let me lay at your feet my deeply reverent congratulations on the occasion of this day, and for the great honor of serving your entire family."

His words struck her as overly obsequious even by Prussian standards.

"Sir, you are—?"

"Lieutenant Herbert von Bismarck, Your Royal Highness."

Of course, the Chancellor's older son, said to be his close confidant, although aged only twenty-one. He resembled his fa-ther, not just in looks, but in the vaguely taunting, know-it-all manner lurking under his courtesy. She had met the whole Bis-marck family at the April ceremony during which the Chancellor was formally elevated to the status of Prince. Herbert, she re-called, had been using crutches, having sustained a bullet wound in the leg while on army service in France.

"Oh yes, Lieutenant, good afternoon. I am glad to see you walking without crutches. You are acquainted with Prince Wil-helm? I was not aware."

"I had the profound honor of meeting the Prince for the first time just now. I sought him out to commend him for his splendid appearance today. The Fatherland is indeed blessed to have such a handsome, noble, and I discover now, brilliant, heir—a worthy son to his magnificent father."

She felt the barb in the young man's fawning. William, brilliant? Herbert had probably quickly taken the measure of her smug and silly boy. But she felt too tired to appropriately counter this play-acting. She gave a curt nod and said, "I must return to my husband."

"Before you go let me offer a future service," the young Bismarck replied. "Your son tells me he will join us in the First Regiment of Foot Guards in a few years' time. I would be pleased to act as a guide to the young prince in his first months as an officer. Please call upon me."

Vicky laughed. "It will be many years before the prince takes up military duties, Lieutenant. We have other, better plans for him." She summoned up her vision of William at Oxford. "Good afternoon," she said, and turned on her heel. She hoped the young Bismarck would tell everyone what she had said. How satisfying to thrust back at the son a small measure of the contempt she felt for the father.

Her mood lifted further as she spied ahead of her, between clusters of people, Fritz's fine fair head and broad shoulders. He was leaning forward slightly talking to a short woman all in black, maybe the widowed Duchess of Mecklenberg-Strelitz. How he stood out in this company for his authentic graciousness and great integrity! She mustn't be so consumed with anxiety, she thought. Later, they would all look back on today and see it for what it was: an electrifying, intoxicating observance of the nation's birth when the real work of nation-building was still in front of them. Even the Chancellor had said privately there could be no more wars. In the future, it wouldn't be people like Bismarck and his son who represented Germany, but Fritz and her and their like-minded allies. She nodded, reassuring herself. William would come to understand this as he got older. There was so much time. Once he had the model of his own father as kaiser—quite soon, she secretly prayed—he would have decades to grow into his responsibilities, become an exemplary man. Still, she would be unstinting in her efforts to improve him. He'd appreciate that she knew best in the long run.

Fritz looked up and caught sight of her moving toward him. He smiled, his face tired, but his spirit true. They were unbreakable, and even in this noisy room she could feel the silent, steady current that linked him and her. She smiled back, confident and in love, ready for all that lay ahead.

Epilogue

Doorn, Occupied Holland, November 21, 1940

*H*e has filled his house with pictures, many of them portraits—life-size painted figures, elegant oils of aristocratic faces, scores of photographs. Yet only three are of his mother, all from her last years. "Here she is forever the widowed matron, dressed in black," his daughter, also Victoria, commented once. "But she was pretty in her day. You don't want to remember her like that? As someone to be admired?"

At the time he smiled, not disputing. Perhaps it's true. Perhaps his ambivalence for the woman who bore him is revealed in how he has chosen and arranged his pictures. His grandfather, the first kaiser, has pride of place in nearly every room.

Today, on what would have been her one hundredth birthday, he plucks from the flock of framed images on the study sideboard one small photograph of his mother. Down in the dining room he props it up next to the crystal water glass as he sits down for luncheon. She's wearing a black ruffled dress, a small black lace cap, and the large star of the Order of the Black Eagle pinned over her heart. Papa's last gift. Her clear, frank gaze looks directly into the camera. No smile. Hers is a serious—but not unfriendly—expression. He notes the soft curve of her cheek, the unlined face, the beautiful white hands holding a folded black fan.

"And so, Mama?" he says aloud, in English, after the footman who served him has left the room and he is alone. "What would you make of the world today, eh?"

Then he laughs. He can't imagine his intense, proper, admonitory mother comprehending the fate of Europe, or his own. Never could she have fathomed such a person as the repellant little Austrian corporal who now rules in Germany. She—a woman who hated obsequiousness, even the proud Prussian version of it—would despise how the noble German people call this scoundrel *"der Führer"* and lift their arms in automatic salute as he drives by in one of his open cars.

Awful, he thinks, summoning up the scene, familiar from the newsreels. True, he welcomed the man's rise when he believed the monarchy might be restored. And, still, that hope dashed, he cheered the magnificent German victories against England and France last spring. Of course, those were the triumphs of his own men, trained as junior officers for the last war and back to take their revenge in the new.

German soldiers guard his home now, not Dutch, and the Lowlands are occupied by the *Reich*. "Can you imagine England, too, Mama, part of greater Germany? A United States of Europe, controlled from Berlin? It may well happen," he says, laughing again, shaking his head.

He shouldn't have let it get around, after she died, that she had requested to be wrapped in the Union Jack and sent back to Windsor for burial. She had wanted nothing of the kind. She was interred, as she had requested, beside her husband and dead sons in the Friedenskirche at Potsdam. Those stories, they were just some fun.

But perhaps it was beneath him to repeat them, he thinks, picking up his fork. Then he rebukes himself. Didn't justifiable rage long ago replace any guilt he felt over her? The fury that engulfed him when he learned how Fritz Ponsonby, the swine, planned to publish her letters, smuggled out of Friedrichshof a few months before her death. Ponsonby had kept them hidden, only producing them after he himself had written a memoir—it was an outrageous effort to sully and contradict his own account.

For the first and only time in his long years of exile he had made a legal fuss, retaining a lawyer in London to sue Ponsonby for theft. Those letters belonged to him, her eldest son and heir. But his solicitor concluded that a thievery case was impossible to prove, and because his cousin the English king did not stand in Ponsonby's way, and his mother's sister Louise, Duchess of Argyll, along with his own two youngest sisters, had approved, *Letters of the Empress Frederick* couldn't be stopped.

So, instead, he took the lawyer's suggestion and purchased the rights to the German edition so he could write his own preface, urging the reader not to believe implicitly what the Empress Friedrich wrote, since she "was very sensitive and everything wounded her . . . and her temperament made her use bitter words about everybody."

He was correct there, he thinks as he eats. Mama could never accommodate herself to things. So often unreasonable. When Papa fell ill, Mama kept disputing with the doctors, bringing in that disgraceful English one to look down Papa's throat and declare he saw no cancer there. By the time Grandfather died, aged ninety, and Papa ascended as Kaiser Friedrich III, he could no longer speak, wrote his remarks on a pad of paper, and the ministers had to listen to their monarch's breathing as it gurgled through the cannula in his neck. Mama should never have allowed it! Better the crown pass directly to him as regent, sparing Papa's dignity. But his mother hungered for power, desperate to promote her pro-English cabal, and to marry Moretta off to that despicable Battenberg, whom his silly sister claimed to love. Well, it all came to naught, as Papa died after a mere ninety-nine days.

He sighs. A noble man, his father, even in death, but inordinately fond of his wife. Quite unbecoming.

The meal finished, he picks up his mother's photograph again, and as he's climbing the stairs he reflects that he's been married twice, and both times to trivial women. Poor Dona, a small-minded creature obsessed with precedence. Admirably fecund, of course. She'd given him seven children, six sons and the baby Victoria, before dying of a malfunctioning heart. Hermine, livelier than Dona ever was, is a welcome female presence at his table when not away on long visits to her children in Germany. She often extolls the regime, applauding the attacks on the Jews. He agrees that his homeland has been too long in the grip of an evil Semitic influence, but the stories one hears nowadays are distasteful: indiscriminate arrests, even of Jewish officers, those who earned the Iron Cross! In any case, Hermine shouldn't talk about politics—she can't carry it off. She's not an intellectual like his mother, nor an artist.

Doesn't he have one of Mama's watercolors somewhere? A seascape she did at Cannes years ago, when they were all there together, before the French war? Maybe in the back passageway, he thinks, turning in that direction to get it. He wonders: who else in this life remembers Mama? Sophie and Mossy, of course. But they long ago gave up discussing her with their older brother. To them she's a kind of martyr, persecuted by Bismarck, lonely in widowhood, but brave for remaining in Germany when she might have left. His sisters refuse to recognize that so much of what their mother did was for effect. She longed to be seen as a saintly do-gooder, a particularly magnanimous woman, but she was never generous or loving to him—he had to join the Guards to find his true family.

In the old days, in Germany, at drunken dinners or off on long afternoon sails, he confessed this aloud sometimes. He was a man revered by millions whose own mother didn't care for him. Listeners would gasp, or murmur that this could not be so, but no less a figure than the famous Viennese psychoanalyst Sigmund Freud concurred. Sometime after the war he gave a speech reproaching Mama for excessive pride and for withdrawing her love from him because of his lame arm.

And yet, Freud never met either one of them.

Back in his study he sits down astride the mounted saddle that has always acted as his desk chair. He puts the photo aside and examines her watercolor for a long minute. It's surprisingly good. She's captured the sea's texture and shafts of sunlight beaming down between clouds. He admires the delicate washes of color and small, precise rendering of the black rocks on the shore. She took great care over it. Typical of her. "*Ach*," he says aloud, suddenly grief-stricken. Wasn't it he who withdrew? She was once to him like the sun—warm, dazzling, vital. But her gravitational pull was so strong. He couldn't stay close to her and become the man he desired to be. He couldn't remain her boy.

That's it! Bigelow remembers Mama, and the rice pudding she used to make. They discussed it when the American visited Doorn last year.

He opens the desk drawer, fishes out one of the blank white postcards he keeps for this sort of missive, and sets down upon it in his large hand the familiar address: Poultney Bigelow, Malden on Hudson, New York, USA. He writes: "Today the 100th birthday of my mother! No notice is taken of it at home. No 'Memorial Service' or committee to remember her marvelous work for the welfare of our German people. . . . Nobody of the new generation knows anything about her!"

He signs it William.

Acknowledgments

$\mathcal{I}$ am indebted to the novelist Sandra Newman, who gave me both exacting instruction and generous encouragement at every stage of writing this book.

I am grateful to Professor David Kaiser for the excellent course on European diplomatic history he offered at Harvard College in the long-ago spring of 1980. David's lectures brought Otto von Bismarck alive in my mind—and I find that the wily old Junker has been stomping around up there ever since.

My father, Dr. Paul McHugh, renowned psychiatrist and neurologist, spent hours discussing these characters with me. As so often in the past, I relied upon his humane outlook and keen intellect to improve my own thinking.

Laura Dail, a wonderful friend turned perspicacious agent, matched me with editor Lucia Macro, whose deep knowledge of British royal history and nuanced appreciation of Vicky's personality made *A Most English Princess* a better book.

I asked numerous friends to read early versions of the manuscript. Ashleigh Bennett, Wendy Breitner, Joan Goodman, Wendy Greenbaum, George Kimmerling, Beth Lipton, Katherine McNevin, Faith Moore, Tom Schwartz, and Hilary Sterne slogged through the entire novel, providing excellent feedback. Mary Hockaday, sister in spirit, cast her discerning eye over the last draft and pushed me to sharpen it. Two German friends, Corrina da Fonseca-Wollheim and Janine Weitenauer, corrected my

German and provided valuable perspective on German history. I thank Natalie Allen, Alissa Dufour, Michael Guarneiri, Alison Gwinn, Jacqueline Lawrence, Peggy Noonan, and Elisabeth Rosenthal for their comments on various chapters.

Charlie Lasswell is ever the affectionate son Vicky could only dream of. And my dear husband, Mark Lasswell, believed in me when I didn't believe in myself. There aren't sufficient words to say thank you for that.

About the author

About the book

Insights,
Interviews
& More...

Meet Clare McHugh

Hannah La Follette Ryan

Born in London, CLARE MCHUGH grew up in the United States and graduated from Harvard University with a degree in European history. She worked for many years as a newspaper reporter and later magazine editor. She has also taught high school history and reviewed books for the *Wall Street Journal* and the *Baltimore Sun*. The mother of two grown children, she lives with her husband in Washington, DC, and Amagansett, New York. *A Most English Princess* is her first novel. ❦

Behind the Book

Quite soon after the marriage of Kate Middleton and Prince William in April 2011, a new law was passed by Parliament, having first been endorsed by the heads of the Commonwealth nations. No longer would the order of succession to the British throne favor males over females. Now the eldest child, regardless of sex, would be heir.

When I read about this change, I had a wistful thought: Might the measure be dubbed "Vicky's law" to honor Queen Victoria's eldest child, a girl of intelligence, energy, and commitment, who was the last person passed over for the crown because she was female? All the sovereigns since Queen Victoria either had boys first, or, in the case of the current queen's father—George VI—only girls.

The poignancy of Vicky's story has long fascinated me—perhaps because I'm the eldest in my family and have a brother only a year younger, as she did. It was easy to imagine how painful it would be: relegated to second best when you were firstborn just because you were a "lesser"—a girl.

I also had a particular interest in the Royal Family and the late Victorian era from what my mother told me of her own mother's childhood. My grandmother, born in 1889, grew up ▶

Behind the Book *(continued)*

in Gosport, near Portsmouth, where boats departed regularly for the Isle of Wight. Her parents worked in the household of General Robert Montgomery, General Officer Commanding South Coast Defense— her mother as a housekeeper and her father as a coachman, later chauffeur. Royal persons could frequently be spotted passing through Gosport en route to stay at Osborne House, and we have a much-cherished photo of my great-grandfather driving King Edward VII, Vicky's brother Bertie, and his nephew, the kaiser, Vicky's son. In the photo below, which dates to 1905, the King is far left, with the kaiser beside him, and Henry George Lampard, my great-grandfather, holds the reins.

Courtesy of the author's family

My interest in Vicky deepened in college, when I studied the rise of Germany as a nation-state, the outbreak of the First World War, the country's tragic turn to fascism, and the horrific Nazi regime. The reasons for the German descent into barbarism and genocidal madness are still debated by historians. But the seeds of later tragedy were planted in the late summer of 1862 when King Wilhelm of Prussia contemplated abdication in favor of his son, Fritz, Vicky's husband, and instead chose another path. Historian John C. G. Röhl writes: "We know that the King finally decided to appoint Bismarck . . . [but] right to the end, the struggle might easily have ended differently. We are dealing here with one of those eerie moments where history holds its breath before revealing the fate that lies in store for future generations."

Vicky was a close witness to this hinge moment, and while I relied on imagination to conjure up the discussions between her and Fritz, her letters to Queen Victoria detail her deep distress at Bismarck's ascendency and the choices he made for Germany in subsequent years. Going from young bride to Crown Princess, and eventually to Empress of Germany for a scant ninety-nine days, the Vicky I discovered in these letters is an affectionate daughter and ▸

a surprisingly modern thinker, who
is determined to be the best wife,
mother, and public servant she can be,
who rages at events outside her control,
who discusses her excitement with new
ideas—political, scientific, psychological.
Vicky read Marx's *Das Kapital* and
Darwin's *On the Origin of Species* with
great interest. She worked tirelessly for
educational opportunities for young
women, and for the better care of the
sick. When in the late 1870s Bismarck
fanned the flames of anti-Semitism
in the German Empire, she and Fritz
defied their advisors to express openly
their abhorrence of this invidious
prejudice. Vicky accepted the honorary
chairmanship of an orphanage for
Jewish girls, and during the height
of the anti-Semitic riots in Germany
in January 1881, she accompanied Fritz,
wearing his full-dress uniform as a
Prussian field marshal, to services at
a Berlin synagogue.

Her progressive attitudes earned
Vicky the enmity of many in her
adoptive country, to whom she would
always be "*die Englanderin,*" an anti-
Prussian agent of a foreign power.
Bismarck's allies encouraged rumors
that she dominated her husband.
For many years, Vicky stood strong
against these calumnies, but the double
blow of her eldest son, Willy, turning
his back on his parents and joining the

reactionary camp, and the illness and
premature death of Fritz at age fifty-
seven, just as he inherited the throne,
threw her into a depression for several
years. The building of a new home
outside Frankfurt, called *Friedrichshof*
in Fritz's memory (now the glamourous
Schlosshotel Kronberg), revived her, as
did her relationship with three of her
daughters. (Charlotte and she were
not close.) Her youngest son, Prince
Waldemar, tragically followed Siggy
to an early grave, dying of diphtheria
in March 1879, at age eleven, just four
months after Vicky's beloved sister
Alice died of the same disease at her
home in Darmstadt.

My awareness of all the sadness
in Vicky's life did not deter me from
spending two years in her company
composing this story. Her most sterling
quality—her desire to be good and do
good—inspired me. And the
contradictions of her life intrigued me.
How did this woman who was used in
an archaic way—married off for dynastic
and political ends—find purpose and
fulfillment as an individual? How did
she use her influence to shape events?
What did it feel like to enjoy great
privilege and yet cope with crushing
disappointment? In truth Vicky often
made mistakes and got in her own way.
Her beloved Fritz once said her greatest
flaw was over-confidence in her own ▶

Behind the Book *(continued)*

opinion. But her life's journey was a noble one, and I hope *A Most English Princess* will inspire readers to learn more about Vicky and the turbulent times in which she lived. ⌒

Exploring Vicky's World: Pictures of Victoria, Princess Royal

The 1846 family portrait of Franz Winterhalter hung in the dining room at Osborne House. Today it can be seen in Buckingham Palace's East Gallery. (Courtesy of the Royal Collection Trust / © Her Majesty Queen Elizabeth II 2020)

Exploring Vicky's World: Pictures of Victoria, Princess Royal *(continued)*

Vicky with her parents on her wedding day, January 25, 1858. (Courtesy of the Royal Collection Trust / © Her Majesty Queen Elizabeth II 2020)

Vicky and Fritz on honeymoon at Windsor. (Courtesy of Hulton Archive)

Exploring Vicky's World: Pictures of Victoria, Princess Royal *(continued)*

Vicky's eldest son, Prince Wilhelm, later Kaiser Wilhelm II, as a ten-year-old—he's been given a glove to hold in his left hand to lengthen the appearance of his shorter arm for the photo. (Courtesy of Everett Collection Historical / Alamy Stock Photo)

Vicky as a widow in 1900, already ill with cancer. Kaiser Wilhelm II kept a copy of this photo in his home in exile in Doorn, the Netherlands. (Courtesy of Thomas Heinrich Voigt / Royal Collection Trust) ⌒⌣

Learn More

The letters between Vicky and
her mother—exchanged starting
immediately after Vicky's wedding
in January 1858 until January 1901,
the month of Queen Victoria's death—
have been published in five volumes
and they are the primary source for
A Most English Princess. Kept safe
by Fritz Ponsonby, the voluminous
correspondence between mother and
daughter today lives in two different
places: Vicky's letters to the Queen are
at Windsor Castle, and Queen Victoria's
replies can be found in the archives of
the Princely Hessian Family at Schloss
Fasanerie near Fulda, Germany. Also,
two excellent biographies of Vicky
exist. The more comprehensive is the
meticulously researched *An Uncommon
Woman* by Hannah Pakula, published
in 1995. An earlier account of her life,
*Vicky: Princess Royal of England and
German Empress* by Daphne Bennett,
came out in 1971.

To understand the family Vicky grew
up in, and the key influence of her father,
Prince Albert, it's worth diving into
two books by A. N. Wilson: *Prince
Albert: The Man Who Saved the
Monarchy* and *Victoria: A Life*, both
published during the last decade. There
are dozens of other biographies of the
famous Victoria—the classic *Queen*

Victoria by Elizabeth Longford holds up very well fifty years after it was first published. Julia Baird's *Victoria: The Queen* and Helen Rappaport's *A Magnificent Obsession: Victoria, Albert, and the Death That Changed the British Monarchy* are both wonderful reads. I have enjoyed several recent film adaptions of Victoria's life, but the lavish TV series *Victoria* broadcast on PBS takes too many liberties with the facts for my taste. The most historically accurate filmed account of the events covered in *A Most English Princess* is a thirteen-part BBC series first broadcast in 1974 called *Fall of Eagles*. You can find episodes on YouTube.

There are only academic biographies of Fritz published in English, but Bertie is the subject of a terrific book by Jane Ridley, *The Heir Apparent: A Life of Edward VII, the Playboy Prince*.

Vicky's son Willy finally got the attention he deserved when Anglo-German historian John C. G. Röhl completed a magisterial three-volume life of the last kaiser in 2008. For my novel, I studied closely volume one, *Young Wilhelm: The Kaiser's Early Life, 1859–1888*, and was impressed by the details Röhl has gleaned from the archives, in particular the unpublished correspondence between Vicky and Fritz housed now at Schloss Fasanerie. I consider Röhl's very critical view of ▶

Vicky's parenting somewhat unfair. However, any reader interested in assessing what went wrong in the future kaiser's upbringing should delve into Röhl's book. William's contradictory nature—his grandiosity and his warmheartedness, his wit and his racism—is on full display in his correspondence with his childhood friend, the American journalist Poultney Bigelow. The Bigelow family donated these fascinating letters and postcards to the New York Public Library, where the public can access them in the Brooke Russell Astor Reading Room.

Otto von Bismarck has been written about—and debated, deified, misconstrued, and slandered—for decades. No other statesman in the second half of the nineteenth century accomplished more than Bismarck; only Abraham Lincoln, savior of the Union, comes close. And, I would aver, we are living in a world that still bears Bismarck's fingerprints. Not only did he found Germany as a nation, he also pioneered the modern welfare state—establishing workers' compensation, disability insurance, and old-age pensions in the *Reich*. His innovations inspired the Progressives in the United States, who, witnessing the industrial unrest of the 1880s and 1890s, believed only the Iron Chancellor had found a way to make capitalism work for everyone. Later, Franklin Roosevelt modeled the US Social Security program on the system established by Bismarck in 1889. But Bismarck—brilliant, cynical, dictatorial—ultimately played a baleful role in his country's development. His suppression of free speech, his disregard for parliamentary authority, and his embrace of militarized monarchical autocracy smothered liberal democracy in Germany in its infancy. Valiant Vicky didn't live to see Berlin in ruins in 1945, but she was correct about where Bismarck's machinations could lead. Henry Kissinger called Bismarck "The White Revolutionary" in a famous essay published in 1968. Like Lenin, Bismarck altered the society he lived in, but he did so from the right rather than the left. Along with Kissinger's article, I recommend two excellent biographies of the chancellor—*Bismarck: A Life* by Jonathan Steinberg and *Bismarck* by Edward Crankshaw.

The monarchy was abolished in Germany in 1918, and Vicky's son Willy lived until his death in 1941 in exile in Doorn, in Holland. But today Elizabeth, Vicky's great-grandniece, the great-granddaughter of her brother Bertie, is Queen of England. And Elizabeth's husband, Philip, is the great-grandson of Vicky's beloved ▶

sister Alice. Vicky's own descendants live all over the world—many in Germany, but others in the UK, and some in the US.

I'm a fan of New York City's High Line park, for its amalgamation of beautiful gardens and modern urban design. A young architect named Tatiana von Preussen—Vicky and Fritz's direct descendant, the granddaughter of their great-grandson—was part of the High Line's design team. Strolling along the park's wooden pathway on a sunny afternoon recently, I thought how fitting it is that Vicky, who loved gardens and art and promoting the general welfare, is connected in a small way to this marvelous public space. None of us know what our legacies will be, and Vicky, who strived so hard to do good, is no exception. ∾

Reading Group Guide

1. Papa allowed Vicky, his cherished eldest daughter, to be engaged when she was not yet fifteen years old, and to be married and leave home when she was seventeen. He pursued the Prussian marriage to serve his own political aims. Did you think his decisions concerning Vicky were selfish or well-meaning?

2. Why do you think Fritz fell in love with Vicky, when he was quite a bit older than her and came from a different royal milieu? What about her made her a good wife for him?

3. How much responsibility did Vicky bear for the antagonism she encountered in Berlin? Would someone with a different personality have found it easier?

4. What prevented Queen Augusta and Vicky from having a strong and enduring friendship?

5. Papa never anticipated Bismarck's rise to power. Do you think he could have helped Vicky and Fritz cope with him had he lived longer? ►

6. What do you imagine Bismarck really thought of Vicky? He liked to complain to colleagues that she had too much influence in the royal household, and yet his associates noticed that he wanted her good opinion. Were these two strong characters doomed to be irreconcilable?

7. Did Vicky give Fritz good advice when she urged him to speak out in Danzig?

8. Fritz was considered a passive man in royal circles but a brilliant and inspired leader of men in battle. Why do you imagine he felt more empowered in a military role?

9. Why did Vicky cherish Siggy in particular among all her children?

10. In what ways was Vicky a good mother to Willy? And in what ways did she fail him? What kind of example did Mama, Queen Victoria, set as a mother? How did Vicky's own sense of self-worth get mixed up with her feelings about Willy?